J. P.

John Mooers

J. P.

Published by riverrun
16310 Sandalwood Street
Fountain Valley, CA 92708

ISBN: 978-0-9886486-4-7

First published March 31st, 2013.

Front cover photograph:
"J. P. Morgan walking to office from yacht landing, New York"
Library of Congress Reproduction Number LC-DIG-ggbain-00215

Back cover photograph:
"J. P. Morgan's body taken from his library"
Library of Congress Reproduction Number LC-DIG-ggbain-12204

www.riverrunusa.com

To Carl Sherbondy, the J. P. Morgan of my world

CONTENTS

Game of Chess

It was night in the city. The automobile pulled up to the entrance of the Willard Hotel. It worked its way to the curb between all the other cars coming and going. Several cars honked their horns. The doorman, tall with a long grey cape-like coat and a tall black top hat with white gloves approached and opened the rear door.

Jack Morgan, better known to the world as John Pierpont Morgan, Jr., 45 years old, partner in J.P. Morgan & Company, wearing dark grey pants, black spit polished shoes, a waist coat, a long overcoat and a derby hat got out of the automobile and stretched his arms out while standing on the sidewalk. He had a full, dark, neatly trimmed moustache. He held in his hand a walking stick that he used more for show than utility. The night air was cold and crisp. Lights from inside the hotel splashed out across the sidewalk. A great many people were going in and out of the hotel. The door constantly swung open and closed.

The doorman held out his hand to help Louisa Satterlee, Jack's sister, get out of the car. She wore a long overcoat, a pink pearl necklace across her white lace bodice, a flat flowered hat and black leather gloves. Once cleared of the cab she glanced around at the rushing crowds. It was near Christmas and shoppers were out in abundance.

Louisa turned and bent down to look into the back of the cab.

"Come, father," she said.

The door man reached out to assist the man getting out of the cab but the man waved him aside with a low grunt.

Using his walking cane to help steady him, the old man slowly emerged from the dark interior of the cab and came out into the illuminated night.

Wearing dark striped pants and an equally dark striped waist coat, a pinned white ascot silk tie, a black frock coat with open silk peaked lapels, a shiny black top hat, and gold watch chains across his robust waist, John Pierpont Morgan, president and senior partner in J.P.

Morgan & Company, stretched up to his full six feet. His moustache and thick side whiskers had grayed and even whitened a long time before. The seventy five year old Morgan glared around at the crowds as he cleared his throat with a deep rumbling sound. He tapped heavily the sidewalk with his mahogany cane.

People stared at him as they walked by.

He stared back.

Looking into his eyes under his bushy eyebrows, it was said by the photographer Edward Steichen, was like confronting the headlights of an express train bearing down on you. It could be terrifying.

He hated to be on display like this. It was his hideous nose. From his grandfather and mother he inherited acne rosacea rhinophyma, the excessive growth of sebaceous tissue on the nose. People said that his nose looked like an overripe pomegranate, a strawberry nose, bulbous and flaming red, monstrous in size, with warty growths that changed and increased in size as he grew older. One who met him called it 'a Cyrano nose of vast blue oozing glands.'

The art dealer James Henry Duveen: 'I was unprepared for the meeting with him. I had heard of a disfigurement, but what I saw upset me so thoroughly that for a moment I could not utter a word. If I did not gasp I must have changed colour. Mr. Morgan noticed this, and his small, piercing eyes transfixed me with a malicious stare. I sensed that he noticed my feelings of pity, and for some time that seemed centuries we stood opposite each other without saying a word. I could not utter a sound, and when at last I managed to open my mouth I could produce only a raucous cough. He grunted.'

The Renaissance painter Domenico Ghirlandalo painted a portrait entitled 'Old Man and His Grandson,' in which a lovely little boy is being embraced by a horribly deformed grandfather wracked with the acne rosacea rhinophyma. Once, when Morgan took the art expert Wilhelm von Bode and his daughter on a personal tour of his art collection at Prince's Gate, Morgan's own grandson came running up to him and he bent down to pick him up. The daughter turned to her father with a clever look on her face.

She whispered: "Ghirlandaio, father."

Morgan overheard and turned to the daughter.

"What is that about Ghirlandalo, miss?"

The father froze for a moment.

"We were just saying we admire the magnificent portrait of Giovanna Tornabuoni by Ghirlandalo that you recently acquired."

But Morgan was not fooled.

"Will you be needing the car this evening?" the cab driver asked.

Jack bent down and spoke into the cab.

"No, I think not."

Morgan told Jack once about how he felt. He hated this. He felt like a circus baboon or something. Jack said it was because they realize who you are, you are famous, and they are in awe of how important you are. Morgan just grunted. He was as famous as Cyrano de Bergerac, and for the same reason. When a woman was so nervous that her young daughter would say something when she first met John the mother drilled the daughter over and over not to say anything. John met the daughter who was very nice and polite and when she left the room, now out of danger, the mother, serving tea, turned to John and said 'Would you like some sugar with your nose?'

An irritated John stared at those staring and then followed Louisa and Jack into the hotel.

He loved to walk into the lobby of the Willard hotel because he felt as if he were walking into a gorgeous painting, a fine work of art. The large lobby was a golden caramel and crème with a multitude of tall marbled Greek columns veined with burnt sienna. The lobby was enormous, like an ancient Parthenon, with its highly polished parquet inlaid floor and its high Renaissance carved ceiling panels. Each Greek column was adorned with a large potted palm, chairs and a small dark mahogany table.

John looked around while he walked as if it were his first time there seeing one of the wonders of the world. The three of them walked over to the Concierge behind the marbled counter.

John stood off to one side as Jack talked with the Concierge. The man's black hair was slicked back on his head and there was a tiny touch of a manicured moustache.

"Yes, Mr. Morgan. We are very glad to see you once again. Welcome back."

John nodded as Jack picked up the pen in order to sign the large guest register.

"I have all of your rooms ready for you."

"Thank you."

"Mr. Herbert Satterlee has already arrived and is I believe, already up in his room."

"Yes thank you," Louisa answered.

"Are you in town for business or for pleasure, sir?"

Jack looked straight at the man.

"I assure you, sir; it is certainly not for pleasure."

The man smiled.

"And your luggage?" he asked, looking around to see if it had already been brought in.

"They are unloading it now. We would like to go up to our rooms now. Please have the luggage sent up when they come in." "Certainly, sir," the man said as he banged the silver bell on the counter and waved over a bell hop with his right hand.

He handed the bell hop the keys. The bell hop was very tall and thin. His clothes hung on his frame unfitting properly.

"Please take the Morgan family up to their rooms."

"Certainly. Please, follow me."

As they walked toward the elevators a group of giggling children suddenly swarmed around them. John had to stop suddenly so not to trip over them. A frantic mother came running over.

"Oh I am so sorry, sorry. Children, be careful. Behave. You almost knocked this man down."

She turned to John.

"I am ever so sorry."

John smiled a quick smile and looked down at the children. Several of them were staring up at him with gaping opened mouths. He could see that they were staring at his nose. They continued staring at him as the young woman led them away. John watched them walk away as one of the little girls asked her mommy 'what's wrong with that man's nose?'

The young woman shook the girls arm and hushed her. A young man, apparently the father, was joking with one of the small boys, poking him in the sides to make him laugh.

John looked back toward Jack and Louisa. They had already started walking toward the elevator again.

John used to play with them when they were young, and Juliet and Annie. When he came home they ran around him laughing and giggling holding his legs so he could not walk and he had to eventually kneel down on the floor where they swarmed over him tweaking at his moustache and pulling out his watch chain and bob and exploring each of his pockets for where he had hidden the candies or cookies this time rumpling his hair as he growled and tried to gobble them up.

Or in the yard in the grass by the wooden bench with the roses, he picked them up and swung them high into the air. They giggled so much when he swept them up into the sky so fast holding them tight.

Or when they all ran down the hill at Cragston racing each other and shouting toward the river through the tall grass, at times taller than they were, and then stopped in their tracks when the fourth of July fireworks boomed out loud in the sky almost directly overhead with tracer sparks shooting across the dark night sky glittering over the water of the river their eyes wide open with wonder.

Oh how they giggled so when he swept them up into the heavens hanging on so tight.

"Come Father," Louisa called back to him.

John looked at her. She stood looking back.

"Are you coming?"

John frowned and walked toward them.

But when he reached the elevator where they stood he stopped. On the opposite wall was a large framed photograph. John stared at the picture hanging on the wall opposite the elevators. He left the group and walked slowly over to the picture. People walked back and forth behind him as he stood motionless staring at the picture. He recognized it. It was a print of a photograph of an American Indian. Proudly sitting on his horse, bare chest, a spear in his hand, the Indian gazed off at something in the distance. John bent down to read the small acknowledgement on the frame of the picture. He had to pull his reading glasses out of his coat pocket and adjust them up and down in order to read the small print. But it was as he suspected.

"'Mounted Cheyenne,'" John read aloud. "'Edward Sheriff Curtis: 1902.'"

"What's that?"

It was Louisa. She had just noticed him standing apart from them.

John grunted a small laugh, pointing at the picture. Jack turned his head to see his father standing in surprise. John turned to look at Louisa, pointing his finger toward the picture.

"The picture, it's one from Curtis, from the book, The North American Indian. It's from the first volume if I'm not mistaken."

"Edward Curtis, the Indian photographer?"

"Yes," John said.

"Now isn't that very odd," Louisa replied. "Think of all the places, what a coincidence to have it here in the hotel lobby."

"You helped finance him didn't you?" It was Jack.

John turned back toward the picture. He slowly shook his head yes.

"Yes," he quietly said.

James brought the man into John's office. John did not look up or in any way acknowledge their presence. He was reading a report and had an assortment of papers spread out on his desk.

James waved the man in and said: "Please have a seat; he will be with you in a moment."

The man nodded and sat in the chair in front of the desk. He held his black leather satchel in his lap. He took off his fedora and sat it on top of his satchel. The man waited.

After a moment John reached over and took his cigar from the tray and took a long puff as he eyed the gentleman sitting across from him.

Edward Sheriff Curtis: photographer. Thirty eight, sharp looking, handsome, new dark woolen jacket, neatly trimmed moustache and goatee beard.

Edward, thinking that the interview had now begun, nodded and smiled.

"I want to thank you for allowing me to see you sir."

John nodded.

Curtis, nervous, began talking.

"Well, 1906, a brand new year, sir. Did you have a good Christmas?"

John turned his cigar around in his mouth, as if thinking, before he answered.

"No."

It stopped the conversation. Edward, a little surprised, tilted his head to one side.

"How so, sir? Nothing serious I hope."

"Well, first a close relative died on December twenty first. We had to cancel the family dinner at our house, but we still went around and saw the grandchildren separately."

"I am sorry to hear that."

"And then on the night of the twenty-eighth my son-in-law, Herbert, happened by our house to see large fire flakes coming out of one of the chimneys. We were out at the time so he rushed in to find a large fire going in the fireplace shooting out sparks into the room. He drenched a table cloth and held it up against the flames to keep the sparks from flying. Two firemen had to come and put the fire out. I dare say he saved the house from burning down."

"Oh, that would have been awful. And to think of all the art works and paintings and the rare books that you have. They could have been lost."

"Yes, well my son-in-law is quite the hero around our house these days."

"Tell me sir, of all the art treasures you have, so many to chose from, if ever there was a fire what would you grab to save as your ran out the door?"

"My father's portrait," John snapped back without the slightest hesitation.

"Interesting," Edward said.

"Now," John boomed, reaching across and pulling out a portfolio. He sat back and opened it. He pulled out a letter. It was on White House stationary. It was signed Theodore Roosevelt. John read a section from the letter out loud.

"There is no man of great wealth with whom I am on sufficient close terms to warrant my giving a special letter to him but you are most welcome to use this letter in talking with any man who has any interest in the subject."

Edward smiled. "Yes sir."

John pulled out another letter.

"You propose detailed plans to publish twenty large format volumes of photographs with accompanying text and drawings, on the finest paper, finest binding, and finest photogravure work available. In addition you propose to publish seven hundred separate portfolios with large prints of what you deem your most important pictures."

Edward shrugged his shoulders. "Yes sir."

John watched him for a long moment.

"That is quite a bold undertaking."

"Yes sir, I suppose that it is."

The two of them sat silent for a moment.

"You went on the expedition to Alaska with E. H. Harriman back in 1899 did you not?"

"Yes I did. I was the photographer. Wonderful trip."

"Do you know that Mr. Harriman and I are business adversaries?"

"That is really none of my concern, sir."

Silence.

"So, tell me then, how was the trip?" John finally asked.

Curtis, puzzled, asked: "The Alaska trip?"

John did not break his stare.

"It was, as I said, wonderful. Despite what you may think, sir, I have found Mr. Harriman to be a most kind, caring and thoughtful man. It began, as you perhaps know, as a vacation for him and his family but when he realized how large the ship was that was needed to travel into the wilds of Alaska he came up with the idea of making it a scientific expedition. He saw no reason to waste the space on the ship."

John, watching Curtis as he talked, sat silently.

"A series of articles and books are being published on the scientific discoveries that were made during the trip so it has proven to be a most worthwhile vacation."

"Yes, I know about that."

"As a matter of fact Mr. Harriman actually piloted the ship at times into areas that even the captain would not sail."

"Foolish," John grunted.

Curtis raised his eyebrows. "Perhaps," he said. "But it allowed us to make discoveries that otherwise would not have been made: a glacier, for example, that is now named after him. Daring is the word I would use, sir, rather than foolish."

John stared down at a letter on his desk.

"And this letter from President Roosevelt, do you realize that at the moment Mr. Roosevelt and I are not on the best of terms?"

"That also is none of my concern."

John watched him. Edward was steady. He did not move.

"You seem to prefer associating with the more rugged and outdoor type of gentlemen."

Curtis smiled.

"Perhaps that is true, sir. But it is a difference of character. Harriman vacations in the wilds of Alaska, Roosevelt in hunting, and you," Curtis shrugged his shoulders, "you prefer the spas of old Europe. People are different."

"And you are of the former frame of mind?"

"Yes. If I were not then I would not have these photographs to publish for the enjoyment of those who are not of that frame of mind, such as yourself."

"Why are you not asking Harriman for your funding?"

There was a pause before Curtis carefully replied.

"Because, sir, I am asking you."

John waited. Curtis sat. He put his elbow onto the arm of the chair and cradled his chin in his fingers of his hand.

Then John spoke, more to himself: "Do you know I saw some Indians myself once, a long time ago."

"Sir?"

After a long pause John sat forward in his chair and put his elbows on his desk.

"Mr. Curtis, I want to see these photographs in books, the most beautiful set of books ever published."

Edward smiled.

"Thank you ever so much, sir. You know that you refused the first time I asked."

"I did?"

"Yes, to quote the entire rejection exactly: 'Mr. Curtis there are many demands on me for financial assistance. I will be unable to help you.'"

"Yes, well. You are very lucky. I very seldom change my mind."

"What caused you to do so now?"

There was a very long silence as John stared at Edward without even as much as a flicker of his eyes.

"I saw your pictures," he said.

Louisa walked over to John. She stood with him for a moment, and then carefully touched his arm.

"Father," she whispered.

"What," he grunted.

"Everyone is waiting."

John looked at her and then at Jack and the porter standing waiting in the lobby by the elevators. A lot of other people were walking back and forth. Everything was so busy, so rushed.

"Yes, yes," he snapped as he looked back at the picture, brushing her off.

"Come on, Father."

They stood together for a moment in silence.

John agreed to fund the field work for the photographs with $75,000 in exchange for 25 sets of the final books and 500 prints. Curtis wrote asking how John wanted to be acknowledged. John had Belle his librarian write back: Morgan would leave "the matter of mentioning his connection with the work entirely to you: he says, 'the less the better.'"

"It is time," Louisa said.

John looked at her again, irritated, but then he nodded. He turned and walked with her toward the others. Louisa glanced at Jack as he turned away with a sigh, slightly shaking his head.

John nodded to the porter, and smiled. His spirit seemed to have lifted.

Yes, he thought; I saw some Indians myself once, a long time ago.

There is a vast world out there. He wanted to see it.

July 5, 1869, at 5 p.m., they left by train from Jersey City, his wife Frances and her sister Mary Tracy and their cousin Mary Goodwin, and went on a trip. The transcontinental railroad had just been completed. They were going to California and back.

John remembered well.

John stood on the station platform. Nebraska. There was no cover where he stood. The sun beat down. The sky was cloudless. He stood on the edge looking out across the tracks and across to the meadow beyond. They had to await a new train. All the others were in the station out of the sun. But it would be stifling and still in the station. At least out here at the edge of the platform there was a breeze, a warm breeze with a hot sun, but a breeze nevertheless.

"Look," a voice from the meadow called out. John looked over, it was Mary Tracy. She held up a handful of wildflowers she had pulled from the meadow.

"Aren't they just lovely?"

John held up his hand to shade his eyes from the sun.

"Yes, very much so," he shouted out to her across the open space.

Both Mary Tracy and Mary Goodwin were wandering around in the field looking at the wild flowers. John watched them with a sense of peace. The breeze was stiffer out in the open. It tugged at their hair sending loose strands flying about. They bent over here and there to look closer to the ground. The field stretched on and on. He had never seen the land so flat for so far. Not a mountain, not even a hill was in sight. Miles away it seemed was a small clump of trees but there were only a few and they were so far away. Where did all the wood come from to build all the little towns? And when a strong wind came up what was there to stop it?

John glanced back at the station. Lined along the platform, in the sun, sat the luggage of all the passengers in the regular cars, waiting for the next train. He could see Frances on a bench in the shade under the eves of the station. The benches lining the wall of the station were filled with waiting passengers. Frances had her bonnet on her head with a ribbon tied beneath her chin to hold it in place. She fanned herself with a folded newspaper. The paper was more important now as a fan than it was as a source of the news of the day.

They were all waiting for the next train.

The different rail lines across the United States had connected just a few months ago at Promontory Summit. In theory one could travel the entire breath of the United States from New York City to San Francisco. But different lines were owned by different companies, different men, and one train could only travel on one line. When you came to the end of one line you had to change trains to one owned by the next line before you could travel on along their line.

John, from where he stood, could see, beyond the station, into the rail yard where they were building the train: the locomotive, then two baggage cars, then the three regular passenger cars, and finally the Pullman car. John watched the puffs of smoke swirling up into the cloudless sky as the small yard engine connected the cars. Only the Pullman car was the same from the prior train.

John and his group were on the Pullman. Everyone else had to get off the train, unload their baggage, and now wait to reload their baggage onto the new train.

The Pullman car was wonderful. They were only a few years old and were still quite a novelty on the lines. George Pullman himself got his start by moving houses out of the way of canal builders. Now he built small hotels on wheels.

Whenever they stopped at a station people on the platform stared into the car pointing with wonder at what they saw. Plush carpets, sleeping couches and seats, tables, glass chandeliers that rattled a little when going across the bumpy rails, heavy curtains that could be closed to block out either the sun or prying eyes, and wood paneled walls and ceilings. The world of train travel was changing. On this trip they only had the one car, named the Minnesota, and no diner car.

They ate at the local eating houses along the way. Some were nothing more than log huts whitewashed inside and with ceilings made of canvas that flapped and tugged at the ropes holding it in place when the wind got strong. Frances would glance around, unsmiling, at the tin plates and the bent forks and the rough cut unclothed wooden tables wondering perhaps if the whole roof was going to be torn away by the wind at any moment. And when it rained? Do you sit and eat with a leaking roof?

Sitting at one, next to the two cowboys who had seemingly not bathed in quite some time, Frances, fanning her face because of the heat, and smell, opened up the Pullman brochure about the dining car and read allowed to John the description, eyeing him after each sentence: the dining car is sixty feet long by ten feet wide. It runs on eight wheeled trucks giving sixteen wheels, and with steel springs it makes the ride very smooth. The kitchen is in the center of the car and is the entire width of the car except for a small passageway on the left. Dining is at either end of the car with six tables in each section; four at each table means that a total of forty eight passengers can dine at any one time. When you are ready to order then pulling a small bell on the side of the car near the window brings a waiter to your table with refreshing iced drinks or chef prepared gourmet food. With the side paneling a black walnut the snowy white linen and solid silver knives and forks make a nice contrast.

"And what is this meat we are eating?" John asked Mary Goodwin, sitting across the table from him and devouring her meal.

"Antelope," she mumbled.

"It is tasty, no?"

Both Mary's shrugged their shoulders.

"It is different to be sure," Mary Goodwin said, breaking apart a piece of bread.

John did not need to query the opinion of Frances.

After they finished eating they came outside into the hot sunshine and the wind. Down the dirt road a long row of wagons were passing by with white canvas tops, creaking turning wheels, and rattling and banging pots and pans. Most of the wagons were pulled with mules and old horses that had seen better days. Several men on horseback rode up and down the line.

Mary Goodwin pulled her hair back, wild in the wind.

"People still go this way?" she asked.

John looked down the dirt path toward the horizon. The flat prairie seemed to stretch on forever.

"I read somewhere that they only do twenty or twenty five miles a day. Imagine being cooped up in a wagon like that for months and months."

"Thank God for the railroad," John said.

On one side of the path there was a large pile of bones. Antelope bones, deer, bison, maybe even horses; it was a large pile of skulls and bones bleaching white in the sun. It buzzed with flies.

Francis, turning away from the wagon train and the pile of bones stopped and with a small shriek grabbed John's arm. John looked in the direction she was staring. There, standing off to one side of the station platform, watching the wagons passing by, holding their horses, were two Indians.

"I'll never get used to seeing them," she said as she began to walk away toward the station itself.

They first spotted Indians earlier that morning out the window from the train. The train was slowing as it approached the small town and coming up to the station. John sat at the table in the middle of the cabin playing solitaire. Frances and her sister Mary Tracy were sitting on the sofa on the side of the car with their backs to the windows. Both were sewing and talking. It was Mary Goodwin who saw them first. As she walked down the length of the car, just as she passed Frances she looked over to see what Frances was sewing and her eyes wandered to the window.

"My God," she whispered.

Frances and Mary Tracy looked up at her and then turned to look out the window to see what she saw.

"Goodness," Frances said, taken aback.

"Pierpont, Pierpont you need to see this."

John, disturbed that his concentration was broken, looked out the window as well. Slowly John stood and walked over to the sofa and stared out the window.

Riding alongside the train was a party of Indians on horseback. There was a group of at least ten horses without riders and riding with them, surrounding them, were five Indians. They had long black hair, shoulder length. One, in the lead, was older than the others which looked to be twenty or twenty five. Three of them were shirtless and deeply tanned.

"Those must be real Indians," Mary Goodwin said, surprised herself by what she was seeing.

"I've never seen a real Indian before."

"Aren't they horrid looking wild creatures?"

Frances looked around at the others as if seeking confirmation of her comment.

"They certainly aren't wearing much in the way of clothes," Mary Tracy said.

Frances quickly piped up: "You should not be looking at that young lady."

Mary Goodwin laughed, "For heavens sake why not?"

Frances turned her head away.

"Are they going to attack us?" Mary Tracy asked.

"No," John said. "Look just ahead, leading the whole group, is some U.S. Calvary. They are escorting them into town."

"Now that is interesting. Aren't they supposed to be fighting each other?"

"Maybe they are going to trade the horses."

John nodded. Exactly right.

The train slowed as it pulled into town and came to a stop at the station, the engine hissing and belting out steam. From the windows they looked at the freshly built wooden buildings, the people walking around the station, and, across the street, horses tied to the railings, another group of U. S. Calvary.

Mary Goodwin spoke up. "It certainly does not look like New York, does it?"

Standing on the platform in the sun John watched as a second train was getting ready to depart. People were piling into the waiting cars.

They were all poorly dressed and most did not carry luggage at all but rather large blankets bundled up with rope. All of their possessions were wrapped up inside. The luggage that a few did carry was old, torn, dented, and a few were held closed by rope tightly wrapped around. They all seemed European, eastern European, and only a few spoke English. Everyone flocked around those who did speak English in order to find out what was going on.

The station master told John that it was an 'immigrant train.'

"Cheap trains, cheap fares, they come by the thousands, we just try to herd them on through."

Going west.

The trains, the wagons, they are all going west.

"What about the Indians?" John asked.

"Naw, around here they are Pawnee. They're friendly. They make raids against the Sioux further north and steal their horses and bring them down here for trade."

"What about further on?"

"Yeah," he said waving away a fly, "further on down the line there's been some trouble, but that's not my jurisdiction so it's no concern of mine now is it?"

John watched as they stumbled onto the train, hot and overcrowded. West was the end of the rainbow where the sun set and the land was golden. John thought of the passionate drive of so many who traveled through such hardships in order to get somewhere that life might be better.

It was amazing to him. To give so much just on the hope that it will be better.

John, standing on the sun drenched platform, was growing a little impatient. It seemed absurd, a ridiculous waste of time, to change trains like this. Why can't they load onto a train in New York and travel the whole distance on the one train? Certainly the different owners of the different lines could come to an agreement allowing passage of each others trains.

John made a mental note to bring that up when he got back to the office. Surely something could be arranged. The railroad owners were so consumed in such petty wars with each other, why can't they see the larger picture, why can't they see how beneficial it would be for everyone to seamlessly integrate all of the lines and for all the trains to run as an efficient whole?

John looked out across the prairie. It was so big, so endless, and as flat as far as he could see. The grass and weeds rippled with the wind.

John watched as Mary Goodwin stood up straight. In her hand she held a bunch of wildflowers and put the back of her hand up against her forehead shielding her eyes from the sun. With her other hand she waved to John.

John waved back.

The two of them in the endless field, one bending over, the other standing tall and waving, sun drenched, the long grass rolling with the wind: John smiled.

If I were an artist, he thought to himself, a painter: that would be a painting I could hang on my wall.

The bellhop slid open the gate to one of the elevators. As the people in the elevator filed out they glanced at John. He watched their eyes, each glanced at his nose. Some quickly looked away; others stared as long as they could. It was always the same.

John and the others finally entered into the elevator. The elevator operator began to close the door when suddenly a small boy appeared. The operator stopped and opened the door again. The boy started to get on but then stopped when he looked up at John. The mother of the boy, wrapped in furs, came up behind him and held him back. The woman stared at John; he stared at her. He sees her eyes looking at his nose.

Do they think I do not notice?

The woman pulled the boy back.

"That's all right," she said to the operator. "We will catch the next one."

Did she pull her son away because it was him, J.P. Morgan standing there, or because it was a scary old man with a big ugly nose?

The elevator operator closed the door. Jack glanced at his father. He must have noticed.

The elevator heaved and with the clanging sounds of chains and gears began to rise. John, Jack, Louisa, the bellhop and the operator all stood in silence as the elevator rose up.

A bell rang and the elevator came to a stop. The operator clanged the door open. Before them was a long hallway, richly carpeted, chandeliered, with rows and rows of doors. The squeak of the gate being held open was loud in the silence of the hall. The bellhop got out first, then Louisa, then John, then Jack. They walked single file down the hallway.

The hallway was empty except for a small boy half way down standing before a door quietly knocking. The four of them continued walking down the hall. No one spoke. John watched the boy. He listened to their approach: the swish of fabric from Louisa's dress; the thumping of all their footfalls, heavy on the cushioning carpet; a small tinkle of the keys dangling from the hand of the bellhop.

The long line of them gets closer to the boy in the center of the hall. The boy raised his hand again to knock but then holds it in mid air. He does not knock. His head turns and he watches as they approach. It is as if the boy freezes in time, watching. John watches the boy watching them approach. Their footfalls get louder as they approach him. His eyes move from one to the next as they come up to him. The bellhop ignores the boy, staring blankly ahead. He walks around behind the boy, taking into consideration his presence but not acknowledging it. Louisa comes up to walk around behind the boy. The boy stares up at her, wide eyed. She looks down at him and smiles. The boy moved his stare to John. The swish of their clothes and coats was loud in the silence. The sound of their footfalls on the carpet was like a rolling thunder, now at the boy's feet. He felt their vibrations. The wood under the carpet must be trembling a little from the weight of their walk. John stares down at the wide eyed boy as he passes behind him. There was a look of fear on his face as the boy stared up at the tall man dressed in black walking back behind him staring down deep into his eyes. John walked past the boy but then, just as he passed he turned his head to look back. The boy was still staring at John. Soundless. He must not have looked at Jack, fixed as he was on John. As John continued to walk away from the boy the boy still stared and John still stared.

There was something.

John turned his head away and faced forward. From behind he could hear the small knocking on the door resume, a little louder and a little more persistent.

"Dad," the boy whispered aloud, and then a bit louder: "Dad."

There was something there.

Images flooded in.

John remembered; he remembered vividly well.

1853: he was fifteen.

The Silva Hotel; City of Horta; Island of Fayal; Azores, Portugal.

John knocked on the door. It was a small, quiet knock. He stood in the hotel hallway. It was dark and long and empty. Down the long hallway door after door was closed, locked, silent. There was a kerosene lamp at the end of the hall near the stairs. The heavy storm outside in the night banged against the window by the stairs. John watched and listened. In the deadened quiet of the hall he could hear the small hiss of the lamp. The sound of the wind and the rain outside the hotel was suppressed by the emptiness of the hallway. He smelled the moist air, the old damp and thin worn rugs. With the wind and the rain everyone must already be in their rooms all locked in and safe. The naked floorboards beneath the throw rugs creaked.

It was night but not too late. Doc should be in the room, John thought. Where else would he be? He would not be out, not in this storm.

John leaned in closer toward the door.

"Doc," he said as he knocked again.

John called Doctor Cole 'Doc.' Doctor Cole called John 'Pip.' It was like a secret bond between them.

Doc was sick. He had consumption. Just the other day his lung had hemorrhaged. John sat with him in his room. Wrapped in his white sheets and his creaking bed Doc tried to talk as if nothing was wrong. But he looked very old and tired, very tired. Doc suffered spasms of coughing and the blood spit up into his handkerchief. Crimson splattered on white. When the handkerchief became too stained John carefully picked it up and put it in a growing pile on the dresser and then got a fresh one from the top drawer and gave it to Doc. There was only one unused one left. Best do the wash soon, John thought to himself.

"That one was bad," John said, trying to smile.

Doc laughed. "I've had worse."

John reached over and ran the side of his hand along Doc's forehead. It was hot.

"Remember when I was sick that time and you took care of me?" John asked.

"Yes," Doc said. "You had a bad attack of influenza."

"Yes," John remembered.

John, sitting in his room, wrapped in blankets even though the sun was bright, Doc sat with him and they talked and watched the day go by out the window. John talked about all the things he could be doing if he was not sick and Doc talking about all the things he can do once he gets well. Then Doc smiled and reached over with his hand. He ran his fingers through John's hair and his fingers were so cool and soft against John's fevered forehead that he felt momentarily refreshed and relaxed and he closed his eyes. It was peaceful.

"I want to take care of you like that," John said with a firm boldness.

"But my boy," Doc tried to smile: "You already are."

John, standing outside in the dark hallway, was worried; he wanted to know that Doc was alright. He knocked on the door a third time and called out his name again. The sound fell flat as if wrapped in cotton. The dull roar of the wind outside made everything else seem trivial.

John tried the door. It was locked.

Earlier that afternoon the two of them were sitting together in the café watching out the windows as the rain come down. A side door in the back of the kitchen was ajar and even in the café itself you could hear from the open door the slap of the water outside coming down the pipes as it hit the cobblestone walkway. A cold breeze came in through the open kitchen door. Every time someone came into the café from the front door there was a rush of cold wet wind and a roar of the rain.

Whenever it rained it was usually a much warmer rain, a tropical rain. But this one was cold, this one was different. From where had it come?

They were going to play Chess. Doc slowly placed the pieces onto the board. It was a wooden board with carved wooden pieces. John watched the rain and then turned to Doc.

"Are you sure you want to do this?" he asked.

"Certainly, why would I not?"

"Well, are you feeling up to it?"

Doc stopped for a moment and looked at John.

But then his face seemed to soften, as if he changed his mind and decided not to say what he was going to say. After a moment Doc said: "Illness or no you have to keep going forward."

John shrugged his shoulders.

"I was white last game," Dr. Cole said. "You are white this game."

John moved his King's pawn.

Doc moved in reply.

John was sick when he first boarded the ship. His father Junius and mother Juliet were with him in the carriage as it came down the wooden wharf toward the ship. The wheels thumped across the uneven slats of wood. It was November and his mother wrapped him in coats and quilts, a woolen scarf around his neck. John watched with wonder at all the activity as the carriage slowly made its way down the wharf weaving through the throngs of people, passing ship after ship. There were stacks of crates and boxes as workers carried the cargo onto the ships. John had seen ships in harbor but he had never been this close.

The driver of the carriage had to stop several times to wait for the people to clear a pathway. Usually they would have parked the carriage at the entrance and walked down the wharf but John could not walk. He was very ill. The horse was nervous and skittish. The driver focused his whole energy on keeping the horse in control.

There seemed to be bells and horns being rung everywhere, shouting back and forth from the ships to the workers on deck. People talked loud as they walked back and forth.

When they finally stopped aside the square rigged barque 'Io' his father got out. John poked his head out of the window of the carriage and looked up at the side of the ship. It seemed enormous, the masts reached high up into the clouded sky.

Charles Dabney was waiting for them. He wore a heavy coat but it was open, John could see his brown checkered waist coat and tie. Mr. Dabney always dressed sharp. He walked over and shook Junius Morgan's hand.

"You've made it," Dabney said. He looked into the carriage and tipped his black hat.

"Mrs. Morgan. Pierpont."

"Quite a chilly day," Juliet said, rubbing her upper arms with her gloved hands.

"Yes, well: it is November, after all."

"I cannot thank you enough for doing this for us, looking after our sick little Pierpont for us like this."

John turned away slightly from his mothers touch.

"My pleasure; my pleasure indeed; I seriously doubt that he will be a bother and with the warm Mediterranean climate of the Azores he will be well in no time."

"Like we explained to you when Pierpont went to stay with his Grandfather in Medford the open country air seemed to help him, but then when he returned to New York he just got sick again. It is so discouraging. I so hope a long stay in the open country air of a warm climate will do him wonders."

"Well, as ambassador to the islands I was returning with my daughter and her friend anyway so the timing is perfect. I don't mind having him under my wing until his health returns."

Two men appeared with a stretcher for John to take him aboard. He hobbled out of the carriage and held onto the shoulder of one of the men. He did feel weak.

John looked up the stairway to the ship.

"Surely I can walk onto the ship."

"No you will not," his mother answered right away. "I will not allow you to exhaust yourself like that."

She motioned to the two men and they helped John onto the stretcher as his mother adjusted his blankets.

"You'll catch a death of a cold in this weather. Are you warm enough?"

"Yes, yes. Don't fuss so much."

"I worry so much about you."

"I'll be fine mother, I'll be just fine." As he said this he glanced at his father standing next to them. His father stood straight, a long grey jacket reached down to his knees, the belt tightly wrapped around his waist. He was expressionless.

Soon the two men hoisted up the stretcher and began walking toward the steps to board the ship. They had to hold him up high so the stretcher did not hit along the banister of the stairs. John was sitting up and looking all around. At the very top of the stairs they carefully, one foot at a time, stepped on the railing of the ship. They held him up high above their shoulders and John looked all around him. It was as if he were atop a mountain looking down on the world. As far as he could see there were ships lined along the wharf, hundreds of masts like naked trees pierced the skyline. A cold breeze washed against his face, a slight salt spray.

Watching from his lofty height, John looked down at his father and mother still standing on the wooden dock below. It seemed as though they had shrunk, they were smaller than just a moment before when he was down with them. His mother waved and he laughed and waved back. She had her handkerchief to her face, crying. His father stood still, like a chiseled statue. Only the flap of his coat moved in the chilly wind. His father did not wave back. He did not cry. He did not smile. His father just stood and watched, watched as his son was taken away, taken away for at least several months.

There was a sharp screeching sound of gulls overhead and John looked up to see them struggling for position on the cross beams of the masts. But then, just at that moment, in a soundless flight way above the clamor of the dock and the ships and the screeching gulls on the masts, way above it all high in the sky, soared a long white slender egret moving across the gray cloudy heavens. Its long thin body stretched out as it slowly and quietly flapped his long white wings. John was transfixed for a moment watching as the bird soared out to sea.

Soon you will be me, John thought to himself as though he were talking to the bird; and it answered by its flight, soon I will be you.

John moved his chess piece.

The rain poured. Sitting in the café with Doc playing chess John turned as a man entered the café. The roar of the rain increased as he opened the door but then he quickly shut it. The man's raincoat was dripping wet. John turned back to Doc. Doc had his eyes closed for a moment.

The man on the train had his eyes closed. Most of the way the man sitting opposite him dozed, his hands on his walking cane, as if holding him in an upright position the whole time, the man had his eyes closed. John did not understand how the man could sleep. They were riding one of the new trains.

John was only eight years old. His father was sending him by train to Boston to see Grandfather Pierpont. It was his first trip alone.

His father brought him in and showed him his seat. It was by the window. When he sat down he looked up at his father. His father stood there, pulled out his watch that he kept in his waist coat on a long chain and glanced at it before he put it back into his pocket. He looked up and down the car.

"Do you have the money I gave you?"

John felt his front pocket, felt the coins, and then nodded to his father.

"Be very careful and do not lose it."

John again nodded to his father. John sat forward in the seat. He could swish his legs forward and backward under the seat.

"The porter will look out for you and your grandfather will be at the station waiting for you."

John looked out the window to all of the people on the station.

"You are very lucky, son, to be able to ride like this on the train. We did not have trains when I was your age."

"Will it go fast?"

His father took a deep breath. "Fast enough," he replied.

"Well," his father said after a moment, "goodbye and have a nice trip. Say hello to your Grandfather Pierpont for me."

"I will."

John watched as his father walked away, down the center of the car and then out the door onto the wooden platform. John jumped when there was a loud shrill whistle. Men walked along the side of the train and closed all the doors with loud clicking snaps.

21

John remembered the trip. Once the train started the car swayed and rattled and bumped up and down. John watched out the window as the houses and trees and fields all went by. The wind came through the window and washed against his face. And he could smell the smoke from the engine up in front.

It was his first trip alone. It was on one of the new trains so he would have stories to tell the other boys when he got back home.

John stared at the man asleep in the seat opposite him. How could anyone sleep through this?

Doc had moved his chess piece. John had not even noticed.

Sitting in his chair back against the wall Doc sipped his hot tea and then smiled. To John he had changed. Even though John had only known him a few months recently he seemed more withdrawn and quiet, more internal, reflective. John knew he did not feel that well, even though Doc always said he felt fine and not to worry, it was obvious that Doc did not feel that well. John was concerned.

John moved his piece automatically, without thinking.

Doc glanced down at the board and then back up at John. He smiled. John returned the short smile.

Doc reached down and hesitated for a brief second but then he made his move.

It was very early in the morning when John came up onto the deck of the ship. He hugged his coat as he walked over to the railing. It was cold. The sky was just beginning to show streaks of dawn. There were large clouds hugging the eastern shore as the sun tried to climb and break free of its watery bed. Behind him the sky was still a dark and clear night dome. Stars still twinkled overhead and behind the ship. The ship rocked back and forth as it ploughed through the water. John could tell they were moving pretty fast. He could hear the splashing roar of the waves as the ship cut through the water. It seemed as though they had picked up speed from the prior day. A slight spray of water sprinkled the skin of his face. John walked back toward the rear of the ship along the starboard side. As he walked he had to adjust to the heavy sway of the ship.

As he walked he looked up at the sails. They were full of wind. The ropes creaked as they were pulled tight and twisted. The sails heavily flapped and rippled as the wind at their stern pushed them full. John listened as he walked at the twisting creak of the wooden masts. Through the ropes and the beams high above he could see the dark blue sky that stretched forever.

He felt much better than when he boarded the ship ten days ago. He actually felt better as soon as he got on board. Once he felt the ship moving through the water he managed to climb upstairs. The ship pulled out of harbor. John watched as the sea opened up wide before his eyes, it was as if the whole world was opening up in front of him. Sea gulls flew overhead and he turned to watch them pass over. Several others were flying along side the ship. John had a lot to write in his log book. It was noon when they passed Boston Light and the captain discharged the pilot. It was eight that evening when they passed Cape Cod Light and left it behind. It was the first time he sailed into open water. There were other sails sprinkled along the horizon but he watched as they grew more and more distant as the night closed in. Watching out the stern, the light house light sweeping the horizon grew dim and smaller as they continued to sail out into the night. He felt apprehensive, expectant, but not scared.

The courage it must have taken the early sailors, casting off into the night and the unknown. It would have been a grand adventure.

This morning he walked the full length of the ship as he felt the morning unfold. He stood by the rail at the stern and watched the white foaming wake the ship left behind. Captain Pillsbury and several sailors came over toward him.

"Well, Mr. Morgan. You are up awfully early."

"I could tell that the wind has picked up. Our speed has increased."

"You're a smart one you are. We're making very good time. We've come to measure, want to watch?"

One of the men held in his hands a chip log. It was a spool of thick twine attached to a roller. At one end of the twine was attached a chip of wood in the shape of a triangle with a lead weight attached to one end. As one sailor threw out the line another watched and as soon as the chip hit the water he turned over an hour glass. The sand started streaming into the glass on the bottom.

"Knot one."

The sailor holding the spool of rope let the rope slide through his gloved hand. At intervals the rope was tied into a knot. At each time a knot slipped through his hand he called out.

"Knot two."

Then as the twine unwound from the spool, and the spool creaked as it turned, the man called out again as a knot passed through his fingers.

"Knot three."

The man with the timepiece was looking very intently at his glass as the sand filed through.

"This measures out a half a minute," the Captain said.

"Knot four."

"That's how you tell speed?" John asked the captain.

"Knot five."

He nodded.

"The chip gives resistance in the water and more or less stays in the same place.

"Knot six."

"So we measure the distance we travel in thirty seconds."

"Knot seven."

"One nautical mile equals 6067 feet. In the rope there is a knot every 42 feet."

"Knot eight."

Bells rang at the bow of the ship.

John looked up at the creaking ropes above him. The thing about a ship is that everything is always moving.

"Knot nine."

John noticed how much lighter the sky seemed. The sun was just about to breach the horizon.

"Knot ten."

The man bent over and watching the time piece quickly stood up.

"Time," he called out loud. "Time," he repeated even louder.

"Just shy of eleven sir."

The captain, holding his log book, did the calculation as he explained it to John.

"So we measure how many knots we travel in thirty seconds. Eleven knots in thirty seconds, eleven times 42 feet between knots is. . ."

John, calculating in his head, said: "462."

The captain looked up from his calculations.

"So it is."

"I have a good head for figures."

"So you do. Now that is in thirty seconds so it is 924 a minute, which makes in an hour. . ."

Thinking to himself John replied first.

"55440."

After a moment the captain nodded with a look of amazement on his face.

"You do have a head for figures my boy. So then," he said, "55440 divided by 6067 of a nautical mile gives. . ."

John shook his head. That was beyond him without paper and pencil.

24

After a moment of calculating on a spare sheet of paper the Captain finally spoke.

"9.14 miles per hour."

The two men both began pulling in the rope.

The Captain looked to the sunrise and then back at John.

"You know that Christopher Columbus kept two sets of books on speed and location?"

"Really?"

"Yeah. He kept one set for himself that told where he really was and how far out they really were, then he kept another set of records to show his men, to show that they were still not far enough out that they could not return. If they ever went out further than their supply of food and water could keep them alive on a return trip then they went out too far to come back. He was a very bold man, Columbus. He believed in himself and his ideas so much that he was willing to put his entire crew at risk."

"But is that good?" John asked. "Suppose he had been wrong?"

"Only when you are right is it good. If he had been wrong then no one would have lived to tell the tale now would they? So be bold my friend, but, most importantly, be right."

The Captain laughed a hearty laugh and then nodded.

John nodded back. "I will keep that in mind. But tell me another thing."

"What's that?"

"Why are you called the Io?"

"Because that's our name."

"But why Io?"

"Well, my boy, as I understand it Io was this beautiful young Greek girl. But then the god Zeus fell in love with her."

"As he seemed to do," John added.

"So it seems, just like our Joe here."

"What's that?" the time keeper asked, looking up from pulling in the rope.

"You always seem to be falling in love with young maidens."

The man raised an eyebrow and smiled. Half of his front tooth was chipped away. "Oh yeah, nothing wrong with that is there?"

"Watch what you say," said the knot counter, "there's a young lad here."

The time keeper winked. "I bet a lad like him has his own maidens back home."

John smiled. "A true gentleman never says."

They looked at him. Then the knot counter piped up. "That makes Joe no gentleman for sure."

They all laughed, including John.

There were the Draper girls; the Draper School for Young Girls out on Pratt Street. There was a large tree next to the dormitories so at night if you could climb over the wall and then climb up the tree without being seen then you could whisper to the girls through the window. They would open the window and lean out and giggle and talk in low whispers so the head mistress would not hear them. John used to climb up the tree and Jim Goodman came up with him. One night they were in the tree and he was leaning out far, holding onto the branch of the tree, trying to give the girls a box of chocolates. The girls were leaning out the window trying to get the box when suddenly John could see down the hall behind them the head mistress walking right toward them. It shocked him and he let go of the tree. Before he knew it he hit the ground with a loud painful flop. He lay there for a moment before he realized Jim was standing over him pulling him up.

Hurry he said, hurry.

All John could think about was that they had to get away. He stood and painfully ran to the wall and he and Jim were up and over to the other side just as the head of the head mistress poked out of the window. He could hear the girls screaming back into their rooms.

Then the Captain continued the story.

"So this here Zeus, trying to hide Io from his jealous wife, he turns her into a heifer. But see the wife is wise to all of his tricks and she sends a wasp out to torment the poor woman. So Io can never find rest, she is trying to escape and wanders all over the world, trying to have a moments rest from the sting of the wasp. Well then, see: that is us. This ship is always moving, always traveling the open sea, always in search of friendly port."

"Always in search of peace," John added.

"Yeah, that too."

"But the story ends when she finds peace in Egypt," John said, concluding the tale.

"Say, so you already know this story? Well," the Captain said, "I guess it was too hot out there for the wasp but we've never been to Egypt yet so there you go."

The men had gathered in all of the rope and were ready to leave.

"It was a bit rough last night," John said, wanting them to stay a little bit longer.

"Yes, last night the waves were a thing to master. It's the back end of a storm passing through. That's what gives us this wonderful wind this morning."

"Some below are sea sick," John added.

"Well, my boy. I take it you are not?"

"No, sir, not I; not I sir."

"On such a good morning remember this. Not everyone has it in them to ride the waves. Well, nice chatting with you young Mr. Morgan, but I've a ship to bring to port and it don't do it on its own."

John moved his chess piece.

Antonio brought some more hot water over for their tea.

"This rain is a cold rain," he said. "That means it comes from the north. It is usually not this cold."

John piped up.

"Maybe it will wash the island away."

Antonio flipped his towel at him, and then laughed.

Doc enjoyed the company of friends. Doc dabbed his lips with his handkerchief and looked to see if there was any stain.

"It is nice on a cold day to have warm friends," Doc said as he reached down to make his next move. He held the piece in the air for a brief moment and then, apparently satisfied, placed it down into its new position.

John swirled the tea into the hot water.

John sat in the café. Antonio brought him some flat bread and cheese. John watched an older man sitting in a corner. He was well dressed and wore a stylish fedora; tie, coat, waist coat, and a polished mahogany cane with the tip on the floor the man seemed to rest his hand on the handle. He had a small pot of hot water and a cup of tea. He had black hair and a small black moustache. John thought that at his age his hair should be gray or even white but it was not. The man seemed totally absorbed in a game of chess he was playing by himself, and with himself. He moved the carved wooden pieces slowly across the board, moving first a white piece and then a black. How could he play with himself?

John watched him. There was something a little odd about him.

At one point the man looked up at John. John tried to look away, as if he were not watching the man.

"Do you play?"

John turned to the man as if he had never seen him before. "What was that?"

"I asked, young man, if you play."

The man nodded toward the board.

"Yes."

"Then perhaps one day you can indulge me in a friendly game."

John nodded yes. The man had an English accent.

"You have just arrived today, I think?"

"Yes. I came from the United States with Charles Dabney."

"Ah yes. I know him well. Tell him that Doctor Cole passed on his hello. Are you staying at his home or here at the hotel?"

"Here."

"Then we shall see a bit of each other for I am staying here myself. For me it is for my health. I am, alas, a bit sickly. And you?"

John got up and walked over to the man.

The man motioned him to have a seat.

"I am sick too. I am here to get well."

"A young lad like you is sickly? I am so sorry to hear that. When you get as old as I am sometimes being sickly comes as a bonus, like an extra treat, but not for someone as young as yourself."

"I will get well."

"Yes you will. And what is your name?"

"John Pierpont Morgan."

"Sounds like a noble name to me."

"I like it."

"Pierpont, it is derived, if I am not mistaken, from a 'stone bridge,' a 'Pierre ponte' built by Charlemagne in the eighth century. A bit before even I was born."

"You are playing chess with yourself?"

Doctor Cole looked down at the board.

"Yes," he replied with a grin. "But that way I always win."

"Yeah, but you always lose too."

"Ah, yes; quite. But such is life my boy."

John laughed. He liked this man.

"I also play a lot of solitaire. Whist. Do you play that as well?"

John shook his head no.

"Shall I teach you?"

"Sure, Doc."

John froze and put his hand up to his mouth.

"I am sorry," he said.

"For what are you sorry?"

"I accidently called you Doc. I apologize."

"There is no need."

"But it is disrespectful."

"It is in some circles a familiar. Let us let it be that. That shows we are going to be friends."

"I have a younger brother and my parents call him The Doctor, so I just call him Doc."

"How old is this doctor?"

"Six."

"Cute?"

John shrugged his shoulders.

"I do not know. I guess. Father likes him the best I think."

"Ah, I see. Well, I will tell you what. You may call me Doc but only if I can call you a nickname."

"Well, my sister calls me Pip."

"Pip?"

"Yes. I got that from the other boys at school."

"And why is that?"

"Well, it was when I was six years old and it was the first day of school. I went to the West Middle District School. Mr. Thomas K. Beecher was the teacher and on the first day he called the roll. Each of us, one by one, had to stand up and give our name. When it was my turn I stood up and called it out: 'John Pierpont Morgan, sir' I said. Mr. Beecher looked at me with his big glasses down around his nose and asked me to repeat it. It was an uncommon middle name he said. So I said: 'Pierpont, sir. John Pierpont Morgan.' But I could hear the other boys giggling behind me. 'What's that,' they said, 'Pier, Pont, Pipont.' And then one of them, Jimmy Calhoon it was, shouted out loud: 'Pip is it?' And then they all laughed. They all called it out then and the teacher had to shush them."

"You sound as if you do not like the name."

John shrugged his shoulders.

"I did not at first but then after my sister started calling me it then I got used to it."

"I do not want to be as presumptuous as to interfere with any intimacy with your sister."

"No, it is all right."

"She will not mind if we share the nickname?"

John smiled wide.

"She is not here."

"Very well, then Pip it shall be."

John moved his chess piece.

The rain beat down.

Doc quickly moved in response.

Doc sat back and watched through the window.

John moved to castle his king.

John noticed that Doc at times withdrew into himself, even if but for a moment. He noticed and understood. He himself had bad mood swings and became withdrawn at times. 'Why are you so melancholic?' his mother asked him once. He did not know at the time what that meant. He was just being himself.

Once he was in a foul mood because he was enraged. He would not even talk to his mother. He sat in his room staring at the fire. His mother even sent his father in to find out what was the matter.

What is wrong with you, his father said once he came into the room and stood over John slumped in his chair.

John did not reply.

Maybe you did not hear me the first time, his father said. I asked you a question and I expect an answer.

John told him. He had gotten a mathematics problem marked wrong but it was not wrong. His answer is correct, I checked it over and over, my answer is right. The textbook is wrong.

Son, the textbook is written by mathematicians. They do not make mistakes.

Yes they did, John shouted, enraged.

All right now, let us keep a level tongue. Perhaps you are missing something. Let me see the problem.

His father sat down at the table and pulled over John's slate. He picked up the small piece of chalk. John showed him the problem.

His father worked the problem and when he came up with the same answer that John did he glanced at his son.

Let me see, he said as he wiped the slate clean and started the problem a second time. He came up with the same answer.

See, John said. The book is wrong. Now I have a bad mark even though I am right. What is the point?

John remembered that his father stared at him for a long time. But then he smiled. John would never forget that.

You are right. The book is wrong. You and I will go and see the teacher tomorrow, we will show him.

Then, after a pause, his father said: Always remember, my son, that what is right is right and it does not matter that someone thinks it is wrong.

John's grandfather was brooding, Grandfather Pierpont. John inherited a lot from his Grandfather Pierpont. His grandfather had the red sores that flared up on his face too. His nose too was slightly disfigured. John inherited a lot from his Grandfather Pierpont.

John noticed that Doc had moved.

John woke one morning with his face broken out. The acne, the red blotches, his swollen reddish nose. The attacks come and go, but they seemed to be more intense lately. John stared at himself in the mirror and then picked up his pillow and held it up so that he could not see the mirror.

There was a gentle knock on the door. John did not reply. Maybe they will go away. He did not want to be seen, he did not want to see anyone the way he looked.

There was another gentle knock on the door.

"Go away," John shouted at the closed door.

"It is me, Pip." It was Doc.

"I can't see you now. Go away."

There was a pause.

"But we planned to go on a morning walk together."

"I changed my mind. I don't want to go."

Another silence.

"Let me in so we can discuss this a bit further."

"No. I do not want to discuss it anymore."

"But, you see, I do; therefore, Pip, the door, please."

John finally went across the room and unlocked the door and then returned to his bed.

Doc slowly entered, carefully closed the door behind him, walked over to the bed and then sat down. He put both of his hands on the top of his walking stick and used it to balance himself as he sat on the bed. He looked at John.

"Well," John almost shouted. "Don't you see?"

"I see you. What is it that I am to see?"

"It is one of my flare ups. I am ugly, people will stare at me."

"I certainly doubt that they have nothing better to do in their lives than stare at your face, but so what if they do?"

"You do not understand."

31

"Let them stare: stare back."

John did not respond.

"Pip, you are what you are. If they cannot accept that then they are not worthy of your attention."

John still did not respond.

"I am an old man. I am not as young and dashing as I once was. My face is wrinkled. I do not like to have people look at me as a wrinkled up old man but many do, so there it is. Should I let that stop me from going out and about and being what I am?"

"It's not the same."

"Pip, my boy, believe me when I say that when you are as old as I am now you will then know that it is the same. When they look at me they see an old man, so be it. They do not see that the young dashing youth is still there inside this mask. And when they see you they will see a young boy with acne."

Doc shrugged his shoulders and opened his eyes wide: "So what?"

John could not help but smile.

"Be true to yourself, Pip, and all things will come. It was the Greek playwright Aeschylus who said 'It is not the oath that makes us believe the man but the man the oath.' Be true to yourself, it does not matter what others believe. Besides, we will walk in nature, up the hill toward the top of the island. There is a wonderful view of the mountain Pico across the waters. We will pack a lunch. The weather is simply inviting."

John finally nodded.

Doc had the café make up a boxed lunch for the two of them: flat bread and cheese with a small container of water. Once outside they immediately turned up the hill and began the steady ascent. It was heavy going. Doc, walking with his cane, had to stop at times to rest. But they finally reached a plateau and walked out toward the edge. They sat on an outcropping of rocks. The sun was warm on their backs. The rocks were almost too hot to sit on. The sky was a clear blue as far as they could see: cloudless. It was the kind of sky that seemed to go on for ever.

"This is much more vast than England."

"There are parts of America that go on forever, and I do mean forever."

"You have seen these parts?"

"Well, no. But I have heard said there are."

"Then you must make it a point to see these parts."

They looked across the water to the other island and Mount Pico, the highest point on the Azores. There was a touch of clouds shrouding the peak.

They ate their flat bread and cheese together. They shared the water container. They talked.

"Some day I want to walk up that hill," John said, indicating Mount Pico.

"Pip, I do believe that this particular peak is not referred to as a hill, it is referred to as a mountain."

John turned to him puzzled.

"When is a hill a mountain, or a mountain a hill?"

Doc thought about it for a moment.

"Well I suppose that when a mountain is in your way you can just think of it as a hill. That makes it easier to overcome. Any one can climb a hill."

"So that is what I said, some day I want to go up that hill. Do you want to come with me?"

Doc laughed.

"No, no, that is not for me; that would take far too much energy for me to do."

"What do you want to do, then?"

Doc thought about it for a moment, he then turned to John with a new found energy.

"If everything goes well I would like to see America in the spring. Perhaps I can visit your forever parts. I have never been."

"Great. I can show you around."

Doc nodded.

"That would be grand."

John quickly moved his chess piece and took a piece.

John would later write a letter to his father. He wrote his family everyday. But they did not write back. Looking back from his stretcher, being lifted onto the Io, John looked back and saw his father standing on the wooden wharf. His face was expressionless. His son was sick, so sick he had to sail away to a remote island and he would not be seen for months, perhaps for ever, and his fathers face was expressionless.

And he did not write letters in return to his son's letters.

A coldness enveloped him. Maybe it was just the cold and damp of the rain.

John had been sick a lot. He missed school. He spent days in bed. He heard his father once, outside in the hallway where he did not think John could hear. His father was talking to one of his business partners, he was saying how he had hoped to bring his son into the business with him soon, and he had hoped to bring him in as a clerk. John was surprised: his father actually wanted him. But then his father said in a depressing tone of voice, but now, he said, but now I do not know what I am going to do with him.

Doc moved a piece and took a piece. John watched him, the move had been expected. Doc carefully placed the taken piece on the side of the board. When he took pieces he liked to line them up in a row.

They were sitting in John's room when Doc saw it. Looking out the window, John's panoramic window view of the harbor, Doc saw the three mast ship coming into port. John was talking about something but Doc interrupted him.

"John. John. Look," he said as he pointed.

John turned and then stood at the window wide eyed at the sight.

"I bet it comes from America. Look, is not that the flag on the stern?"

"I can not see that far."

"I bet it brings mail. What do you think?"

Doc shrugged his shoulders.

"I am going to go down when it docks. What about you?"

"Go, my boy. Go. I'll be in the café. Bring me the news."

With that John bolted out of the room and into the hallway. Doc heard his footfalls run toward the stairs and then down them at least two at a time. He did not even close the door behind him.

Doc, sitting in the chair with his walking cane set on the floor between his legs with both his hands resting on the top of the cane, closed his eyes and shook his head.

Youth.

He watched the sky, clouds sliding by; so white against such a deep blue.

Slowly he stood, using the cane to balance himself. He made his way to the window and stood watching as the large three mast ship sailed into port. It did not happen everyday. It was something of a joy when it did.

Oh great ship, what word do you bring. Father from across the sea, any word will do.

The heart of your son aches.

It was better than an hour later that Doc sat in the café: a pot of hot water and a cup of tea on the small table before him.

John came in. Doc knew as soon as he saw him.

John sat down next to him.

"Nothing?" Doc asked.

John shook his head.

"There was mail, but nothing for me. I do not understand. I write, I write almost everyday. Whenever a ship comes by I send it. Why do they not write to me? I do not understand. Have they forgotten that I am here?"

"Don't be silly my boy."

"Well?"

"You know what? I have a present for you."

"What present?"

"Here, follow me."

The two of them left the café and walked up the street, and then down a side street.

It was a bird shop.

When they were done they came back to John's room with two cages. In one were two yellow canaries and in the other a blackbird. They set them on the open window ledge of his room. The warmth of the sun and the coolness of the breeze washed the room.

The canaries began to sing. John laughed.

"You are lucky that you are on the second floor, otherwise a cat could snatch them away."

John moved his chess piece.

Have you ever heard of a man named Paul Morphy?" Doc asked.

"No."

"He is this genius of a chess player. He's from New Orleans, in America. Just about your age I think."

Doc did not talk for a moment as he studied his next move. Carefully he reached down and made his move. He took another piece and then carefully placed it on the side of the board in his neat little row.

"Maybe I should play him some day," John laughed.

"Actually in a way I think you will. You see," he said as he waved his hand across the chess board. "It is just a game, life is a game, you can not change it but you can arrange clever ways of moving."

John moved as Doc spoke as if by moving when he talked Doc would not notice the implications of his move.

John looked back as someone came into the café from the rain outside. He was soaking wet. Why does anyone go out in this? Doc continued to talk even though John had looked away.

"But his genius is to see things, to see moves, which no one else can see because they all follow the same patterns. We live in these patterns. It is hard to see outside of them. They are our daily lives. The genius is to break out of that and see things from totally different perspectives."

When John turned back around he saw that Doc had already moved his piece.

"You will see a thing like no one else does and then they will wonder why they did not think of it themselves."

John knocked softly on the door again.

"Doc, it's me. Pip."

John came up from the café, Doctor Cole was not there. He surely would not be outside in this. John waited for a moment more. He heard the winds and the rain outside. At the window at the end of the long hall branches from the tree outside slapped against the glass. John walked down the hall, glancing back once to see the closed door for one last time. It was just the other day that John was in the room beside Doc's bed. He had a lung rupture. He wheezed when he breathed. John brought up a tray of tea and sugar with a saucer of cream. John sat by the bed and poured out his tea for him. Dr. Cole took a sip and then lay back. John held his hand.

"Has your father written?"

John shook his head no.

"There was only the one letter."

"He will write. He is a very busy man."

Doc laughed.

"Perhaps he wrote you everyday but they were all on a ship that sunk."

"I don't really see that as funny."

Doc shrugged. "Life is a fragile business."

"When I was at home my father a lot of times was away on business."

"There, you see; you are a good boy."

"Thank you. I try."

Doc coughed a little bit. "He will write," he declared. "The world rights itself after a bit."

"You helped me when I was sick so now I can help you now that you are sick."

Doc smiled, but then coughed. John did not realize that he had said that several times as if by saying it Doc would be nursed back to health.

John did not really know what else to do.

"In all things fairness," Doc said as he watched John. "In all things love and respect."

"Return a good deed with the same," John said, trying to match Doc's little sayings.

"But more importantly," Doc replied as he closed his tired eyes, "return a bad deed with a good."

John walked to the hall window and looked out at the night. It was dark and the wind howled. Tree branches beat against the glass. He is afraid that it will break. If the glass ever breaks then the black howling night will come in. It will howl through the hall and leave nothing untouched. It is so dark he cannot see outside, just the branches looming out of blackness. Far off in what would be the water he sees small specks of light where the ships would be moored. Surely a storm like this will play havoc with the ships in the harbor. John felt the cold air seeping through the window. Maybe there was a crack around the edges of the glass. Even now a bit of the wind got in somehow. John reached out and touched the window. It was cold and seemed moist to his touch. The glass trembled a little each time a gust of wind hit it. It scared him. It seemed so fragile.

As fragile as Doc.

As fragile as himself.

What was trying to get in? You must always be on the move so that it will never catch you. It was a race with the wind to the end.

John moved again and this time took another of Doc's pieces.

John pulled an orange out of his coat pocket and began to peel it. The juice from the outer peel popped into the air and onto his hands.

John loved oranges.

Dabney grew them in his back yard. Once John went up to their house but they were not there so he sat on the stone wall by their trees and, one by one, ate twelve of them. He picked them and then lined them all up on the top of the low wall in a single row and sat down in the middle of them and began eating them one by one.

John loved oranges.

He offered Doc a section of the orange and they sat there and ate it together. Doc watched him very closely.

Doc, holding the sliver of orange up to his mouth with one hand reached out and moved with his other.

The next morning John heard voices in the hallway just outside his door. People were walking back and forth. He quickly dressed and opened his door, carefully peeking down the hall. Three men stood outside one of the rooms. The door to the room was open. It took a moment before John realized that it was Doc's room. John opened his door, stepped outside and then carefully closed his door behind him. It was as if he did not want to be heard or noticed. He walked down the hall, hugging close to the wall. As he walked he could gradually hear what they were saying. The three men were guests in the hotel, John had seen them before.

"It was the maid who found him," the tall man in a white suit was saying.

"Really," the second man, large with a beard, replied.

"It certainly was a shocker. I heard her run by my room gasping for breath."

"Here, stand aside," the third man with the moustache said. "It looks like the Doctor is done."

The two men stood to one side as another man came out into the hallway. He was carrying a small black leather bag. He was speaking Portuguese to a man who came out of the room after him. That man was the Manager of the hotel.

John walked around them and between them until he could see into the room. As they talked he glanced at each one of the men outside the room and then back into the room. John could see Doc's black suitcase open on the chair by his window; his grey coat on the coat rack. Several other men were standing about in the room.

John walked in. No one really noticed him as he entered. It was Doc's drawing room. His pants and a shirt were draped over the wicker chair by the window. Doc did that before retiring to bed. Several books were on the table by the sofa. The pillows were propped up just as Doc liked them. Whenever they played chess in his room he would go through a ritual in propping and fluffing three large pillows into a certain way. 'Best for my back' he said as John watched him, waiting.

John knew the room. He walked past the sofa and looked around the corner into the other room through the door, the bedroom. He could see the bottom of the bed. The covers were pulled up. Someone was in the bed under the covers. Another man stood by the bed, his back to the door. John stood still for a moment but then he entered. With each step more of the room came into view, more of the bed came into view. As he stepped into the room itself he could see the entire bed.

Doc was lying in the bed, the covers pulled down to his waist. He wore his pale and well worn light blue bed shirt that he wore. His white robe draped across the covers as if he had just taken it off and set it down. His head faced the door. His eyes were closed. If he opened his eyes he would look straight at John. Doc was still. His face relaxed and his mouth was slightly open.

There were two men standing in the room, one on either side of the bed. They talked in Portuguese and John did not understand what they were saying. All John could see was Doc on the bed. Still. Not breathing. It was as if at any moment his eyes would open up, see John, and then look around the room startled, wondering who are all these people and why were are they all here in my room and I am not properly dressed to meet them.

John waited, he stood watching. He did not know exactly what he was waiting for. But Doc did not open his eyes. He did not move. He did not breathe. He was silent. The voices of the men talking faded away until John could not hear them anymore. A deep heavy and empty silence arose out of the bed and enveloped the room.

The man on the opposite side of the bed came over to John. He felt the man place his hand open palmed against his chest.

"Mr. Morgan," the man quietly said.

John at first did not hear him. But slowing the voice seemed to emerge from somewhere. He knew the voice. It was the desk clerk. Antonio. Not the Antonio of the café but Antonio the desk clerk. John did not look up. He could not take his eyes off the face of his friend. He felt a slight pressure as Antonio pressed his hand against his chest.

"Come, Mr. Morgan. Let me take you away."

John still did not look up.

"He is my friend," John was just able to say. He spoke just above a whisper.

"I know, Mr. Morgan. I know. Come with me. You don't want to be here."

John had to study his next move. It seemed that things were not going so well. Were the tables turning? Antonio brought over a small dish of sliced cheese.

"My friend is perhaps confused?" Doc said to Antonio.

John studied the board.

"You see, Antonio, he does not even hear us. He has such focused concentration when he wants."

John started to make a move but then stopped. He knew nothing of their conversation. He had been so confident but now, in one move, everything seemed different. How could one unexpected move change the whole carefully plotted game? He had to expect that, to look out for that, and to know how to react to that, the unexpected move.

It was when John went to the Cheshire school in Connecticut, he was about thirteen, at that time the school did not have a boarding house so the students all stayed with different families in the town. John's father arranged for John to stay with The Reverend Dr. Seth Paddock and his family, two boys and a daughter. Dr. Paddock was the principal of the school. John's school friend Jared Starr boarded in a house down the block and he would walk by Dr. Paddock's house each morning on his way to school. John would be on the porch, in the porch swing, or leaning over the railings of the porch. Jared knew that Reverend Paddock was ill so he shouted out to John each morning.

"How's Dr. Paddock today?"

"Oh, he is just about the same," John replied each morning, busy doing whatever he was doing at the time.

This went on day by day. But then one morning Jared called out: "How's Dr. Paddock today?"

John, absorbed in something, shouted out as always: "Oh, he is just about the same."

Jared walked on but then John suddenly shouted out to him.

"Oh, I forgot, Dr. Paddock is dead."

It took a long time for John to figure something out but John finally made his move. He moved his Queen and took a piece. There was a twinkle in his eyes as he watched Doc's face as he put Doc's taken piece aside.

Later John sat in the café. He was writing a letter. The tip of the pen scratched across the rough surface of the paper.

"My poor friend here Dr. Cole died last evening at 5 o'clock he was a very nice gentleman and was a great source of pleasure to me."

On the table off to one side were the remains of his breakfast: eggs; bread; hot tea. John sipped his tea as he stared out the window. The

40

storm from last night had gone. The sky was still overcast with heavy dark clouds but the rain, at least for now, had stopped. He watched the people as they walked by. The streets and trees and buildings were all still very wet and cold. The doctor said he died around 5 o'clock. It was not long after their chess game.

I was standing outside his door. I was knocking. And he was already dead. He was there inside and heard me call out to him but did not reply. He could not hear the living. He was already dead. Where did he go? How can someone just disappear like that leaving their body behind? Where do they go?

Already John felt emptiness inside where warm thoughts of Doc use to dwell.

He was writing a letter to his father. How can I describe that to him?

John put the cup of tea down into the saucer and picked up his pen. He stuck the tip of the pen into the inkwell and hunched over his letter. Holding the paper with one hand he began again to write.

"I miss him very much, for he was a very agreeable person."

John remembered something that Doc had said once: they were on the hill above the town of Horta on a picnic looking out across the waters to the mountain of Pico. The sun was bright and warm, the sky clear. Cherish the beauty you find wherever you find it for it is a very precious gift.

Nothing lasts forever. Everything is fragile.

John watched Doc's face. It was the end. Doc was doomed. For a brief moment it looked like Doc had turned the table and John was going to lose the chess game. But then John focused. He applied his full energy to the task. How do I not only get out of this but turn the tide for me to win? He sacrificed his queen, no one did that, but it was a trap.

John sat back. He was going to win and the realization was slowly coming over Doc's face. But it felt empty. John almost felt ashamed. Doc had the look in his eyes. It was written on his face.

When he was ten John was pulled out of school. His Grandfather Morgan was dying and he wanted to be with his grandchildren up until the end. So John and his two sisters were pulled out of school and taken to see their grandfather. Grandfather Morgan went to church on Sunday and spent the whole day in Church, service after service. That was the way he was. But when John got to Grandfather Morgan's house he was in bed. John went in to see him. His grandfather held out his hand and held John's hand. His sister's were there as well. The next day was Sunday and John got up and got dressed in his Sunday best in order to go to church with his grandfather but his grandfather did not go to church that day. His grandfather did not even get out of bed that day.

John knew then that this was serious. Something was dreadfully wrong.

For days John sat around the house. They could not go anywhere. They could not go to school. They could not go into town.

John stood on the stairs staring into Grandfathers room. The door was open and John, standing on the stairs, could see in. He could see the chairs, the desk, the drawers, and the bed where Grandfather lay moaning. His back hurt bad and he had bad pains in his stomach.

John watched day after day. He would go in and see his grandfather who smiled and squeezed his hand but then grimaced from the pain. John could see it in his face; he could see it in his eyes. This was the end.

But the end took a long time.

Then one morning while he was still in bed his father came into the room and stood by his bed. John, in bed under the covers, looked up at him. It was still dark. His father held up a lantern. The flickering flame shimmered the room with soft light. Father spoke.

"Grandfather Morgan died early this morning."

John did not know what to say. He did not know what he was supposed to feel.

"When you get dressed come up and you can say goodbye to him."

His father left the room. The light left with him. Darkness of night closed in and filled the room as his father left. He could hear the creak of the floorboards as his father walked away down the hall.

John got dressed. He went up the stairs. When his father saw him standing in the hallway he waved him into the room. John came in and stood at the bed. His grandfather was under the sheets. His head was turned away. He did not breathe. He did not reach out and hold John's hand.

John left the room. He walked down the stairs. He stood in the kitchen and looked out at the morning. The sun was just coming up. Maybe now he could go out and play.

John waited for Doc to make his next move. Doc studied the board but it seemed that he was not that focused on the game. At first he had played well but now he was wandering. It seemed to John that the game did not have that much to offer Doc anymore now that they were near the end.

Doc finally reached out and moved a piece as Antonio brought over more hot water for the tea. As he placed the pitcher on the table there was a sudden loud clap of thunder followed by a rolling roar as the sound washed across the heavens.

Antonio wiped his hands on his apron. "If this storm keeps up it will be the death of us all."

"More is to come," Doc said. "The gods are not yet satiated."

When John was eight years old he almost died. Charley Beach, eighteen, and his two younger brothers Frank and Ike one day went down the road toward Little River to wade and fish. Charley walked with their fishing poles across his shoulder. Young John wanted to come along but they said no. He followed them from behind as they walked down the road calling to them the whole way to let him come with them but they said no, go away.

The Beach boys got to the river and started to fish. They told John to go away. John instead climbed up a tree by the riverbank that stretched out over the water where they were fishing. He shook the tree branch again and again in order to scare the fish away. Whenever he saw a fish in the water he threw a twig at it. It splashed away.

"Stop it," they called out to him.

"Go home and leave us alone," the Beach boys shouted.

John continued to shake the tree. But then he lost his balance and before he knew it he splashed into the river. When he surfaced he could hear them all laughing.

"Serves you right, see," they shouted.

John, choking and inhaling water, disappeared under the water again. When he came up they were still laughing but it did not matter because he could not get his breath. He inhaled but water rushed in and he disappeared under the water again. It hurt his lungs.

The next time he came up he briefly saw Ike on the embankment near him. They were no longer laughing. It looked like Ike was throwing out his fishing line to John. But he almost blacked out and everything hurt and there was no air and they were shouting something about grab the line grab the line and John reached out and clung to the line as he went under the water again and he could not see because it was dark in the water.

He felt hands pulling him and he felt dry land but no air and he hurt all over and gagged and coughed until he passed out. The next thing

John knew they were holding him up and he was choking and spitting out water.

That night Grandfather Morgan made a small notation in his ever present diary: "Pierpont came near drowning while fishing in Little River near Finlay's Upper Mills with George Beach's sons. He was rescued by Isaac T. Beach reaching him his fish pole."

And with that Grandfather Morgan put his quill down and closed his book and went to bed.

Suddenly the outside door swung open.

"Pierpont," a man called out. John looked up. It was Charles Dabney standing in the doorway. He walked over to John and stood looking down at him.

"Are you all right?"

John nodded. "Doc died."

"I heard; that is why I've come."

"He was my friend."

There was a very long pause as Dabney stood there looking down at John. He did not know what else to say. John placed his pen down upon the paper.

"Come and see the damage from the storm," Dabney said. "The Io cracked two masts."

"What?"

Charles waved him up. "Come on and see."

John went out the door with him. It was cold and John did not have his coat but they walked down the street toward the harbor. There was litter on the street. Broken palm branches were scattered around the street. The ground was wet. Everything had a fresh wet smell, washed clean. Roofs dripped.

But when they came in view of the harbor they both stopped short. It was a scene of utter destruction. Usually boats were set side by side in neat orderly rows. But now they were tossed about at random. Facing every which way, torn from their moorings, a collection of smaller boats were all bunched up banging against each other and against the stone sea wall. Broken masts lay across several boats. One larger ship was seriously listing to the port side.

"Look," Dabney said as he pointed out further to sea.

It was the Io. It was still tied to its mooring but two masts were snapped off. One plunged straight down into the water. Ropes and tangled canvas kept it tied to the side of the boat. The second mast had split and was leaning against the third, hopelessly entangled. Men were trying to tie up the ropes.

The sea was still choppy and stray boats banged against each other floating which ever way waves pushed them.

John thought about his Grandfather Pierpont, about one of his sermons, something about frail mortals crushed by the Hand of God: he remembered that it scared him the way his grandfather shouted it out in a deep angry voice.

From the north there was a heavy roll of thunder. John looked toward the sound. The sky was almost black in that direction. Heavy black churning clouds were coming in as if they all had a life of their own. Crawling across the sky they were like creatures swarming in from the deepness of the heavens.

There was a light spray of cold rain on his face. His clothes were growing damp to the touch.

"Come along," Dabney said as he looked up at the clouds. "We should get inside. It looks like rain again."

John heard him but did not answer. He was too fascinated with the churning clouds.

Dabney put his hand on John's shoulder.

"You do not want to be here."

Mere frail mortals are we: what are we to the Power and Majesty of the Almighty?

John watched as Doc closed his eyes. John listened to the wind and the rain outside while watching peace come over Doc. He looked so tired sitting in his chair against the wall. When he finally opened his eyes again John reached to the chessboard.

He moved.

"Mate in two," he said, apprehensive. Part of him felt proud: he won. But part of him felt rotten: he was losing something more important.

Doc looked from the board to John and smiled.

He knew.

"I am tired," he said. "I think it is time to retire."

John nodded. "See you later."

"Yes. I hope too."

Cards of Queens

John stepped out onto the balcony of his hotel room. The night air was cold and felt damp against his skin. He smoked his cigar. He rested his palms on the cold railing. Looking out across the city he saw the lights flooding the streets in all directions. There were lights on in the buildings. It seemed like a sea of lights that kept the city alive. As a boy if he stood here and looked out the city would have been dark, black, perhaps a few kerosene lamps here and there. This late at night the city would be asleep. And as a grown man if he stands here the busiest streets would be softly illuminated with flickering gas lights. But now, with electricity everywhere, the city was alive with activity.

Louisa stepped out onto the balcony.

"Why are you out here in the cold night air?"

"Look out at the city," he said.

She stood next to him and looked around.

"I helped bring this about," he said.

"Brought what about?"

John swept his hand across the wide panorama of the city below them.

"This is Thomas Edison; the electric light. Someone said that Edison invented the twentieth century, and I think that is right."

"You backed him right from the start, didn't you?"

"I deal with larger and financially proven companies; reorganizing, merging, refinancing. I never deal with unproven gambles. It is too risky, and I do not gamble. But with Edison I did. When I met him I knew that he would make it."

"It's a very pretty night," Louisa said looking out across the city. "It's very Christmas like."

John took a drag on his cigar. The tip glowed with burning brightness.

John remembered.

It was 1879. It was late afternoon. The sun was already low in the sky when the train pulled into Menlo Park, New Jersey. John stepped off the train onto the almost empty platform, followed by his two companions, Egisto Fabbri, a fellow partner at Drexel, Morgan & Company, and Hamilton Twombly, representing the Vanderbilt clan. Looking around John found who he was looking for sitting on a wooden bench outside the Lighthouse Tavern.

Grosvenor Lowrey stood when he saw them.

"I am glad to see you all again. Hope you had a nice trip up here."

"It was good," answered Twombly.

Grosvenor Lowrey was attorney for Edison. He had enlisted and organized the financing for Edison's 'light' project. A group of investors had put up the money. On October 15, 1878 they formed the Edison Electric Illuminating Company. Egisto Fabbri was treasurer.

"Follow me, gentlemen, and I'll take you up to the workshop."

Lowrey took them through the Lighthouse Tavern and out the front to the wooden sidewalk on Christie Street. As they walked single file through the tavern John looked around. There was a long wooden standing bar with a rail at the bottom to rest your feet. Several men standing at the bar turned and watched as they walk by. The men all wore blue overalls. Several stood at the billiard table playing pool. The air was thick with cigar smoke.

John felt very conspicuous. He felt he was on show, almost as if a circus. Well dressed New York City bankers filing through their tavern, John could not imagine what the men must be thinking.

Outside the wooden sidewalk wormed its way up the hill. The road itself was dirt, muddy from a recent rain. Lowry pointed out that the house towards the top of the hill, some two hundred feet up, was where Edison lived.

As they walked John puffed on his cigar. A slightly chilly breeze pulled on the flap of his coat as he walked. He wore no hat and the breeze played though his hair.

Several months before, sitting with several of the investors in John's office at Drexel, Morgan & Company, Lowrey tried to explain that Edison was facing a few set backs. Several of the investors were concerned. All that money they put up and as of yet there was nothing to show for it. Others were having success with arc lighting, so why did Edison feel he had to invent something else, and why should they keep their money behind him. What was happening?

When Lowrey first entered the office Fabbri joked with him, asking if he knew of anyone who wanted to buy his shares. He said he was joking but Lowrey explained to Edison later that he 'looked serious.'

Lowrey tried to explain that scientific discovery was a process of trial and error. Others asked Lowrey pointed questions that he tried as best he could to explain.

John sat and listened.

The wooden board walk gave out at Edison's home. The men carefully stepped down onto the dirt, now slightly muddy, road. John watched the house as they walked past. It was a three story white clapboard house with a creaking windmill in the back yard. A picket fence surrounded the house and yard. Two little children, a boy and a girl, were playing on a swing in the yard each watching the strange men walking up the hill.

Lowrey pointed to a group of wooden buildings up the hill even further, yet another one hundred yards or so beyond the house. He said that they were the laboratory buildings where Edison worked.

The men marched on.

John and his firm had agreed to handle the lighting patents in Europe for the Edison Electric Light Company but the details were not yet worked out. Edison wanted to draw eighteen hundred dollars from that fund. The partners told John that maybe he should reconsider this draw if he was losing confidence in the project.

But after listening to the debate between Lowrey and the partners John told them that he was looking forward to negotiating the deal and that he was quite prepared to go ahead with the deal as planned.

It was then that Lowrey suggested that to ease their fears perhaps the investors should come to the laboratory, come to Menlo Park, and meet personally with Edison. If the investors could see with their own eyes, among the rubbish and the rejects, the progress that had been made they might form some idea of the actual operation and its present difficulties. Edison, he assured them, would speak quite frankly in his discussion. Lowrey explained that Edison strongly believed that it is through failure that you gain success.

The men finally reached the laboratory. It was a two story framed wooden structure about thirty feet wide and one hundred feet long. It had an arched porch and above that a second story balcony. From the rear of the building John could hear sawing and hammering, and from another building behind a small smoke stack spewed smoke into the air.

John noticed, as they climbed the steps to the first floor of the building, that the white walls were in desperate need of fresh paint. There were patches where the paint had chipped away exposing the bare wood underneath.

Once inside the building John, with the rest of them, walked up a second set of wooden stairs to the second story. The bare wood creaked from the weight of so many coming up at a time. The center area of each step was well worn. Many a footfall had come this way. When he reached the top of the stairs John stood and looked around the room. It was a long room, thin, worn wooden floors. There were several long wooden tables with chairs sitting around seemingly at random. Along the walls were shelves from floor to ceiling stacked with multicolored bottles of different chemicals. Some were jarred with caps and others corked. Some held powers of different shades and consistency while still others held fluids of different colors. The overwhelming odor of the room was chemical and sawed wood. Interspersed along the walls were tall floor to ceiling windows. Without curtains, the windows let the setting sun flood in.

The men moved around the room, shoes shuffling across the not recently broom swept floor, wooden slats creaking as they walked about looking at this and that. There were two of Edison's workers in the room. One had a dark full beard with a huge drooping moustache.

John walked the length of the room. Lowrey talked but John did not really listen. John was watching the tables. They were cluttered with batteries and microscopes and large magnifying glasses; there were hammers and files and telegraphic and telephonic equipment; there were jungles of wires wrapped around wooden spools, jars, and strips of tin foil; pieces of dismantled machinery, pieces and scraps of non-descript metal, and rubber tubing; and on one table a well worn clay pipe.

Edison made his way to the center of the room where his phonograph sat on one of the tables.

"This, gentlemen, is my little baby," he said as he patted it with his hand. He cranked it and then looked about as a cracking voice, his voice, began to recite 'Mary had a Little Lamb.'

As his disemboweled voice could be heard about the room he laughed, a wide opened mouth laugh. John could see his tobacco and coffee stained teeth.

"This is my baby," Edison said. "And I hope that it will grow up into a big fellow so it can support me in my old age. Whenever I fail on something I come back to this because it shows that I can be successful and I can do something right."

Egisto smiled. Lowrey, a bit nervous, stumbled for words.

"Surely, Tom, your successes exceed your failures."

John, standing off to one side, toward the rear of the room, watched.

Edison walked over to another of his gadgets near a window. He walked a little stooped, odd, John thought, for a man in his early thirties. He trailed his hands along the tables as he walked as if gaining support. Edison turned toward the others when he reached a strange looking thing near the window.

"This here is my ear trumpet, or telescopophone I officially call it."

There were three huge funnels mounted on a tripod. The center one had a mouthpiece attached, and each of the two outside funnels had rubber tubing to be held up to each ear. He demonstrated by putting the end of the two rubber tubes to his ears.

"I stood here the other day and put one of these to my ear. I heard a child cry; I heard the telegraph instrument tick down at the station, one thousand feet away; and I heard one curious, softly grinding sound that I could not identify till I followed up and found it to be a cow biting off and chewing grass, two fifths of a mile distant."

He looked at each of the men as if to gage their reaction. Egisto laughed a small laugh. John smiled and nodded.

"Just think, gentlemen, if I make it a big enough why we could hear the man in the moon walking around."

Edison laughed at his own joke. John noticed that it did not really matter to him whether anyone else laughed.

John liked that.

Edison stood by the table. He was about five foot eight to John's six foot. He had straight dark brown hair, a little uncombed, that wandering down over his forehead so that he was constantly brushing it aside with his stained hands. He stood with a curious bend in his waist. It was as if his legs thrust his hips back and he bent his upper torso a little forward, rolling over his slightly paunchy stomach.

John noticed on the table where Edison stood sat a half drunk cup of coffee and a pie tin almost empty. From the fork cuts in the pie he obviously ate it straight from the tin without the intermediary need of a plate.

John tapped his own developing portly waist. He, after all, loved to devour his elegant wine and fine foods at Sherry's or Delmonico's. Edison, it appeared, gorged on his beloved bitter black coffee and home made pies.

It was growing darker as the sun began to set.

The assistant with the drooping moustache was lighting several kerosene lamps. The glass scraped across the prongs as he lifted the glass, lit the wick, and then lowered it.

John walked all the way to the back of the room. There, against the back wall, was a small pipe organ with the pipes all in a row shooting straight up toward the ceiling.

A pipe organ, here?

As John stared at the keyboard Edison came up along side him. John looked over at Edison.

"Do you play?" Edison asked.

"No, I am afraid not."

Edison turned his head slightly as if to let his ear better catch what John said.

"And you? Do you play?"

"What's that," Edison asked as he cupped his hand around the back of his ear, slightly bent over and looking up at John.

John swept his hand toward the keyboard.

"I take it that you yourself play," John said slightly louder.

Edison smiled. "Oh just a bit of this and that. It's great at the end of a long day, for the boys. It takes the edge off. So you say you don't play?"

John shook his head. "I like a good hymnal now and then, but I can only sing it, not play it."

"Hymnal you say." Edison walked over to a shelf of books and began rummaging through them. They were all song books. Finally he pulled one out and handed it to John. It was a new edition of hymns.

"Pick one," Edison said as he slid into the seat and adjusted the distance to the keyboard.

John opened the book and glanced down the page. There was a new one that was becoming his favorite. Surprisingly it was there. 'O Zion, Haste.'

John held the book open so that Edison could see. Edison began to play, slow and unsure, but John recognized the tune. He mumbled the words.

O Zion, haste, thy mission high fulfilling,
To tell to all the world that God is light,
That He who made all nations is not willing
One soul should perish, lost in shades of night.

Someone from behind them deeply cleared his throat. It was Lowrey.

"Tom, I hate to interrupt but it has grown dark. We need to get to the matter at hand."

Edison, it seemed, had to think for a moment as to what that comment might have meant. But then he remembered. He stood up.

"Well, then, gentlemen, to the demonstration."

The room was darker. Night had come on. John was surprised; he did not notice until then that the day was done. Outside it was already dark. The two kerosene lamps were the only light in the room.

John listened as Edison talked about his experiments on his high resistance platinum lamp. He talked about different filaments he used, something about needing a greater vacuum, how he was going to put in a Gramme type generator, about how he used an ordinary air pump with limited success and then used a Sprengel pump that created one or two millimeters of full exhaustion of air, got a light of 25 candle power for some time where as in open air it raised only to 4 candle power, and how this experiment they would see tonight with platinum coils is useful but they only get a few hours of light and had a tendency to pop, so therefore he was already moving toward using carbon and he was sure that carbon filaments would be the answer he was looking for.

John tried to follow.

On the main table in the center of the room Edison pointed out four globes of glass. Each sat in a container tied with wires that ran from each globe to a tall wooden framed machine on the table with a large dial. Edison called it his coiled resistance wire rheostat. On the first floor of the building was a steam engine driving a generator that created the electricity that flowed upstairs to the rheostat. By turning the knob it controlled the amount of electricity flowing to the tubes.

As Edison gave his rambling introduction John glanced outside the window several times watching as a large bright moon rose over the empty fields. It was just past full.

When Edison was finally ready he asked his assistant Charles Batchelor to extinguish the kerosene lamps. They all watched as Charles lifted the glass and snuffed out the flame. The room darkened. Charles walked over to the other lamp and did the same thing. With the last one out the room went almost pitch black. The light of the moon coming in through the windows streaked the wooden floors and gave the room a silvery ghostly glow.

John could only just make out the shapes of the tables and men.

John Kruesi, the man with the long drooping moustache, stood by the rheostat.

Everyone was silent, waiting.

It was Edison who spoke.

"Turn on the juice slowly," Edison said.

John could hear the slight scrapping sound of metal against metal as Kruesi began turning the dial.

Slowly the four globes on the table began to glow a cherry red. John thought they looked like large glow bugs in the evening sky. He used to chase them when he was a kid. They made him wonder at the beauty of the world.

"A little more juice," Edison said a little louder than before.

The lamps glow increased. John watched. He almost could not believe his eyes. There was no flickering flame; there was no fumes and smoke rising up from the light. The light began to distinguish the objects sitting around on the table. As the light from the glass globes slowly brightened it changed hue, shifting from a red to a dull yellow.

"A little more."

The lamps grew brighter. The color of the light turned to white. John could distinguish the faces of the men, looking back and forth at each other. It worked.

But suddenly there was a crackling pop sound and instantly the room went totally dark.

"Ah. It was number four."

Kruesi turned the dial to off. Edison made his way over to the globes. John could distinguish in the moon light that Edison was replacing the burned globe with a fresh one.

"Now," Edison said. "Give it some juice."

Again the metal scrapping sound of the dial, and again the four globes began to glow a cherry red.

"More."

Kruesi turned the dial and the globes again brightened growing in intensity and changing again to yellow and then an almost pure white.

Suddenly there was a cracking pop again and the room lapsed into darkness.

"That was two," Kruesi said with his German accent.

"Charles: the lamps."

John watched as the men walked about in the moon light. Charles pulled the glass of the kerosene lamps up, scraping the sides of the prongs, and then struck a match. It hissed and flared and he quickly lit the wick and the slid the glass down.

Edison began pacing, hands buried into his trouser pockets.

Lowrey spoke up.

"We thought that it would be educational for you gentlemen to see the great progress that has been made so far, but the difficulties which still remain."

John watched Edison. Pacing, pacing.

Fabbri and Twombly glanced back and forth from Lowrey to Morgan. It was as if they did not quite know what to think. Displeased, perhaps; concerned.

John looked out the window. The fields were washed in the silvery light of the moon.

It had to work, he thought to himself. It had to work. In most of the country they still use tallow candles or whale oil or kerosene. In the cities they use gas. Each light had to be individually lighted, and individually extinguished. And the glass globes had to be eternally cleaned because when the candles and the gas burn it gives off ammonia and sulfur and carbon dioxide. This not only darkened and stained the globes but also entire rooms: carpets, drapes, and furniture. And it depletes a room of oxygen and in the winter it helps to sicken the inhabitants. And if the lines cracked they can explode.

We desperately need something else.

Electricity has none of these drawbacks.

John turned back and looked around the room.

Edison stopped next to the globe that had failed. John walked over to him. John bent down and whispered loudly into his ear.

"So tell me," John said. "What I am to walk away with this evening is the knowledge that indeed it works, but it needs work."

Edison thought for a moment and then smiled and nodded.

"Couldn't have said it better myself."

John placed his hand on Edison's shoulder. Edison laughed.

"You know, I heard that this German mathematician named Karl Friedrich Gauss once said 'I have the result, but I do not yet know how to get it.'"

He stopped for a moment as if to let what he said sink in.

"That's how I feel. It's there, I know it is there, but I just have to get there. You understand what I mean?"

John smiled.

"I understand perfectly."

John held out his hand and they shook hands. John thought to himself: rough skin, calloused hands; he works like he says he works.

John liked that. He knew right then that Edison would do whatever it took to achieve whatever he wanted to achieve.

They built the first power station on Pearl Street in New York. They formed a new Company, Edison Electric Light Company, and found the money to finance it. Edison perfected the lamp and wanted to demonstrate its wide commercial appeal by electrifying business buildings and entire sections of the city. The offices of Drexel, Morgan & Company would be one of the first. He bought the Pearl Street location in August of 1881 and went to work installing steam engines and large "Jumbo" generators. Trenches along the streets had to be dug to hold the wiring, and the office itself had to be wired.

Finally the day came. September 4, 1882.

In the morning Edison was at the power station tending to a thousand last minute details. He was nervous. A thousand things all had to not go wrong for the one demonstration to go right. He washed his hands; he tried to wipe off the grease on the knee of his trousers; he rolled down the sleeves of his shirt; he put on his starched shirt front; he tied on his white cravat; he put on his Prince Albert coat; he donned his high crowned white derby hat.

Standing with John Lieb, his chief electrician at the power station, Edison matched the time on his watch with the time on Lieb's watch. Then, with Edward Johnson and several others at his side, Edison and troop began their walk down the street to the Drexel Building on Wall Street.

When he arrived John met him at the door.

Everyone was waiting, including the newspaper reporters. Edison chatted with them. He tried as best he could to be calm. He kept glancing at his watch. Then the time arrived. Edison stood by the switch and watched the minutes tick by. At exactly three o'clock John Lieb at the station pulled the lever to let the electricity flow. Edison at a second after flipped the switch.

Everyone watched as the 106 light lamps throughout the Drexel offices began to glow.

It worked.

Edison was always amazed when things worked.

As the hours passed the steady white glow of the lamps continued. Night came on. Through the windows the steady white light washed the sidewalks outside. People walking by stopped and looked in. The steady white of the electric light was so different than the pale yellow of the flickering gas lights.

John and Edison stood next to each other watching out the window. The faces of people outside emerged out of the darkness, painted by the light.

Edison looked up into John's eyes.

"I have accomplished all I promised."

John agreed. "That you have, sir."

Edison offered John a cigar.

"Why thank you," he said looking down at the cheaply bound cigar. "Where does it come from?" he asked, expecting the name of some

Cuban company.

"It comes from the Lighthouse Tavern. I don't know where he gets them but they are cheap and he keeps getting them so that's all that matters to me."

John smiled.

"Well, here," John said as he pulled a cigar from his pocket. "Have one of mine."

Edison took the cigar.

They watched the amazed faces in the window of the people in the street as they puffed their cigars together.

"This is very good," Edison finally said.

John smiled. Edison's cigar was not very good.

"I will tell you what," John said. "Just for you I will give you a whole box."

"We can trade a box of mine for a box of yours."

"No," John said, "that is all right. I insist: allow me the honor of a gift."

Edison turned back to his cigar.

Edward Johnson, Edison's chief executive for the Edison Light Company, was summoned to the Morgan household in the fall of 1883. He was shown into the library where John sat at his desk in the center of the room. John wanted two things. Last Christmas Johnson had put on display in his home a set of small walnut sized electric lights on his Christmas tree. The tree rotated by a small electrical motor attached to the base, and the lights turned off and on in either a red or a white or a blue.

"I heard that it was quite beautiful. I wish I had seen it. You invented this yourself?"

"Yes, I tinkered with it a bit. I wanted to do something special for the children."

"And I bet they loved it."

Edward smiled. "Oh yes they did. They brought all their friends in to see it. The look of wonder in their eyes made it all worth while."

"Good. I want the same thing for myself, this Christmas. Can you arrange that for me?"

Edward was taken aback. Was this the reason for the summons? Morgan was a major backer of the Edison Company. When he called for you, you went.

"Of course, if you wish."

But that was not all.

John was the first private citizen to electrify his house. Underneath his stables in the back yard they dug a deep cellar where a steam engine, boiler, and generator were installed. They dug a trench and constructed an underground brick passageway where they ran wires from the generator to the house. Using the gas fixtures they wired the entire house installing electric light bulbs in place of the gas burners.

John loved it and loved having the lights at night, when they worked.

Next to his bed they even put in a switch where with one flick he turned on or off all the downstairs lights at once.

The engineer from the Edison Company arrived at his house every day at three o'clock to start the steam engine. By four there was enough steam built up to start the generator, and thus the lights. But there was more than once when guests were over for the evening that John forgot the engineer went home at eleven by switching off the power. A plunge into darkness and the subsequent fumbling for candles followed.

Electricity was a wonderful thing, but some things had to be ironed out.

The steam engine and generator, when turned on, were so loud that all his neighbors complained. Mrs. James M. Brown complained that the vibrations made her whole house shake.

"Does it have to be so loud?" John shouted to the engineer as they stood next to the generator.

The engineer turned his head.

"What's that you say?"

So to fix the problem they padded the machinery with Indian rubber supports, lined the machines in felt, and padded the cellar with sandbags.

The smoke from the steam engine filled the air with black smoke. Mrs. James M. Brown complained that it entered her pantry and tarnished her silver. So to fix the problem another trench was built in order to funnel the smoke away and into his chimney.

Mrs. James M. Brown complained that it still tarnished her silver, but not as much as before. John told Frances that Mrs. Brown's silver would never be as bright as she thought it should be.

But then during cold winter nights neighborhood cats gathered along the warmth of the exhaust and howled at each other for position.

John explained to Edward Johnson.

"I want you to look over my system here and tell me what you think. It seems to be shorting out more frequently and after seeing how it works at the office I wonder why I can not have the same efficiency here."

Edward went throughout the house and outside to the cellar looking at this and that and testing this and that. He finally came back into the library.

"Well," John said, looking up from reading his reports strewn all over his desk. "What do you think?"

Edward cleared his throat. He was nervous.

"Do you want an honest and candid reply?"

"I do."

"If it were my own I would throw the whole damn thing into the street."

John chuckled.

"That is precisely what Mrs. Morgan says."

There was a long pause.

"But replace it with a newer system, of course," Edward said, wondering if he had just lost his best customer.

"That is precisely what I say," John replied.

"All of this is hopelessly out of date."

"But I just had it put in a year ago."

"But you were the first. A lot has happened since then. It is the nature of electrical innovation. It is innovating and last year will be outdated by today."

"And tomorrow will outdate today?" John asked.

"I am afraid that is the nature of invention. Last century was the age of steam. You could try to destroy the engines and be a Luddite or you could build railroad empires with it. We are entering a world of electricity and that will change the world."

"It is frightening to think what the world will become."

"Not frightening, exciting."

John stood up and put out his hand. Edward stood and they shook hands.

"I hope that the Edison Company appreciates the value of my house as an experimental station."

"How is that?" Edward asked.

"I want you personally to do the work. Make what changes you think best, I trust in your judgment."

"But sir, I do not think that I. . ."

"Just make it right, Mr. Johnson," John said as he walked him toward the door. "Just make it good, and make it right."

Edward reworked the entire system. But he was faced with a new problem. The desk in the library was in the center of the room. It sat on top of a large rug. John wanted an electric lamp on his desk but not wires across the floor. But the desk had to be occasionally moved when the rug was pulled up for cleaning. Edward brought wires along the ceiling of the basement and then up into room to insulated plates set in the floor of the library. He then put contact pegs in one of legs of the desk in order to penetrate the rug and make connection with the plates, conveying the electrical current to the lamp. The pegs were not large enough to damage the rug, nor were they permanently attached so the desk could be easily moved.

He tested it before he left for the day. It worked fine.

But he was frantically summoned early the next morning. When he arrived and the servant Henry opened the door and Edward entered the marble vestibule of the house and removed his brown derby hat he instantly smelled the problem. The strong smell of wet charred wood and burnt carpet was everywhere. Henry, much shorter than Edward, looked up at him with a frown and shook his head.

"Mr. Morgan and Mrs. Morgan are at breakfast, but I will show you in."

As he took him into the Library he explained what had happened. Last night the Morgan's were at the opera. Henry turned on the lamp on the desk. There was a loud pop and flames shot up out of the rug and up the leg of the desk. He ran to fetch water and by the time he got back the rug was aflame. He dumped the basin of water and put the fire out but there was a horrible fountain of sparks.

Edward stood looking down at the torn and burned rug and the burnt wood of the leg of the desk. The wet smoke stench was strong.

How was he going to explain this?

Edward heard heavy footsteps. Henry shyly stepped backward. John appeared in the doorway. He held a newspaper in one hand and a coffee cup in the other. He was wearing his reading glasses down on his nose and tilted his head down in order to see over the tops of the glass.

"Well?" John barked loudly.

Johnson tried to formulate what he could say. He started to speak but stopped. He saw Frances Morgan standing behind John. Catching his eye she put her finger to her lips and slightly shook her head. Then she vanished down the hallway. Edward stood staring into John's piercing eyes. He looked back down at the mess on the floor.

"Well, what are you going to do about it?"

Edward swallowed hard.

"Mr. Morgan, the trouble is not inherent to the thing itself. It is my own fault, and I will put it in good working order so it will be perfectly safe."

John paused and narrowed his eyes.

"How long will it take to fix it?"

Edward looked over at him.

"I will do it right away."

They stood staring at each other for a moment.

"All right," John finally said. "See that you do."

John turned and walked down the hallway, heavy footed.

Henry took a deep breath and then walked away.

Edward, alone, looked back down at the mess.

John sat at his desk in his office at Drexel, Morgan & Company reading financial reports when his secretary James approached. John looked up, a cigar held between his fingers in his right hand.

"Yes, James."

James read from a slip of paper.

"Sir, do you know a Darius Ogden Mills?"

John thought for a moment. The name seemed familiar somehow. He tapped his desk with his left hand until he finally remembered.

"Yes," he finally barked.

A financier, made a fortune in the gold rush out in California. He owns a railroad and helped to found the Bank of California. He and Billy Ralston. Mills was at the party last night at John's house showing off his newly wired electric lights.

"Well, he is here sir, in the lobby."

"He does not want to see me does he?"

"No sir, he just placed an order to purchase one thousand shares of the Edison Electric Illuminating Company."

John sat back in his chair. He was speechless for a moment.

"You are joking with me."

"No sir."

John turned and stood up slightly. The walls of his office were made of wood up to a certain height but then the top section was made of glass. He could look out and see the whole office. John carefully peeked above the glass and looked toward the lobby. It took a moment, for there were a lot of men in the lobby, but there he was, the man he had just met last night at his house. He wore a thick drooping moustache that covered his mouth.

John quickly stood up and went out of his office. Holding his cigar aloft John almost ran down the hallway toward the lobby at the front of the office. People seeing him coming down so fast and determined got out of his way. When he reached the lobby Darius was just beginning to leave.

"Mr. Mills," John almost shouted out in order to stop him from leaving the building. Darius turned and stopped. John approached him.

"Well, well. What a surprise. I just met you last night and here you are today. Welcome."

The two of them shook hands. People coming in and out of the bank had to walk around them.

"Mr. Morgan. You have a wonderful bank here, wonderful. Your staff is quite good."

"Glad to hear. I pride myself on my people; I try to select the best."

"And I want to thank you for last night. It was wonderful. I was amazed at the demonstration of your electrified house. I have been reading about the practical application of this electricity concept and I saw it for the first time with my own eyes last night."

"It is certainly a wonderful thing. It opens up a lot of possibilities."

"Indeed it does. I have placed an order for my house to be so wired."

"Really. Care to come to my office?" John asked.

Darius waved his hand.

"No, I am afraid that I have an appointment to which I am already a bit late."

"What then can I do for you?"

"Well, I think I have already done it. I purchased one thousand shares of the Edison Company. This I feel is going to be a very big thing."

"What do you know of the Edison light?"

"I have been reading. I know all about it. And last night it has been confirmed with my own eyes so I am here."

"All right, we will take your order and any other orders of the same kind, but I am going to put a condition on my partners with respect to such orders."

Darius looked puzzled.

"What kind of condition?"

"That for every share of Edison stock they buy for you they buy one for me."

Darius laughed.

"You too, then, are a man of vision."

John, for the first time since he left his office took a puff from his cigar. He did not say anything in reply. He had to squint his eye from the smoke.

"Well, Mr. Morgan. It has been a profitable pleasure but I must now be off."

They shook hands and Darius left.

John spun his cigar in his mouth as he watched Darius walk out the door, down the steps, and into a waiting brougham.

You too, then, are a man of vision: indeed.

"All right, enough of this, father. You need to get inside before your cold gets worse."

It was Louisa. She grabbed John's arm and started to pull him inside the hotel room. They stood on the balcony over looking the city at night.

"It is beautiful out here," John protested.

"Not a word," Louisa said, "inside with you right now. I insist."

John, knowing she was right, and feeling a little chilled anyway, sighed and went back into the hotel room. Louisa came in after him and closed the door leading out onto the balcony.

Just as they entered there was a knock on the door. Jack, sitting on the sofa, stood up.

"That's probably the lawyers. They wanted to meet one last time before the session tomorrow."

Jack stood watching John as if waiting for his approval to open the door.

John waved him on. "Well go on then."

As Jack went to the door John sat himself at the desk near the end of the sofa. He picked up the deck of cards and shuffled them several times as the men came into the room.

Henry P. Davidson, partner at J. P. Morgan & Co., came in first. John, shuffling the cards, nodded when their eyes make contact.

Then Thomas W. Lamont, a fairly new partner at the firm, came in next, followed by Joseph H. Choate, principal lawyer for the firm. He was followed by a young clerk that John did not recognize. He must work with Choate.

"Please, gentlemen, be seated," Jack said, motioning to the sofa and several chairs.

As they all sat John pulled out his handkerchief and had to blow his nose. It was beginning to run again.

Louisa, standing behind him, leaned over and whispered to him.

"You see, I was right."

John just grunted and set the white handkerchief onto the table beside him in case he needed it again. Everyone, glancing back and forth at each other, waited until John had completed his task.

It was Choate who spoke first.

"Thought we'd go over some last minute details of what they will ask tomorrow."

Jack nodded. "Yes, certainly; would that be okay with you father?"

John, before he started his game of solitaire, before he started any game of solitaire, had to light his cigar. He nodded to Jack as he held the match up to the tip of his cigar and took several deep puffs. He loved the first taste of a cigar, the first swirl of smoke.

"We need to know what to expect," Jack said.

John cleared his throat. "I expect questions," he said, sharp and to the point. Several of the men shuffled in their seats. John picked up his deck of cards and began laying out the hand.

"With all the recent talk in the papers and on the campaign trail of a money trust controlling and manipulating the economy the Arsene Pujo committee wishes to determine if there is a money trust that, through interlocking directorships and stock ownership, controls the primary sources of money and credit and can thereby wield power and control of the economy at large."

"I would agree to that, Joseph," Thomas spoke up, "but with one changed point, they are attempting to show what they already believe is a money trust. It is not a fact finding expedition to come to a conclusion but rather a fact finding expedition to confirm what they already believe to be true. Why else would they call for the investigation in the first place?"

"True," Jack agreed. "And the difference is an important one to make for the first is an inquiry but the latter is a glorified witch hunt. It fits the overall pattern of the government's war against business. The Standard Oil suit, our own Northern Securities, the ICC filing against the Harriman interests, Roosevelt brought forty suits under the Sherman Act, but Taft has brought eighty, and now with Wilson in the White House who knows what will happen. All we can be sure of is that the trend will continue."

John moved his cards back and forth. He had heard it all before.

"The world is changing and they do not like it. But the political class, instead of riding along with the change and adapting to it, they want to control it and direct it to where they want, that best benefits them and, in their view, the public."

"Joseph," Jack replied, "Since the end of the Civil War in 1865 we have become a nation of business where captains of industry are the kings and the rulers for they create what makes the nation function and the political class does not like that. They want that power and since they cannot create it themselves all that is left for them is to steal it away by governmental decree, that is in a nutshell what is happening here."

John took a long draw on his cigar, stared at the glowing embers and collecting ashes of the tip, and then carefully placed it down into the ashtray. He picked up a card and turned it over.

Queen of Hearts.

A sudden flash of memory washed the room.

Voices faded.

You are my queen of hearts, he told Memie.

When. When and where was that? And where did that thought come from?

John smiled to himself staring at the card. You are my Queen of Hearts: and that certainly is true.

It was wedding day. John stood and looked at himself in the full length mirror. He looked his best, he thought, with his black pants, waistcoat and coat, and with his ascot tie and collar and his favorite pocket watch bob and chain across his waist. He stroked his newly grown mustache with his finger. John smiled and winked at himself in the mirror.

"Today; today is the day to remember. October 7, 1861. Remember this day for ever, my good man."

There was a voice behind him.

"Indeed we will," the voice said.

John turned to see his Cousin James Goodwin leaning against the door frame. His coat was open and his two thumbs were in the pockets of his waistcoat. He had thick side whiskers but a clean shaved face. He was young but his hair was already beginning to thin.

"My, my, my, do we not look quite exquisite."

James began walking around John as if admiring a statue. "It is indeed a sad day for all the fair young maidens of the land to lose from the available pool of potential mates someone such as you."

"I go to a better future."

"Perhaps, my good man. Only time will tell us that. But in the here and now the time has come. I have been sent to fetch you. She awaits upstairs."

John stood erect. A sudden chill went through him. It is time. He started to walk toward the door when James stopped him by putting his hand upon his shoulder. They looked into each others eyes. James grew serious.

"Pierpont. Are you sure about this?"

John stood for a moment staring into James's eyes.

"I am," he finally said.

"I love you as my own and I would not want you to get hurt."

"How could I get hurt marrying the one I love?"

"I just thought, perhaps you should wait. Her being as ill as she is, maybe it would be best to wait until she is better. This has all been very sudden."

"Look, we have been friends for a long time, Jimmy, and I know that you wish me the best. But I am sure about this. Even if we assume the worst, as many seem to do, and Memie dies, then I am still going to get hurt regardless. It is best that if she dies she dies as my wife for at least then I will know that she died as my wife."

James nodded and then looked down. John still fixed his gaze on James.

"Besides, Jimmy; she will not die."

James glanced back up. He nodded again.

"Then you best be on your way old man for she awaits."

"Wish me luck?"

James seemed to be overcome. James put his arms around John and hugged him hard.

"With all my heart," he whispered.

Amelia was up in her room, sitting on her bed, fully dressed; waiting for John to come in. Her mother was there with her. When John turned and walked into her room he stopped. He had to take a moment to absorb the whole thing.

She sat on her bed. She seemed so small on the vast white quilted bed cover, sitting underneath the white laced canopy. Pale, she sat like a small frightened doe. But when she saw him enter the room her eyes lit up and her face opened into a deep wide grin. She shrugged up her shoulders and almost squealed his name.

She was beautiful.

The windows were wide open and the breeze from the garden beyond and the sunshine flooded the room. The sunlight streaked across the floor and across the bed. She sat half in sun. White lace curtains fluttered as the cool breeze filtered through. Vases of fresh full flowers were all about the room. The room was alive with life.

"Pierpont," she exclaimed as she clasp her hands together with her fingers out long.

Her dress was colored a rich deep ivory, trimmed in watered ribbed silk with wide pagoda sleeves, laced white, with secondary cap sleeves above. She wore a full knife pleaded skirt with a crinoline bustle and long train. Her buttoned high neck bodice gave her an air of elegant grandeur.

She was beautiful. It was like a scene from a long ago fairy tale

65

suddenly coming true.

He nodded to her mother Mary standing off to one side, and then he walked slowly and stately over to Amelia. He bent down as she reached up and put her arms around his neck and hugged him ever so tight.

"Hello dear Mime."

"Hello dear husband to be."

They laughed as he stood back up.

"Pierpont, dear, are you very sure about this?"

"Yes."

"I was well when you first met me, but now that I am ill it changes everything. I do release you from obligation if you wish."

"No, it changes nothing. Ill or not ill you are still you. You are still inside the woman I love."

"Are you sure?"

"As sure as anything I have ever done."

Then, after a short pause, he spoke again.

"Or ever will."

"But it is on such short notice; none of your family is here. Do not you want to wait for a proper wedding and celebrate with everyone here? Perhaps they do not wish this to happen."

John shook his head no. And then with a realistic coldness: "We cannot wait, Memie."

Amelia glanced toward her mother. She understood.

"Yes, I suppose you are right."

John noticed on the small dresser by her bed sat The Common Prayer Book he had given her just yesterday when they took communion together at St. Georges Church. He reached over and picked it up. He smiled down at her and then opened the book to the flyleaf where he read out loud the inscription he had written yesterday.

"Memie from Pierpont. St. Georges. Communion Sunday,
Octo. 6, 1861"

He closed the book, he kissed the book, and then he put the book back down on the dresser.

"Of course we may have to postpone the wedding anyway," she coyly smiled.

"Oh?"

"I still have not gotten use to your cute little moustache you are growing, it may take some time. It makes you look older than your twenty four years."

66

John waved it away: time to take charge.

"Here we go," he said. "The time is now."

John held her hand and helped her stand up. She was weak and shaky.

Mary came over to steady her daughter.

"Let me help you."

The three of them together walked over to the door and then awkwardly made it through the door.

"Look," John finally said, "I do not think this is going to work." He looked at Amelia. She seemed exhausted already.

"The folding doors separating the back parlor from the front are closed. I'll carry you downstairs into the back parlor and when you are ready the doors will be opened and everyone will watch the wedding."

"Carry me?"

"Yes, you cannot walk down the stairs, look how winded you are already. The folding doors are closed, no one of the guests will see, they will not know."

"But carry me?"

"Enough of this," he firmly said as he reached behind her with one arm and swept her up into his arms. She laughed a small scream. "Please do not hurt yourself."

"There, light as a feather. Now Mary, you lead the way and we will follow."

In the garden room the Reverend Stephen Tyng, the bridesmaid and James Goodman were all waiting. John carefully set Amelia down standing up and took several deep breaths. She was small and light but she certainly was more than a feather. They all got into their place with Amelia standing next to John and the bridesmaid and best man standing on either side. The Reverend stood behind. They could hear the people in the other room talking; a few laughed. The back French doors were all wide open and the sound and scent of the garden beyond filtered through. The bright sunlight flushed the October trees and foliage a dazzling mixture of rich warm greens and reddish yellow. Small chirps of birds could be heard.

Amelia whispered to John.

"I am frightened."

"You are not alone."

"I feel weak, will you hold me up."

"Yes."

Then when John nodded to James he folded back the doors

67

separating the two rooms. When the doors pulled back there was a sudden hushed silence from the front room as all eyes turned toward John and Amelia. Everyone was quiet for a moment, as if stunned. Then as John and Amelia smiled and bowed everyone began again talking and laughing with several clapping, now directed toward them in awe at the picture the setting presented.

Mary, on the piano, began to play. John and Amelia turned to face Reverend Tyng who stood tall before them in his long black robes.

"It will be fine," Tyng whispered to Amelia as he held up his black well worn Bible, and then he smiled with a deep and warm affection. She felt safer.

Everyone watching was watching to see if she, poor thing, had enough strength to see it through.

When the ceremony was complete John and Amelia walked through the crowd of friends chatting and laughing with each. Amelia stood the whole time but clutched John's arm tight. If she let go she felt she would collapse from exhaustion. After a bit of time John, with Amelia clutching his arm, made his way to the front door. He raised his voice.

"Everyone, everyone, please: in the dining room beyond awaits an elaborate breakfast that the wonderful Mary Sturges has prepared for all of you. Please feel free, and enjoy yourselves as long as you wish. Thank you all for coming and for all the kindness you have bestowed upon us. We, unfortunately, must leave to catch our boat. We are a bit late and must rush so not to miss the departure. We must be off."

And with that he reached down again and swept Amelia up into his arms. She giggled. Some shouted and clapped. John turned and, staggering a little, made it out of the door James Goodwin held open. People came out with them and laughed and shouted as he carried her to the awaiting carriage. They both waved as the driver snapped the reins onto the horses and they started down the path toward the road. The two of them waved out the back window as the crowd, the house, their prior lives all disappeared behind them.

Once they were clear and galloping down the road she turned to him with concern.

"Are we actually late? Is there a chance we will miss the boat."

John put his head back and laughed hard and full.

She grew a little irritated.

"Are we?" she demanded.

"No, no. There is no boat. It leaves tomorrow, tomorrow."

"You scoundrel."

"You can rest all day until tomorrow."

"But what of our clothes, our baggage?"

"They are at the Jackson's house, which is where we are going now. We can be alone and rest. Your mother is coming along as soon as she can."

Amelia did not know if she liked this surprise. He leaned over and kissed her. We had to get out of there because it would have exhausted you, am I right?"

She knew he was right but did not know if she approved. She held off for a moment.

John held out his arms in a questioning gesture.

"Am I right?"

After a long silent moment she smiled.

"You are certainly an extraordinary man John Pierpont."

"And you are an exceptional woman, Memie Morgan."

The next day they arrived at the dock. It was busy with the hustle and bustle of hundreds of passengers and crew going about their business. Amelia kept looking all around at it all, taking it all in. When things are not well with you then the things that are well become fascinating and sacred. It was a little cold; Amelia wore a mauve colored coat and white gloves. They said goodbye to their friends who came to see them off. Amelia hugged her mother, her father, her brother. Mary began to cry and held a handkerchief to her eyes. At the base of the stairs leading up to the railing of the ship John stopped and turned to her. He held her hand.

"What do you think?"

She looked up the stairway. It looked very tall and had a lot of steps. Others passed them by and climbed ahead of them.

"Do you feel up to it?"

"Yes, yes I do," she replied.

They walked up the stairs to the top near the railing. She felt good that she had made it and still felt strong. Maybe John was right about this. A sea voyage to a distant land heals the soul, which then heals the body.

At the top the steward on board reached out his hand to help Amelia on board but John turned to her and kissed her. The steward waited, arm outstretched.

"Now I will carry you across, not because I need to but because I want to."

She glanced around at all the other people around. The line of people behind them climbing the stairs came to a stop. The steward smiled and withdrew his helping arm.

"Not now," she whispered aloud. "It would be embarrassing."

"I do not care," he said as once again he wrapped one arm around her legs and swept her up into his arms. She noticed some people looking over at them, some smiling and some not. She looked down at her family and friends down on the dock. She waved.

"Now, allow me to carry my wife onto her savior ship."

As he stepped over onto the ship, the steward carefully watching out for them, John looked up at the sky. Gulls in the masts were squawking and screeching for space and dominance. The ship bells clanged. But then there, as if coming from nowhere, above them, high above the masts of the ship, quiet, soared a long sleek egret silently flapping its wings sliding across the cloud filled sky.

A flash of memory: Io bound for Fayal.

Once on board he put her legs back down. He hugged her and whispered in her ear.

"You will see. Together we will overcome this. When I was sick a voyage to a sunny land healed me and it will heal you too. There are signs."

"Let us hope that it is true," she quietly replied.

When they reached England they both stood leaning against the rail looking down at the wharf where hundreds of people were standing about. John's eyes searched everyone, everywhere, looking for his father. As the passengers departed the ship and went off with their waiting friends the crowd thinned until there were but a few left.

His father was nowhere to be seen.

"It is fine. Perhaps they were delayed."

John stood cold and silent.

She tugged at his arm.

"Come. We best get off the boat before it sails to somewhere else."

Louisa placed her hands on her father's back and began to slightly message him. She leaned forward and, again in a whisper, said: "If you are too tired, do you wish to retire?"

John looked up at the men in the room. They were talking. It was Thomas Lamont talking.

"Their theory that he is a selfish manipulator is insultingly absurd in my opinion. We need to counter that argument."

Henry Davison: "You cannot say he is a mere money maker, interested in his own temporary gains. He instinctively plans for something permanent in the structure of his money making activity; he has furnished the grooves in which all our industries operate. He is an organizer, or in many ways a reorganizer, he his not a stock manipulator, and never a bear, he is always bullish. Morgan never wrecked a company nor purposely depressed it for his own gain. His work was to reconstruct, to repair, to build up, create. He created wealth both for himself but, most importantly, for others as well."

Jack Morgan: "Examples are the Philadelphia & Reading, the West Shore, the Erie and of course the Northern Pacific. His railroads are real operating railroads, his industries are really working industries where everyone works and makes money, these are not just paper companies, created entities that only exist as manipulated stock on the stock market."

John leaned back, smiled up at his daughter and whispered: "I am fine."

"Maybe we can go down to supper after they leave or room service if you are not feeling up to it."

"Yes, let's go down."

She squeezed his shoulders and then left.

John reached over and brought his handkerchief to his nose. The blowing of his nose silenced the room. They all looked back and forth.

"Sorry," John said.

"Father has a bad cold," Jack added.

John looked back down to his cards. He started to play again but after two rounds he turned over another Queen.

He did not want to be here. Every so often over the years he realized how much he missed her.

John stood at the counter of the telegraph office. It was a hot day. Everyday was a hot day. Every night was a hot night. Coming here with Amelia was a mistake. He realized that now. The doctor said the dry desert air would help her but Algeria was a mistake; his mistake. John looked up at the man behind the counter. The man was wearing white. It was a white robe that fell from his slumped shoulders all the way to his ankles. The man was old and his skin was dark, burned by the relentless sun for ages. His face was deeply wrinkled like a fresh ploughed field. John also wore white: white jacket, white pants. They say that white reflects back the sun. They say it keeps you cooler in the sun. But his shirt was still moist with his own sweat. The air in the telegraph office seemed close, tight. Breathless.

"Can you send these?" John asked the man.

"Yes sir."

There were flies all around. Relentless flies.

John once again read the cables he had just written.

To Mary Sturges:
I do not wish to alarm you nor do I think there is
any immediate danger but I should not think I was
doing right to hide from you the true state of her
health. I can but feel she is very sick. The greatest
mistake I ever made was coming here at all. We can
only trust and hope although it may be against hope
that our Heavenly Father may yet let the cup pass with
out our drinking.

To Junius Spencer Morgan:
I can but feel she is very, very sick. I fear the
worse. I can only blame myself.

John looked up again into the face of the man as he handed him the cables. A small smile flickered across his ancient mangled face.

"Sorry to hear, sir," he said

John nodded but said nothing.

When he went outside he was almost blinded by the sun burning down. Reflecting off of the white washed walls the glare overtook him. Instinctively he moved into the shade of the nearest building. Lucky for him the sun was low in the sky, near the horizon. It was nearly dusk. He started walking up the hill toward his Hotel keeping in the shade as much as he could.

He remembered sitting in the doctor's office, sitting in the leather chair. The one doctor stood next to him, the second doctor sat in his large chair behind a mahogany desk. Behind the doctor were large draperies, colored mauve with golden tassels, pulled back to show the windows behind. The window was open, slightly ajar. The sun shone through and streaked the wooden floor, the rugs. Soft sounds from the boulevard outside filtered into the room.

It was the doctor behind the desk that spoke.

"Consumption is, I'm afraid, irreversible. There is yet no cure."

John sat in silence. He was still trying to absorb the meaning of what he was hearing. The voices from the street outside were so far away.

"She may improve with rest, a remedial diet, and warm dry air. A desert climate would be best."

"She may improve?" John softly said, grabbing at the doctor's words.

But then the doctor standing next to him placed his hand on John's shoulder. It was a firm grip.

"We are speaking merely of her ability to cope with her condition. I fear some things are beyond our grasp."

"Do you want me to tell her?" the first doctor then asked.

"No, no. I'll do that. When it is time I'll do that."

As he turned the corner and his hotel came into view he saw her. Memie was sitting at a table in the outdoor restaurant outside the hotel. There was a patio, open, wood framed, and with a ceiling of palm tree leaves tied together. It gave shade to the patio but let the air and some sunlight through. There was only one other couple sitting in the patio, a married couple from Germany.

John usually carried her up and down the stairs. She was too weak to walk, much less climb the stairs to their second story room. She was upstairs when he left for the telegraph office. How did she get down to the patio café?

Standing in the shade he watched her for a moment. If he did not know her and were seeing her for the first time he would think that she looked concerned, tired, he thought almost in despair.

As he approached she looked down the street and saw him. She instantly broke out into a wide smile. She watched him as he came up and opened her arms out wide. He came up to her and hugged her.

"Oh, Pierpont. How happy I am to see you. Where have you been, it is been so long."

He sat down in the chair next to her.

"What are you doing?"

She laughed her child like laugh and motioned toward the table with her open hands. On the table were a tea pot, a half filled cup, and a tray of flatbread.

"I am having tea, can not you see?"

"Yes, but how . . .?"

"I came down by myself," she said. "I felt a bit better so I came down for a spot of tea. Do not be cross, you always carry me up and down the stairs, it is just silly for you to do that. It is such a burden. Besides, perhaps exercise is what I need, maybe that will help me get stronger."

John sat watching her, looking to see if anything was wrong, if she was strong enough to be here.

"Do not be cross with me. Is everything alright?"

"Fine," he said. "Fine."

He forced a small smile.

"Everything is just fine. But you should not over tax yourself."

"But I sit in bed all day. I want to see a bit of life. Let us go for a drive, around the town, or perhaps out a bit into the desert. Let us experience, it is our honeymoon you realize. It is our one and only honeymoon."

How strong she is when she is with him, showing strength. But alone she is weak, and he caught her crying once.

The sun was setting. It blazed near the horizon. The two of them looked out toward the open desert, the open abyss of the desert. It was painted in deep stark colors as the sun began to disappear behind the distant hills.

Memie changed. Her mood softened.

"This is quite different than the lush trees of home, is it not?"

John agreed by nodding his head.

"Stark," she almost whispered. "Life is so harsh at times, is it not?"

"Cruel," she whispered to herself.

They sat in silence for a moment until he looked over at her. She had combed her hair back into a bun: a tight, neat, well groomed bun.

"I have a surprise for you."

"What?"

"We are going to Nice."

"In France?"

He laughs yes. The glowing joy in her face made him happy.

"Why?" she asked, pausing for a moment, surprised, happy, but careful.

John shrugged his shoulders as if it were simply the thing to do without the need of an explanation.

"Change of scenery," he finally offered.

She watched him as she thought for a moment.

"But what is in Nice?"

John did not know how to reply: Doctors; help; somewhere away from here where you are dying; somewhere away from the emptiness of the desert abyss; anything. Some place where you will live and not die.

John tried to smile his happiness so that it would embrace her.

"Beauty."

"Mister J. Pierpont, you can be so mysterious at times that I never know what you are thinking."

"Good," he replied with a sparkle in his eyes.

John stood.

"Let me take you up stairs, can you walk?"

She stood and took a few steps, holding onto the chairs and table as she walked. Finally she looked over at him. There was a desire but yet an accepting submission in her look. He held her tightly as he brought his left arm down to her knees and swept her up into his arms. He grunted at the base of the stairs.

"There is one positive thing about your illness."

"Oh."

"It is that you are getting lighter."

She laughed as he climbed the stairs. At the door to their room he fumbled at the door knob until it finally opened.

"In the chair on the balcony," she said as they came into the room. He carried her to the balcony over looking the desert, the town, the setting sun.

The day was growing dim.

She brushed her fingers through his hair as he placed her down into her wooden chair. He stood bent over her.

"You are so good to me."

"I love you, you are my wife."

"Pierpont, how long did you know?"

"Know what?"

"Know about me being sick."

"I knew you were sick from the start, of course."

"No, I mean it was the doctors in Paris when they told you how bad it was, is that not so?"

"Yes."

"And you did not tell me then? This whole trip you knew but you did not say."

"I did not want you to worry. It was not going to spoil our honeymoon."

Amelia became very serious.

"You have not been totally truthful with me. It is not going to get any better is it?"

Standing over her with his head bent down, almost cheek to cheek, John whispered: "Do not say that; of course it is. I got better when I was sick and traveled to Fayal. It worked for me: it will work for you. Travel heals the soul."

"But your doctor friend did not."

The sun was well below the distant hills and the sky was draining its light. John felt a chill deep within him.

"Do not talk about it now," he said.

He kissed her cheek. "Not now. You need to just rest."

"I am sorry."

"What could you possibly be sorry for?"

"I have not fulfilled my obligations."

"What are you talking about?"

She turned to whisper in his ear as if there were others in the room who could overhear.

"We have not consummated our marriage."

He shook his head and laughed and kissed her on her forehead.

"There will be plenty of time for that sort of thing later, after you get better."

John stood up, squeezed her shoulders with both of his hands, and then stepped back into the room leaving her to watch the approaching twilight. He stood behind her chair and watched the sky as well. He stepped back and back again into the darkening room. They did not speak. She watched the sky.

So fragile, he thought. She is so enormously fragile. Filled with such life and such desire and hope for life, but yet so fragile are we.

He tried but John could not stop the sharp cut of the pain and the tears down his cheek.

"Do you see this?" she said. "Do you see this wonderful sunset?"

He took a moment, closed his eyes, a deep breath, and wiped his cheek with his hand. The eastern sky blazed orange, cloudless. The room darkened, night crept in.

"Yes," he finally said.

The voices of the men in the room returned.

John was distracted back into the present, the hotel room, the gathered men discussing the Government and the Committee meeting tomorrow.

Henry Davison: "The basic concept of the trust is to stabilize the economy. I don't understand why the government sees that as a threat."

Jack Morgan: "Because it is not them doing the stabilizing and controlling the stabilizing."

Thomas Lamont: "It is also a new phenomenon, they are mistaking Morgan for the captains of industry of old, like Vanderbilt, Rockefeller, Yerkes or Carnegie, or even worse the manipulators of companies like Drew and Gould and Fisk and Heinze, where they build up a company and expand by driving out of business their rivals. But we have created a cooperative effort, where everyone in the cooperative wins, and a banking system that allows others to survive and thrive."

Henry Davison: "We need to focus in that point. They say it is a curtailment of competition, but quite frankly total competition, total Laissez Faire competition is deadly. No one wants that. Before the railroads were constantly at each others throats laying parallel lines and price cutting to the point that everyone was failing and going into bankruptcy. The consumers were not helped by that, nor were the bond or the stock holders."

Jack Morgan: "Right, and my father changed all of that. Now, through mutual agreement everyone mutually benefits. The railroads can now concentrate on creating a strong efficient business which provides the customer a better and more stable market place, and that rewards the stock and the bond holders as well. Why can't they see that?"

Joseph Choate: "They want to control the banking system, not the banking system controlling itself. They want to have a say in industrial integration. So we need to show the greater efficiencies of the market place controlling itself."

John sniffed but his nose was running heavily with fluid. He had to blow his nose. He picked up the handkerchief next to him and as quietly as he could he blew his nose. Conversation among the men in the room stopped. John dabbed his nose and put the handkerchief back down on the table next to his cards. Then, into the silence, he spoke. His mind was still with Memie.

"You do not really realize the difference between the outside and the inside of a thing."

No one spoke. Everything hushed. The men looked back and forth at each other, each wondering, questioning. John noticed. Several stared over toward him. He did not exactly know what they all had been saying just before he spoke. His mind was not focused on what they had been saying. Maybe what he said did not apply to their conversation.

He cleared his throat.

"The difference between what we see as the outside and what really is on the inside."

It was his son Jack who spoke first.

"What exactly do you mean, Father?"

John looked around. He felt confused. He did not feel well. He pointed his hand toward the French door leading out onto the balcony.

"Outside in the night it is cold, it is winter. If you were outside and not properly dressed you could freeze to death."

"Certainly, it can be harsh and unrelenting," Jack said. It seemed to John that Jack was trying to cover for him, to show the others that his father was indeed listening to their conversation but had a deeper and more insightful view of the matter.

"But here, inside," John said as he waved his hand, "there is warmth and comfort, security. These gentlemen only see what appears on the outside, they see a so called money trust, an interlocking consensus of bad men trying to take over the country and squeeze it for all the profits we can. But inside, it is not that at all. We are trying to bring an order and economic security that will be beneficial to everyone."

But he grew tired of it all.

"And I, on the outside I am an old and tired out man with a cold and a running nose," he stopped for a second with a mischievous smile, "but what a nose it is."

There was muffled, almost suppressed, laughter in the room.

One of the lawyers spoke up, the younger one.

"But on the inside you are a caged dynamo of energy and drive. Do not worry Mr. Morgan, you will defeat them. You will show them the fault of their assumptions, and then you will show them the truth and wisdom of yours. They have no idea whom they are dealing with."

There was a general agreement among the others.

John stared at the man for a moment without expression. That was not exactly what John was going to say. But what was he going to say? What words give truth? Words can express facts; words in a limited way can express ideas; but words are seriously empty in expressing feelings.

But the man was right in one way: more and more he did feel caged.

John remembered a day in Fayal.

His windows were opened wide and the sun flooded in. His cage of two canaries was on the window shelf. The little birds were hopping back and forth from one cross bar within the cage to another. He was happy. He was going home. He was packing his clothes in the trunk on the floor. The canaries sang in the sunshine. Everything was right.

He pulled some pantaloons out from his dresser and turned to kneel down by the trunk but his elbow bumped the cage. In that moment of recognition of what happened he dropped his bundle of clothes and reached for the cage. But it was too late.

He watched helpless as the cage sailed through the air and fell straight down to the side street two stories below. It spun as it fell and it hit the street with a loud crack and the cage broke into pieces.

John watched, frozen in the moment. What could he do?

Then, cautiously, the two canaries both hopped free. They stood on the pavement chirping and looking around, wondering, perhaps, what had just happened. But then, both together, they took flight and disappeared into the trees.

John, from his window perch above, smiled.

The inside flew free.

John waved his hand in the air, as if he waved the men away. But they took it to mean that they should carry on. John tried to focus on his game of solitaire. He studied the cards laid out on the desk. The game was against him. He was not winning. Not seeing a move he turned over another card.

It was again a queen.

John stood at the counter of the telegraph office. It was raining outside, a cold February day. His hat and coat were dripping water onto the floor and counter. He walked from the carriage to the telegraph office oblivious to the rain. The agent behind the desk stood, glancing at the trail of wet foot steps.

"I need to send a cable to London," John said, emotionless.

The clerk pulled out a form and set it and a pen in front of John. John seemed dazed, staring into the face of the clerk for a long time before he looked down at the paper.

"Thank you," he mumbled.

He picked up the pen and addressed it to his father. He wrote "Father" but then stopped, holding the pen just above the paper. How do you say it? What words?

John tried to make Amelia as happy as he could. They finally made it out of Algiers and on to Nice, France. It took two tries. The first time he booked a passage for the three of them, Amelia, the maid Anna, and himself but when they all arrived at the dock the captain of the boat stopped them. The man took one look at Amelia sitting in her wheelchair and turned John aside.

"Sorry sir but you'll have to book a different passage. I'm not taking you across. Not on my boat."

"What do you mean?"

"Just look at her. I don't want nobody to die on my boat. Sorry, but I don't think she'd make it across."

"She will not die on your boat, sir."

The captain shook his head no.

"You may not want to see it, and I am truly sorry, but she is a very sick lady and needs a hospital. Look at her."

John turned and looked at her, sitting in her wheelchair at the end of the ramp, white shawl wrapped. So fragile, he thought. So pale. He suddenly knew. She is not going to get any better.

The Villa St. Georges in Nice was atop a hill. It was surrounded by groves of olive trees, and orange trees and lime trees. It is said that in season the scent of the blossoms fills the air like heaven.

"You should be here then," the gardener told them as John wheeled Amelia around the gardens. "Come back then."

"Oh lets do, Pierpont. Can we?"

During the day if it was warm enough John wheeled her out among the trees, down the leafy and shady paths, and then through the rose gardens. At the white wooden gate you could see the snow capped mountains so far away.

On colder days they stayed indoors. John built a fire and Amelia rested. She stayed in a downstairs room near a plant filled conservatory where several canaries flew about freely. She tried walking out everyday to great them and say hello. She could listen to their song from her room. And in the room next to her were two caged nightingales.

John had two canaries and a blackbird in Fayal and he was healed of his sickness. He wanted her to have the same. If it worked for him then it should also work for her.

But there was the ever present cough, the vomited mucus, and the small pellets of turpentine after every meal, and the 'nice jelly' of cod liver oil twice a day, and the iodine. There were times she coughed most the night and could only find sleep during the day.

John seldom slept more than a few hours at a time. Between John and Anna someone had to be with her at all times. So it was a grand and happy day when her mother Mary and brother Edward arrived. Amelia hugged her mother over and over again throughout the day as if afraid that if she let go she would disappear. Her mother was with her most of the time. Mary tried to talk about home and friends in order make life as normal as possible.

Mary sat staring out the window. She loved watching the birds in the early morning. They seemed happy and active jumping from branch to branch, never staying in any one place long. Chirping back and forth she wondered what they were saying to each other. Gossip? Comments on the weather?

In the bed beside her Amelia was asleep. Her breathing was regular, although raspy. It is good when she sleeps. Her eternal coughing gave her few opportunities so when she could finally relax into sleep the last thing Mary wanted to do was to accidently wake her up. After she relieved Anna early this morning she gave Amelia some eggs and tea, feeding her with a spoon. She was holding a spoonful when Amelia closed her eyes and fell into sleep. Mary carefully put the spoon down on the tray on the table by the bed and sat back into her chair. She watched her daughter for a long time but then turned to look outside. The birds were very active in the garden. But it was a dark and cloudy day. Drops of rain began tapping the window.

Amelia coughed, and the tone of her breathing changed. A look of pain was on her face. Her breathing became deep and gurgling. Thinking her choking Mary tried to sit her up.

"Amelia."

She did not wake up.

"Amelia. Amelia," Mary called out louder, shaking her thin shoulders.

Amelia breathed deeper and with more difficulty. Holding Amelia up into a sitting position Mary called out for Anna. She had to call several times, each time louder until finally Anna arrived. She instantly rushed over to Amelia and held her face in her hands. Anna looked at Mary. They both knew.

Mary, holding her own hands to her mouth, rushed out of the room and across to the stairs.

"Pierpont," she screamed. "Pierpont."

Like an arrow shot from a bow the tension flew through the house.

Mary stood at the base of the stairs frozen. She did not know what to do. Race up the stairs to his room; go back to her daughter; scream out again.

But from above came the thunder of boots and then he turned at the top of the stairs and paused.

"Hurry," she said as she turned back and ran toward the room.

Anna was just laying Amelia back down onto the bed when John came in. He knelt down beside her and held her hand up to his lips. Her breathing was heavy and very labored. Her eyes were closed but her face seemed twisted in agony.

"Speak," he said. "Speak to me."

Her face grew calm.

"Please. Memie. Speak to me just one last time."

Her breathing grew shallow, then more shallow.

John moved closer, his face was next to hers, their lips almost touching.

"Please," he barely whispered.
Breathing stopped. Amelia relaxed. Silence.
John closed his eyes.

John sat on the side of his bed in his room. Strewn about on the bed were cables he had received. In his lap lay The Book of Common Prayer he had given her on the day before their wedding when they both took Communion at St. George's Church. It was odd: Communion at St. George's Church; death at Villa St. Georges. Death was the dragon they could not slay.

He held her Bible in his hands. The Reverend Childers had come to help, to comfort, to help heal. He had read from Saint Paul's Epistle to the Philippians. In her Bible John underlined the passage:

"For to me to live is Christ, and to die is gain. But
if I live in the flesh, this is the fruit of my
labour: yet what I shall choose I wot not. For I am in
a strait betwixt two, having a desire to depart, and
to be with Christ; which is far better: Nevertheless
to abide in the flesh is more needful for you."

John opened the book to the beginning of the New Testament and carefully wrote:

"Amelia S. Morgan. Died at the Villa St. Georges near Nice France at 8:30 a.m. Monday February 17, 1862. 'Her end was peace.'"

John closed the book and set it aside. He opened her Common Prayer and reread what he had written on the flyleaf of the book just 134 days before.

"Memie from Pierpont. St. Georges. Communion Sunday.
Octo. 6, 1861."

John thought for a moment and then took his pen and, as if she could somehow, somewhere, still hear him, added the words: "I go to prepare a place for you."

John closed the book and held it up to his forehead. He hurt more than he ever had; he hurt more than he ever would. He carefully placed the book on top of her Bible.

There was a slight knock on his closed door.

"Yes," he said.

"They are here, for her." The speaker paused. It was her brother Edward. "Let them take her?"

John waited. They were taking her coffin to the Church of the Vaudois. They were here. It meant releasing her forever.

He cleared his throat.

"Yes," he said. "They can take her."

John could hear as Edwards footsteps disappeared.

He picked up one of the cables on the bed. It was from Junius. Father. "I cannot tell you how much I am grieved by the sad, sad intelligence conveyed in your telegram."

He looked to the window. It was open a jar and he could hear footsteps below in the gravel. He read on: "It is a hard blow for you my Dear Son—but I feel sure you will resign the precious one into her Saviour's arms without a murmur. He gave her to you and has taken her away."

Without a murmur?

What about the question Why? Why her, now?

John picked up another telegram. It was from his father again. "We know that our lives and all that we have are in the hands of a kind Heavenly Parent who never afflicts but for our good."

There were more footsteps in the gravel below. Voices. John stood and walked to the window and pulled aside the thin curtain. He looked down. Two men were loading the long black coffin into a hearse. The horse seemed nervous; it kept pulling on its reins. Edward and Mary stood by and watched in silence.

This is for my good, John thought to himself. How can I accept this as being kind and just and for my own good?

They all stood on the dock. It was pouring rain. Relentless rain. They stood on the dock under large black umbrellas. John, Mary, Edward, Anna. They watched as the undertakers slid her large black coffin out of the hearse and set it on a pedestal on the wooden dock. Two men, one from the Church and one from the ship stood together under another umbrella and signed the necessary papers. The coffin sat in the rain glistening from the wet.

They were all motionless and silent as workers from the ship lifted up the coffin and took it on board. It was being shipped home. They all turned to leave except John. They asked for him to come but he waved them away. Mary held the umbrella for him but even she eventually walked away. They had a train to catch.

John stood alone in the rain for a bit longer.

Then he turned to walk away.

On board the train John sat by the window and stared out. Edward and Anna were sitting opposite in the cabin. Mary entered and sat down. She looked over at John. He was soaking wet. His hair and clothes and coat were dripping into a puddle of water on the carpet floor of the train. He was slightly shivering.

"Pierpont."

He did not respond.

"Pierpont," she said again louder.

Without a word he turned his head and looked at her.

"Would you not want to change your clothes, you are soaking wet."

John did not respond. He shivered as he looked down at himself.

Trying again Mary said: "Please change your clothes. You will catch a death of a cold like this."

John looked back out the window. He watched his reflection in the window glass as he smiled.

Why would that be a bad thing?

John, sitting in his hotel room, reached out and touched the lamp on the desk. The shaft had a vine like pattern: Art Nouveau like. His son and the others were still all talking. John turned and looked into the bedroom. Louisa had gone in there awhile ago. The lights in the sitting room were all on but in the bedroom it was dim. She only had a small light on next to a chair by the bed. She sat in a pool of light reading a book.

"Well, my friends," Jack was saying as he stood up. "As we have quite a day before us tomorrow perhaps we should adjourn for the evening."

The others all stood.

John, distracted, turned away from Louisa and watched as the men prepared to leave. He nodded and said good night to each as they all waved goodbye. He did not get up from his chair.

"See you tomorrow gentlemen."

"I am sure we will get through this."

"We have before."

"Take care."

"And take care of that cold Mr. Morgan."

"Yes, exactly.

Jack walked out into the hallway with the men leaving John alone in the room. He once again turned and looked into the bedroom, the darkened bedroom where Louisa sat in her chair by the bed reading her book in a small pool of soft light. It was just enough to read by and nothing more.

John took a deep breath. Death lingered in the room like a scent of sulfur from a long since extinguished match.

It felt like the office after everyone left for the day and he remained behind, alone.

Work was a lonely place after the work day was done and everyone left for home. He liked the excitement of the office with the people buzzing around, transactions being fulfilled, things happening.

It was life.

But after hours it became empty and alone.

It was very late. John, sitting at his desk in his office, took off his reading glasses. He rubbed his eyes. Sitting back in his chair he could not help but yawn. He was tired. He felt melancholic. After a moment he stood up. The office all around him was dark. Only a few lights here and there were left on. Across the office he could see the janitor bent over sweeping the floor.

Slowly he took his coat from the coat rack and put it on; his hat from atop the rack and put it on; his walking stick and tapped it on the rug. He reached over and turned off his light. His office was dark.

Walking down the hallway toward the front door he found one office where the light was still on. He stopped and looked in. Charles Coster sat at his desk in the pool of light from his lamp on his desk. His desk was cluttered with papers.

"Do not work too late, Charles."

Charles, startled, looked up. He had short chopped hair, sprinkled grey, and a large moustache. He squinted to see who stood at his door. John walked out of the dark and into the pool of light; he sat down in the wooden chair in front of the desk.

"No, sir; I was just finishing up a few things."

John nodded.

"Well see that you get some rest. You look tired."

"I will sir; I will be leaving in just a bit."

"I need you to be around for a lot of years to come."

Charles watched John closely before he spoke.

"I have not had a chance to tell you, sir, how sorry I am to hear about your father."

"Thank you, Charles."

"It must have been quite a blow when you heard."

John took a deep breath and then nodded. He turned and for a moment looked outward from the pool of light made by the lamp.

April, 1890. John set out with his daughter Louisa on the White Star Line ship the "Teutonic" to join his father for their birthday celebrations. It was a tradition for them to celebrate their April birthdays together. John would be 53 and his father would be 77.

When they arrived at Liverpool they stood by the banister watching as the ship pulled in. They made their way to their cabin and were packing the last of their things when there was a knock on the door. It was a messenger from the White Star Line. He handed John three envelopes.

"What are they," Louisa asked as she packed her shawl into her suitcase.

"They are telegrams."

"Who are they from," Louisa asked.

"Strange, one is dated April 6, one April 7, and then one today, the ninth."

"Who are they from," Louisa asked again.

"They all seem to be from Walter Burns," John replied as he looked at each envelope.

"Walter? Are they all from London?"

"No, that is what is strange. They are from Monte Carlo."

"They are at your father's already?"

John looked at Louisa with a puzzled look and then dropped the two early telegrams and tore open the third.

"Read it out loud," she said.

John adjusted his reading glasses and began to read.

"'Your father passed away at quarter before one on the morning of April eighth he never. . .'" John's voice trailed off for a second as he swallowed hard but then he resumed "'he never recovered consciousness and doctors say never aware of pain there is no need your coming Monte Carlo unless you specially desire. . .'"

John looked over at Louisa. They were both in shock. John looked back down and started to read it again. He could not finish. His hand trembled. He dropped the telegram onto the desk. He stood for a moment but then he crumbled onto the bed like a wounded deer.

Louisa grabbed another telegram. It was dated April 7. She tore it open. She began to read.

"What?" John managed to ask.

"'Father had very restless night and has lost ground since yesterday feel very anxious but not hopeless.'"

"Lost ground, lost ground from what?"

Louisa tore open the first telegram.

It told of the accident, but 'symptoms improving general strength maintained.'

John, sitting on the side of the bed, turned his head and looked up at Louisa. He began to understand. She watched as his eyes swelled with tears.

"When is the funeral?"

John turned his head back to look at Charles Coster sitting across from him.

"May the sixth."

"Why are you here, sir? You should be home with your family."

John began to trace his finger up and down the stem of the lamp.

"I have always believed that burying yourself in work is the best remedy for depression."

Charles did not say anything for a moment, watching as John traced his finger up and down the stem of the lamp.

"Well, I suppose that can be true. I am too busy," Charles said. He smiled. "I'm afraid that I do not have time to be depressed."

"You, Mr. Coster, are working yourself to death. You need to slow down. I want you around here for many years to come."

"Yes, sir. You have already mentioned that."

"Did I?" John asked as he tapped the lamp with his finger.

"Are you all right, sir?"

John looked at him: searching, wondering. Am I all right? He thought about it.

"To be honest with you Charles, I do not know."

Charles stared for a moment. He was not expecting that reply. He did not quite know how to respond. This was J.P. Morgan sitting across from him: J.P. Morgan. How is it that he does not know? Charles had never seen him wounded.

There was a very long pause.

"I had a close friend die once," Charles found himself saying, talking about something he never talked about.

There was just something in the moment that brought it out.

"He fell," Charles said as he gently lifted up his hand as if pointing to the roof, or a ledge, or the top of a crevasse, or the peak of a mountain.

After a moment he brought his hand back down.

"You know you never get over it. They say that you do but you do not. It just fades back into your memory and you do not think about it as much. But when you do: there it all is. It chills your sense of well being, your sense of place and order."

Charles paused but then asked.

"Were you there when he . . ."

"No," John answered sharp, cutting him off.

John turned once again away and looked out into the dark office. It was easy to hide in the dark.

When the carriage arrived at Villa Henrietta John was out before the horses came to a stop. He crunched across the graveled driveway toward the stone steps to the house. His sister Mary was standing at the top of the porch stairs near the front door. Seeing her over took him. By the time he reached her he was crying. They hugged hard, intense, grasping. He was breathing heavy but he closed his eyes and in her embrace it slowed. When they separated she reached up with her fingers and wiped away the tears on his cheek.

"Where?" he asked.

"He's in the front parlor, on the left."

John went into the house and approached the closed door on the left. She followed him but he turned and held up his hand. She stopped.

John opened the door and entered the room alone.

The furniture in the room had been pulled to the sides. In the center of the room on a long table sat the closed casket, a polished dark mahogany. It dominated the room, as if the room had been built to contain it. The French doors were open with the drapes pulled aside. Sunlight streamed in across the floor. There was a small garden outside, tree shaded.

John slowly walked over to the casket. He carefully placed his hand onto the wood. It seemed cold to the touch. He stood for a moment motionless. John placed both hands onto the top of the casket, palms down, and brought his head down. Bent over the casket he touched the wood with his forehead and stood like that for a long time.

He envisioned his father's death. They said he went out for a ride in his small black Victoria. Jack, his coachman, rode out along the road between Beaulieu and the village of Eze. It was a nice spring day. The sun was warm against his skin. At the point where the road runs alongside the railroad tracks a train, approaching from behind, blew its whistle. The two horses, startled, bolted into a run. The Victoria bounced along the path as Jack tried to rein in the horses. Junius, rather than sitting back and holding on, stood up in the carriage in an attempt to help the coachman with the horses. He was thrown from the carriage and slammed against a low stone wall. By the time Jack stopped the horses and turned them around two men walking along the path ran over to Junius. He was bleeding from deep cuts in his head.

Over the next several days he never regained consciousness.

John stood up. He took a deep breath. Carefully he reached under the lid and unlatched the lock. He opened the top of the casket, it opened soundless, and his fathers face and torso came into view.

They dressed him in his brown pinstripe suit. His snow white hair was carefully combed; his bushy eyebrows under more control than when he was alive.

Embalmed.

John brought his palms together and touched the tips of his fingers to his lips. He started down at his father asleep.

It was soundless.

Absolute stillness and silence.

There was no breathing; no motion of his chest or his nose; no small twitch of his eyebrow that he used to do at times when he slept. John remembered once when he was a little boy he crept up on his father, asleep on the couch. John watched the twitch of the eyebrow: wondering, watching. But suddenly his father's eyes popped wide open. He reached out and growled like a bear. John squealed and fell back. Even though his father started laughing John was still scared and cried. They hugged.

John stared down at his father's face.

It was as if he was waiting for the eyes to open.

They did not.

There was absolute silence: absolute silence.

Is this what death is?

John carefully reached down and touched his father's forehead. It was cold to his touch. White; pasty.

Father is not in there.

It all returns to Egypt in the end. They so desperately asked the question that we all ask sooner or later, the question to which everything else is but a footnote. Why do we have to die, and if we have to die then why do we live?

He could hear from outside in the garden the birds chirping. The drapes moved as a breeze filtered into the room.

He watched his father. He did not move. He listened to the birds outside in the sun.

It brought thoughts of Memie.

John lowered the lid back down. He watched as the shadow of the lid covered his father, his father disappeared inside the dark mahogany. The lid squeaked a little. The latch under the lid clicked against the lock on the casket. When he slightly pushed down there was a loud resounding snap of the metal hinges. It echoed the room.

It was closed.

"You know, my father was against this at first."

Charles Coster tilted his head to one side.

"Against what?"

John tapped the shade of the lamp.

"Electricity. The Edison Company. He did not see a future in it."

"I am surprised. I thought your father gave you wise advice."

John laughed. "Mostly, I suppose he did, but, I am afraid, not always. I wrote to him every Tuesday and Friday, for years, decades, every Tuesday and Friday. He wrote me back. It was mostly about business, what the firm was doing, what he was doing, that sort of thing. But he was trying to shape my character. 'You are altogether too rapid in disposing of your meals. You can have no health if you go on in this way.'"

"He wrote you that?"

"Yes, oh yes, that and much more: my Father. When I was very young and away at school he wrote me to 'not to get intimate with any but such as are of the right stamp.'"

"Oh my. Were you prone to that?"

John nodded. "And he also wrote that 'now is the time for you to form your character and as it is formed now so it will be likely to remain.'"

"It certainly sounds as though you took all of them to heart enough that you memorized them."

"But he did give me the best advice a father could ever give his son: 'do not let the desire of success or of accumulating induce you ever to do a single action which will cause you regret. Self approbation and a feeling that God approves will bring a far greater happiness than all the wealth the world can give.'"

"That indeed is very sound advice."

"You know, Charles; my son is quite tame, quite reserved. I do not think he knows how to do anything bad. I was a bit of a wild one myself.

90

It must be very difficult for a father to try and tame the flaming and passionate youthfulness of a son. And passionate and youthful I certainly was. He tried to temper my compulsions. When I first started out in this business there were several major things I did that he chastised me for. And looking back I would have to say that he was right."

"And what were they?"

"Well, I speculated in gold during the war. I bought up a lot of gold and then sent some overseas to England. That spiked the price here at home so I sold what I had and made some money. It seemed innocent enough at the time but it was during the war. It was legal, of course, but not exactly ethical. Too many I have found will narrowly follow the first but totally ignore the second. I was young and believed that what was important was making money however you could. But I was wrong."

John tapped the lamp with his finger.

"And the second?"

"I was in New Orleans on business when I found this shipment of coffee that had been delivered to dock but the buyer had failed to follow through with payment. The captain was bound to lose a lot of money. So I bought his full shipment with a draft on company funds, which I technically was not authorized to do."

"You bought the full shipment?"

John smiled. There was a gleam in his eyes.

"Yes, but you see I had done my homework first. When I heard about it I went around the city to hotels and coffee houses with samples and got from them firm commitments to buy different allotments of the coffee if I could produce it. It was only when I had enough to sell the entire shipment that I wrote the draft, bought the coffee, and then turned right around and sold it all with a tidy little profit. By the time they found out I had bought the coffee, and were ready to cancel the draft, they also found out that it was all sold with a handsome profit."

"What did they do?"

"What would you do? They chastised me for over stepping my authority, but then they kept the profit."

"But certainly the end did not justify the means. And they could not let that stand as a policy for it could be disastrous in the hands of someone not as clever."

John waved his hand.

"Of course not, but that is age and experience talking. Again, I was young and, as you say, clever. But that can be a deadly combination."

"Dare I ask if there was a third?"

"Critics in the papers have plagued me for years on this one. It was at the beginning of the war. The union was desperate for men and material. In August of 1861 a certain Simon Stevens came to me for a loan. He was a politically well connected lawyer. He had a Purchase Order from General John Fremont, commander of the Western Department at the time, for the purchase of five thousand refitted breech loading Hall Carbines for $22.00 each, a total of $110,000, to be delivered to Missouri. Stevens said that he could buy the carbines from a certain Mr. Arthur Eastman for $12.50 each, for a total of $62,500. That was quite a profit. All that he needed from me was an initial down payment of $20,000 to start the transaction. The carbines were breach loading smooth bores and they were to be re-rifled and fitted for percussion cap firing and sent on to Fremont in allotments, payable upon delivery, and once I began receiving payments I would advance the remaining funds to complete the deal. So, upon the authority of the Purchase Order I lent him the $20,000."

John paused for a moment.

"I told him that I wanted to see the carbines in question. He was a little reluctant at first but then finally agreed. Well, as it turns out neither he nor Mr. Arthur Eastman actually owned the carbines. Eastman, who was familiar with firearms and ordinance, found the five thousand Carbines, left over from the Mexican war, in a federal warehouse on Governors Island off the southern tip of Manhattan. In May of 1861 he offered to alter the guns to more modern standards but the Ordnance Chief, a man named James Ripley, thought that the carbines were worthless and he said no. Eastman then proposed to buy all of the guns outright and Ripley agreed to sell the lot for $3.50 each just to get them off of his hands. But Eastman did not have the $17,500 needed. So Stevens makes Eastman an offer of $12.50 per carbine, which Eastman agrees to, and then Stevens turns around and sells the carbines to General John Fremont for $22 per carbine."

"So you bought carbines from the government to sell them to the government?"

"Well, I did not: they did. My $20,000 was needed to actually buy the carbines from the government. It took longer than expected to re-rifle them so the first shipment of 2,500 carbines were shipped the end of August. On September 10 I received a payment from Fremont of $55,550 for the carbines and freight charges. I deducted my $20,000, interest on the loan, and a commission of $5,400, for a total of $26,344 and sent the rest on."

"What about the rest of the carbines?"

"Well, it was at that point that I got out of the transaction. I gave the deal over to one of my father's partners, Morris Ketchum. I was no longer involved. When they sent the final shipment they were not paid and the War Department charged them with war profiteering. The suit went on until the Supreme Court ruled in their favor in 1867 and they were finally paid."

"So there was nothing illegal that happened?"

"No, not technically, but I did learn a very valuable lesson from that affair. Always do your homework. Know what the transaction is and who you are making the transaction with and why. I was only interested in making a profit; the money alone was my focus. But that is wrong. Focus on the transaction, be knowledgeable of that, make that a prudent and clean and wise thing and the profit flows from that alone."

"I always thought," Charles replied, "that it is best to be straight with everything, that way you have nothing to fear and you will not worry that you will be found out in anything."

John smiled and slapped his knee.

"You sound like my father."

"That I take as a compliment."

"I have to say that my father was right most of the time. You must have a clean soul, he used to say. You have to watch yourself, you see, because it is a far too easy and slippery slide to corruption. I have dealt with different men in my life that I wish I had not. They seek only for themselves and take for themselves everything that they can. They do not look to build, to make something long lasting, something that will benefit everyone. They do not care. All they want is to take for themselves all that they can and the rest of the world be damned."

"Nothing works best save that which works for the most."

"We all slide down that pathway a bit, I am afraid, it can not be helped in business, it is the way of the world. But catch yourself before you slide too far and walk back from it. My father was right: once there is a stain on your soul it is a stain forever."

"You were very lucky, sir, to have the father that you did. Count your blessings."

John looked at Coster for a long moment before he finally nodded in agreement.

"You know, Charles, I thought about this on the ship coming home. Sitting on deck watching the clouds go by I thought about how it is strange in a way that your mother and father give you shelter, they serve as a roof over you protecting you, and you feel that they will always give you shelter no matter how old you get or how successful you become, you know in the back of your mind that there is a place to go, a sanctuary where you can escape and all will be well, and all will be fine, and they will watch over you and take care of you no matter what. It is silly, really, to think about that when you yourself are married and raising a family."

"But you become the father to your children and they look to you in the same way," Charles said.

"Think about how frightening that is."

"I know. And there are times that, just for a little bit, you do not want to be grown up."

"But then when your parent dies you are it, the roof over you protecting you is gone and you have to face the elements alone. And not only do you have no one to protect you any longer but, as you say, you have to protect your own children who feel the same way about you as you felt about your father."

John continued to run his finger up and down the lamp, lost in thought.

"My father worked hard and was buried in work all of the time. I remember as a child he it seemed he was away working, it was a great adventure to go and see him. When I was in the Azores for my health I wrote to him almost everyday. In the Azores for the longest time I never got a response. It was the loneliest I have ever been. You see, it was like I was cut off, separated from what protects me. I have kept some of that with me all my life. I can not shake it. Every once in awhile it gets overpowering."

"But sir, you have so much."

John shrugged.

"Sometimes what you have is not what you really want. Sometimes that is lost before you even realize it is what you wanted."

"And what is that, sir?"

John sat for a long time staring at the lamp. Finally he looked up with a wounded look in his eyes.

"I do not know."

"I think we should enjoy what we have."

"On the boat coming back I watched the ocean, the sky, clouds. Those things are always there every time I sail but I suddenly saw them. It is hard to explain. I watched the people on the boat going about their things, their little daily things. My father's body was in a box in the hold and they all went about their little daily things as if nothing were different. I remember going to the Azores how free I felt in the open water for first time. The wind in my hair; staring up at the sails; the ropes pulling taut; the creaking mast; flapping sail; huge white clouds; and a deep blue sky that went on forever. I am truly free, I thought. Freedom

94

tasted so sweet. But my father was always there, safety, and that is what made my freedom taste so sweet."

John paused. Charles never knew John to talk as much as he was talking now.

"And now that your father is gone?"

"It is a different feeling all together, I suppose I am free from him but now that feeling is tempered with obligations and responsibility. Freedom is not free. Like everything it has a price. And that price is high enough that it destroys the very thing it is buying. Like the passion to buy a work of art is very strong and can consume you. But once you acquire it then there is a feeling of satisfaction I suppose but that is no where near the strength of the passion of desiring it."

"Well, what is that saying that there are two sides to every coin?"

"I suppose it is with the death of your last parent that you finally and ultimately mature."

After his father's funeral John sailed for London. There was his father's house. There was the estate. There was the art. Arrangements had to be made.

When John entered his father's study it immediately felt strange. He had been here many times. When he was in England he even worked here at the very same desk reading reports and sending cables. But his father was here. Even when he was not physically present he was still, nevertheless, present in the room. That is, until, today.

John stopped and looked around at all of the familiar things: the room (the wallpaper on the wall, the drapes on the windows, and the rugs on the floor); the furniture (the desk, the chairs, the cabinets, and the sofa); the art work (the paintings on the walls, the statues on the tables and cabinets, and the books on the shelves along the walls). It was all too familiar. It invoked his father. It defined and characterized him.

But the one essential difference between now and all of the other times that he had been here was that all of the other times the room invoked what his father is, it gave definition to the world what his father is, but now it invoked what his father was.

John walked over to the desk and sat down on the chair. This was his chair. This is where he sat, where he read, where he wrote reports, where he wrote letters: letters, perhaps, from father to son; and where he read letters: letters, perhaps, from son to father.

John looked around the room from the perspective of the chair. He noticed across the room, on the bottom shelf of a cabinet of books, a set of letter boxes. Curious, John walked over and knelt down with one knee on the floor. Each box was carefully marked with dates in his father's perfect script. One box in particular attracted John. The writing on the outside binder said: 'Horta.'

That was the town on the island of Fayal. John pulled the box off the shelf and went back to the desk and sat down. He untied the small string that kept the lid closed. He opened the lid and looked in.

On top was a letter. He began to read:

"Horta, Fayal
    November 23, 1852

My dear Parents:
    Since I left you, now 15 days ago, I have crossed nearly the whole of the broad Atlantic, and am now writing you in my room at Silva's Hotel at Horta on the Island of Fayal. After a very short passage of eleven days and a half at noon of Saturday, November 20, the IO entered this harbor. During the voyage I was not seasick in the least and enjoyed myself greatly. The voyage was rather rough but we had westerly winds nearly the whole of the passage. . ."

John looked up. He felt a strange tightness in his chest. He held in his hand the first letter he wrote after he landed in the Azores.

His father kept it.

John pulled others out of the box. They were the letters he had written. His eyes fell on one, talking about when he bought a blackbird and two canaries in a cage "in order to have something to take care of and to make the time pass pleasantly."

He held up another: he was writing about seeing a native funeral and "there is no solemnity in it at all and unless it was for the coffin I should never know it was a funeral."

He put it down on the desk and pulled out another: he asked for them to send pantaloons for "the two pair which were so small for me I cannot now button within at least an inch and a half."

He pulled another: "rode a donkey today for the first time for it is the main means of transportation on the island."

He pulled out another: "I wish I received letters as often as you do. I have received but one in ten weeks."

John looked into the binder. There were many more, many. John realized that not only did his father get all of his letters, and read them all, but he carefully filed them into this box and kept them all. It has been

96

thirty eight years. Why did he keep them all of this time?

Why did he not write when I was there?

John could imagine his father sitting at his desk reading a letter from his son: I am lonely, why do you not write I know you must be very busy. Then he would carefully straighten out the creased letter with the palm of his hand, hold it up one more time to see, and then carefully place it into the binder with all of the others, wrap the string around the hook closing the binder, and then slide it onto the shelf, making sure the edge of the binder was flush with the edge of the shelf. He then sits back down at his desk and brings the days work.

And John, sitting on the hilltop overlooking the Harbor, a fresh windy sun lit day, watching for a ship to arrive on the far horizon that just might have a letter from his father, but does not.

He picked another letter out of the binder: it was about the Dabney house, the girls, and all of the fresh oranges he ate, juicy and sweet, sent a crate home but the ship hit bad weather and had to return until the storm passes, afraid the oranges when you finally get them might not be as fresh when they arrive please write and let me know.

Dr. Cole says sometimes you must enjoy things when they are not what you want them to be. I worry about my friend Dr. Cole. Stayed up with him, he had a hemorrhage in his lung, blood was on his kerchief.

"We can amuse ourselves together very well. He intends if nothing happens to go to America in the spring."

I feel sad for him.

The canary cage fell and broke and they escaped. Hope them happiness in their new life.

John stopped reading. He looked up.

He remembered that day, the day the cage fell. It was toward the end. He was coming home. The window was wide open and the cage was on the window sill. John was packing his belongings in his suitcase. He pulled some pants out of the chest of drawers and turned. That was when he bumped the cage. It tilted out the window. In a fraction of a second he knew, he reached for the cage, but it was too late. He helplessly watched as the bamboo cage spun in the open air around and around as it descended out the window. It splintered into pieces with a loud crack as it hit the pavement two stories down.

John stared down. All he could see was the splintered remains of the cage. He waited. He could not see the birds. There was no noise from the cage. All he could think about was how now they were exposed to the cats.

Finally he heard a chirp. It was a dazed and confused chirp. He could see one of the canaries hop out from under a section of the shattered cage. It hopped out and fluttered its wings. Then there was the second canary. It too stood on the ground for a moment next to the other. John didn't know if they were hurt or not. Should he rush down and scoop them up? But then John watched as the two of them, one after another, flew up and disappeared into the trees. John tried to see them in the trees but he could not. They were gone.

John closed his eyes and breathed a sigh of relief. They were free. He remembered Dr. Cole. By then he had already died, buried in a grave atop the hill. But when he saw how attached John was getting to his birds Dr. Cole asked one day: what will you do if they escape and fly away?

John did not know how to answer. What should I do? Dr. Cole smiled, his palms resting on the top of his cane.

You wish them well, he said; you just wish them well.

John gathered up several of the binders and carried them out the back door into the small yard. There was a red brick fire pit at the edge of a patio. John put the binders down on the small brick wall on that side of the patio. He gathered up some dry leaves and twigs that had fallen from the overhanging trees and carefully placed them in the fire pit. When he thought he had enough he struck a match and lit the leaves. The fire increased.

John took out one of the early letters he had written to his father. He looked it over and then carefully placed it upon the fire. The page blackened and crunched together. Small flames licked around the sides.

He picked up another letter.

Why do you not write? With every ship that comes into port from America I look to see if there are any letters from you, but I find none. I believe that you still care for me but with each passing day with no word I cannot help but question.

John placed the page down onto the flames. They quickly licked around the edges of the paper and curled it up into a ball of ash. One by one he read each letter. Some he placed aside on the brick. Others he placed into the fire.

Footsteps approached. John looked up. It was Thomas Hand, his father's valet and butler. Thomas watched as John placed another letter to the flames. A strand of smoke curled into the air.

"Are those not important papers, sir?"

John smiled at him.

"Yes, perhaps; at least at one time."

"But your father was a great man, sir. Won't you be needing those for the historians?"

"No."

"Why, sir."

John looked at Thomas. Thomas was a good help to his father for a lot of years. He was more than just hired help.

"History does not need to know everything. A lot of these are personal. Sometimes there are things that no one else should know."

"I do not think that I agree with you sir. I seriously doubt that there is anything in those that will dishonor his memory. He saved them, after all, so he must have wanted them saved."

"He saved them for himself, Thomas. He saved them only for himself."

"Just the same, sir."

"It does not really matter. My father's greatness will and should live on by his ideas and his accomplishments, not on misinterpreted salacious details of his person."

"But sir, those are letters that you yourself wrote. Are you burning him or are you burning yourself?"

John did not answer. He did not have an answer.

Thomas stood silent for a moment but then turned to leave. John mumbled something.

Thomas turned, "What is that sir?"

"I said 'perhaps both, Thomas.'"

John looked at Thomas, and then back at the fire.

"If this is what your heart speaks, sir, then you must listen."

With that he turned and walked away.

After a moment John took out another letter written from Fayal. He read. I fear for my friend Dr. Cole for his health does not seem to be improving. We are both here for our health however I am improving, but he is not. Did I tell you that if nothing happens he wished to visit America in the spring?

John placed the letter onto the flame. He watched as the tongues of flame curled around the edges of the paper. He could hear himself in his mind, he could hear that day.

"Some day I want to walk up that hill," John said, indicating Mount Pico across the waters.

Doc, standing, leaning against his walking cane, smiled at him.

"Pip, I do believe that this particular peak is referred to as a mountain."

John turned to him puzzled.

"When is a hill a mountain, or a mountain a hill?"

Doc thought about it for a moment.

"Well I suppose that when a mountain is in your way you can just think of it as a hill. That makes it easier to overcome."

"So that is what I said, some day I want to go up that hill. Do you want to come with me?"

Doc laughed.

"No, no, that is not for me; that would take far too much energy for me."

"What do you want to do, then?"

Doc thought about it for a moment, he then turned to John with a new found energy.

"If everything goes well I would like to see America in the spring. I have never been."

The afternoon breeze crossed the yard. The branches of the tree that stretched out above the brick fire pit swayed. The shadow of the leaves danced across the ground and the brick, dappling flickering sunlight and soft shadow. John watched. It was like that day, the day he went to visit Dr. Cole again.

Dappled shade and light.

He visited the island of Fayal again, late in life.

It was a hot day; the sun bright. He and Louisa left the rest of the party, he said there was something he wanted to see, he would be back, no you all stay here, enjoy the sites, it will not take long, no I insist, stay here, I will be back. He and Louisa drove off in the car. They had cars then, not like when he was there before, back when he was but a lad of fifteen. The driver eased the car up the slope, up the narrow dirt path. The hot sun poured through the window. The gears of the car would grind each time the driver shifted. Finally they stop atop a slope. John got out and surveyed the area. Once Louisa got out of the car he pointed. 'Over there,' he said. He marched off climbing the hill, stepping over large stones and around bushes. Louisa tried to manage her dress through the bushes as best she could. It was hot. In one hand she held an opened umbrella, her face shaded. John was a portly man of sixty nine years old in a waistcoat and jacket: he grew tired. He sweats under his coat. Finally, near a large tree over looking the sea far below John came to a stop. He rested one foot on an outcropping rock. Louisa made it up to him. John was out of breath, heavily heaving. He took off his white fedora and wiped his brow with his handkerchief. He pointed to the small white gravestone beneath the tree. 'Here,' he said. 'I found it,' he said. The weather had worn it down. John stood for a long time staring down at the small white stone. Dr. Cole; Prometheus Bound; devoured by life. Spark of life, spark of dreams, and spark of beauty: hold onto these things because they can otherwise disappear. The branches of the tree overhead swayed with the breeze. Dappled shade and sunlight danced about the grave.

John closed his eyes and with a bowed head mumbled a prayer. Louisa watched him. He was crying. She watched as he wiped away the moisture from his eyes. She glanced down when he looked over at her. Best not said.

It had been fifty four years but it was as sharp as yesterday. John looked out across the sea as he had that day.

"Look at the sea," Doc said. "Look at the sparkle of the sunlight on the surface of the sea."

John looked out across the glisten of the water; he looked out across as far as he could see. To him at that moment it was as far as eternity.

"In my mind I think of the sea as life and the sky as spirit. Each sparkle is that of a soul emerging from the water of life and bursting into the sky of the spirit."

Doc paused for a moment before he continued.

"One day we will sparkle like that."

John looked back at Doc sitting on an outcropping rock.

"When the time comes, Pip, I wish to be buried here. Here."

"Stop talking silly," John said.

But Doc only looked up into John's eyes.

"As best you can, Pip, seek that which is eternal. Nothing else matters."

John stood over the grave. He turned away. It was enough. He took several steps toward the pathway leading down the hill. Louisa, nearer the path, turned away as well and began walking away, her back turned. John briefly looked back. Shade and shadow from the sun through the trees danced about the ground.

It is done.

Dappled in sun and shade the day drifted away.

John sat smoking his cigar, sitting alone in the room. They had all left and were standing in the hotel hallway outside the door. He could hear their muffled voices. He noticed on the wall opposite, near the door, was a painting. Impressionist: it was a young woman in the sun among the wildflowers.

He could remember standing at a gallery. It was after Memie's death, years had passed. Time moved on. He stood in the gallery surrounded by hundreds of paintings either hanging on the walls or stacked on the floor leaning against the wall. It was in the late afternoon and there was no lights lit in the gallery except for the sunlight streaming down from a skylight in the ceiling. Motes of dust floated freely in the streams of light. It was a bit close and stuffy and you could hear sounds from the street outside echo quietly in the silent chamber. John stopped when he saw it.

There was a painting of a young woman. It was slightly impressionist in style, dabs of paints, like thoughts or memories, instead of line. Color bright unblended. Pure. Sunshine sparkled the scene. The woman in the black hat had her head tilted down. Why a black hat on such a warm and sunshined day? It was perhaps remembrance, recognition that even the joyous sunshine of the moment is tainted.

Wedding in the autumn; buried in the spring.

Is not that the reverse of the natural order of things?

The woman was Memie.

He froze.

The agent approached him.

"Do you like this piece?"

John turned to the man.

"There is an uncanny resemblance to someone I know," John said. But then, returning to the picture: "Someone I knew."

"Art can be like that."

John bought the painting and hung it over the mantle. He never told Fanny about who the picture reminded him of, although she probably figured it out.

"Art," he once told someone while they were standing looking up at the painting, "Art is the closest thing we have in our world to the eternal. Just look at the pyramids and statues from Egypt, they are as old as they come but yet we can enjoy them still."

"Indeed," the man mumbled turning to look at other things.

Flesh decays but art reminds us of our immortality.

John set his cigar down into the ashtray and stared down at his cards. He turned over the next card.

It was the last Queen.

John sat at his desk in the West Wing of the Library when the two of them entered. John kept reading the letter he held before him and did not look up even though he heard them enter. He twirled a lit cigar in his hand as he read. Before him were several piles of papers, letters, and documents. There was a large stack on side of the desk and a much smaller pile on the opposite side. There was silence as John finished reading his letter and then, placing it down upon the smaller stack of papers, he finally looked up.

It was his nephew, Junius, and a woman.

"Uncle, I hope we are not disturbing you too much."

John did not respond except with an expressionless stare.

"I would like to introduce the woman I was telling you about: Belle da Costa Greene. Miss Greene, my uncle, Mr. Morgan."

The woman made a slight bow of her head.

"It is a pleasure to meet you, Mr. Morgan."

The woman who stood before him was small in height and very slender. She wore a fur felt cloche hat, a high neck buttoned lace white bodice, a black sleeved jacket with a small red tea rose in the lapel, and a long close fitting black skirt that accentuated her slender figure. She stood up with a very erect carriage, and she titled her head slightly. But it was with her facial features that John became intrigued. Her dark hair curled about the base of her hat, suggesting much more tucked up inside, her soft and smooth skin was a richly dark olive in color, but her large searching, almost blazing, eyes flashed a penetrating green.

John's expressionless stare gradually dissolved into a slight smile. He put his cigar into the ashtray and then pushed his chair back and stood behind his desk.

"Junius spoke very well of you, Miss Greene. Please, have a seat."

Junius had already dragged a chair across the rug and placed it next to the desk. Belle stepped over and sat down, closing her ivory gloved hands together in her lap. Her manner was elegant with dignity and poise. She sat near the edge of the large chair; poised, nervous, ready.

Junius turned toward Belle.

"Well, I shall retire and let you two discuss things. I promise you his growl is worse than his bite."

Laughing, Junius looked to John as if signaling him to behave and be nice. Once he had left the room John turned his undivided attention back to Belle.

"My nephew tells me he met you over at the Princeton University Library where he works."

"Yes sir. I work as a clerk at the Library."

"You work for him?"

"No, I work with him."

"You are a librarian there?"

"Yes sir, although that is not my official title."

John nodded.

"He explained to you what I want?"

"To help catalogue and maintain your book and manuscript collection."

"Not to help but to do."

She nodded.

"My books are scattered around at different places. I have finally built a single place to put them."

"You must be very excited about that."

"Well, I have been collecting books and manuscripts for some time now. I use Junius a great deal. He has a strong love of books, the knowledge, and a strong passion for what he does."

"Oh yes he does sir. He is quite inspiring."

"I must say that he has been quite a help to me."

She smiled with a knowing smile.

"But my collection has grown to the point that I have no where to put it. That is why I had McKim build this building, a library, so that now I can properly catalogue and display what I have."

Belle sat, listening.

"That is where you come in. I need someone to do exactly that task for me."

"It would be my pleasure, I assure you, sir."

"Junius explained to me that you do not have a degree."

"No sir."

"Do you have any formal library training, other than working there as a clerk?"

"No sir."

"Do you have any experience managing or overseeing a library collection?"

"No sir."

John chewed on his cigar for a moment and grunted.

"How old are you, exactly?"

"Twenty-four sir."

"What is your ancestry?"

"Portuguese."

John stopped for a moment.

"I spent some time on Fayal, in the Azores, when I was young. Were you born in Portugal?"

"No, it was my grandmother on my mother's side. I inherited her complexion, and, according to my mother, her fiery personality. Did you enjoy it there?"

"Yes. I was young; at that age one enjoys almost everything."

"Yes sir."

"Miss Greene, I appreciate the formality but it is not necessary to continue calling me 'Sir.'"

Belle looked down, nervous, embarrassed perhaps.

"Sorry," she said.

There was a long silent pause as John watched her and she tried to look around, not noticing his stare, but she finally turned her eyes back at him.

"I do," she began to say weakly but then cleared her throat and spoke strongly: "I do, Mr. Morgan, have a strong and very passionate love of rare books and manuscripts that serves me well."

John placed his cigar on the rim of the ash tray on his desk and leaned back in his chair.

"Why?"

"Why?"

"Yes. Why do you love books?"

"I knew definitely by the time I was twelve years old that I wanted to work with rare books. I loved them even then, the sight of them, the wonderful feel of them, the romance and thrill of them. Even the smell of them is exquisite to me. Before I was sixteen I had begun my studies, omitting the regular college courses that many girls take before they have found out what they want to do."

John smiled. He looked at his cigar as he rolled it back and forth in his hand.

"I do not think I could have said it better."

"Thank you Mr. Morgan."

"What brought you to Princeton?"

"I chose Princeton because of their library and because of their program. But in a word, sir, it was because of Ernest Cushing Richardson, the head librarian."

She spoke his name respectfully, even adding his middle name, with careful pronunciation carefully articulating each syllable as if she were reading it from an honorary plaque or a granite statue. John noted the tremendous respect she had for the man.

"I met the man. Junius works for him."

"Yes he does. I feel that Mr. Richardson is the best bibliographer in America. That is why I came to Princeton."

"Junius did say that you had as strong a love as he does."

"Yes Mr. Morgan I do have that."

"But you also have a lack of the necessary experience."

There was a strong pause before she replied.

"But I feel that with this position that inefficiency will quickly be eradicated."

"Perhaps."

Belle pointed to one of the paintings on the wall behind John.

"Is that a Botticelli?"

John twisted around in his chair to see the painting she pointed too, and then turned back toward her.

"Yes."

"It is marvelous."

John spoke up.

"That is an important trait to possess."

"Sir?" she asked, confused.

"Passion."

"I think it is perhaps the most important trait to possess, Mr. Morgan. A passionate love for a thing will sustain you through everything."

True indeed, John thought to himself.

"Mr. Morgan, if I may be so bold as to ask, I was wondering at the stacks of mail on your desk. It seemed when I came in that you were sorting through your mail. What criteria do you use to separate them into two stacks and why is that one so large and that one is so small?"

John put his hand on the smaller stack of papers.

"This represents matters that I must attend to. That stack represents matters that others wish me to attend to."

"But there is such a discrepancy."

"I have found over the years that on some things if you set them aside long enough they either die out or they resolve themselves. It is much more time saving that way."

"That is bad Mr. Morgan."

"But it works greatly to my advantage," John replied with a smile.

Belle laughed. It was the first time. She seemed more at ease.

John, after a moment, stood up.

"Come with me," he said. "I want to show you something."

"Alright," she replied as she stood and followed him toward the door. He walked briskly out into the rotunda and then out through the large bronze doors into the daylight. Belle had to rush to keep up with him.

They walked together down the street toward a large house on the corner.

"I have my manuscripts at different places, but most of them I kept in my house," he was explaining as they walked. She followed him as he walked up the steps onto the porch of the house. He opened the door and let her into the front room. When he closed the door behind her he said "This way."

She followed him down a long hallway and then into a kitchen.

"Here," he said as he opened a small door, "follow me into the basement."

They climbed down the wooden stairs to the basement. Wooden crates and trunks used for traveling were piled high and lots of furniture sat around draped in white sheets. John came to a room built within the basement. He pulled out a ring of keys from his pocket and flicked through the many keys until he found the one he was looking for. He inserted it into the lock on the door and with a snap the lock opened. He dropped the key ring back into his pocket and then opened the door. The door creaked as it opened. It was dark inside. He waved her in.

Belle walked into the dark room, looking around, waiting for her eyes to grow accustomed to the dimness. John mumbled something as he reached up to a light switch.

"Now we have to be careful because this light does not always work right."

As he spoke he flipped the switch. A lone light bulb dangling down from the ceiling blazed on. It caught her by surprise and she shielded her eyes for a moment.

"Sorry," he said. "It can be a bit bright at first."

All of the walls from floor to ceiling were shelved with stacks of large folders. In the center of the room, directly below the light, was a wooden table with a small wooden chair. The chair scrapped across the bare floor as John pulled it aside.

"Here," he said, "let me show you something."

He reached up to one of the shelves and pulled down a large folder and placed it onto the table. Then, eyeing her, he carefully pulled something out of the folder and pulled the folder away leaving its contents on the table.

Belle looked closely but could not believe what she saw. It was a manuscript.

"Oh my goodness," she said as she placed a hand upon her chest. Belle leaned against John for a brief moment and held his arm as if she had suddenly grown faint and needed to be supported. She glanced up at him, and then quickly turned to the manuscript spread out in front of her. She bent over the table.

"Look at the colors," she said, "they are exquisite. It is in such excellent condition, the colors are so clean and clear."

The light from the naked bulb sparkled across the page like jeweled sunlight dancing across the waves of a lake. She held out her gloved hands as if to touch but held back, it was too sacred to be touched.

"Feel the paper," he said.

She looked at him, knowing that he had read her mind. Ever so carefully she pulled off her glove and ran her thumb and fore finger along the edge of the parchment. She could feel the grain of the paper.

"It looks Medieval French. The Book of John?" she asked as she looked back toward him.

John was carefully watching her, her every move.

He nodded.

As she bent over the table she looked closely at each line, each colored figure.

"Look at the lines, so perfect."

She laughed and closed her hands together in front of her as if in prayer.

"Just imagine a medieval copyist sitting at his desk in a monastery, outside the open window is such a beautiful day with the sunshine and the birds prancing about but he is inside drawing out the lines with such devoted precision. He ignores the day for the sake of his art writing out the words of our Savior for the centuries of devoted believers hoping to find peace and solace in their troubled lives."

"Is that what that is to you?" John asked.

Belle stood up straight and turned to him. There was a slight look of fear on her face.

"Yes," she said. "When I see something like this that is what I see. Think about it. This only exists because someone somewhere was passionate enough to make it exist. Here he is, that scribe, that day, alive in our hands. What he did that day is still here."

"Indeed," John said. He had found someone who felt like he did.

She looked all around at all of the shelves, floor to ceiling, packed with manuscripts and artist portfolios.

"Such delightful treasures," she gasped as she tried to take it all in. She was almost breathless.

"Here, look at this one," John said as he pulled out another sleeve of paper and pulled a manuscript out. He gently laid it on the table. She again bent over and studied it. It was a parchment, hand written with black ink. It was in English. When she got to the signature at the bottom she stood up.

"Thackeray, William Thackeray?"

John nodded, smiling.

"It was my nephew, Junius, who helped me get this one. He said he came across a Thackeray manuscript that he wanted but he could not afford it. I said I might help, let me see it. He bought into my office a very young man named Wheeler.

'What have you got to show me?' I asked him.

'I have a Thackeray manuscript that came to me from Thackeray's daughter, Mrs. Ritchie.'

He pulled the manuscript out and put it on my desk. I looked it over, turned it, felt the paper.

'Are you sure this is in Thackeray's own handwriting?' I asked the young man.

'Quite certain,' he boldly replied.

'You are too young to be quite certain.'

'I think not, sir, because I have been dealing in manuscripts since I was seventeen.'

He seemed very proud of that fact.

'Very well. What's the price?'

'One hundred pounds.'

'Is that cash?'

'No sir. Ninety pounds cash.'

'Very well. My Secretary will give you a check. Let me know if you get any more really good author's manuscripts.'

That was it. It was now mine."

Belle laughed.

John liked that she had laughed.

Oath of the Man

Louisa came into the sitting room of the hotel from the bedroom. She walked over behind John as he sat in his chair.

"Are they gone?" she asked.

John waved his arms as if bringing into focus the empty hotel room.

"Magic," he said as he tried to turn in the chair to look up at her.

"Things do not look good," she said, nodding toward the cards spread out on the desk.

"Yes, well," he turned back toward the desk.

"I could do with some supper."

"That sounds inviting."

The front door opened and Jack came back into the room. He stopped and looked over at the two of them.

"Conference complete?" John asked.

Jack nodded.

"I wish you would take this a little more seriously."

"I do, Jack: I do. I take it very seriously. But what am I to do about it? They will ask questions and I will answer them strong and true. I certainly will not give them any ammunition but I will answer them true. I have nothing to hide."

"It is not that simple."

"I think that it is."

"Jack," Louisa broke in, "we wanted to have some supper. Are you interested?"

"Surely. Should we call for service in the room?"

With that John stood up.

"No, I would like to go down to the restaurant."

"Good idea," Jack replied. "It will take our minds off of things.

"Let me just call Herbert to see if he wants to come."

When they arrived downstairs the lobby was still filled with people, even this late. In the restaurant they were sat near the window where they could watch the people walking back and forth along the sidewalk outside.

"Looks like a busy Christmas season," Louisa said after they sat down and held the menu in their hands.

Her husband Herbert sat next to her.

John grunted in reply. He had to adjust his glasses in order to read the menu.

Through the chatter of the hotel guests John could hear a piano from behind him. He turned in his seat, pulled off his reading glasses, and saw a large grand piano off in one corner of the restaurant. Several people were standing around as the man played.

John turned back around.

A piano.

He remembered then: a piano; Frances playing the piano at the Ralston Mansion in California. The notes resounded in the room.

John remembered.

Ralston took them on a tour of his home.

"I like to call it Belmont," Ralston said as they all followed him around the enclosed verandah that encircled most of the house. It was modeled after the promenade deck of a Mississippi River steamboat.

"As a boy I worked on a steamboat down the Mississippi River. I use to love the feeling, standing on the decks with a slight sway as we plowed down the river, you could see all around and the wind in your face."

"Sounds very nice," Mary Goodwin said.

"Oh it was. So I built a verandah around the house but enclosed with large glass windows and doors. That way with the doors open I can have the wind in my face, but with the doors closed I will not have the rain in my face."

Ralston, smiling at himself, stroked his below the chin Lincoln like beard.

Each small narrow room was filled with large potted plants, white wicker furniture from China, and assorted bric-a-brac with large throw rugs on the highly polished wooden floor.

"The house was originally owned by an Italian Count, a Leonetto Cipriani. In 1852 he fabricated a house in Italy but then he took it apart and shipped the whole thing in large crates to here."

"The whole house?" Frances asked.

John noticed as they walked the large number of bay windows with seats of colorful upholstery. He chuckled to himself. From the bay window seats you could actually see in the distance the actual bay.

"Yes," Ralston continued. "He shipped all 120 tons of it in carefully

111

marked crates to San Francisco. He then had the pieces hauled down the peninsula in wagons and carefully rebuilt the house here. I bought it in 1864 and have been adding to it ever since."

Through one of the large open doors they walked into the interior of the house, into an enormous mirrored ballroom with a highly polished intricately inlaid floor. They walked across to the main foyer at the base of the main stairway.

"This is where my wife Lizzie surprised me. I was away to Virginia City for a bit and she called in the carpenters and at her direction they tore out the walls on the second story and circled the ballroom with these spacious protruding balconies."

"They look like a series of opera house balconies," Mary Goodman said, looking up.

"How delightful," Mary Tracy piped in.

"I am afraid that I am not much of a dancer myself so when I have a party I can sit up there and watch the whole extravaganza from up there."

"Wonderful," Frances said. "And your wife, you say she is in Paris?"

There was a slight pause.

"Yes, with the children," he said. John noticed it. There was a slight pause in his voice. John sensed that there was something not right.

But then they walked into the music room. There, to one side, sat an enormous grand piano.

"Look at this, Francis," John said.

Francis smiled a deep smile. "Beautiful. Beautiful."

Ralston noticed her joy.

"Care to play?" he asked.

She looked over at him with a look of 'really, can I' in her face. As she sat on the stool Ralston spoke.

"It is one of my prize possessions. It is handcrafted here in San Francisco, a master piano maker moved here recently. It is made of Hawaiian koa wood."

"Hawaiian?" John asked amazed.

"Yes Mr. Morgan, it is Hawaiian. Now how many times do you come across anything Hawaiian in New York City? Think of the opportunities Mr. Morgan. I think in the not too distant future San Francisco will rival New York. The old belief that the west is the wild untamed west is a thing of the past Mr. Morgan."

It was obvious that they had struck a nerve in Ralston; this was a passionate belief of his.

"Think of the investment opportunities, why it reaches the sky in its limitlessness. And with the railroads interlacing the entire continent now," he shook his head as if he still was amazed and could not yet grasp the whole thing.

John thought of earlier that very day.

Rather than staying in a hotel in the city they were instead staying in a small white cabin on the cliffs over looking the Pacific Ocean. They could stand on their porch looking out and fill their lungs with the salt smell of the sea. He bought a bag of oranges from a local vendor and pulled them out one by one and lined them along the railing.

"You will love these," he told the women as they watched him line them up in a row.

"I ate these when I was in the Fayal when I was a boy. They are wonderfully sweet and juicy."

Mary and Mary watched with suspicion and giggled. They never had an orange before.

On the wooden porch they had chairs and even a small hammock like swing and they sat down and, one by one, started eating the oranges. They watched the sun go down into the waters of the ocean. How strange to watch as the sun descend down into the water rather than rise out of it. Sea gulls and large pelicans used the updrafts of wind coming in and up over the cliffs to fly overhead. John watched as ships sailed up and down the coast. There was a small telescope in the cabin and he watched the ships.

Standing in the yard John watched as a long train rumbled by. The Engineer waved to him and he waved back. The train scared the crows up into the clouded sky. It carried fruits and vegetables, oranges, bringing them into San Francisco from the rich farmlands to the south. Think of the possibilities, John thought. With interconnecting railroads food from here could be transported across the United States. He could have oranges for breakfast every day.

His thoughts were cut short when Frances began playing the piano. It was a deep and rich sound. It echoed about the almost empty room.

When she was done John held her shoulders and bent down and kissed her cheek.

"That was beautiful" he whispered into her ear.

Ralston clapped his hands.

"Wonderful, wonderful," he repeated over and over.

There was a pause before Ralston again spoke.

"So tell me, how did you spend your day?"

"We rented some horses and went riding," John replied.

"Oh, you should have used mine; I have a few beauties you could have used."

"I did not know. Anyway, the three of us," he said as he nodded toward the two Mary's, "my wife, as it turned out wisely, remained behind, went riding."

"Oh."

"We had a bit of an adventure. I had this huge black horse with an overly thick mane."

"Yes, that would be Pelman's I assume."

"Yes, that is the one. Kind man."

"And you enjoyed yourself? There is nothing like a quick ride to boost your spirits. I love to ride, and ride fast. Swimming as well; they both energize you, help to electrify the skin."

Mary Goodman exclaimed: "We raced each other shouting out to each other."

"Yes, along the top of the ocean cliffs," Mary Tracy said.

John nodded. "There are a lot of quite lovely meadows and tress around here. But when we stopped I saw in this ravine that went down to the water some wild growing blackberries."

"Yes, they are around."

"So I climbed down to get them. It was quite precarious."

Mary Tracy: "He almost fell."

Mary Goodman: "He cursed too."

Mary Tracy: "He had to hold onto a branch so not to fall."

John turned again toward Ralston.

"Well, then, we sat in the grass and feasted on blackberries watching the sea. It was cloudy all morning but I did not really pay too much attention."

Ralston laughed.

"So you were caught in the rain?"

John nodded. "Downpour. We raced back on the horses but it poured the whole way back."

Mary Tracy: "We were drenched to the bone."

Mary Goodman: "And you were screaming the whole way."

Mary Tracy: "But there was lightening. You saw it. And then the thunder chased us. We could have been hit with lightening."

John laughed. "There was a thrill in it I must admit."

Mary Tracy: "Pierpont made a hot roaring fire when we got back and we all took off our clothes and hung them up in front of the fire to dry."

Mary Goodman: "Down to our underwear."

"And Mr. Morgan?" Ralston asked.

The two girls giggled. "Him too," Mary Goodman said.

Frances spoke for the first time. "My husband spent the rest of the day walking around barefoot in his long johns puffing his cigar. Not a pretty sight, Mr. Ralston, I assure you.

The girls giggled again with their hands to their mouths.

"Well, wait until this story circulates around the banking world."

"I will have the chicken," Louisa said to the waiter.

"Excellent choice madam," the waiter said.

John looked up at the man. He seemed very thin. You could clearly see the bones of his cheeks. His eyes were such a deep blue.

"And for you, sir?"

John looked back down at the menu but then folded it and handed it to the waiter.

"Chicken as well," John said as he took off his reading glasses and put them back into his waist coat pocket.

"And have we chosen a wine for dinner?"

"Bring me a glass of port," John said.

"Certainly, sir."

Everyone else nodded in agreement.

"A bottle perhaps?"

"Yes," Herbert said. "That makes the most sense."

John turned again to look toward the piano. The music had stopped. The player was sipping on his drink as he listened to two men talking to him. They then all laughed. They all laughed the way you laugh when you want the others to think that you are having a fun time in their company but, perhaps, are not.

"Do you recognize someone? Louisa asked.

"What is that?" John said as he turned back around in his seat.

"You seem to have recognized someone."

"No, no," John said. "I was just. . ."

He did not finish the sentence. He just grunted and waved his hand, waving away the thought.

Jack, with a raised eyebrow, looked at Louisa. She saw his look but frowned and shook her head.

John looked out the window.

John could remember sitting in his office and reading the newspaper accounts of the death of Billy Ralston. There was talk of scandal, the Bank of California had collapsed, some claimed there were misappropriated funds. John shook his head while reading the accounts.

It was a hot August morning and looked as if it would be a blister of a day. John had just arrived but already he had taken his coat off. He hated to read things like that, especially about bankers. Any sign of corruption in a banker was bad, bad for the whole industry. People had to trust in banking, and to do that they had to trust in their banker. The character of a banker had to be exemplary.

Oh Billy, Billy, John thought to himself. What have you done?

But how easy it is to slide down that slope. A little bit here, a little bit there, no one will notice and I'll have it paid back by then. It happened to more than he would like to admit.

So many fall into temptation.

So many into greed.

John read on. Ralston said he would pay back the monies, every penny. But the directors asked him to leave the room. A resolution was offered asking Ralston to resign as president of the bank and for Darius Mills to present it to him. When Darius told Billy he was calm and quiet. He left the building. At the front door he stopped Dr. John Pitman who was just entering the building and asked if he was up for a swim. They often swam in the bay together. But no, I have an appointment, sorry. Billy patted him on the shoulder and said good bye.

He walked the two miles over hills to the Neptune Beach House at the end of Larkin Street. It was a wooden building, stained by the salt winds coming in over the bay, and had a short pier. Swimmers walked out to the end of the pier and dove directly into the cold water.

It was a hot day and by the time he reached the Neptune Beach House he was perspiring heavily. He went in, took a shower, rubbed himself down, and then came back out onto the pier in his bathing suit. He walked to the end of the pier. A few hundred yards down the beach was a much longer pier and the Thomas Selby lead smelter plant. Black smoke rose out of their tall brick chimneys and whirled away with the wind. Beyond the large pier was moored the stern wheel steamer 'Bullion,' owned by the Thomas Selby company.

Billy looked up and down the beach and then dove into the water. People watched as he swam out, he swam out beyond the 'Bullion' into the open bay. They knew he was a strong swimmer; he swam all the time, so they were not concerned. But then he began flaying in the water. They watched. He was in trouble. People on the pier shouted out and pointed to him. But what could be done? Swimmers moved in his direction.

People on the shore watched as the 'Bullion' sent a small boat out to him. They pulled him into the boat and made their way to shore. People ran over and helped pull the boat up onto the sand. They took Billy out of the boat. His body was limp. They lay him out on the sand and began artificial respiration. They tried. Soon a doctor that had been called for arrived in his wagon. But there was nothing left to do.

John sat back. Without really seeing them John watched the Christmas shoppers hurrying back and forth by the window. Louisa and Jack sat without speaking. They knew that John's attention was somewhere else. They knew from experience that it was pointless to try and break in; a gruff wave of the hand would silence them. They merely looked around at the others dining in the restaurant and waited. At some point John would come around.

The waiter brought a bottle of port and, standing beside the table, opened the bottle and placed the cork before John. Jack reached over and smelled the cork. He nodded to the waiter who then poured out the four glasses. When the waiter poured out the glass in front of John he did not budge.

It was like this then, John thought to himself. When he returned from the trip, the trip to California, when he returned, it was rushed like this, excitement and crowds of agitated people coming to and fro, shouting. He had to think fast. After such a peaceful trip he walked right into a crisis. Samuel Sloan, his friend and neighbor, had wired him while he was on his trip. There was trouble, he said, and it was getting bad. It seemed that the 'black slime' of Jay Gould and Jim Fisk were trying to take over the Albany & Susquehanna Railroad and the tactics were getting dirty.

Joseph Ramsey, the president and founder of the A & S Railroad, went to Samuel Sloan, president of the Hudson River Railroad, and asked what he could do. Gould and Fisk were in a hostile takeover and Ramsey feared that they were going to win.

"Call on J. P. Morgan. Consult him. If any one can save you he can. He is due back from a trip on the first of September. I will bring him over."

When John arrived back in New York Sloan picked him up and rushed him to see Joseph Ramsey, the president of the Albany & Susquehanna Railroad. The room was filled with Ramsey's 'men.'

"So what exactly is the situation," John asked after they sat him down on a small wooden chair. The table was stacked with papers and ledger books, the wood of the table stained with coffee.

Several of them began talking at the same time. John closed his eyes and waved his hands in the air.

"Stop, stop; one, just one tell me what is going on. I want a written statement of your exact situation. I want a brief report on what Gould and Fisk have done so far. After I examine all the reports then come to my office the day after tomorrow and I will tell you what I think."

The men looked back and forth at each other.

"Agreed," Ramsey said. He liked a man who could instantly take charge.

In the carriage on the way back to his office John pointed to Samuel Sloan sitting beside him.

"Fill me in."

Daniel Drew, Jay Gould and Jim Fisk had wrestled ownership of the Erie Railroad away from Cornelius Vanderbilt. They did it, to John's way of thinking, backhandedly by corrupt politicians, corrupt judges, and falsifying the value of stock securities.

It was, after all, Daniel Drew himself who invented the concept of 'watering the stock.' As a cattle merchant when he brought his cattle to market he had his cattle drink vast quantities of water just before a sale. The price was based on weight so a temporary well 'watered stock' fetched a better price. By over inflating the assets of a business, and thus a higher price for its stock, he could manipulate the price of the 'watered stock' for his own benefit.

Once they had control of the railroad the next step was for them to turn on themselves. Gould and Fisk cut Drew out, and eventually into bankruptcy. Thieves were thieves, even among themselves.

But then Gould and Fisk wanted to expand the Erie Railroad so they looked around at who they could next devour. There was a smaller, 143 mile line called the Albany & Susquehanna that ran through the Catskill Mountains between Albany and Binghamton, New York. It was much smaller than the Erie, with only 17 locomotives and 214 cars verses Erie's 317 locomotives and 6643 cars, but it had several attractive features.

Founded by Joseph H. Ramsey in 1852, construction began the next year with one million dollars raised by individuals along the right of way. But by 1854 money had run out. The New York State Legislature passed a special act allowing cities along the line to subscribe to the stock. Twenty two towns participated. Construction began again in 1857. Several other subscriptions were issued until again they ran short of money in 1868. Ramsey went to Wall Street and raised funds enough to finish the line by January 12, 1869.

There was already dissent with the board of directors over Ramsey's management of the railroad. About half of the board was against Ramsey and the leader of the opposition was Vice President Walter S. Church. Ramsey had already said that at the next board meeting in September one or the other faction had to go.

As Gould saw it once he connected the Albany & Susquehanna with the Erie not only would it give direct competition with Vanderbilt's New York Central for regular traffic between Albany and Buffalo and west to the lakes, but with a railroad bridge over the Hudson River at Albany it would link the Pennsylvania coal fields with energy starved New England.

Gould saw his opportunity in the up coming board meeting. He approached Walter Church with a deal. Gould began buying as much of the stock of the company as he could get but it was thinly traded and he could not obtain controlling interest by stock purchase alone. Townships and municipal governments that were being served by the railroad had underwritten parts of the line and held large blocks of stock. Under law they could only sell their shares at par value or above, and they could only sell it for cash. Gould invited a dozen or so of the township commissioners to Manhattan and set them up at the fancy Fifth Avenue Hotel and provided a lavish dinner.

Then, on August 1, he made them an offer. If they voted with him, allowing the Erie to take over and merge with the line, Gould would buy up their shares at par with Erie cash. Most agreed to the proposal, seemingly not concerned that once they voted for Gould to take ownership the verbal proposal was not legally enforceable.

He certainly would not lie to them would he?

The officials from the town of Oneonta, however, insisted on their shares being purchased first. The Board of Directors meeting and vote on September 7 was to be based on all stock ownership of record as of August 7. So on August 3 Gould got a Supreme Court Judge in Owego to issue an order to record the Oneonta transaction on the transfer books of the company prior to the seventh.

The treasurer of the company, William L. M. Phelps, who actually backed Ramsey in the dispute, refused to put the transfer on the company books without the proper sales documentation. Allied with Church and the other dissenting board members, and with the voting power of not only his own shares but also that of the pledged votes of the other shareholders, Gould felt confident of victory. Gould got a judge that was friendly to him, Judge George C. Barnard, to not only order the transfer of the stock of Oneonta, but also to suspend Ramsey from the board.

Meanwhile, to counter Gould's moves against him, Ramsey, as president of the company, arranged for the company to issue more stock. Originally the company was authorized to issue 40,000 shares but only a portion of that had been issued. The company still had 12,000 held in reserve. Ramsey smuggled the subscription books out of the company office and at his home he and friends issued 9,500 shares of stock to themselves at $100. They put down a deposit of 10% ($95,000), which the company charter required, which Ramsey borrowed from David Groesbeck using $150,000 worth of Albany & Susquehanna bonds as collateral. The treasurer, Phelps, to be careful, took the transfer books of the company and hid them inside a tomb in the Albany Cemetery.

Walter Church called for a board meeting on August 6 without either Ramsey or the treasurer being present. He hoped the board would fire the treasurer and establish another one that was more sympatric to Gould. But just as the meeting got underway a team of lawyers representing Ramsey arrived at the meeting and served Church and three others board members with orders from the Albany State Supreme Court Judge Rufus Peckham suspending them from the Board. Without Ramsey and Phelps, and now without Church and the others, there was not a quorum of board members so the meeting had to be dissolved without a vote.

Hearing of this, Thomas G. Shearman, lawyer for Gould, decided that the next best move was to turn the company over to a receiver. But to do that he need a court order from a judge.

But by then Judge George Bernard had left New York and was in Poughkeepsie where he sat at the bedside of his dying mother. That did not faze Shearman. He wired Bernard: "Come to New York without fail tonight. Answer care 359 West 23 street."

This was the address of Josie Mansfield, Jim Fisk's mistress. Bernard had a choice to make: be with his dying mother or please Gould.

He picked Gould.

Bernard traveled back to New York and raced through the streets to Josie's lavish apartment. Sitting in her bedroom, with muffled drunken laughter through the walls from a party in the next room, he signed the papers assigning Jim Fisk and Charles Courter of Cobleskill, an existing board member sympathetic to Church, as receivers for the Albany & Susquehanna.

By 10:30 that night the papers were fully executed and Fisk, as a nice touch, traveled on Vanderbilt's New York Central with the order in his pocket. He also brought along a set of body guards. They meet Courter in Albany at the Delavan House Hotel where they took rooms for the night.

At eight o'clock the next morning, Saturday August 7, Jim Fisk, with his waxed moustache twirled into two points and his flaming brilliant red shirt, and his dazzling assortments of rings on his fingers, and with his bodyguards, and with Charles Courter in tow, arrived at the offices near the Albany waterfront in order to take possession of the Albany & Susquehanna Railroad.

To their surprise they found a Robert H. Pruyn, a man sympathetic to Ramsey, already installed as the receiver of the company. He was protected by John W. Van Valkenburg, the General Superintendent of the railroad, who had at his command more than a dozen railroad mechanics. Unknown to Fisk, last night Ramsey had his Judge Rufus Peckham also execute an order of receivership for the company placing Robert Pruyn as receiver.

Van Valkenburg allows Courter to enter the office, since he is a board member, but he does not allow Jim Fisk to enter. Upon comparing the two orders they find that the order of Peckham pre dated that of Bernard by several hours. Pruyn therefore stands.

Fisk, outside the office was fuming with rage. He called to his bodyguards.

"Rush in, boys, and take possession."

Van Valkenburg, standing at the door, orders them to stand down.

"This, sir," Fisk shouts back, pacing back and forth before the door, "this is the twenty seventh such raid that I have made and I propose to take your men."

"I hope you a good time trying."

"Sir, I will take possession of the railroad if it takes millions of money and unlimited number of men."

"I order you to leave by the authority of Mr. Pruyn, the legally appointed receiver by Judge Peckham."

"I don't give a damn. Boys, throw them out."

He and his bodyguards try to rush the door and force their way into the office but Van Valkenburg and his men physically stop them.

Fists fly.

Chairs are smashed over the heads of Fisk's men.

Fisk is literally shoved and thrown down into the dust. It ruffles his greased hair and carefully twirled moustache. His guards help him up but then a police officer arrives. His men scatter. The policeman places Fisk under arrest. He is taken down the street to the police station and the detective tells him to enter and wait there for him to return. Fisk goes in but the policeman walks away. Other police in the station stare at him as he takes a seat. Finally one of the officers approaches him.

"Can I help you?"

"What? That detective told me to wait here until he returns."

The man, looking out the window, then asks: "Which detective would that be?"

It turns out that the policeman was actually one of the mechanics posing as a police detective.

Laughing, the mechanic walks away.

Fisk wires Bernard. He tells him the situation. Bernard then wires Fisk back with a court order not only voiding the Pruyn receivership but also ordering the police and 'the whole country' to enforce his order.

Fisk brings the police back to the offices. But the order from Bernard is just a cable. Without an original signed and sealed document of the court the order is not enforceable.

All of the parties then agreed that they were in a deadlock and they would reconvene on Monday morning. Fisk immediately left by train for Manhattan where he met with Gould. He returned back to Albany on Sunday night by boat with Bernard's properly executed order in his pocket.

At eight o'clock the morning of Monday, August 9, Van Valkenburg sent orders from Judge Peckham all up and down the railroad line for everyone to ignore any orders favorable to the Erie contingent. The war of the railroad was now the war between combating judges.

Realizing that the city of Albany was strongly in favor of Ramsey, Fisk had their judge, Judge Bernard, wire his orders to the other end of the line at Binghamton to Sheriff Browne, the Broome County Sheriff at Binghamton. He, on the power of the order, seized the Albany & Susquehanna terminal in Binghamton at two o'clock that afternoon. He was able to lock up three of the four locomotives at the terminal. But before they could get their hands on the fourth locomotive mechanics fired it up and escaped toward Albany. As it pulled out of the station yard the sheriff's men ran along side waving and yelling and trying to stop it. The mechanics on board just waved good bye to them as the engine picked up steam.

Fisk appointed H.D.V. Pratt as the new superintendent of the railroad and within thirty minutes they put together a train with the engine 'Roswell McNeill,' named after Erie's rolling stock superintendent. On board were Pratt, the sheriff, and some twenty mechanics. They pulled out of the station heading out toward Albany. They called ahead and ordered the tracks cleared so they could travel as fast as they could. They wanted to seize each station along the line as far toward Albany as they could.

Meanwhile, at the Albany end of the line, Van Valkenburg ordered all scheduled trains to immediately turn into sidings and then he too ordered a special train, loaded with 150 armed men and their attorney Henry Smith, to travel directly east toward Binghamton. They too stopped at each station and left some guards at each one to help protect Albany & Susquehanna property from the Erie forces.

The two opposing engines finally met at the town of Bainbridge. Smith arrived first. When Pratt, with the Erie train, came into the station that evening they saw Smith's special train, empty, sitting on a siding. Pratt stopped and waited and watched from inside his car wondering what had happened. Where was Smith, where were his men? Had they left?

Finally he ordered the train to progress down the line. But without seeing it they crossed over a 'frog' routing devise purposely left on the tracks derailing the locomotive. Trapped and motionless Pratt hopelessly watched as Smith and his armed men appeared out of the trees surrounding the station and surrounded the train. Pratt had no choice, he had to surrender.

Smith had his men put the locomotive back onto the tracks and then sent it on to Albany.

By this time all customer traffic on the line had come to a complete stand still. The company was completely shut down.

Fisk, from the Delavan House, ordered another train to leave Binghamton on the afternoon of August 10. On board were about 600 of his men armed with clubs and pipes as weapons. From the opposite camp Van Valkenburg sent out a train loaded with about 450 men. The two trains met at a railroad tunnel near Harpursville, New York. The Erie train stopped just outside the tunnel when they spotted the Albany & Susquehanna train coming up the grade toward the tunnel from the east. The Erie conductor tried to flag down the on coming train while the engineer tried to reverse the train.

With belching smoke the Albany & Susquehanna locomotive rammed into the sitting Erie locomotive and demolished both cowcatchers, the headlights, the smoke stacks, and partly derailed the Albany & Susquehanna engine. Van Valkenburg's better armed men flooded out of the train and quickly scattered the Erie men who fled back through the tunnel. The Erie engine managed to reverse back up into the far side of the tunnel where their forces regrouped. Once the Albany & Susquehanna forces got their engine back onto the tracks they proceeded down the tunnel and met the Erie defenders at the other end. A massive fight broke out.

Having heard of the coming conflict the Forty fourth Regiment of the State Militia was sent to break up the fight. By nightfall the two opposing forces occupied either end of the tunnel. No one was killed but ten had been shot and many had more were wounded with beatings and stab wounds.

The next day, August 11, the Governor Toots Hoffman appointed Major General James McQuade, Inspector General of the State Militia, as the new interim superintendent of the railroad. Both sides agreed to the appointment.

The two sides were in deadlock. All waited for the upcoming shareholders meeting of September 7.

Enter J. P. Morgan.

It was then that Ramsey approached John. Ramsey and several board members arrived at John's office as requested. John sat them down and went right to business. They were all older men and they sat across the table from the thirty two year old John.

"In my opinion you will have to fight this in the courts. I think you can win. Do you want me to proceed?"

Without hesitation Ramsey almost shouted out: "Yes."

"Good. I have a plan. Gould controls too many local judges. We need to raise this matter higher into the Supreme Courts. I have State Supreme Court Judge Rufus Peckham in mind. I'm going to retain my father-in-law Charles Tracy, he is a fine lawyer, and I will also retain Samuel Hand of Albany. You must grant me full control of action without hindrance. What I have planned will save the railroad but it may alter the structure of the ownership. Do you agree?"

The board members looked back and forth.

Ramsey spoke: "Will I still be a part of it?"

John stared at the man for a long moment. He, after all, is the one who built the railroad.

John, without speaking, nodded his head yes.

The board members looked back and forth at each other again before Ramsey finally, again, said "Yes."

"Good. We have a lot of work to do in preparation to the stockholders meeting I suggest we start right now."

John promptly placed an order to buy 600 shares for Dabney, Morgan & Co. He told the board members to look over the list of stock holders to make sure that they were all present, and could be present, at the stockholders meeting.

Meanwhile Gould and Fisk, hearing that Morgan had been hired, got an injunction from Judge Barnard restraining Dabney, Morgan & Company from receiving their 600 shares and restraining the owners from disposing the 9500 shares they had issued. It allowed for an arrest of Ramsey, Treasurer Phelps, and several other officers.

John spent the day of September 6 at the Delavan House, the day before the meeting, with Ramsey, Phelps and Samuel Hand preparing for the next day. They made a list of the shareholders and all legitimate proxies. Men at the front door would make names to the list and only those absolutely authorized to vote could enter the building. They prepared the minutes for the meeting. They wrote out the report for the inspectors of elections. They prepared affidavits whereby they could instantly get restraining orders against anyone attempting to vote illegally.

Late that afternoon Samuel Hand picked up his hat and approached John. He had to go down to the wharf to see a friend off to New York.

"I'll be back in no later than a half an hour."

John agreed.

"Hurry back as soon as you can."

Samuel left and disappeared.

He did not return in a half an hour, or an hour, or two hours.

He did not return for supper.

He did not return all evening.

No one knew where he was. John finished the papers, waited, but then went to bed after midnight. He was worried since he was relying on Samuel for any legal confrontations that may occur the next day. But he was also worried for his safety.

It was in the early predawn hours that Samuel burst into John's room and shook him awake.

John lit the lamp.

Samuel was in a frightful and agitated state. His clothes were wet and dirty, the cloth of his pants was torn around the knees.

Samuel sat in the chair by the window.

"Calm yourself, please," John said.

"Yes, yes. I am all right."

"What happened to you?"

Samuel carefully, told his tale.

He was saying good bye to his friend on the steamer and did not pay attention to the signals to get off. Next thing that he knew the steamer pulled away from the dock and was under way down the river.

"I pleaded with them to let me off, go back to the wharf, but they refused. 'We have a strict schedule to keep, sir.' 'We can't afford the time.'"

"But when is your next stop?"

"There are no stops. We are straight into New York; we will arrive by daylight tomorrow."

"New York? I can not go to New York. I have to return to Albany right away."

But the crew members did not care. And the captain just shrugged his shoulders. You can arrange for passage back from New York tomorrow. Nothing I said could persuade them. I was raging but all to no avail. It grew dark. I thought of jumping overboard and swimming ashore but I was not that good of a swimmer and it was now dark.

For awhile I simply resigned myself to my fate but then I came up with a plan. With the cash that I had in my pocket and with more cash that my friend had I made the captain a proposition. I offered to buy one of the life boats. It was much more than the life boat was worth. I would go ashore and he could mark the spot where he let me go and then pick up the boat the next time he came through.

The captain said that he would. When we came to the lights of the next town he slowed the boat and lowered the life boat and let me push off.

But I am not a sailor and the boat was difficult to row and there was a strong wind. It chilled me to the bone. I do not know how far I drifted down stream but I lost the lights before I touched land. Trying to get out of the boat I fell into the water. In the darkness I stumbled over rocks and brush. I even tripped over some railroad rails. It cut my knee and I had to limp in great pain. But I followed the rails and finally came onto another light. It turned out to be a station.

I asked the lone teller when the next train to Albany was due and he said just about now. But he would not sell me a ticket. I had spent all of my money on the boat. I had nothing in my pockets. I explained to him who I was and that payment would come as soon as I returned to Albany but he would have nothing of it. As far as he was concerned I was nothing but a vagrant and he slammed the teller window down.

I was near the end of my rope. My leg was hurting me but I managed to walk over to a group of trees and stood there in the dark until the train came in. I waited while it refueled its water.

Then, after the teller walked the platform and shut the doors and waved his lantern to the engine he turned to go back inside the station. The train began to move. I managed to painfully run toward the train and grabbed the railings of the last car and pulled myself up onto the platform. I stood there for a moment trying to let the pain in my knee subside.

Then I reached for the door.

The car was lit up with lights and there was loud voices and singing coming from within. Just as I started to turn the knob I looked into the window and right there, sitting facing me, was James Fisk himself. The car was filled with his gang of boys. They were drinking and playing cards and through the cigar smoke I could see that the car was full.

He is here, Mr. Morgan. He and his gang are here to do God knows what physical mischief at the meeting.

I did not enter the car, thank God. I sat on the platform holding on to the railing and hoping that no one would come out onto the platform and find me. They might have thrown me into the river if they had. I jumped off just as soon as we pulled into Albany and came right here to warn you.

He is up to no good.

John immediately got out of bed and got dressed. He sent for a doctor to see about Samuel's knee. He went over to awake Ramsey and Phelps. They informed the police but they said that nothing could be done and they could only be called if there was a disturbance of the peace.

"Then we will have to deal with it ourselves," John said.

"He and his boys will be barred at the door," Ramsey said. "He owns shares but his boys do not. We cannot let them into the building."

A few minutes before the meeting was to begin Fisk, wearing a bright yellow speckled straw hat and a blue ribbon sash, arrived at the front entrance. His boys were with him. They were blocked at the desk where they were checking names.

"Sorry, sir but only you can pass. The others, unless they are shareholders, will have to wait outside."

Fisk looked beyond them and saw some of the mechanics from Ramsey standing around waiting. Fisk did not want a repeat of when he tried to storm the offices.

"Come on," he said to his men. "Follow me."

He went around the back and opened the rear door. A closed stairway led to the second story of the building. Fisk started to climb the narrow stairs. Only one at a time could climb. His men followed behind him, one at a time.

But it was not until he was near the top of the stairs that he noticed

Ramsey and John standing at the top of the stairs blocking the way.

"What is this," Fisk snarled.

They said nothing.

Fisk stood for a moment. Ramsey was small, about 115 pounds. Fisk could handle him with ease. But Morgan? He stood six foot and was strong and robust. Fisk wavered. Who else was behind them? But his men were all filing up behind him. Fisk started again up the stairs.

"Get out of my way Ramsey," Fisk was shouting when it happened.

He felt strong hands grab his shoulder and shove him back. He fell backwards onto the man behind him, and he fell back against the man behind him. The whole line of men crumbled and Fisk tumbled head over heels for several steps.

Ramsey slammed shut the door at the top of the stairs. He shoved the bolt down locking the door.

As John and Ramsey made their way to the main floor Ramsey was shouting with glee but John just shook his head. What is this? This is not business. This is a ridiculous circus. If this is the way business is going to be run I do not want any part of it.

At the board meeting of September 7 the room filled with men from both sides. The books were brought in from the cemetery and lowered in by a rear window. When the official meeting began the Barnard injunction was brought forward and Ramsey, Smith, and the treasurer were all arrested for stealing the books. It was a ploy to diminish the pro Ramsay forces. But in anticipation of this their bail had already been posted. After they all returned the doors were locked, another roll call was taken and the vote was cast.

Ramsey won.

John was elected as Vice President.

John immediately left for New York.

Gould and Fisk got Judge Barnard to file injunctions against the Ramsey board from action.

But it was too late.

Before the injunctions took effect John had acted. He had a signed contract, voted on by the board, to lease the Albany and Susquehanna Railroad to the Delaware and Hudson Canal Company for ninety nine years on a seven percent basis. John was placed on the new company's board of directors. The Delaware and Hudson Canal Company now ran the railroad and it was out of reach of Gould and Fisk.

Litigation lasted for months but it was to no avail.

John won, and he beat them at their own game.

And he was also pleased that to combat the war of the judge's the New York Bar Association was established in order to police judiciary abuses.

But the whole affair gave him a feeling of being soiled. Business should not run like this.

John turned away from the window. He glanced at the table and then he looked over at Louisa sitting across from him at the hotel restaurant. She smiled at him. He returned her smile.

"You are back," she said.

"What?"

"Nothing," she smiled, "nothing Father."

John looked toward Jack.

"Nice port," Jack said as he held up his glass. John looked at the glass of wine sitting before him as if wondering where that had come from. He picked up the glass, swirled the wine in the glass and held it to his nose. He then took a small sip.

"Nice," he said to Jack.

Two servers arrived at their table with their meals.

"Ah," Herbert said, smiling. "Our feast."

After dinner, still sitting at the table John asked the waiter for a glass of brandy. He turned to Jack.

"No thank you. I believe I am going to turn in. I want to be fresh in the morning, as you should do."

"A brandy will help put me to sleep."

"Madam," the waiter asked Louisa. John noticed Herbert glance at his watch.

"No. I do not want one. But I will sit with you while you have yours."

"There is no need for that. You two go to bed. I'll just have a small brandy, a smoke, and then I will be off myself."

"Are you sure?"

"Yes. Good night."

"Good night."

The three of them stood up, pushing their chairs back, and turned to leave. Jack looked back at his father.

John smiled and waved a small wave to him.

They left.

The waiter brought John his glass of brandy.

Brandy after dinner. He had a brandy after dinner when he visited

Anthony Drexel.

That turned out to be the most important glass of brandy he ever had.

John stood on the wooden dock waiting for the ferry to take him across the Hudson. He was on his way to the train station. His black satchel and his small leather overnight bag both sat at his feet. Packed in it he had a change of clothes for one day. He took his watch out of his pocket and glanced down. Five o'clock in the afternoon: Wednesday, March 8, 1871. He slipped the watch back into his coat pocket. He looked around at the crowd of people standing and waiting for the ferry. Soon they would all load onto the ferry and cross to the station where everyone would board, each bound for somewhere different. He was going to Philadelphia this evening. His mission was somewhat secret. He did not understand it himself.

John took in a deep breath of the fresh air blowing in across the water. As the late afternoon dissolved into early evening the air turned a little chilled.

John was tired. He was tired not just from a long day of work, but he was tired in a deeper sense of exhausted, exhausted physically, mentally, emotionally. At only thirty four years old he was tired of all of it.

Wall Street was filled with scoundrels. He had to work with far too many of them every day. They seemed to be legion. There were so many untrustworthy men that he had to deal with that it made him sick.

John regularly wrote to his father in England. Is this what constitutes business? Is this how it is? It seemed that more and more there were only men who through back stabbing and money grabbing ripped and tore everything to shreds for their own wealth, aggrandizement and personal gratification. If destroying everything in your path simply for the sake of yourself alone was the way of business then John was done with it. It did not appeal to him at all.

His father repeatedly tried to reassure him. He himself, he wrote, was graced in his daily dealings with true and noble gentlemen: like Peabody, like Belmont, like Rothschild. You will also, my son, find such men. Build on that network of trust and shared goals and values and it will reward you a hundred fold. Wade through the chaff and you will eventually find the true grain within.

If noble men abandon the field then it truly will be taken over by charlatans and your own worst fears will be realized. Stay true, his father wrote to him repeatedly: stay true.

John looked around at the people waiting for the ferry. Most of them were all simple wage earners. They were not rich. They had to work to survive. They did not have the power to change an entire company. They were the ones hurt when a business was destroyed to further enrich someone already rich enough to destroy the company in the first place.

How many here were hurt by the Erie Railroad wars of Vanderbilt and Drew and Gould and Fisk? How many lost their small savings on Black Friday when Gould and Fisk tried to corner the Gold market?

John watched as the steam ferry came toward the dock. The smoke from its chimney curled up and back into the air as the small ferry made its way toward the landing. There was but a handful of people coming across. In the morning, of course, it would be full with workers crossing into downtown for work. Now all of those same people were standing on the dock with him waiting to cross back to their home across the water. John took out a handkerchief from his coat pocket and rubbed his nose. It was sore. He again had a cold. The red rash on his face was there again aflamed. His nose was tender to the touch.

John was tired of it. Why would any man want to take over a business by back handed stealing in order to then destroy it by sucking it dry? Why not take over the business by legitimate means and help it to grow and thrive where it will reward you a thousand fold over? He just did not understand it. He wanted to deal with men of honor and integrity but it seemed to him that lately everyone was drowning in a sea of corruption.

Was there no end?

He wanted no more of it.

And, as luck would have it, the opportunity for a drastic change had arrived. His business partner, Charles Dabney, had announced at the beginning of the year that he would be resigning from the firm in July. There were other interests he wanted to pursue. It was the chance John hoped would come and now it was here. John had other interests he wanted to pursue as well. He announced to his other partners George Morgan and Jim Goodwin that, in light of Charles Dabney leaving, he was going to leave as well. The partnership will dissolve.

John was not a well man.

That was a second reason he wanted to quit. Ever since childhood John was sick from time to time, it seemed to be his natural state. And the inflammation in his nose and face was getting more pronounced, more intense. John always seemed to have a cold. And he seemed tired and exhausted most of the time. He was plagued by migraine headaches and dizzy spells, even at times fainting.

131

His heart was just not in it anymore.

He could rest. He could raise his prize collies. If he bought the land then he could raise prize cattle. He could travel. He had enough money built up that he could stop working and still be comfortable. He had his growing family.

Yes, and he could travel. He remembered sitting in the Pullman car, slightly swaying, the glass in the chandeliers slightly tingling as the iron wheels clicked along on the rails, watching as the miles and miles of grasslands raced by the window.

There was a whole world to see.

That would be grand.

The ferry blew its whistle long and hard as it came in toward the dock. John watched as the captain navigated the ferry to turn the starboard side toward the crowds of people waiting. He eased the boat in. It blew the steam whistle a second time. The attendants stood on the dock ready for the ropes.

John closed his eyes for a brief moment and tilted his head back. He did not feel that well. He did not fully understand why he was going to Philadelphia. It was his father's wish. If it were not for that he would decline and go home to rest.

He felt the moist and cooling wind on his skin. He heard ship bells clanging away across the water; sea gulls screeched; churning of the ferry's engine; splash of the waves against the dock. There was a slight bump and sway of the planks beneath his feet as the ferry softly hit against the dock. He heard the slap of the ropes thrown onto the wood and the attendants grabbing them and rapidly wrapping them around the cleats on the dock.

John opened his eyes, his head tilted back, looking up into the sky. People began boarding the ferry. The sky was a sharp clear blue washed with the afternoon sun. Seagulls flew back and forth crisscrossing the sky. He could see flapping flags all about. Tall masts with folded canvas sails tightly rope wrapped. John watched the gulls crisscrossing, circulating. John watched them. But then, higher still, near the roof of the seen, it was there again crossing the sky in slow steady strokes, a long thin white.

It took a moment.

Flash of memory, a blaze in the mind: he held Memie in his arms on the top of the stairs and her dress was white and looking up into the sky and then a long sleek of white swimming through the heavens there, just there and then as a boy of fifteen on a stretcher held up high over the banister bound for the open sea he looked up into the blue and the long thin bird all alone flapped across toward the forever unknown it seemed to say without words come, yes, come with me.

Again; there.

Clang of bells.

Take me across the waters.

People bumped against John as he stood motionless. Move along, they said. Move along.

John realized where he was, he looked around at those looking at him, get on with it, he picked up his satchel and his overnight bag and he walked with the crowd of people onto the ferry.

Memory lost.

He boarded the boat, crowding in toward the bow.

With a grinding shutter that shook the whole boat the captain brought the engine back to life and turned the ferry away from the dock. John, standing against the banister near the bow of the boat, held the railing to steady himself as the boat turned into the width of the river.

The blow of the whistle announced their departure from the dock. Smoke poured out of the stack as the boat came to life. The seats across the center of the boat filled up first. Everyone wanted a seat. But John preferred standing against the railing near the bow of the boat. He liked to watch where they were headed. He liked to watch the other boats as they passed by. Fully exposed, he squinted his eyes against the wind.

He and Fanny were thinking about buying a house in upper state, near Highland Falls. On occasion they rented the Stonihurst house, next to Cragston. There, on the front porch, they could look out through the tall cedar and elm trees, down the sloping grass covered hill toward the small wooden dock on the river. They, with friends, went boating up and down the river. It was quiet at night. The star sprinkled sky twinkled through the trees. He awoke each morning with the birds chirping and singing outside hopping from branch to branch. In the chilled early morning of autumn the mist from the river crept up through the trees carpeting everything with a moist hushed quiet.

Samuel Sloan, his neighbor and now friend, who lived across the river, climbed up into the trees to help tie the ropes for a swing for little Louisa and baby Jack. On the night of the fourth of July John and Fanny along with the Sloan's and the Osborn's and Charles Tracy all sat on the porch chairs watching the fireworks across the river shoot up and ignite the night sky. Shrapnel from the fireworks fell and splashed into the darkened water.

133

John, on the ferry, watched the birds sitting in the water bobbing up and down as waves rippled by. If he could afford it then why should he work? Why not live in Highland Falls, boat along the river, raise his beloved prize collies, raise a family, and take better care of himself?

Looking around at all of the people on the ferry, they all had spent their day working because they had to work to survive. Now they were going home to spend a few hours with their family before they had to get up the next day and do the whole thing all over again. Why should he? He knew how lucky he was. He was well enough off that he did not need to work, not for the money. If not for the money to survive, then why do it at all?

Why not live to live? Why sacrifice that just to have more? And in the end: more of what?

The ferry slowed its pace. A large frigate passed across their path. John looked up and watched the sailors on board. Some where high up the mast opening up the canvas sails. They were busy at what they did. Others stood along the rail. Some waved at the small ferry coming up toward their starboard. A wave of hello: a wave of good bye.

The captain cut the engine and let the boat drift, waiting for the frigate to pass. The ferry rocked back and forth in the waves of the frigates wake. Fresh out of port and bound for open sea, destinations unknown, it could be months on the ship before the happy waving sailors stepped once more onto dry land.

John raised his hand and waved. He could have been a sailor bound to ports unknown. Sailing to the Azores opened his eyes.

If I had not become a banker what would I be?

I could have been a sailor, or a ship owner, or a shipping company owner.

I have a good head for numbers. My teachers in Germany wanted me to further my studies in mathematics. I could have been a mathematician, a Gauss, a Euler; or, more likely, a professor teaching Gauss and Euler.

I am growing fonder of art and collecting. I could have been an art dealer, or a scholarly critic.

John watched as the frigate passed by. He once again could see the far side of the river; he once again could see his destination.

The engine once again roared to life, rattling the whole boat as the captain cranked the engine up to full power. A deep plume of smoke belched out of the chimney and John held the rail as the boat stopped drifting and lurched forward.

My father blazed the path and my footsteps followed his. John shrugged his shoulders. A banker I became.

His father once told him that you work and give it the best that you have not primarily for yourself, and not even primarily for your family. But you do it, rather, for the betterment of the community at large. It is out of that better community that you gain your own security, wealth, and, most important of all, your own self worth.

"You do what you can for the whole and that is your reward," he wrote in a letter.

All of the Vanderbilt's, the Fisk's, the Gould's, they were all certainly out just for themselves and could not give a damn for the whole. Was that the root of the problem? He was being so sucked into the particular, drowning in the selfishness of individuality, that he was losing sight of the whole.

Were his father's wise words once again the light to see him through to the end of this dark tunnel?

To the Jay Gould's and the Jim Fisk's of the world life was all out war and you won by taking what you can and then devastating everything else.

The ferry steamed across the water bobbing in the wave wakes of larger passing ships. John watched as the opposite shore grew closer. Pilgrims of the day returning home, John carefully searched the faces of the people on board. Some were young, eager workers at the end of a work day; some were older, the joy of youth long since departed from their faces, their eyes; some were older men and women, waiting.

Why must it be like this?

Was it indeed true? If you do for the all then the all will do for you. Certainly as a Christian he had to admit that there was something to it: Our Savior certainly gave his all for everyone and now everyone, in turn, through their faith and their love, give back to Him. Sometimes it was very hard to practice your faith in the day to day struggle.

John looked up at the incessant seagulls flapping back and forth as if, for some reason, they were all hovering above the boat. Then he saw the young boy standing on the opposite side of the ferry tossing what looked like pieces of bread up into the air and out over the water. A gull swooped down and grabbed a piece of bread in midflight. Others dropped down into the water to fight each other over the bread floating on the surface of the water.

The boy laughed. The birds swirled all around him, above him. The birds, if they could, would kill each other for the small loaf of bread the boy held in his hand. But he laughed and kept tearing pieces off and flinging them into the air out away from the boat. John watched as a woman reached over and pulled on the boy's shirt and pulled him back, forcing him to sit down. The woman scolded the boy, the boy looked hurt and mad and of the young age that John expected the boy to start crying. To the boy a greater tragedy had struck: his joyful abandonment to his glee was cut short.

John again watched the opposite side of the river as they neared the landing. He had to shield his eyes from the sun. Low in the western sky it cast long shadows across the water from the buildings and the docks along the shore. It was as if the shore was reaching out to embrace the incoming ferry before it actually reached its destination. John watched the shadows approach. The ferry blew its shrill whistle just as the first of the shadows crossed the bow of the boat.

After he got off of the ferry it was a short walk up into the Jersey City Depot. The depot was bustling with people. With twelve tracks heading in all directions anyone could go almost anywhere from here. With multiple ticket booths, station platforms and restaurants it was all a wonderful insight into how the world could be, and would be, if the forces of corruption and greed could be contained.

John boarded his train to Philadelphia and sat in a seat next to the window. The train had recently made connecting links which now made it possible to go direct into Philadelphia in a matter of hours. Not that long ago it took days. In the invitation to come and see him Anthony Drexel wrote that John could leave work, have dinner and spend the evening with Drexel and, after spending the night, take the 7:30 train to New York and arrive back at work the next day by 10:45. That way, Drexel explained, "we would then have ample time to compare views without your losing any business time."

As the train pulled away from the station John thought abut Anthony Drexel. Why had he written requesting a meeting between them? Telegraph or write to me on what train you take and I will be at the station to meet you, he wrote.

John did not really know Drexel. He had heard of his firm but that was about all. But yet six days ago John received the first letter with an invitation:

"Some time since I received a communication from your father the nature of which and my reply thereto he has no doubt written to you about. Should these matters strike you favorably, I will be glad to have an interview with you to talk it over. Could you come over here any time next week, or when convenient to you?"

There was no explanation from his father. The only mention was in a letter last January where he wrote "I have had a visit from Mr. A. J. Drexel, of Drexel & Co., Philadelphia. It is possible he may want to see you about a certain matter, and if he does I hope you will go to see him."

That was it. There was no mention then or since about what "the matter" was.

When the train pulled into the station at 8:20 that evening John at once saw Drexel standing on the platform waiting for him. Bald on the top of his head, his hair just above his ears was slightly bushy. He looked a bit ordinary, forty five years old, nothing fancy in his dress to indicate his prominent position, medium height, slightly portly, a large busy moustache, and a noticeable double chin.

They went up the street in his carriage to his mansion where he, his wife Ellen and their seven children lived.

They had dinner and pleasantly discussed this and that: business in general, the stock market, the nice spring weather they were having, the joy of raising a family, Ellen asked about Frances, what did she like to do with her time.

But then, as the clock on the wall struck ten, Anthony rose and asked if John would care to retire to his library.

"Surely," John replied.

"Perhaps I can offer a nice cigar and a glass of brandy. From what I hear you do enjoy both."

"I do, and that would be most generous."

The library was a cozy room, a soft sofa, comfortable chairs, a large desk. There was a painting on the wall above the fireplace. It was of an artist sitting at his easel painting a self portrait. With a high collar, sideburns, it was a handsome face.

Anthony noticed John's gaze.

"That is my father. He was a painter in his youth, had that artistic temperament and all of that. He had a few wild adventures during the Napoleonic wars."

"From an artistic painter to currency trading and banking, now that is not a usual story."

"No it is not. But then again my father was quite an unusual man. He still had a burning fire in him even as a banker. I, on the other hand, provide a stabilizing counterpoint to him even though I wish, at times, that I had inherited more of his flame."

John sipped his brandy. He felt relaxed. He liked Anthony, he was kind and warm hearted.

"I am of a dual myself," John said as he swirled the brandy in his glass.

"Oh, and how so?"

"Well, what I inherited from my two grandfathers could not be more different. Grandfather Morgan, my father's father, was a business man true and true. He was careful and frugal man and, step by slow step, built up his empire. He was a successful merchant, owned a store, owned some stages, a hotel, formed an insurance company, and became a banker. He was everything my father now is."

"But I take it that this was not so your other grandfather?"

"No. Grandfather Pierpont was a preacher and a poet, a fiery preacher from all accounts, who passionately and continuously expounded upon his sacred causes: abolition of the imprisonment for debt, temperance not only in drink but in all things, and, the main one, the complete abolition of slavery. He was passionate to the core on all of those things and spoke out even to his own detriment."

"His own detriment?"

"Yes, he was the preacher for the Hollis Street Church in Boston for, oh, twenty some years. But then a group of them tried to have him removed for his outspokenness. But he stood his ground and forced the issue in a trial before the Ecclesiastical Council. He was fully vindicated and then, on his own, resigned his pulpit."

"Sounds like a man of principal."

"He told me once, when I was just a boy, that he stood for 'love of right, freedom and men, and corresponding hatred of everything that is at war with them.'"

"And what happened to him?"

John took swirled his glass and took another sip before he answered. He spoke in a low tone.

"Well he pretty much lost everything. But when the Civil War came there he was, a seventy six year old man, joining the army as a chaplain to help end slavery. He could not stand the cold. He would walk around at night beating his arms trying to keep warm. He appealed to Secretary Chase for a job, any job. Chase knew of him from his preacher days so he gave him a position as some clerk. He died without much left."

"I'm sorry to hear that."

But John smiled: "But on his eightieth birthday, in 1865, he was told a few friends were waiting for him. When he arrived there was a swarm of old abolitionist friends waiting for him. They came to honor his role in ending slavery. William Lloyd Garrison gave a speech. My grandfather broke down and wept."

"He was vindicated."

John nodded. He waited a moment before he spoke.

"And that was more important to him than owning all the hotels and banks in the land."

Anthony glanced up at the painting of his father.

"I learned a lot from my father, as you do from yours no doubt."

"Yes, we write every week." John laughed. "He never wants for advice on how I should be."

"And the advice is good is it not?"

"Oh yes. Good advice, mostly. It is the wisdom of age and experience you know, I suppose. You can not buy that in a store."

"No."

"But my Grandfather Pierpont gave me some advice that I remember to this day. When I was about sixteen he gave me a jack knife. 'It's for whittling my boy,' he said. 'Take what you find and whittle it into something better.' Strive for the beautiful, he said, for it is always there."

"Unfortunately my father has passed on. He may still be alive today if it was not for an unfortunate accident. It leaves quite a hole in your heart."

"What happened, if you do not mind my asking?"

"He was returning from a business trip, seventy one years old and still going strong. The train pulled into the station and he was about to get off but he held a large portfolio of documents under his arm. To steady himself he asked this boy behind him to hold the portfolio for a moment while he stepped onto the station platform. Once he was on the platform he turned around to get the papers but just then the train moved and he lost his balance. He fell onto the tracks and the train crushed his legs. He died that evening."

"I do not even want to think what I will feel when my father dies."

"You must absorb all that you have for one day it will be gone."

"I suppose you are right."

"We must carry on, for what else is there to do? Someday it will be resolved, in heaven perhaps."

"Perhaps."

"But this brings me to the point of the trip."

John set down his glass and sat up in the chair.

"Yes."

Anthony said that he and John's father were much alike in their view of business. In talking with him we found that our two situations were a perfect match. He has a strong presence in London and New York but wishes a strong one in Paris. I have a strong presence here in

Philadelphia and in Paris but a weaker one in London and New York. I am looking for ways to expand and strengthen my international business, and so is he.

"He presented the solution and I was amazed at its simplicity."

"And what was that?"

Anthony sat back in his chair.

"Mr. Morgan, I want you to come into my firm as a partner."

John was stunned. He could not speak.

Anthony explained some of the details as John still sat silently.

John protested. He was not well. He was going to dissolve his partnership and completely retire.

Anthony shook his head. "That would be a tragic loss. It is time for this wild financing and speculative excess that we see so often to come to an end. Together, you and your father and I, we all think of business in the same way. We can help build a solid financial foundation to help build good companies that will prosper and grow."

John had to agree.

"If you are not well then take a vacation. Take an extended vacation. Take all the time that you need. Would a year off be enough?"

"Perhaps."

"Mr. Morgan, I believe in long term relationships and to that end what is but a year?"

Anthony stood and walked over to his desk and sat down. He took up his pen and found a used envelope and began writing on the back. "Here," he said as he wrote. "This is the proposal."

When he was done he handed John the creased envelope. John glanced at it and then folded it and put it into his pocket.

"I want a man with boldness to his step but honesty in his intent. I think you are that man."

John sat on the deck of the steamer making its way up the Nile. It was a hot and bright sunny day but comfortably cooler in the shade beneath the canvas canopy. A long trail of smoke rose from the smokestack leaving a trail behind that slowly evaporated in the sunlight. John watched the stark desert pass by as they made their way up the river. Ducks, in the water, aroused, flew up into the sky and down stream. John had to turn around to watch them quack their way away.

On his year long quest for peace John traveled to England, to Paris, to Frankfort, to Munich, to Rome. Never did he find the quiet peace that he sought. It was only here, in Egypt, on a steamer plowing up the Nile that he finally found his peace. It was his first trip to Egypt; it would not be his last.

He watched the eternal desert pass by. He waved at the occasional people he saw on the shoreline. Some stood and waved back to him, others continued to work, bent over in the fields.

Here and there the guide brought the boat in and tied it to a dock. John and has family and friends got out to see what tomb or ruin there was to see. They rode on donkeys into the interior. Louisa jumped onto the back of the donkey without fear but little four year old Jack was afraid and cried and held onto his mother.

Francis stroked the boy and whispered in his ear that it was all right, there was no need to cry. John walked on into the sand toward whatever there was to see.

Egypt was old, pure, clean; the ruins were thousands of years old and yet here they still stood for him to see.

Back home the job with Anthony Drexel was still there waiting for him to return.

"Take your time," Drexel told him, "we will begin when you return."

This, John thought as he walked in the sand, this, he thought, this is what I want to build; this is what I want to leave behind as a monument to my having lived, I want to build something strong, something clean, something eternal.

When the ancient Egyptians built their tombs and their pyramids they did not simply build it for this years profit, caring not whether it lasted beyond tomorrow. No, they built for the ages, for the eternal.

I want to build something equally strong, clean, and eternal.

He did not know it at the time but as he sat on his steamer in the shade watching the day go by back home the shallow and the corrupt was being washed away.

William 'Boss' Tweed, the center of the corrupt and corrupting Tammany Hall of New York, lynchpin in the world of Jay Gould and Jim Fisk, was arrested, charged with corruption; he would eventually die in jail.

And Jim Fisk met his fate.

In 1870 Jim Fisk and his mistress Josie 'Dumpling' Mansfield, whom he had found several years before in Annie Wood's 'establishment' and lavished with her own apartment suite, clothes, jewelry, introductions to high society, and a bank account, had a falling out. It seems that she and one of his friends, who he had introduced her to, an Edward S. Stokes, who Fisk had financially helped out when he managed to lose a small fortune at the horse races, had begun having an affair.

Josie told Fisk that she wanted to continue being his kept woman (the money was good) but she also wanted to have her freedom to be with whomever she wished.

"It won't do Josie," Fisk said. "You can't run two engines on one track in contrary directions at the same time."

Josie demanded a $25,000 settlement to end their affair. Fisk said no. Josie threatened to publish his love letters and expose secret business dealings he had told her about. Fisk brought suit against them for blackmail, they brought suit for libel. That news proved as surprising to Stokes's wife as Jim Fisk's affair with Josie proved to be to Jim's wife.

In the court trial for libel Fisk's lawyer took Josie apart in cross examination. On January 6, 1872 Justice Bixby threw out the Stokes and Josie case, and then in a separate action on the same day a grand jury indicted both of them on Fisk's charge of blackmail and issued warrants for their arrest.

Edward Stokes, when he heard of this, went to visit Josie for one last time. With his short curly hair and his full Van Dyke goatee and moustache, he took a cab to the Grand Central Hotel. He jumped out and went in through the Ladies entrance and then up the stairs to the second floor. There he paced back and forth and back and forth.

Jim Fisk arrived with his black scarlet lined military cloak and silk hat and gold headed walking cane. He also entered the Ladies entrance to the hotel. He spoke with a hotel employee and then started up the stairs.

Thomas Hart, a bell hop at the top of the stairs, watched as Stokes came to the top of the stairs.

"I've got you now," he said.

Fisk looked up to see Stokes at the top of the stairs with a colt revolver. He fired. The bullet hit Fisk in the stomach. He reeled back but caught himself from falling. Stokes fired again and the bullet hit Fisk in the left arm. He fell to the floor at the bottom of the stairs.

Stokes turned and walked across the second story lobby, hid the gun under a sofa cushion, and then started down the main entrance stairway toward the front door.

The bell hop followed him, watching him. Shouts about someone being shot could be heard. Guests stopped to look around, wondering what was going on. Stokes turned and entered the saloon. The bell hop frantically waved over the hotel manager H. L. Powers, the manager pointed toward Stokes.

"Stop that man," he shouted as they ran toward him. Stokes looked back and went out of the saloon into the barber shop toward the outside entrance on Mercer Street. By them Powers and Hart reached him and held his arms back. Patrons sitting in the barber chairs with their faces lathered for their shave watched it all.

Jim Fisk died at 10:45 the next morning.

When John returned to New York in September 1872 he read the old papers about the Fisk affair and simply shook his head. It was such a sordid ending to such a sordid way of life. No true gentleman would act in that way. Things now would be better.

He was rested. He was refreshed. He was ready now, with Drexel and with his father, to build their own Egyptian kingdom: something pure and something eternal.

When he met Anthony Drexel upon his return they shook hands.

"A good man in my past," John told him, "once quoted the Greek playwright Aeschylus who said 'It is not the oath that makes us believe the man but the man the oath.'"

Anthony smiled. "This is so," he said.

"Let us make it our motto for the future."

"I agree," he simply said.

Cards of Kings

John finished his glass of brandy, signed the check for dinner, and left the restaurant. As he passed the reception desk he saw a telephone and had a sudden urge to call Belle de la Greene at the Library. He did not know why. It did not really make any sense because he had nothing in particular to ask.

John pulled his pocket watch out of his waistcoat pocket and popped open the lid. It was late. She would be home by now, perhaps even asleep, or, possibly, out with one of her friends at dinner or a show or a dance.

John smiled at the thought of her; she certainly had her wild side. She thought that he did not know, or did not want to know, but he enjoyed hearing about her. She was not the usual librarian. What is it she had said? Just because I am a librarian does not mean I have to dress like one.

She was life, burning and passionate life.

When he first hired her she spent the first year simply unpacking crates of books and manuscripts and carefully cataloging them. He started using her more and more. But it was not simply for the Library.

More than once he had stopped to admire her beauty. Exotic, with a whirl of black hair, huge green eyes, dark and soft olive skin, she was small and slender and walked with such a proud and upright carriage.

He liked her. She had a calming influence on him. When he was restless or agitated he called her into the west room and they talked. He found himself confessing things he never shared with anyone else. He had her read to him while he sat with his eyes closed. She read from the Bible. Other times he just had her there while he worked, both sitting in silence.

Once she read the story of Jonah and the whale. When she was done she put the book down.

"Do you believe the story is true?"

John looked at her over the top of his reading glasses. He was a little taken by the question.

"Of course it is true," he said so matter of factly.

"Do you think everything in the Bible is true?"

"Of course," he replied without hesitation. It made him wonder whether she did or not. She did not say, and he did not ask.

When he felt she was more capable John eventually sent her to England. He had purchased a great many things on his recent trip and needed someone to arrange for their shipment home. But there was another purpose as well.

Lord Amherst was selling his collection of books at auction. Among the books were sixteen Caxtons, some of the earliest printed books in England. John had already bought twenty four Caxtons from Richard Bennett in 1902. He wanted to expand his collection. John wanted to buy them privately, before the auction, that way he could be assured of the whole set, and perhaps at a less expensive price than open bidding, but Lord Amherst declined. John sent Belle.

"Do your charm," he told her when she was leaving.

"What is my charm?" she asked.

John just smiled.

Belle arrived a week before the auction and requested an immediate audience with Lord Amherst.

Sitting on the sofa in his drawing room one afternoon she talked about Morgan, the Library, the beauty of the architecture and the red patterned walls. It was such a wonderfully beautiful place to store such wonderful treasures.

Belle could feel the disapproving stares of Lady Amherst and other members of the family.

"You see, Lord Amherst, Mr. Morgan simply has to have them. He has asked me to offer the following," she said as she reached into her small pocketbook and pulled out a small piece of perfumed paper. She held it out to him. He hesitated a moment. Out of the corner of her eyes Belle could see the family members glancing back and forth.

Finally he bent forward and took the small piece of folded paper from her white gloved hand. He stared straight into her eyes as he opened the paper. He briefly looked down at the paper and then steadied his stare back up at her.

She smiled, raising an eyebrow.

She had simply written on the paper '$125,000.'

That was all.

"That, of course, is with immediate payment."

"I see," he said.

That was all.

At the door, as she was leaving, she turned and in a lower tone of voice, as if sharing a secret with only him, said: "I might be speculating beyond my station but, from overhearing discussions, I fear that if Mr. Morgan cannot purchase the Caxtons by private sale that he may forgo bidding in the auction altogether."

She smiled again and then nodded: "Good day, sir."

Days passed with no word.

Surely he understood the implication. If John did not bid in the auction then prices for all things would be lower.

The night before the auction arrived she dined with other bookmen who would be actively bidding against her tomorrow. They all tried to find out what she was interested in, what were her plans, what did Morgan want to buy. 'Gentlemen, never ask a woman her secrets,' she replied with a wink of her eye. But an older man, with gray peppered hair and a monocle eyeglass, turned to her and asked point blank.

"Miss Greene, will you promise me that in the morning you'll not bid against me for the Caxton 'The History of Troy?'"

Belle hesitated. She took a sip of wine in order to delay her answer. Just as she was putting the glass down a tall man in black walked over to the table.

"Pardon me sirs, Madam. Are you Miss. Greene?"

"Yes."

"There is a telegram for you," the man said as he handed her the telegram. She tore it open and, shielding it from the others, read the message. It was from Lord Amherst. It read: 'Offer accepted.'

Belle laughed, her gloved fingers to her mouth. She turned to the older man with the gray peppered hair.

"Yes," she said, "I will promise not to bid against you at the sale tomorrow."

As soon as she got back to her hotel she wired John. He was sitting in the west room when the message was brought to him. When he opened it he sat back and read the words. "Good news. Offer Accepted. Belle."

John, alone in the room, shouted out. He held his hand up into the air and clenched his fist.

"Oh Belle, I knew you could do it."

John loved working with her. He loved being with her. When he was there he demanded her full attention. Once, when he came to her long after it was time for her to go home for the day, he asked her to compile a list of books on loan to the Metropolitan. She looked up at him with an irritated and tired look. He was electric; he filled the room as though a gale were passing through.

"Pierpont," she said, "you are the most exhausting man I have ever known."

"Good. So; on my desk first thing tomorrow morning then?"

His passion overtook him once and it changed their relationship forever. He returned from a trip and entered her office in the back of the Library. He was happy and joyous, the trip had been good, he had bought a lot of good things, he was happy to be home and rested, and, surprising to him when he fully realized it, he was filled with anticipation and joy at seeing her. She laughed and stood up when he entered her office. He went over to her and she put out her arms for a small hug but he swept her up into his arms and spun around. He hugged her tight. She smelled and felt so good.

When he put her down he realized that he had over stepped the bounds. He was going to apologize but her reaction stopped him.

"My goodness," she said, slightly giggling like a school girl; "That is a side of you I have not had the pleasure of seeing before."

He smiled a deep and wide grin.

It was later, toward the end of the day, after he called her into his office that they talked.

He had to get it out. It had to be said. He could not let it go on.

John told her that he realized how much he missed her when he was on his trip.

"But you were with Adelaide Douglas; certainly she can keep you company."

John waved her away.

"It will be our last. But all the while I deeply missed you. I have grown very fond of you, Belle. You have become something more than just my librarian; you have become a close and intimate friend. I have told you things, and discussed my feelings about people, more than anyone else."

"That, sir, certainly is true. I have wondered if you realize what you are telling me at times."

"I do, but it is because I find it so easy to talk to you, almost confess to you."

"Yes, we have become something more than an employer and his employee. It is such an honor to work for you, and to have become such a friend to you is even a greater honor."

147

"Do you suppose. . ." he slowly asked.

She smiled and tilted her head.

"Do I suppose what, Mr. J. Pierpont Morgan?"

It suddenly knifed him; the difference in their age.

"What if I were thirty years younger?" he asked, desperate perhaps, but already knowing the ending answer.

"Then," she said, calculating in her head, "I would be negative one."

They laughed.

But then he grew serious.

"No," he said. "Seriously."

She waited and smiled. She reached out and touched his chin with her forefinger.

"Perhaps forty years younger."

There was a long painful pause as the meaning of her response sunk in.

"What we have transcends that. Why cheapen what we have by making it merely sexual."

John was surprised at her open frankness. He tried to make the most of the painful impossibility.

"Enrich is perhaps the word I would have used," he finally said. "Not cheapen."

"But you are already rich enough, what more could there be?"

He could not help himself from saying it.

"You," he quietly said.

"But you have me, forever. I do not plan on going anywhere but here. You have my word."

One evening while dining at Sherry's John spotted Lady Alice Murano and her husband Frank. John went over to pay his regards.

"So you have returned from Europe I see," he said as he bent over to greet them.

"Oh, Mr. Morgan, how kind," Lady Murano said. She had such long black as coal eyelashes and such pasty white skin. Her attempts at preserving her youth were meeting with diminishing returns.

"Yes, indeed. Just yesterday as a matter of fact," Lady Murano said. "What a strange thing we have run into you, Mr. Morgan."

"Why is that so strange?"

"Well," she said, "we happen to have seen your girl over there, in Venice. Miss Greene?"

"Yes, she's doing some business for me."

"Well," Lady Murano said with that inflection in her voice suggesting a 'if you say so' attitude.

"She was traveling with Bernard Berenson, the art critic. Her maid, she said, was with her; her chaperone I presume." Lady Murano smiled, tapping the top of her wine glass with her gloved finger. The rings on her fingers were far too large, and too many.

"After all, Mr. Morgan, Bernard Berenson is quite a handsome man and when we spotted her they seemed to be in the midst of an engrossing discussion."

"About Giovanni Bellini no doubt," John said as he stood up.

"Of course," Lady Murano replied, hackling her forced laughter.

John quickly walked away as if seeing someone else he had to go see.

Another time when he was dining at Delmonico's Charles Robbins took John aside.

"Might I have a word? I say, Pierpont, it is a delicate thing."

"What is a delicate thing?"

"Well, you may want to have a word with your librarian, Miss Greene."

"And what should I have a word with her about?"

"Well, you know. Her manner is bound to make things a bit more public than would be agreeable. I heard that while on her way to dinner with friends Miss Greene noticed that her lace sleeve was torn, exposing her upper arm. She laughed it off, it is said, by flippantly saying 'the black blood really shows through, doesn't it?'"

John stared at the man without saying anything.

"People talk, of course, but that is just idle gossip. But if she makes comments like that then it may become more widely known, you see."

"Charles, I do not understand. What may be more widely known?"

Charles had a little panic and surprise in his voice.

"Why, Pierpont, surely you know. I mean how can you not? I just assumed that you knew her because of her father."

John tilted his head to one side. He was trying to make sense of the whole thing. John did not know who her father was. They never talked about him.

"Richard Greener, her father is Richard Greener. You worked with him years ago on the Ulysses S. Grant Monument Association. It was back in, what, 1885 or so."

John thought back. Greener. Yes, he remembered him. Sharp young man. He was the first Negro graduate from Harvard.

John froze. Charles watched John's face.

"Please tell me that you knew. I thought you hired her because you knew her father."

John could not speak for a moment.

"Pierpont?"

John turned and looked at Charles.

"Yes, yes, of course, of course," John stumbled.

"Thank goodness. I have always told the others that I think it bloody well bold of you, I must say."

"Quite."

When John got back to his hotel room he began to undress. Both Louisa and Jack were in their own rooms. He carefully removed his jacket and waistcoat and hung them up in the closet. He sat in his chair by the table and removed his shoes and his socks. It felt good to have his feet naked. He could feel the thick carpet with his toes. He saw the cards sitting in a stack on the table. One more game, he thought. One last game before the day is done.

John carefully shuffled the cards and then laid them out on the table. Clearing his throat he pulled over the first card.

It was the King of Clubs.

There had been kings in his life.

February 4, 1895.

It was already dusk when the train arrived. As the train pulled into the station John watched from his window the people standing on the station. Standing on the platform, cold, bundled in their coats and shawls, looking in as if trying to see whoever it was they were waiting to arrive. The train gradually slowed and as it came to a halt John picked up his coat draped across the seat opposite him and stood to leave. He swayed a bit and held himself up against the side of the car. As soon as the car was at a complete stop he stepped out into the pathway and began walking toward the door. He glanced back to see Stetson and Bacon getting up out of their seats and gathering their folders and coats. John put his woolen coat on as he walked down the aisle toward the door. As he stepped down from the train and onto the platform he felt the sting of the cold against his face. He glanced back and forth, saw the cab station at the end of the platform, and began to walk, tapping his cane on the wooden platform as he walked. He assumed that Stetson and Bacon were just behind him. If they were not they should be. He wove through the people on the platform as it filled with people getting off the train. He eyes were trained on the cab station.

But standing before him was a man in grey with a high collar. It was Secretary Daniel Lamont. John stared as he approached and slowed his pace. Lamont was staring directly at him. Is he here for me? The Secretary of War, why was he here for me? Is this who they send? Lamont stood shorter than John. His bald head was uncovered. His full thick moustache protruded out from under his nose, almost hiding his lips. It had a dash of grey just under his nose. When John came up to him Lamont nodded.

"Mr. Morgan," he acknowledged.

"Mr. Lamont. Kind of you to be here."

"I've been sent by the President."

"And?"

"I regret to say that you are on a wasted trip. We cabled but you had already left New York."

John waited, silent.

Lamont was nervous.

It was then that first Bacon and then Stetson came up from behind John and stood next to him. They finally had caught up with him. Bacon stood still but Stetson and Lamont nodded.

"Hello Daniel," Stetson said.

They knew each other. Stetson had been a law partner with Cleveland and Lamont had been his private secretary. 'Lamont is a wonderful man' is how Cleveland characterized him. 'I never saw his like. He has no friends to gratify or reward and no enemies to punish.'

Lamont looked back at Morgan.

"The President will not see you. He has decided on a new public bond offering."

Lamont seemed to be waiting for some kind of reply from John but John remained silent, staring.

"He is going to push the issue through Congress."

John tapped his cane on the floor.

"He offers his sincere regrets for any inconvenience he may have caused you but that is the course of action he has decided."

John did not reply. He tapped his cane on the wooden platform. He tapped his cane slow and steady.

Everyone glanced around at each other except John who stared relentlessly at Lamont.

Then, finally, with a last tap of his walking stick, he spoke.

"I have come down to Washington to see the President and I am going to stay here until I see him."

All eyes were on Lamont. He did not reply.

"Inform him of this," John ordered.

Without waiting for a reply John walked on past Lamont and tapped his cane with each step as if he were walking on three legs in order to get where he was going faster. Stetson and Bacon, stunned, looked at each other and then at Lamont. They both shrugged their shoulders and then followed John one by one as he quickly made his way to the cab stand.

John came to a stop at the edge of the sidewalk and then walked over to the cab station. He watched the horses standing in the cold, mist exhaling from their nostrils. Several stamped their feet. The cab dispatcher came over. He was bundled in a large coat, woolen cap pulled down over his ears, and woolen gloves.

"Cab sir?"

"Yes. Two."

John turned toward Stetson.

"Go to the White House and try to set up a meeting, tonight if possible, but definitely tomorrow. We will see you later tonight at the hotel."

"You come with me," he barked to Bacon as John stepped into the waiting cab. Bacon followed.

John pulled out a small folded piece of paper from his coat pocket.

"Here, give this address to the driver."

John settled into his seat. The cab started and John watched out the window as they started down the street. Bacon had long ago learned not to disturb John when he was thinking. If you were lucky he would simply ignore you, possibly not even hear you, and your words would fall silent to the floor. If he did hear you and disturbed him then he would turn his eyes toward you and his stare would melt you like ice.

Finally, when he was ready, John turned and leaned toward Bacon as if what he had to say was secret and he did not want anyone else to hear.

"The President's position is impossible for me to understand in view of the immediate situation. I do not think they appreciate what the next twenty four hours could bring, especially if word were to get out that our negotiations have been called off. Panic will ensue. That is why I have to speak with the president personally. Understand. I want to avoid as long as I can being seen at the hotel. I want you to go on to the hotel but stay away from reporters. Belmont should be there. Tell everyone to say nothing. And see if you can set up a meeting, tonight, with Olney. In case Stetson fails we can perhaps convince Olney to intervene. I will be at the home of a friend. J. Kearney Warren. I can hide out there until a meeting is set in place. Call me there when you have something."

Standing on the doorstep Morgan rang the bell. A small Negro woman answered the door.

"Why, Mr. Morgan."

"Hello Bessie. How are you this evening?"

"Oh fine, just fine. Come in, come in out from the cold."

John walked in as Bessie closed the door behind him.

A voice came in down the hall.

"Who is at the door Bessie?"

"It's Mr. Morgan, Mrs. Warren. Mr. J. P. Morgan."

There was a momentary pause and then the sound of footsteps coming down the hall. Bessie helped John take off his coat. John turned when he heard a voice in the hallway behind him.

"Goodness gracious, Pierpont."

"Hello Roberta."

John held out his arms as he walked over to her. They hugged.

"What on earth are you doing here?"

"I'm in town unexpectedly and I could not be here without coming to visit."

"Is Francis with you?"

"No, I am on business."

"Well come in."

They went into the parlor. There was a fire in the fireplace. As he entered the room he could at once feel the warmth of the fire.

"Sit here in front of the fire, warm yourself. I'll get Bessie to bring some tea."

"Roberta. Actually this is a bit of business."

"When isn't what you do a bit of business?"

"I cannot tell you why but I need a place to hide out for an hour or so. Someone will call for me later."

"That is all right by me. In the mean time we can chat. How are you, how are the children? Here," she said as she held out a box of small cigars. "Have one of Kearney's cigars."

John peered into the box.

"He will not mind?"

She waved her hand in the air as if to dismiss the entire question. "He is not here," she laughed.

They sat and talked for an hour. She did most of the talking. John glanced several times at the timepiece on the mantel over the fireplace. But then the phone rang. Bessie came into the parlor.

"It's for Mr. Morgan, madam."

John went to the phone in the hallway. It was Bacon. Richard Olney, the Attorney General, finally arrived home. He could see them at his home. Now. A cab is on its way to pick you up. We'll meet you there.

"Good," John mumbled into the phone. "Good, good."

Soon they were all sitting in the parlor of Richard Olney. John was forceful.

"I need to meet with the President face to face to discuss this matter."

Olney shook his head no.

"But he has changed his mind from last month," he said. "The President wants to present a bond sale. It is too politically delicate for him to be seen in collusion with Wall Street interests."

"No, that will not work. If you break off negotiations it will be more disastrous than if we had never spoken. I must see him and convince him of the gravity of the situation."

"But he has said no. Lamont explained all of that did he not?"

"But I insist on seeing him, nevertheless."

"Tell me what proposals you have and I will convey your position to him."

"No, that will not do. I must speak with him directly."

"But even if he agrees to meet with you, and he has not, that may be difficult on this short notice. You have a much better chance for him to hear your proposals through me. I can speak for you."

"I have already said no to that. It is urgent that I speak with him directly."

"Like I said, that. . ."

"Like I said, sir, I am John Pierpont Morgan of J.P. Morgan and Company and I must speak with President Cleveland with the utmost haste. I fear he does not realize the seriousness of the current situation."

"I am sure he is aware. . ." Olney began but he was trapped by John's eyes boring into him. Olney held his hands up in the air as if to signal stop, all right, stop.

"Let me see what I can do."

"We will wait."

"I will call you at your hotel when I get a reply."

"No, we will wait," John replied sharply. He sat back into the chair and placed his open palms onto his thighs as if to signal that he will wait forever. If there was any hope of Olney getting to bed tonight he had to handle this now.

Olney went into the next room. After a moment John and Bacon could hear Olney's muffled voice on the telephone. There was pleading (he won't take no for an answer, should not discount what he has to say, it is J.P. Morgan for gods sake man) and then finally Olney came back into the room. He seemed nervous.

"His secretary says you can meet him in the morning. When he gets in he will fit you in, he will call you with the times."

"Good. He does not need to call. I will be there at eight o'clock."

Bacon piped up. "Perhaps we should now let the Attorney General retire. I am sure he has had a long day."

"Yes, quite right," John said as he instantly stood up. Everyone else then stood as well.

"I thank you for your efforts, Mr. Olney, but I feel strongly about the present situation. It is far more dire than the President has been led to believe. I leave you with a good night."

The next morning when John came down stairs and into the lobby Robert Bacon was already there waiting for him.

"Morning, sir."

"Good Morning. Where are the others?"

"Stetson is at the reception and Belmont is already over there."

John pulled out his watch and looked at the time.

"Good," he said as he snapped down the lid and dropped the watch back into his waistcoat pocket.

"Sir," Bacon asked, "after I left you last night how late did you stay up?"

"I played solitaire. I think better that way."

"I know, sir, but how late did you stay up?"

John shrugged his shoulders.

"The last I remember I think it was around three. Why?"

"Because, sir, I have been personally entrusted with looking after you and making sure that you do not over do it."

John turned and looked directly at Bacon.

"Entrusted by whom?"

155

"Your wife, sir."

John paused. My wife?

Bacon gave one of his quick boyish smiles. Robert Bacon was new to the firm. John got him away from Lee, Higginson & Co. just last year. Bacon had graduated from Harvard, Class of 1880, and as an undergraduate gained high achievements in football, baseball, track, boxing and crew while graduating in the top third of his class. He was tall with curly blond hair and was, as was said, 'handsome as Adonis.'

"If you are looking after me then did you call the office this morning for the latest gold drafts?"

"Yes. There are many but one in particular is a ten million draft waiting to be filled."

John closed his eyes for a second and sighed: "Good God."

"I told them to delay it as long as they can."

"Good."

By the time Stetson came over to them John was already walking toward the door. They fumbled with their overcoats as they walked. Outside, on the porch of the hotel, they stood for a moment adjusting their coats and gloves.

Snow was falling freely and a cold stiff wind whirled the white around. Walking out from the hotel the air was sharp and cold against their skin.

"I'll get us a cab," Bacon said as he began walking toward the cab stand.

"No," John snapped. "We'll walk."

He began down the stairs, thrusting his cane ahead of himself, stepping into the falling snow.

"Walk?" Stetson said. He and Bacon looked at each other and then at John, now standing on the sidewalk at the bottom of the stairs. The snow floating down was already gathering on his coat and hat.

"Of course," John said, "it's just over there across Lafayette Park."

"But sir, it's. . ." but Bacon did not finish his sentence.

"Come on, we don't have time to waste. The cold will wake you up; clear your mind."

By then John was already crossing the street.

Stetson laughed.

"Well, you heard the man."

"My mind is as clear as a summer afternoon and that's where I'd like to keep it, warm."

John was already across the street when first Stetson and then Bacon rushed to follow him. John walked with a heavy and determined pace.

Their breath turned into mist. They did not talk as they walked for too much energy was spent in trying to get where they were going as fast as they could.

They were shown directly upstairs into the library. President Cleveland sat at the end of a long table on the far side of the room with two of his secretaries. Standing around him were the Secretary of War Daniel Lamont, Treasury Secretary John Carlisle, and Attorney General Richard Olney. John noticed too, at the other end of the table, sat August Belmont.

As they took off their overcoats and handed them to the receptionist who showed them upstairs, Lamont noticed them and quickly came over to them.

In a hushed whisper he tried to explain the situation.

"I have explained to the President the outline of what you propose. He still is for the public sale. Right now we are working on the wording of a draft to congress. Please, Mr. Morgan, be seated. He will see you in a short while."

Lamont showed them to three chairs along the wall opposite the table where everyone else was standing about.

They sat in a corner of the room.

They waited.

John pulled out a cigar and looked around the room for matches. Bacon pulled a small box of matches from his waistcoat pocket, lit it and then held it out toward John. John leaned toward it but stopped. He knew that Cleveland was a cigar smoker. John decided to wait and share cigars with Cleveland after a deal was agreed.

"I'll wait," he said to Bacon.

Rolling the unlit cigar back and forth in his fingers, John watched and listened. He did not like being set aside like a messenger waiting for a reply.

But he waited and watched.

Messengers came in and out of the room.

The telephone on the desk rang several times. Cleveland's secretary answered and jotted down notes. He gave the notes to Cleveland to read.

John watched everyone, every move.

Messages came in for Carlisle. He read them with a sour look on his face.

John overheard Carlisle read one of the messages to Cleveland. The amount of gold in the New York Sub-treasury was now down to Nine

Million.

Everyone at the table took the news in silence. No one knew of what to do.

It was then that John spoke up, loud and clear.

"I know of one draft alone for ten million. If that is presented you cannot meet it. It will be all over before three o'clock."

No one spoke for a moment.

The gravity of the situation slowly sunk in. The government of the United States of America will go into default.

Grover Cleveland pushed his chair back and stood up. He walked over and stood looking down at the seated John. Cleveland stood for a moment with his hands in his pockets.

"Do you have anything to suggest?"

John stood up.

"Yes," he said.

It was time.

Quickly he walked over to the table and took a seat. Cleveland followed him, sat down, and then leaned back in his chair.

John talked fast.

In his hand, under the table, he twirled his unlit cigar back and forth as he talked.

There is a drain on gold; government bonds have been advanced several times in the past year but they were only temporary fixes; those who bought government bonds simply borrowed the gold to pay for the bonds and then exchanged the bonds for government notes and then took the government notes to the Treasury and exchanged them for gold. Reusing gold to buy the same gold is not a solution.

When Belmont and I were approached by Assistant Secretary Curtis then we, acting on good faith, and using our international connections, arranged to secure fifty million dollars of new fresh gold from European markets. The mere hint of these negotiations helped stabilize the markets. This, sir, is your solution.

A syndicate of international bankers can provide the Treasury with all the gold they need.

But now, simply for political reasons, because you think you are going behind the back of Congress, you have reneged on these plans and wish to solicit a new bond issue through Congress. This will take too much time and once word that negotiations with us have collapsed the markets will destabilize making the drain more severe and the new bond issue useless.

"This is a financial problem and to let politics dictate a solution is absurd."

John stopped talking for a moment. He wanted all of that to sink in. He watched their faces and, under the table, he continued twirling his unlit cigar around and around in his fingers.

"But there is a solution," he finally said.

President Lincoln was faced with a similar problem during the Civil War; Congress passed an Act in 1862 authorizing Secretary Chase to purchase gold coin with government bonds. If we draft the loan as the purchase of gold coin rather than the sale of government bonds then you do not need the fresh approval of Congress because you already have their approval from the 1862 Act.

"What is this Act?" Cleveland asked.

"Section 3700 of the Revised Statutes," John replied.

"Is that so, Mr. Olney?" Cleveland asked.

"I do not know, I'll go and look it up."

Olney left the room.

"If it is still in force then I believe we have our solution."

"It sounds as if we do."

When Olney returned he held in his hand a huge book of Statutes. He handed it to Cleveland. Cleveland read the passage to himself.

"Is this still in force?"

"I believe it is, sir," Olney replied.

Cleveland read the passage to himself a second time. He handed the book to Carlisle.

"Read it aloud," Cleveland said.

"'Passed on March 17, 1862: An Act to authorize the purchase of coin and for other purposes. The Secretary of the Treasury may purchase coin with any of the bonds or notes of the United States, authorized by law, at such rates and upon such terms as he may deem most advantageous to the public interest.'"

Everyone looked at each other around the room.

Finally, it was Cleveland who spoke: "Well gentlemen, it seems that we may have ourselves the solution."

It broke the tension in the room. Everyone seemed to relax. Cleveland, for the first time that morning, smiled at John.

Cleveland stood up. John, as well, stood up. But before he moved away from the table the secretary sitting next to him pointed to his pants.

"Mr. Morgan, what is that brown powder on your trousers and clothes and all around your chair?"

Everyone looked. There was a brown stain of dust in his lap. It was the cigar he held and twirled in his fingers throughout the meeting.

Without realizing it the cigar had come apart and crushed tobacco was all over his pants. He quickly brushed it away. Cleveland laughed out loud.

"I admit, Mr. Morgan, that things got a bit tense but to crush such a fine cigar is a travesty. Here," he said as he reached for his own box of cigars on his desk, "please, have one of mine."

John, laughing with all of them, accepted.

Cleveland motioned him aside and, as they walked across to the other side of the room, put his hand on John's shoulder.

"We will work out all the details but what guarantee do we have that if we adopt this plan, gold will not continue to be shipped abroad and while we are getting it in, it will go out, so that we will not reach our goal? Will you guarantee that this will not happen?"

John answered instantly.

"Yes, sir, I will guarantee it during the life of the syndicate, and that means until the contract has been concluded and the goal has been reached."

Cleveland stared into John's eyes for a moment, still holding his hand to John's shoulder. There was a flicker across his face.

"Thank you," he said.

Cleveland then turned and returned to the others at the other side of the room.

Robert Bacon leaned in toward John and whispered to him.

"You can't make that promise. You don't control the entire gold market."

"I know," John whispered back.

"How can you do that, sir?"

"I have no idea."

John, sitting at his desk in his hotel room, naked feet on the rug, continued to play his last round of cards. He had been thinking back a lot lately, especially today. He usually was thinking ahead, thinking about tomorrow and what was to come. But lately, it was what had already come, where he had been. It was like a summing up, a collection of what he was and what he had done with his life. The Egyptians do that, when they cross over. All that they have done is put into a weight balance, and your life is measured. John turned over another card.

It was the King of Diamonds.

December 12, 1900.

It all began, of all unlikely places, at a dinner party. There was a speech.

And then the world changed.

It was a cold December 12, 1900.

It was being held in the dining room of the elegant University Club on Fifth Avenue. When John was taken to his seat he found that he was at the head table, sitting to the right of the guest of honor, Charles Michael Schwab, the new president of Carnegie Steel Company, the largest steel manufacturer in the United States. J. Edward Simmons, President of the Fourth National Bank of New York, and prior president of the New York Stock Exchange, as well as the host of the dinner party, sat to the left of Schwab.

When John approached Simmons stood and held out his hand.

"Why Mr. Morgan, how good of you to come."

"I thank you for the invitation."

"You know Mr. Schwab?"

"Yes," they both said as he stood to shake John's hand. John nodded and smiled toward Charles Stewart Smith, founder of the Fifth Avenue National Bank, who sat next to Simmons.

"It looks like you have quite a turn out," John said as he looked around at all of the people.

"A good eighty or ninety have come."

It seemed like an exclusive who was who of New York. He saw Edward Harriman talking with August Belmont, the Rothschild representative, and at one table sat Henry Rogers, vice president of Standard Oil, James Stillman, president of National City Bank, and Chauncey Depew from the Vanderbilt family. Jacob Schiff of Kuhn, Loeb and Company stood in the corner laughing at a joke with Right Reverend Henry Potter, Bishop of New York, and the Right Reverend George Worthington, Bishop of Nebraska.

"Well then," John said as he pulled out his chair and sat down.

Schwab smiled a nervous smile.

"I was disappointed that I did not hear from you when I contacted your office a month ago," John said.

"Yes, I am sorry about that. I was tending to a lot of different matters at the time and could not come."

"I wanted to talk with you about the new Tube plant that is rumored you are building at Conneaut."

"Yes, I actually spoke with Charles Steele and he mentioned that."

"Are you going forward with the project?"

"Well, we are investigating the possibility."

"I hear your board authorized the purchase of the land just yesterday."

Charles was a little taken aback.

"You know of this?"

"I suggest that we will get along much better if you do not be coy with me, sir."

Charles took a deep breath before he replied.

"Mr. Morgan, Carnegie is indeed going forward with the Tube plant at Conneaut." He held his gaze steady.

John could see something in his eyes. He was a torn man. Something was amiss.

Then Charles added: "And with others as well."

It was a remarkable statement. Schwab worked for Carnegie, why would he be telling John this?

"You do know," John continued, "that Carnegie will be directly competing with my National Tube Works."

"Yes, I think he is well aware of this."

"And he is in talks with Gould to lay a competing rail line to the Pennsylvania. That will trigger a deadly rate war. I have spent my entire life trying to convince the railroads to all avoid such devastating activity; it serves no one and ends up being wasteful to everyone."

"Yes, sir; this I know."

Again Charles held his gaze steady. There seemed to be something more that he wanted to say. Something was going on, John thought. He did not quite understand what it was.

At that point Simmons stood and in a louder than normal voice called out "Mr. Carnegie, are you off then?"

Charles Schwab stood as Andrew Carnegie came to the table. Short, burley, with full white whiskers and a black derby hat, Carnegie placed his hand on John's back as he leaned in. In his Scottish accent he begged for forgiveness since he had to leave for another engagement at the Pennsylvania Society to speak on Industrial Pennsylvania.

"You will miss quite a feast," Simmons said.

"Oh I am sure that I will but, alas."

As he spoke waiters came to the table with the first course of the meal: bowls of Green-turtle soup.

"Oh my, look at that, and the aroma. Now I must hurry off or else I will never leave. Mr. Morgan," he said as he patted John on the back, "a very good day to you."

"And to you as well," John replied.

Carnegie nodded toward Simmons while pointing to Schwab: "And honor to whom honor is due."

"Well gentlemen," Simmons announced to the table at large, "shall we begin?"

The dinner was brought out in wave after wave of courses. After the Green-turtle soup came a mousse of bass, with cucumbers; breast of guinea, with Madeira sauce; oyster crabs with mushrooms; saddle of lamb, served with potatoes and French peas; rum sherbet; Philadelphia terrapin; canvasback duck, with currant jelly; celery salad; ice cream and cake, fruits and coffee. And dashing back and forth came the waiters pouring bottles of wine: Chablis, Bernkasteler, Rauentaler Berg, Chateau Mouton, Chambertin and Pommery.

As he ate John enjoyed the enormous flower arrangement as a centerpiece to the table. The scent of each flower he found wonderfully rich and sweet. And John could hear the soft chamber music floating through the room intermingling with the chattering voices of the well pleased crowd. As he twisted around in his chair he could see the players off to one corner of the dining room.

No one talked of business while they ate. They were all too busy.

J. Edward Simmons stood up at the small podium as the guests sipped their coffee or, for some, brandy. He told of a trip he and Charles Stewart Smith had made to Pittsburgh and how hospitable Charles Schwab had been to them with dinner, lodgings, and hours of his time.

"He is a good man of a good heart," Simmons said.

Many of the crowd clapped. One tapped his fork against a glass to show his approval.

And so, Simmons went on to say, that is why we are all gathered here today, to reply in kind to his open hospitality. Well known within his circle of the steel industry, he may not be as well known outside of that circle.

"We hope, this evening, to help remedy that. And so, gentlemen, I have asked Mr. Schwab to gives us a small speech to honor this occasion."

There was a round of applause as Charles, obviously a bit shy before so many distinguished guests, rose and walked up to the podium. Simmons gave him a pat on the back and returned to his seat.

From the podium Charles began.

Gentlemen, I promise to be short. Mr. Simmons asked me to speak only fifteen or twenty minutes because, as he put it, 'these are old men and they have to go home early.'

There was a round of muffled laughter.

Those are his words, gentlemen, not mine.

John pulled a cigar out of his waistcoat pocket.

I am going to talk about steel because I can not talk about anything else, because I do not know anything else.

John was fumbling for a box of matches in his pocket when Simmons, smiling, leaned in toward him. John stopped and leaned in. Simmons whispered: he starts every speech the same.

John nodded and then sat back, his unlit cigar in his fingers.

Schwab continued.

There are great opportunities alive in the current situation that the steel industry finds itself. Over the years the industry has lowered its production costs, the actual cost of processing steel from both a metallurgical and a mechanical point of view, to where I feel it can go no lower.

But we can cut our costs further because we can cut our costs in distribution. Today manufacturers now think in terms of markets, markets in which they limit production in order to increase their prices and thus make profits. But this hurts not only the consumer but also opens the door for cut throat competition as other manufacturers try to enter the market. As manufacturers come and go it hurts investors, bond holders, customers, and creates instability across the industry.

John, sitting at his seat, holding in his hand his unlit cigar, nodded. It was the same story in the railroads and he had spent his life trying to solve that problem.

"I have a new vision, a new and better possibility," Schwab said, seemingly looking in John's direction as he spoke.

Imagine a huge firm, or a collection of mutually integrated companies, with many different plants, but with plant specialization, in other words each plant specializing in a single product. Instead of a plant tooling for one product and then retooling to produce another product, you have one plant producing one product, tooling only once. Instead of many different companies making the same product, with the overlapping costs of labor, the sales force, the costs of overlapping equipment, tooling and retooling, imagine if they all could join and have a single plant produce a single product, you have as many plants as you have products.

And further, place the plants producing a particular product in the location where that particular product is used. If these plants were located in the same areas where their products were sold then delivery charges to customers could be reduced. Such a firm could consolidate

164

their sales forces, further reducing costs. It would reduce cross hauling, where now one firm moves products from A to B while a different firm moves products from B to A.

If the steel industry were made as efficient as possible, and if its plants were specialized and integrated and centrally managed, and if its leaders were willing to cooperate for long range mutual growth, then an ever widening market for steel could be created. New uses for steel could be found, new and improved methods of production could be invented, and record profits could be attained, shared by all in the industry. Both the producers and the consumers would benefit: producers would make greater profits on their products, while consumers would pay less for them, all because of an increased efficiency and specialization.

There would be cooperation for the benefit of all rather than repeated ruinous industrial wars to the detriment of all. We, gentlemen, with foresight and cooperation, can create an orderly and disciplined industry for the benefit of the industry rather than the wasteful and crazy warfare that now ruins everything, and hurts everyone.

Thank You.

As he started toward his chair there was a loud applause from the audience.

John could barely move. He set his unlit cigar down upon the tablecloth and clapped.

Schwab had it. The perfect solution, it was the perfect solution for the railroads and now it could work as the perfect solution for the steel industry: or any industry.

John stood with the others as they gave Schwab a standing ovation.

When Schwab was free John instantly pulled him over to a recessed window and they sat on the cushions, their feet dangling down. John wanted to know more. How would it be done? Who could integrate with whom?

Time passed but they did not notice.

It was night, well past nine o'clock at night, when the carriage pulled up in front of Morgan's home. From inside the carriage Charles Schwab peered out the window and looked up at the tall brownstone building. Snow was falling coating the street white. He had never seen the home of the great J. P. Morgan. It seems less, somehow, from what he was expecting. John W. Gates, also in the back of the carriage, threw the butt of his cigar out the window.

"Well," he said. "Here we are."

Schwab came by train from Philadelphia and he and Gates had dinner together.

It was several days after his University Club speech that he received a call from Gates. Morgan wanted to meet; when can you come by his office?

Schwab said no, there was no way he could meet in Morgan's office. How could he meet with Morgan behind Carnegie's back? Frick met with outside investors behind Carnegie's back and it helped lead to a terrible split between them.

Schwab tried to explain the situation to Gates. He did not want to be disloyal to Carnegie. Schwab was the newly elected President of Carnegie Steel and he did not want to lose that.

Schwab remembered vividly when he had done something that made Carnegie furious and he was sure he was going to be fired. They were outside, it was a bright sunny day, and Carnegie climbed into his carriage. Schwab closed the carriage door, not knowing what he should say if anything, and Carnegie leaned his head out of the window. In very fierce and piercing words he said: 'You can make as many mistakes as you like, but don't make the same one twice.'

Was he making the same mistake as Frick?

But yet they had to meet. He had to talk with Morgan, he had to convince Morgan.

Well, then, Gates surmised, what if on a particular day you were at the Bellevue Hotel in Philadelphia, I hear they have an excellent beef steak, and you happen to run into Morgan there, also dining on the excellent beef steak, surely you would want to pay your regards?

"I suppose my schedule could be arranged so that I can sample the fine food at the Bellevue Hotel," Schwab replied.

But when he arrived at the hotel there was a message for him from Gates. Morgan was taken ill and could not make it, could they reschedule?

Schwab was desperate. He called Gates. Schwab convinced himself to come to New York. Gates said that the two of them could dine and then go over to Morgan's house. Schwab agreed and, nervous and a little frightened, he boarded the next train.

In recent years there were a greater and greater number of mergers and consolidations in the steel industry. Bill and Jim Moore had consolidated four different larger firms; John Gates formed American Steel and Wire Company, Morgan himself created three combinations himself. Most of these concerns made finished products, but there were now three large firms who supplied the raw steel. The largest, by far, was

166

Carnegie Steel; but Morgan interests owned the second largest, Federal Steel Company, and the Moore interests owned the third, the National Steel Company. Carnegie was not alone any more.

From the standpoint of the finished product producers it made sense to move into raw steel production, and even ownership of the iron ore fields and mines themselves. Otherwise they would be completely dependent upon the whim of Carnegie. But this cut into Carnegie's core business.

So from the standpoint of Carnegie he could move into the business of finished steel products, in competition directly with the newly consolidated companies.

The resulting competitive war would be deadly.

It had already begun. Gates and the Moore Brothers, and even Morgan, had all cut their orders from Carnegie.

It was Morgan himself who answered the door. He was dressed casually, his face and in particular his nose were flaming red.

It was just a cold, he said. But it was bad enough that he did not want to risk going outside in this snow.

Yes, Schwab replied. I understand.

"Well," John said showing the way with the sweep of his hand. "Shall we?"

Inside the parlor sat Roger Bacon and George Perkins.

John's chair was closest to the fire.

When everyone was comfortably seated John began the discussion.

Schwab seemed very nervous.

"I do not necessarily want to buy Carnegie out," John explained. "I just want to stop him from expanding into fabricated goods, and definitely I want to stop him from going into railroads. He will demoralize railroads like he has demoralized steel."

"But he will expand unless you buy him out. You and everyone else pose a threat that he cannot let pass. You don't understand him like I do. He will fight all of you out of spite and the need to win until all of you are bankrupt. It will plunge the steel industry into a war that will be disastrous to some of the weaker companies and costly and damaging to the strongest."

"Surely he can see reason in a negotiated settlement," Robert Bacon added.

"You do not understand," Charles desperately said.

He looked at John sitting in the chair opposite him. "You do not understand," he repeated in a much lower voice.

Charles closed his eyes and sat for a moment taking in a long deep breath. He remembered it well. Schwab was sitting on the stone wall down in the grasslands. It was a windy day. He was visiting Andrew at his castle in Scotland, the Skibo Castle. Andrew stood on the grass with his right foot resting on the top of the stone wall with his elbows resting on his leg. He was staring off across the grounds. Directly in front of him Schwab could see the huge magnificent castle.

They had been discussing the plant at Conneaut, the new Tube plant Carnegie wanted to build; the location, the costs, and the new advanced equipment.

"You will be going directly against Morgan. You have never done that."

"Yes, I know," Andrew replied.

Charles could not take his eyes off of the shining white castle. If it were he who owned it why would he want to leave it?

"Charles," Andrew finally said after a long pause.

Schwab turned to look up at him. From where he sat the sun was directly behind Andrew. It made him glow.

"How much cheaper, Charlie, can you make tubes than the National Company?"

How could you be asking this, how can you be thinking of doing this; to Schwab it was suicide.

"Perhaps ten dollars a ton."

Andrew nodded as he once again stared off across the grounds.

"Go on and build the plant. Move into the railroad as we discussed, negotiate with Gould."

Charles watched as several birds soared above the castle. You could lose all of this, he thought to himself. You could lose all of this, and for what? How can I tell you this and not be seen as a traitor?

"Are you quite sure?" Charles asked.

"My boy, it was Cardinal Richelieu who said 'First, by all means conciliate, failing that, all means to crush.'"

The wind tugged at his jacket. Andrew placed his hand on Charles's shoulder.

"There is no use in going halfway across a stream," Andrew said.

John watched Charles very closely. There was something amiss and he began to suspect that he knew what it was.

"Charles, tell me. Are you breaking with Carnegie?"

"No sir. I will stand with him and serve him no matter the outcome."

"And he knows nothing of you being here?"

"No. And he may very well have my job if he knew."

"Then why are you here?"

"I hope to do what is best for him. I hope to do for him what he would do for himself if he only let himself see the whole picture."

"You do not agree with his expanding into finished goods?"

"No, because of the war that it would bring."

"But, as you say, what other choice is there for him?"

"Open warfare is not inevitable. The current situation is such that there is a great opportunity for anyone to take action who is concerned with maintaining industrial stability."

"And what is that action?"

"Andrew is tired and he wants to retire. His wife wants him to retire. He has said on many occasions that he wants to spend the rest of his life in doing charity. This could potentially destroy that chance."

"And you propose?"

"Let him retire. Let him retire now while he is at the top of his achievement. Buy Carnegie Steel and with that as the core form the consolidated Steel Company that I outlined in my speech of the other day."

John looked back and forth at the others in the room.

"It is the perfect answer for him," Charles continued, "and it is the perfect answer for you."

John had to blow his nose. Everyone waited.

"I must admit," he said finally. "It does have great appeal."

Charles smiled.

"It is up to you, sir."

"Me?"

"You are the only one who can do it."

John thought about it, staring at the fire.

Charles pulled out a sheet of paper from his jacket.

"I have drawn up a list of companies I think should be included, and those who should not because of duplication. I've given not their book value but rather what I feel is their potential future value."

John nodded to Bacon who stood up and took the list from him.

John narrowed his eyes as he watched Charles.

"If Andy wants to sell, I'll buy. Go and find out his price."

Schwab did not know exactly how to approach Andrew about the deal. Would he take to the idea or would he be furious that Schwab was talking with Morgan without his consent? Andrew could fire him on the spot. And if he did there was no turning back. When Andrew made a decision like that he never turned back.

But the coming war had to be stopped. Everyone would lose. Would Andrew throw away all that he had just to fight to the death?

Schwab went to see Andrew's wife, Louise. She was at their new home directing the painters. It was raining. There were only unfinished wooden floors throughout the house, wet now from the boots of the workmen walking in and out. When Schwab came in to the room it was a mess with ladders and scaffolding along the walls and paint splattered drop cloths carpeting the floor. Louise stood mid room staring up at the molding when Charles entered.

"Louise," he said.

"Oh; Charles. Please forgive this hideous mess. Can you believe it? They were actually going to paint this room entirely the wrong color."

"Really?"

"Yes. I cannot believe it. Must I supervise every last detail myself?"

She laughed and shook her head.

"But enough of this, here," she said as she helped to pull drop cloths from two covered chairs. "Please, have a seat."

The two of them sat down, alone in the large otherwise unfurnished room.

"You said you had a private matter to discuss with me."

"Yes," he said. "Thank you for your time."

She smiled: "Well then?"

Charles took a deep breath before he began. He explained the speech, the call from Gates, the meeting in New York at Morgan's house, the discussion of buying Carnegie Steel.

"Well, you have been quite busy, I must say."

"But you see, Louise, Andrew knows nothing about this."

"Oh, I see," she said.

"I have come for your advice on how best to approach him; or even if I should approach him at all."

"Yes, I see," she said, thinking, staring off.

"I believe that he wants to sell and I am trying to arrange that for him, but lately his moves seem to point in the opposite direction. I do not think that an open war with Morgan and the Moore brothers and John Gates is really in his best interest."

She sat in quiet thought for a moment.

There was the sound of banging hammers from some other room in

170

the house. There was sawing of wood. From the open space where a window was yet to be installed the moist feel of the rain outside blew into the room.

"My Andy is a very proud man, Mr. Schwab."

Charles nodded in agreement.

"And his pride is his work, as it is with most men. All of his drive and creative energy has been for so long poured into his work. It will be very hard for him to let go."

Charles nodded in agreement.

"But let go he must."

"He has spoken of it often enough. But am I reading him wrong?"

"No," she quickly said. "No, you are not reading him wrong. But, you see, he still has very mixed feelings about it all."

"That is why I am afraid to approach him."

"No, Charles. You must. Provide him with the way. He does not want to do the details for at each step of the way the painful conflict in him will show itself. Provide the solution for him and I think he will be grateful to you."

"But how do I present it to him?"

"Ah, yes. The how is a bit of a problem."

They listened to the hammering from the other room.

"Golf, Mr. Schwab."

"Golf?"

"Yes, he has been playing golf for only a short time and he loves it. It relaxes him and pleases him; as a matter of fact he calls it 'Dr. Golf.' He is in the best of spirits after a game of golf."

"All right."

"Meet him tomorrow at Saint Andrews Golf Course. He owns a small cottage there on the green. Play golf and then have a nice dinner in the cottage. There is where you present it to him."

Charles smiled and nodded. "Thank you, you have been a great help."

"Oh but Mr. Schwab," she carefully added, letting her words float through the air, "he is in the best of moods when he wins the game, if you know what I mean."

Charles nodded in agreement.

Louise looked around the room.

"Retirement. It will give our new house a whole new meaning."

The next day Schwab and Carnegie played golf. It sprinkled a little but that did not stop Andrew. A little bit of rain meant nothing. On one of the holes when Andrew shot a long straight drive right to the green he laughed out loud.

"Beat that Charlie," he shouted out.

Charles held his club.

"Sir, you have said that at some point you wanted to retire from business and spend the rest of your life giving to charity."

"Yes. A man should only work half of his life making money and then spend the last half of his life giving it away."

"That still is your goal?"

"Yes."

"But, if I may be so bold sir, you are sixty five. When does it end?"

Andrew stared at Charles for a long time. He wiped his wet beard with his hand and pulled down on his woolen cap. Andrew turned to stare down toward the green. He stood for a long time before he spoke.

"You are quite right, of course. When is enough enough?" Andrew asked in a low slow whisper.

You could hear the splatter of rain on the grass. Charles thought that now was the moment.

"I do not think we should be moving in the direction we are going. Even if you win a war against Morgan and the others it will cost you dearly, both in your wealth and in your time."

"Do you suggest that I just give up and let them trample all over me? That's not in my nature, boy."

"I know that sir. But when is enough enough? Would it not be a greater victory to keep all that you have and live the dream you have envisioned for yourself? What greater victory can there be but that you did what you set out to do?"

Andrew turned toward Charles.

Charles spoke.

"Time is no man's friend. You cannot fight against time, no matter who you are. If you want to do what you have always wanted to do then you have to do it. Now is the time, not when it is too late."

"Why do you have to be so damn right all of the time?"

Charles shrugged his shoulders. The moment had passed. He guessed it right.

Charles placed his golf ball onto a tee and stood over it with his club.

"But how?" Andrew asked.

"I have a plan."

"Somehow I thought that you would."

The rain, a long light drizzle, began to increase.

"I thought I might go over it with you over dinner."

"Why not now?"

Charles looked up at the sky. "Perhaps we should finish the game first and get to a warm dry fire."

"Give me a hors d'oeuvre."

"Morgan asked me to find out if you really wished to retire from business; if so he thinks he can arrange it."

"Well, if anyone can arrange it Morgan is the one who can."

The two of them talked at the cottage over dinner. Schwab laid out the over all plan. Morgan wanted to know what Carnegie's price was.

Andrew thought about it. He picked up a short stubby pencil and wrote things down on a piece of paper. Thinking, figuring. Then, finally, he cut the piece of paper in half and on the fresh piece wrote it out with the same short stubby pencil:

Carnegie Company bonds to be exchanged at par for bonds in the new company:
$160,000,000
Each $1,000 Carnegie Company share to be exchanged for a $1,500 share in the new concern:
$240,000,000
Profits for the past and coming year (estimated):
$80,000,000
Total:
$480,000,000

Andrew handed Charles the half piece of paper. Charles read it in silence.

"What do you think?"

"More than we offered Rockefeller."

"That was then, not now. The environment is different now. And I want half in bonds. I want to be a creditor, not an investor; that way if the concern fails I can take it back over and run it myself."

"Do you think it possible that Morgan will fail?"

Andrew paused, and then: "No."

Charles could feel the warmth of the fireplace against his back. He could hear the rain outside. When he glanced over Andrew was watching the fire, lost in thought.

"Do you have any regrets sir?"

Andrew drew in a long and deep breath as he crossed his arms across his chest and sat back in his chair.

"Of course there are regrets, must be, changes are all devilish, but must come. We ought to have perpetual youth, an option not to leave this Heaven below until we wish to."

"You will be free for the first time in your life; truly free."

"Aye, that I will be. And there is pleasure in knowing that."

Andrew pointed toward a painting on the wall above the fireplace. "Do you know the man?"

Charles turned in his chair and looked up. It was a painting of Shakespeare. "A little bit, sir."

"You need to read him more. I have been there often, at his home, but I am awed into silence as I approach the church; and when I stand beside the ashes of Shakespeare I cannot repress stern, gloomy thoughts, and ask why so potent a force is now but a little dust. The inexplicable waste of nature, a million born that one may live, seems nothing compared to this——the brain of a god doing its work one day and food for worms the next."

The crackle of the fire and the rain on the roof was all that could be heard.

"Well," Charles meekly said, "let us hope for a brighter tomorrow."

James brought Charles Schwab into Morgan's office. John sat behind his desk; Robert Bacon sat in the chair across from him.

"Mr. Schwab, good of you to come. You come with news?"

Charles stepped over to the desk.

"I have seen Carnegie."

"And does he offer a price?"

Charles nodded as he pulled out the half piece of paper from his briefcase. He held the paper out so that John could read it. John pulled up his reading glasses and leaned forward.

He stared at the paper for a full minute.

Then John sat back in his chair and looked up at Charles.

"I accept," he said.

The deal was done. Now all that remained was to put it together. After Charles left John sent Bacon to see Judge Elbert Gary, president of Federal Steel Company.

"Morgan wants to know if there is anything practical, from a business standpoint, in buying out Carnegie."

"Why yes, absolutely," Gary answered almost immediately, but then, after a pause, asked: "Can it be done?"

"Yes," Bacon replied. "Schwab brought us a proposition," Bacon said as he pulled out the piece of paper, "and Morgan wants to know what you think."

"Let me have a look and I'll get back to him tomorrow morning."

The next morning Gary walked into Morgan's office. John looked up and smiled. He pointed to the chair opposite him.

"Sit. Now, how should we start?"

"With Federal Steel as the core around which we attach all the others."

"Will the board agree to that?"

"I've already talked with them: Porter, Rogers, Mills, Ream, Thayer and Field."

"And?"

"The general answer was that if you think you can do it then they are for it."

John sat back and tapped his desk with his left fingers, tapping tapping. "Good," he mumbled, "good, good."

"And who are the other companies?" John asked.

"The same list that Schwab gave you originally. I totally concur with his judgments."

"You need to set up shop right here. I'll put you and a staff up in the conference room. Until this deal is done you will work here."

"Okay."

Then John stared directly at Gary.

"Now, there's one thing I want understood; if I go into this you are to go with me, not only as my lawyer but as my friend, that is, you are to stand by me."

A bit surprised, Gary nodded. Of course.

John had known Judge Elbert Gary for awhile. After graduating from Union College of Law in Chicago at nineteen he worked with his Uncle, Colonel Henry Vallette. He worked as a Superior Court law clerk in Chicago for a few years but then opened his own little practice in an office above a Madison Street restaurant.

He gained a reputation as being quiet, meticulously accurate, painstakingly honest, and gave up smoking cigars when his mother complained about the smell when she kissed him. For eight years, from

1882 to 1890 he served in Wheaton as a judge of Du Page County, organized a bank, and then served as the town mayor.

John first met him when he was pulled in and consulted on a railroad deal in the state of Illinois. When presented with the situation Gary simply shook his head.

"I do not think you can do that legally, Mr. Morgan."

John turned to him.

"Well," he began, speaking very slowly, "I don't know as I want a lawyer to tell me what I cannot do. I hire him to tell me how to do what I want to do."

Gary felt the scorch of John's stare.

There was a brief pause.

"Very well, tell me your purpose and I will see what can be done."

John explained what he wanted the outcome to be. Gary thought about it for a moment before he replied.

"There is a legal way to reach that result."

"Yes?"

"Yes," Gary nodded now that he had yet another minute to think about it.

John took note.

In December of 1892 John W. Gates, of barbed wire fame, hired Gary to help build a consolidated company joining together a group of barbed wire manufacturers. Gary worked for a week with all of the different company owners until he finally patched together a deal. The combination of the Lambert and Bishop Wire Fence Company, the Saint Louis Wire Company, the Braddock Wire Company, the Iowa Barb Wire Company, the Baker Wire Mill, and of course John W. Gates, all became the Consolidated Steel and Wire Company with John W. Gates as President.

Next Gates approached Gary in 1897 because now he wanted to merger and consolidate an even larger combination incorporating not only barbwire manufacturers but steel manufacturers as well. Gary negotiated again with all of the potential partners but he felt that they needed substantial underwriting to finance the enterprise. They loaded into a railroad car and went to New York to see Morgan.

While they all stayed at the Waldorf-Astoria Gary met with Charles Coster at Morgan's office to work out the details. Coster suggested that Morgan take the deal and Morgan said that he would consider it if the various elements all came up with a workable plan.

Coster spent hours with Gary carefully working out the details of the plan. Gates and others spent their time gambling and drinking at the hotel.

Coster took notice and reported back to John. Gary is a man of talent and a man to be trusted.

Gates is otherwise. There is a reason he is called 'Bet-a-Million' Gates. His gambling knows no bounds.

John took note.

In the news the battleship Maine was blown up in Havana Harbor. The United States moved toward war with Spain.

Morgan announced that he was not pleased with the annual reports of some of the companies. And in the current atmosphere he could not fund the enterprise at this time.

At the hotel several of the members backed out as well. They were tired of it, and if Morgan did not want to do it then they were going to back out as well.

To the few who remained Gates threw up his hands.

"The jig is up," Gates said. "There's nothing to do but go home."

The next day in a driving rain they boarded a Chicago bound train. Gary sat separate, by a window, reading a book. The others sat chomping their cigars and drinking their wine. They took turns spitting at the spittoon betting on who could make it further and further away. When Gary mentioned the spit on the floor Gates laughed and mumbled something about giving the porter something to do.

Gary watched as the landscape went by, and tried to read his book.

Gates noticed that the rain on the windows raced each other down the window glass.

"Hey Ellwood, bet you a thousand dollars this here drop will beat that drop down the window."

Ellwood, leaning across him said "You're on."

The rain drops raced and Gates won.

"Double or nothing on those two," Ellwood shouted.

"You're on," Gates replied, laughing out loud.

Gary watched as the landscape went by, and tried to read his book.

Outside of an hour, on the water drop bets, Ellwood was in debt to Gates for ten thousand dollars.

"Damn," Ellwood said, swaying in the walkway of the cabin, "I'm tired of this."

Bored, Gates talked about the deal, lost opportunity, and Morgan.

"Good old Livernose," he began but had to stop when the others began laughing. "Good old Livernose was just scared. The big bad banker was just scared."

"I hear that he just doesn't like us," Ellwood sneered. "Thinks we'd upset the applecart. Wants us Westerners to stay out of Wall Street. Says we're too wild."

"Wild?" snapped Gates. "This is the safest, biggest proposition ever offered to old Livernose and he thinks it's too wild? It could be the start of something really big, I mean really big. If Morgan can't take it then who can? Us?"

They sat silent for awhile. Puffing their cigars and blowing smoke rings into the air they were all quiet.

Gary tried to close his eyes.

But then finally Ellwood spoke up.

"Well, why not us?"

"What's that?"

"Why don't we just do it? The hell with those who dropped out, let's us join our companies."

Lambert, off in a corner, called in: "I'm for that, I'm in."

Gates sat up. "Why not us, alone? When it works it's more for us, right?"

Gates stood up and walked over to Gary.

"Can it be done without Morgan?"

Gary shrugged his shoulders.

"Maybe."

Four weeks later Gary had worked out the details. He consolidated fourteen different plants and on March 18, 1898 the American Steel and Wire Company was formed, with John W. Gates as President.

John took note.

Illinois Steel called Gary for advice. Several of the directors, H. H. Porter, Robert Bacon of J. P. Morgan, H. H. Rogers of Standard Oil Company, and Governor Flower from New York, called on him to help consolidate with several other companies a larger Steel company. Gates was on the board of directors but he knew nothing of this.

But they laid down the law.

Porter told him that "I will have nothing to do with this if John Gates is part of the deal."

And John told him that "I will go with you, Judge Gary, but Gates is out. I don't think property is safe in his hands."

Gary argued that Gates had brought him into all of this and he had an obligation to him for that, and he too was on the board.

But John shook his head no.

"If Gates is in then I am out."

Gary agreed and in four months he help created Federal Steel Company. Gates was asked to step down from the board.

In September, as Gary was heading for the train back to Chicago, he was called into John's office. He protested that he was late for his train. Porter and Bacon were there waiting with John.

It was John who started the conversation.

"Judge Gary, you have put this together in a very good shape. We are all very well pleased. Now you must be president."

Gary was shocked. It was not what he expected.

"I couldn't think of it"

"Why not"

"Why Mr. Morgan, I have a law practice with $75,000 a year and I cannot leave it."

"We will take care of that. We must make it worth your while."

Gary was at a loss for words.

"But I must think it over."

"No, we want to know right now."

"Now? But I have a train to catch. But who are the directors to be?"

"You can select your directors, name the executive committee, choose your officers, and fix your salary."

Gary had to sit down. He could not believe what he was hearing. He had to think this over.

"I need, I don't know, maybe a week to think it over."

"No," John barked. "I will give you twenty four hours. Call me from your home. Now, have a safe journey."

But Elbert Gary had no choice. He took the position.

He now worked for John.

Now all of the principals involved with the Carnegie purchase and the consolidation of the companies Schwab had suggested filed into the conference room at J. P. Morgan and Company and talked with Elbert Gary, chief council for the formation of the enterprise.

All details were working out. Each agreed to the figures offered by Gary and John and one by one the consolidation was being formed.

All, that is, except for American Steel and Wire Company: John W. Gates.

He said no. He had been there from the beginning; he knew the intimate details of the plan because he had helped put it together. He wanted more money for his firm, a lot more.

He showed up at the office with his fellow partners William Edenborn and Max Pam. He wanted to be placed on the board of directors of the new company. They were sitting around the conference table when John walked in. He walked straight over to where Gates sat and placed both of his hands on the table and leaned in close to Gates.

"Mr. Gates," he began purposefully, "the men who are organizing this corporation have decided to offer you and your friends a price for your interest in the American Steel and Wire Company. You have that figure."

"I do not feel that it is nearly enough."

"You may accept it or reject it, as you see fit."

"What about the board of directors?"

"It will be impossible for you to enter the directors of this corporation or to take active part in the management of the company."

"Yeah, why is that?"

John glared at him.

"You have made your reputation, Mr. Gates. We are not responsible for it."

"My reputation is as good as yours," Gates almost shouted back.

John breathed heavily. He smiled.

"It is a reputation that we do not wish to be a part of."

"Yeah, so what's wrong with taking a bet here and there? At least I don't have a string of female travel companions like some people we know."

John did not say a word.

William Edenborn placed his hand on Gate's arm, shaking his head.

John stood up straight and walked out of the room. In the hall he stopped Gary.

"I'm through, I cannot settle with him. I have seen their kind all my life, in Drew, in Fisk, in Gould, I am sick of them. I never want to deal with their kind again."

"I'll talk with them."

Morgan walked back to his office. Gary walked into the conference room.

"Mr. Morgan sent me in to trade with you. Luckily, I know the wire game as well as you do."

"And who was it got you in all this?" Gates asked him.

Gary ignored the question.

"You have been offered all your property is worth, and it is all you are going to get."

180

The afternoon passed. They argued. Gates was adamant. He was there from the beginning, he wanted his due.

It was four o'clock when John sent James in to tell Gary that he was leaving for the day. Gary told James to ask John to stay a bit longer.

Time passed. Nothing.

It was five o'clock when James returned. John wanted to leave for the day. No, tell him to wait just a bit longer.

Time passed. Nothing.

Finally Gary excused himself for a moment. He ran into John's office. He told him what he wanted him to do. John agreed. Gary returned to the conference room.

Gates again refused to change.

Then the door suddenly banged opened. All eyes turned to John as he walked in, a lit cigar in his mouth with smoke trailing behind. He wore his black overcoat and black top hat that made him seem larger than he was.

"Gentlemen," John loudly barked as he took the cigar from his mouth with one hand and brought his fist down onto the table with the other. He leaned in toward the three of them. He focused on Edenborn.

"I am going to leave this building in ten minutes."

He paused.

"If by that time you have not accepted our offer, the matter will be closed. We will build our own wire plant."

Morgan stood back up, put his cigar back into his mouth, and then he turned and walked out of the room and disappeared down the hallway.

The three of them sat silently.

Finally Gates raised his eyebrow and turned to Edenborn.

"Well boys, I don't know whether the old man means it or not."

"I can assure you he does," Gary carefully pointed out. Gary pulled out his pocket watch, looked at the dial, and then snapped the lid closed.

Gary crossed his arms.

"Then," Gates finally said, "I guess we will have to give up."

Gary opened the door and called for John. After a moment John entered, standing near the entrance.

"The gentlemen have accepted your proposition."

John stared at each one and asked "Is that right?"

Each one, one by one, Gates being last, answered yes.

"Good. Now, gentlemen, let's all go home."

John was in his office when Francis Stetson, the lawyer, came into his office. He seemed upset.

"Sir, we are drawing up the papers but we do not have anything signed by Mr. Carnegie."

"Yes."

"Not even a proposal or letter of intent."

"Yes?"

"But sir, we have nothing to hold him to it if he changes his mind."

"But he won't change his mind. He gave his word; he won't go back on it."

"But what if he drops dead, we have nothing to hold against the estate."

"All right, so what do you propose?"

"Since neither of you two has met over this matter perhaps you could arrange a meeting and we could have him sign all of the relevant documents then."

John nodded.

He telephoned Carnegie. Perhaps he could come down to the office for a little talk and sign some things to make the lawyers happy.

"Mr. Morgan," Andrew answered, "it is just about as far from Wall Street to Fifty First as it is from Fifty First to Wall Street. I shall be delighted to see you here at any time. I understand I am a retired man now."

John hung up the phone and laughed.

When he arrived at Carnegie's house Andrew's personal secretary, James Bertram, showed John into the study. James looked down at his watch when they entered.

John and Andrew talked, sitting on two chairs by the window. John pulled out the proposal from his satchel.

"Lawyers seem to think we need this signed."

"I suppose I could sign something," Andrew replied.

"But Mr. Morgan, were you not worried, what if I renege on the deal?"

"You gave your word so I knew that you would not."

Andrew laughed. "Do you remember, years ago, I had an interest in a transaction your father wanted to buy from me. You came to me and asked what I would take. So I figured that my last statement showed fifty thousand already in my account and with accumulation since then, I said I'd take sixty thousand. So next day you came back with two checks, one for sixty thousand and another for ten thousand. 'Mr. Carnegie,' you said. 'You were mistaken. You sold out for ten thousand dollars less than the statement showed to your credit, and the additional ten makes seventy.' I handed you back the ten thousand dollar check and said 'Well, that is something worthy of you. Will you please accept these ten thousand with my best wishes?' But then you did not take it and said 'No, thank you. I cannot do that.'"

They both laughed.

"Do you remember it?"

"Honestly, I cannot actually recall."

"You had in me from that moment forward a firm and honest friend."

"Well, I thank you."

"Thank you, it is so refreshing to deal with true gentlemen."

Andrew picked up his pen and opened up the papers to the signature line.

"Don't you want to read it first?"

"Mr. Morgan, is what is written out here the same as what we agreed?"

"It is."

"Then I need not read it, do I?"

And he proceeded to sign the documents.

Andrew walked John to the front door. Standing on the porch, with Andrew in the doorway, John held out his hand and they shook hands.

"Mr. Carnegie I want to congratulate you on being the richest man in the world."

Early one morning at the office Elbert Gary walked out of the conference room just as John walked by on his way to his office.

"Sir," Elbert called out.

"Yes," John grunted as he continued to briskly walk down the hallway toward his office. Elbert followed him trying to keep up.

"Sir, we need John Rockefeller."

"Why?" John snapped.

They were walking down the hallway toward his office weaving in and out through other men walking in the opposite direction.

"The new company will need a secure source of ore. That means Rockefeller. He owns the Lake Superior Iron Mines which controls the largest deposits of ore in the Mesabi Range. It is currently owned by Rockefeller but leased by Carnegie."

"We have all that we can attend to."

"But sir, it is greatly to our advantage to own the mines and control the flow rather than be dependent on the whim of Rockefeller."

John stopped just outside his office. Others were in his office waiting for him.

"How are we going to get them?"

"You are to talk with Mr. Rockefeller," Elbert replied.

John shook his head no. "I would not think of it."

"Why?"

"I do not like him."

Elbert smiled. He did not know if John was serious or not. He could not read it in his face.

"Mr. Morgan," Elbert began. "When a business proposition of so great importance to the Steel Corporation is involved, would you let a personal prejudice interfere with your success?"

John glared at Elbert.

John finally replied: "I don't know."

John then turned and entered his office greeting the several men sitting there waiting for him.

The conversation with Elbert was done.

It was the very next day that John entered the conference room where Elbert sat pouring over piles of papers. John leaned forward and put both his hands on the table.

"I have done it," John roared, a big smile on his face.

Elbert sat back in his chair.

"Done what?"

"I have seen Rockefeller, yesterday afternoon."

"How did he treat you?"

John shrugged his shoulders. "All right."

"Did you get the ore lands?"

John stood up straight. "No, I just told him that we ought to have them, and asked if he would not make a proposition."

"Great."

John fingered the pockets of his waistcoat as he talked.

"I thought of what you said so I called him and asked to see him. He said that he was quite out of the business and never went downtown but that he would be glad to have a personal chat with me at his house on West Fifty Fourth Street."

"So you went to see him?"

John nodded.

"But every time I mentioned anything business he clamed up and said I needed to speak to his son, John Rockefeller Jr."

"And when is that?"

"I do not know. We called to set up an appointment but he is evasive, he will get back to us. He is an impertinent little twenty seven year old trying to play cat and mouse. How much do you think we ought to pay?"

Elbert shrugged his shoulders.

"I can work up the figures."

"Do it."

"I'll come up with what we would like to pay, and then an outside figure of what we will pay."

"Do it."

It was several days later that John Rockefeller Jr. finally made an appointment to see John. John was deep in conversation with Charles Steele when his secretary James showed Rockefeller and Henry Rogers in. They sat while John continued talking with Charles. John did not acknowledge them. They sat, uncomfortably sat, waiting while John and Charles continued their conversation.

Finally it was done. Charles left, nodding to the two seated men. John leveled his gaze at the two men. He knew Rogers, an old Rockefeller hand.

"Mr. Morgan," Rogers began, "allow me to introduce John Rockefeller."

Before him was a very young looking twenty seven year old, looking more like eighteen, sitting back in his chair with the elbow of his right arm resting on the arm of the chair and his fingers supporting his clean shaven chin. The other arm rested along the straight length of the chair. He was well groomed with his hair slicked back, small wire spectacles, expensive suit with a high white collar; he sat with one leg crossed over the other, slightly tapping his foot in mid air.

"Why has it taken more than a week to get back to me?" John instantly snapped.

"We have been quite busy of late," Rockefeller replied.

"I understand that your father wants to sell his Minnesota ore properties and has authorized you to act for him."

"It is true I am authorized to speak for my father in such matters but I have not been informed that he wishes to sell these properties. In fact I am sure he does not."

John glared at the boy. He noticed that Rogers looked at Rockefeller a bit surprised. This must have not been a part of their talks before they came.

John decided to call his bluff.

"Well," he shot back. "What's your price?"

Rockefeller waited for a moment before he replied.

"Well, Mr. Morgan, I think there must be some mistake. I did not come here to sell. I understood you wished to buy."

John waited and did not move nor speak for a long time. Their eyes did not waver from each other. Finally John abruptly stood up and walked out of his office. As he turned the corner into the hallway he glanced back and noticed that Rogers leaned into Rockefeller whispering into his ear but Rockefeller brushed him off with a frown. John walked down the hall and into the conference room where Elbert and several others were at work.

"Get me Henry Frick. I want him to be our middleman. Gates said not to use him but Frick knows more about steel and ore than almost anyone and Frick knows Rockefeller, Rockefeller the father."

John paced back and forth as he talked. Elbert and the others glanced back and forth at each other.

Finally it was Elbert who spoke: "Not going so well with the son?"

John stopped in his tracks and glared at Elbert.

"He is a cocky impertinent little child and if he thinks he can play games with J. P. Morgan he has a rude awakening awaiting him."

Elbert tried not to laugh but could not help himself.

"What are you laughing at?"

"Nothing. Nothing, sir."

"Get Frick now. Junior and I are done."

John turned and stormed back into his office and sat down and stared back at the two of them.

It was Rockefeller who spoke first.

"If that is all, Mr. Morgan, I bid you good afternoon."

Without a reply John returned to the papers on his desk. The two made their own way out.

It was night but there was a moon.

The carriage pulled up to the gate.

From within the carriage a man's voice called out for the driver to stop there. The driver pulled on the reins. The horse abruptly stopped and began stomping its feet and shaking its head. The carriage door opened and the man from within the carriage emerged into the night as he stepped down onto the gravel below. He was distinguished, well dressed and well groomed, with a white Van Dyke moustache and beard.

He was clothed in an overcoat but with no hat.

He looked up at the driver.

"Wait here until I return."

"Yes sir."

The horse continued to stomp its right front hoof.

The man walked over to the large iron gate and swung it open. It creaked in the still night air. The man walked through into the yard beyond. It seemed so odd that one of the richest men in the world would have a front gate that needed oiling.

The man walked on. His boots crunched loud on the gravel pathway and seemed to shatter the still night air. Surely you could hear him coming from a mile away. He walked beneath the over hanging trees and as he approached the house he wondered how they were going to meet.

"I will find you," he said on the telephone. "Just come in, I will find you."

The man walked in closer to the house looking back and forth into the dark park and gardens, trees and bushes.

Then there was another man's voice.

"Henry Frick," the soft and slightly high pitched voice called out.

Henry looked toward the voice. A man emerged into the moonlight from beneath the dark protection of a tree. He was an older man, thin, walking with a cane, balding, very pale white skin.

Henry waited until the man reached him. He walked softly and slowly. Henry held out his hand and when the man finally made it over to him they shook hands.

"Greetings Mr. Rockefeller," Henry said.

"Mr. Frick. It is always a pleasure."

"Likewise."

John Rockefeller waved his hand forward.

"Please," he said, "let us walk."

The two men began walking side by side.

John began to chuckle. "It was an interesting proposal of yours for you to come at night in order to avoid any press, but won't it make quite a story for the newspapers, our sulking around in the bushes in the dark?"

"It certainly makes things seem more sinister and secretive than they are."

"Oh well," John said as he waved his free hand in the air, "you know how inventive those newspapers can be with the truth."

"Certainly."

"So tell me, how is life now that you are out of Carnegie?"

187

"More relaxed I must admit."

"Rumor has it that you chased old Andy around the desk and out the door threatening to cleave him in two with a hatchet."

"Now Mr. Rockefeller, you must not believe everything you read in the papers, only some of it."

"You must tell me all about it. I love a good story."

"Another time perhaps."

"Yes," John said quietly, reflectively. "For the matter at hand; you represent Mr. Morgan now?"

"On this matter at least."

"As my son told Mr. Morgan when they met, I am not anxious to sell my own properties, certainly not the Mesabi."

"That is unfortunate."

"But as you surmise, otherwise you would not be here; I never wish to stand in the way of a worthy enterprise."

"That is most fortunate."

"I do frankly object, however, to a prospective purchaser arbitrarily fixing an 'outside figure,' and I cannot deal on such a basis. That seems too much like an ultimatum."

"Perhaps it was a poor choice of words."

"Now I want to ask you a question. Nobody is more familiar with those properties than you are. Do you or do you not agree with me that the price these gentlemen propose to pay is less by several millions than their true value?"

Henry waited for a moment before he replied. John did not look up at him; he continually watched the ground in front of them as they walked. John waited.

"In all honestly I must agree."

They continued to walk, staring before them.

"But you represent Mr. Morgan and his interest do you not?"

"Yes. But I do not believe in a price; I believe in a fair price."

John nodded.

"I thought that would be your answer. Now Mr. Frick, I will tell you what I will do. I want only a just and fair price. You know what this is, certainly better than those gentlemen do, and quite likely better than I do. I know that your judgment is good and I believe you to be a square man. I am willing, Mr. Frick, to put my interests in these properties in your hands."

"Really?"

"Now, given the price that they offer where do you stand?"

John came to a halt and stood still. They were on a slight incline over

188

looking a long and wide stretch of grass below them. It was shrouded in darkness near the far trees but the lawn sprinkled with silver moonlight. The moist blades of grass glistened. With both hands resting on the top of his walking stick John stared into Henry's eyes.

"Well, Mr. Rockefeller," Henry began, not really sure of how he was going to proceed. "Being in the industry I perhaps am aware of things that others may not be so aware of. And you, owning the mines of the Mesabi Range, perhaps are a party to like inside information."

John watched his every move and remained motionless.

"You are aware of the new mapping financed by Gates of the range. It shows many new areas of potential ore deposits which are outside of your holdings."

They stood together in silence for a moment. Finally it was Henry who spoke.

"If Mr. Morgan knew of this he may decide it is cheaper to purchase and develop these areas instead."

Far off, across the moon soaked grassland, off in some trees at the far end, there was an echoing call. John turned toward the sound.

"You know," he said, "I have always believed that birds go to bed early because they are always the ones to rise at the very first break of day. But there is this one bird, there, which is always up at night. He flies back and forth and screeches out like that sometimes most of the night. But I have never seen him. I come out at times just to spot him but I never do. It is most strange."

"Some things are elusive."

"Yes," John replied as he turned once again toward Henry, "yes they are."

John smiled.

"Mr. Frick, we must deal in the here and now. What may be in the future may be, or may not be. So I ask again: in the here and now, given the price that they have offered, where do you stand?"

Henry thought for a moment as their eyes searched each other in the darkened night.

"In the here and now, I would say that they are about five million short."

John nodded.

"That was about what I thought. Then, I will trust you to represent me."

"Might I say, then, that we have a deal?"

John turned toward the distant tree line and the elusive bird.

"Perhaps tonight will be the night I finally will see him. What do you think?"

"If that is what is important then that is what you must pursue."

"Have Mr. Morgan draw up the papers," John said as he began down the stairs toward the grassland below.

Henry watched him leave.

It was Elbert Gary who was in shock. They were in John's office where Frick was telling them of his trip to see Rockefeller.

"But sir, that is a good five million more than our price, it is a prohibitive proposition."

"So?" John asked him.

"What do you mean? It is too much, way too much."

John, from behind his desk, glanced at Frick and then back at Elbert. There was a mischievous twinkle in his eye.

"Judge Gary, in a business proposition as great as this would you let a matter of five million dollars stand in the way of success?"

"But I told you, Mr. Morgan, that mine was the outside price, the high price. This is well above that."

"Well, put it this way: would you let these properties go?"

Elbert thought for a moment.

"No," was his final reply.

"Well, write out an acceptance."

It was the final key.

The deal was done.

The official announcement in the papers was on March 3, 1901. He had consolidated the Carnegie Company, the Federal Steel Company, National Steel, National Tube, American Steel and Wire, American Tin Plate, American Steel Hoop, American Sheet Steel, Lake Superior Iron Mines and the American Bridge Company. Out of all this John created the United States Steel Corporation. It had a total capitalization at par value of $1,402,846,817. One and a half of a billion dollars; it became the largest company in the United States.

And it was done in less than three months after a speech; a speech that changed the world.

John sat at his desk in his hotel room playing cards. The game was going well. He could not tell if he was winning or not. You do not really know if you have won until the end, when you win. John remembered Carnegie. It was years later. It turned out that both he and Carnegie were on the same transatlantic liner. John stood at the railing with his daughter Anne, the wind tugging at their coats and dancing with their hair.

Andrew cautiously approached him and stepped up next to him.

"Well, hello Andrew," John said when he turned and saw him standing next to him. "I heard that you were on board."

"Yes. I am returning to New York."

"Are you enjoying your retirement?"

Andrew laughed.

The short Andrew dressed in woolen red and brown plaids looked up at the tall John dressed in cotton solid black. The wind pulled at their coats.

"I made one mistake, Pierpont, when I sold out to you."

"What is that?"

"People think I should have asked you a hundred million more than I did."

John laughed.

"Well, Andy, you would have got it if you had."

Carnegie stared down into the water. "I knew it," he whispered.

"Andrew," John said firmly. "I made you the richest man in the world. What would another hundred have done you?"

"Nothing," Carnegie replied. "But it is the game, Pierpont, it is the game."

John rubbed his bare feet back and forth on the carpet. He turned over his cards and placed them. One after another everyone had a place. Then he turned over another King: Hearts.

Saturday, May 4, 1901.

John left the dressing room and walked toward the spa area. Men all robed in white towels walked back and forth into and out of the spa area. The floor was already getting wet. John walked with his over sized slippers, his bathing suit barely containing his robust stomach, a white towel wrapped around his waist and hanging down like an apron, another towel draped over his naked shoulder. Breakfast done, John was set for his normal spa routine. The exercise walks and the bubbly sulfur spring water drinks he did not like and did not take part in. He picked and chose what healthy traits were healthy for him.

John stopped before the desk to sign the log for the spa.

"Good morning sir," the teller said.

John nodded. It was a new teller. John came to the Aix les Baines resort for many years now and he usually got to know many of the workers at the hotel and spa. This young man was new. There was a second teller there as well. He was new also.

John was especially happy today. Yesterday after he arrived the mayor of the town came to see him and brought a huge bouquet of lush and beautiful flowers. It was to welcome him yet again to their resort, and to their town, but to especially thank him for his financial gift he had given to the city hospital. They were in bad need of funds and, when John heard, he wired a contribution. When the mayor asked him how on earth he could repay John for his generosity John just waved his hand and said, "Make people well."

"That is what we do here," the little man said, "that is what we try and do. And you, you will take part in all of our healthy measures?"

"Some of them, of course, but as I see it the secret of health is contentment, cheerfulness, and not to expect too much from others."

"Wise council, my friend," the mayor said as he winked and smiled, "very wise council."

John pulled his towel up, nervous. He was afraid that it would slip down. And then what, he thought to himself as he looked at all of the old half naked men walking up and down the hallway. He started toward the door into the spa itself when the young man called out to him.

"Yes," John said, turning. The young man came up to him and handed him a telegram.

"You are Mr. Morgan. This just arrived."

John nodded and started toward the door again thinking that he would read the telegram later but then stopped in the middle of the hallway and ripped the envelope open. It was from Robert Bacon at J. P. Morgan and Company, New York.

John read the message to himself.

"UNION PACIFIC INTERESTS BUYING NORTHERN PACIFIC. MAY HAVE CONTROL ALREADY. INSTRUCTIONS."

John froze. He looked up.

"What?" he almost shouted.

Men walking past him stared over at him as he stood motionless.

He reread the telegram.

How can this be? He knew of most of the positions. Between the

Great Northern, James Hill, himself, and several other heavy investors that he clicked off in his head there was no way that anyone could capture the Northern Pacific by purchasing in the open market. Who in their right mind would first of all have the money and second of all go after a $155 million dollar stock?

"It can't be done," John whispered to no one in particular.

But yet; unless; unless someone was selling. And with a rise in price some may be selling to take profit now to buy back later. John sighed. Stupid; it is such stupid short sightedness.

John looked up at the clock on the wall over the desk. He calculated the difference in time between here and in New York. It was before dawn there, Saturday. There was time to send an order and place it before the markets closed at noon. But it had to go right away.

John quickly walked back to the desk.

"I want to send a telegram."

The teller took a telegram order and picked up his pencil.

John quickly called off the address.

"Absolutely buy what ever it takes. Immediately buy 125,000 shares of common and then advise. Get John Keene involved."

"Now, this has to go out right away, right now."

"Yes sir."

The clerk handed the cable to the second clerk and told him to take it to the telegraph office at the main lobby of the hotel. The second clerk went there and gave it to the telegraph operator. The telegraph operator looked at the date written at the top of the form. It was dated May 5, tomorrow. The telegraph operator put it in the stack of telegrams to be sent out tomorrow.

John walked into the spa area and settled down into the hot water. All the time he was thinking, trying to analyze. Harriman? Why does Harriman want Northern Pacific?

Something very big is going on.

But why does Harriman want the Northern Pacific? It is a parallel line with the Union Pacific, there is no advantage to spend that kind of money for a line that you already have.

Unless.

Harriman and the Union Pacific needed a connection to Chicago. He tried to buy the Burlington which would give him that access but before he could the Northern Pacific bought it.

John had it.

"Yes!" John screamed out as he brought his fist down and splashed into the water sending a spray of water in all directions. Everyone looked over at him but John did not notice.

That is it. He is buying the larger Northern Pacific in order to get his hands on the smaller Burlington.

John laughed. Oh you Harriman, you think that you are so brilliant. But I figured you out.

Friday, May 3, 1901.

On the night of April 14, 1901 when James Hill arrived in New York he saw Mortimer Schiff standing on the dock waiting for him. He was the son of Jacob Schiff of the firm Kuhn, Loeb & Company.

Hill waked up the plank and stopped in front of Mortimer.

"Father is waiting for you at Mr. Baker's house. Did you get his note?"

"Yes."

It was a note saying that Schiff and Edward Harriman wanted to meet and discuss the purchase of the Chicago, Burlington & Quincy Railroad. Both Hill of the Great Northern Railroad and Edward Harriman of the Union Pacific Railroad were trying to build transcontinental rail lines. Both needed access into the Chicago system. Both wanted to buy the Chicago, Burlington & Quincy Railroad which would give them access into Chicago. Harriman had tried and failed to buy enough stock in the open market to gain control. Harriman had approached the board of directors to purchase the company but they refused. But now Hill, merging with Morgan's Northern Pacific Railroad, had approached the board of directors and they had agreed. They would sell their line to Hill and Morgan. The deal was to be signed tomorrow.

"Is Harriman there also?" Hill asked.

"I believe so," Mortimer answered.

"Okay."

George F. Baker, of First National Bank, greeted them at the door of his house. He brought them into his library. They thought it best to meet at a neutral place.

Schiff asked Hill why he had told him just a month before that he was not buying any Burlington. We have had a long relationship together, why were you untruthful to me?

"I am sorry that I misled you but it became necessary."

"It was necessary to lie to your friend?"

"I knew of your relationship with the Union Pacific."

Harriman wanted to be a part of the deal. He would pay a third of the price in order to be on the board of directors and be a third partner.

Hill said no.

But it is a part of Morgan's whole community of interest concept, explained Schiff. To avoid ruinous competitive wars it was to the best interest of the community for each of the most important players to mutually share in the workings of a railroad and be on each others board of directors. That way each of the major players had a vested interest in maintaining an orderly and stable railroad. Harriman is a major player in this and he should be a part of the deal.

Hill said no.

But to you it is an access to Chicago, to Harriman it posses a threat to the livelihood of the Union Pacific Railroad itself. It is better to mutually coexist to the benefit of all than to fight. I am sure that Morgan would see the wisdom of that.

Hill said no.

Harriman, pacing the floor as he listened to all of this turned and pointed at Hill. Harriman was hot with anger.

"Very well, it is a hostile act, and you must take the consequences."

The meeting ended.

Morgan, after putting together U. S. Steel, left for his annual vacation in Europe. Robert Bacon was left in charge of J. P. Morgan & Company. James Hill wanted to show Edward Tuck and Amos French, representing French and German investors, the Great Northern line. So they left on April 15 for Seattle.

Both were out of town.

It was then that Harriman struck.

James Hill was in Seattle when he noticed it. There was a great deal of activity in the Northern Pacific stock, but there was a great deal of activity in the stock market as a whole so no one thought much of it. The stock price rose from 101 to 117. But it was not a shaky up and down up, but rather a steady climb. Then at the close of one day's trading a clerk brought in the news. The stock had traded a very heavy 106,500 shares and had risen two points.

Hill knew something different was up.

He took the next train to New York.

When he arrived he went to see Jacob Schiff on Friday afternoon, May 3.

"Are you buying Northern Pacific stock for Harriman?"

Schiff looked at him from behind his desk.

"What makes you ask that?"

"Jacob, I can see it. I know what you are doing."

Finally Schiff nodded.

"I suppose I can tell you because it is almost complete and there is little that you can do about it now. So, yes, we are buying control of Northern Pacific. We shall bring the harmony and community of interest that we could not achieve by peaceful means."

"But you can't get control, impossible. Too much of it is owned by us."

Schiff smiled as he tapped his desk with his forefinger.

"That may be, but we've got a lot of it. You secretly bought the Burlington and refused to give us a fair share; now we're going to see if we can't get a share by purchasing a controlling interest in the Northern Pacific."

Hill stood in disbelief. "It can't be done."

Schiff merely shrugged his shoulders.

Saturday, May 4, 1901.

Edward Harriman was home sick in bed. His forehead was burning up and he ached everywhere. He was coughing so much that he was hoarse. He was furious that he would get sick now, now of all the times to get sick, right when he was closing in on victory.

When he could he tried to think clearly. Staring up at the ceiling he tried to calculate it all out in his head. By his last count they owned in total stock $79 million of a total of $155 million. That gave him 51 percent of the total. That meant he had controlling interest.

He had won.

He closed his eyes briefly and tried to overcome a sudden wave of nausea. When it passed he opened his eyes and started calculating on the ceiling again.

But he was troubled by the breakdown between preferred stock and common stock. Of the preferred stock he calculated he owned $42 million of the $75 million preferred stock outstanding. That was a percentage of 56 which was more than enough. But of the common stock he only owned $37 million of the $80 million outstanding. That was only 46 percent. He figured, at current prices, it would require just 40,000 shares and he would have majority control of both the preferred and the common stock.

Only then could he feel safe.

Harriman looked at the clock. He reached over and sitting up in bed pulled the phone over to him. He called Kuhn, Loeb and Company. Harriman asked for Schiff. He was not available. Harriman asked for Louis Heinsheimer. It was Saturday but it was still early enough. The market closes at noon. Harriman told Heinsheimer to buy 40,000 shares of Northern Pacific common stock and place it right away.

Heinsheimer ran out of the building and caught Jacob Schiff just as he was getting into his carriage to go to Synagogue for prayers. Schiff shook his head and looked at his watch. He was already late. What is the problem? We may be shy in common stock but we have majority control of the total stock and that is what is important. And what can they do about it now? Morgan is in France.

Schiff waved Heinsheimer away. I will take responsibility. We can place the order on Monday. He then left for Synagogue.

Harriman, now secure in the knowledge that he had total control in every way lay back and tried to get some desperately needed sleep.

Tuesday, May 7, 1901.

John sat on the balcony of the restaurant with his friend overlooking the Lac du Bourget. The water glistened in the late afternoon sun. Large rolling clouds passed over at times blocking the sun completely but at times letting the full power of its rays shine through. Across the lake the mountains grew darker on this side as the sun began to set behind them. John sat drinking his coffee and eating his small chocolate cookies.

"I did not know that those were on the regulated diet of the spa."

It was John Stewart Kennedy. Born near Glasgow, Scotland, in 1830, he came to the United States when he was twenty and through banking and railroads had become a millionaire. Kennedy, with his now totally grey bushy sideburns, was down for his usual treatment at Aix les Baines. He frequently stayed here, and frequently saw John here as well. He and John sat watching out over the lake together.

"It is my afternoon treat after a hard morning of the spa," John replied.

Kennedy was a heavy investor in Northern Pacific but had not sold a single share.

"The market is going wild."

The stock in Northern Pacific was indeed going wild. In New York chaos ruled. With the soaring price of the stock due to both Harriman and Morgan buying up shares others had jumped in buying what few shares were left. Speculators bought the stock short figuring that the wild speculation would end, the price collapse, and they could buy back their shares at a considerable profit. But they did not figure on Harriman and Morgan buying and holding. To buy shares in Northern Pacific short brokers were selling stock in others companies to raise the money. Other railroads were dropping in price; U. S. Steel fell to 42.

"Speculators," John grunted with disgust, spitting the word out like a vile tasting piece of gruel.

"I know that you do not like him, but Morgan you do have to hand it to Mr. Harriman, what he tried to do was bloody brilliant and bold and he almost got away with it."

John did not answer. He sipped his coffee as the sun disappeared behind a cloud shading the whole balcony.

John first clashed with Edward Harriman in 1887. Harriman was the chief operator of the Illinois Central Railroad. They had another railroad under lease, the Dubuque & Sioux City, but wanted to terminate the lease and buy the line outright. Majority shareholders objected to this and they, to be safe, placed their shares in the hands of Morgan. At the shareholders meeting Charles Coster of J. P. Morgan & Company showed up and was ready to vote all of the majority of shares he held in proxy against the Illinois Central plan. But Harriman arrived with his lawyer. It seemed that according to Iowa law shareholders had to be present to vote their shares. The Illinois Central got their way and all of the proxy shares that Morgan held were dismissed.

John was livid.

It was the Jay Gould method all over again of using the devises of lawyers and technicalities. It did not care for what was right. It only cared for what in the short term worked.

In 1895 the Union Pacific Railroad board of directors asked John to help reorganize the railroad but he decided against it. He judged that it was not worth it. It was then that Jacob Schiff of Kuhn, Loeb & Company approached John. Would it be all right if he had a go at reorganizing the line?

"Go right ahead. I am through with the Union Pacific."

It was the biggest mistake of his life.

But for all of Schiff's attempts there was resistance that blocked his every move. Could it be Morgan after all?

But when Schiff approached John he said no, it is not me. "I am not responsible. But I will find out for you who is."

And when he found out he called Schiff.

"It is that little fellow Harriman. Look out for him. He is a sharper."

When Schiff confronted Harriman he said yes, it was he. "I intend to reorganize the Union Pacific myself. I can get money cheaper than you and the Illinois Central ought to have the Union Pacific."

Schiff thought about it.

"Can we work together?"

"Sure."

"Are you sure that we still retain control of Northern Pacific?" asked John Kennedy.

John watched as the sun came back from behind a cloud. The whole panoramic view of the lake lit up with a rush of light.

"I believe so," John replied. "I do not think that Harriman understands that the board has the power to discontinue the preferred shares. If they vote to do that then whomever owns the most common shares will be the majority owner."

"Clever. So the outwitted fox outwits the fox."

"But I still want to know who was selling."

"Yes, indeed."

"I feel bound in honor when I reorganize a property and am morally responsible for its management, to protect it, and I generally do protect it."

"Yes, but now once this matter is cleared up maybe you should reconsider your position toward Mr. Harriman."

John turned to him. "How so?"

"Perhaps you two should work more together. I think he has proved himself to be in it for the long run and not just for speculation. And he is very good at running a railroad; you have to agree to that."

John did not want to admit it outright but as it turned out John was wrong about Harriman. The man was not speculating. He was building a strong and long lasting company. One of the first things Harriman did when he became director of the Union Pacific Railroad was to inspect the entire length of the rail. With a small observation car in front and the engine pushing from the rear Harriman left Kansas City on June 17, 1898 with his two daughters and a collection of Union Pacific officials to inspect his newly acquired railroad.

Stories abound about what happened.

Walking along the rails at one stop with a highway engineer Harriman noticed the amount of rock ballast beneath the tracks. He wondered.

"What is the distance of ballast from the edge of the rail to where the ballast slopes off?"

"Eighteen inches."

"Why is it eighteen inches?"

"That is our standard width."

"That is no answer," Harriman barked at the man. "Why is that our standard?"

"Well, sir, I presume that they want a good quantity of ballast outside the rails so that a part of it could be used if necessary in filling in between the rails when it got shaken down."

"But isn't it likely that the outside ballast would slide off down the slope so that a good deal of it wouldn't be there when you wanted it?"

The man shrugged his shoulders. "It might," he said.

"Suppose then that the ballast shoulder was only eight inches, wouldn't that do just as well?" Harriman asked with out even looking at the man.

"It might."

"Might or would?"

"It would do just as good I suppose."

"Good. Now get a pencil and a piece of paper and go and sit down and figure up the quantity and the cost of an eight inch shoulder of ballast as compared with an eighteen inch shoulder over nine thousand miles of track. Let me know how much money we will save."

Sitting in his observation car it seemed that they were stopped for a long time. They were filling with water. Harriman looked back at the water tower filling the engine with water. The opening of the spout where the water flowed out was smaller than the opening where the water flowed into the engine.

"How wide is the opening in the engine for the water?"

"About twelve inches I believe."

"How wide is the end of the water spout?"

"About six to eight inches."

"Why is the spout only six inches when the receptacle is twelve?"

"That is the standard measurement from the manufacturer."

"But wouldn't we be making better time if we were filling up with water through a twelve inch spout rather than a six inch spout?"

"Yes, I suppose we would."

"So then, tell the manufacturer that if they want us to buy from them then from now on make our water spouts twelve inches in diameter rather than six."

Harriman was walking along the tracks with Julius Kruttschnitt, a huge monster of a man, in sharp contrast to short thin and frail Harriman. Harriman saw a track bolt sticking up. He bent down and touched the bolt. It was firmly placed. But then he noticed for the first time that all of the bolts extended a bit above the nut. Bent down Harriman turned his head to look up at Julius.

"Why does so much of the bolt protruded above the nut."

"It is the size of bolt which is generally used," Julius replied.

"Why should we use a bolt of such a length that a part of it is useless?"

"It is the standard size they come in."

Harriman turned back to look at all of the bolts "But why?" he asked.

"Well when you come right down to it there is no reason."

Harriman stood up and they began walking on.

"How do we pay for the bolts?"

"By weight."

"How many bolts do you think there are in a mile of track?"

Julius tried to make a rough calculation.

"I would say maybe twenty five hundred to three thousand."

"Well, then in both the Union and the Southern Pacific we have about eighteen thousand miles of track and there must be some fifty million track bolts in our system. If you can cut an ounce off from every bolt you will save fifty million ounces of iron and that is something worth while."

"That is indeed."

Harriman looked at Julius as they continued to walk.

"Change your bolt standard," he said.

When Harriman heard that there had been yet another train robbery in Wyoming he asked what they did about it. Not too much can be done was the reply. There are several gangs of robbers living out in the badlands and finding them proved near impossible. Some, like Butch Cassidy and the Sundance Kid had become famous. They blocked a railway at a certain point and cut the telegraph line. When the train had to stop they robbed the train and then took off. By the time the crew repaired the telegraph line, wired to the nearest town for help, and the town gathered a posse and rode out to the train, the robbers were long since gone.

The robbers never got caught. The high insurance rates on shipping were just a cost of doing business.

Why bring the posse to the robbers, Harriman asked, why not bring the robbers to the posse?

Harriman hired some Pinkerton Detectives and an Indian guide and put them as random passengers on each train. With each train there was also a freight car full of horses. As soon as the robbers finished robbing the train and rode off then the detectives with the Indian tracker immediately rode off right after them.

From then on the robbers never got away.

Train robbery on the Union Pacific stopped.

Thursday, May 9, 1901.

John was furious.

The stock market was on a rampage.

Speculation was wild.

Everyone bought into the Northern Pacific stock and the price had soared to $1000 per share. With all of the short positions more shares had been purchased than there were shares outstanding. There was no way to accurately determine between Harriman and himself who owned the majority until they had in hand all of the shares.

John left Aix les Baines early and rushed to Paris. He went to the French office of J. P. Morgan & Company, Morgan, Harjes & Company.

He found out that several large shareholders of Northern had sold when the price began to climb in order to cash in on profits. They expected to buy them back when the price fell back again. Even Robert Bacon at J. P. Morgan & Company had sold thousands of shares.

The market was falling apart. Most stocks were drastically falling in price and many broker houses were on the verge of defaulting because they could not cover their short positions in Northern Pacific. Short interest was sky high. Banks set up emergency loans to help tide the panic.

And newspapers were having a field day. It was all the fault of the greed of Morgan, they said. It was a war of the two giants of Morgan and Harriman trampling on all of the small investors.

Morgan, Morgan, the Great Financial Gorgon, vendors called out in the street.

When his carriage pulled up in front of his Paris headquarters John shouted out from the back of his carriage. Newspaper reporters were all over the curb. News had traveled that he was coming.

With his cane and his overcoat swirling John tried to race to the front door. But he was rushed.

"Morgan, why are you doing this?"

"Are you trying to crush the market to take over?"

John could barely get in the door. The teller watched as John approached. He was new; John had never seen him before.

The newsmen where shouting questions at him.

"You owe the public an explanation, sir."

"Get them out of here," he shouted at the teller. "Where is John Harjes, I want to see him and Hermann Herold right now in the forward office."

John started down the hall. But the teller shouted out to him as he raced to catch him.

"Sir, you cannot go in there. You will have to wait here, sir."

When John kept walking the teller shouted out louder.

"Stop, sir. Stop or I'll have to call the guards."

John spun around and stormed back at the teller with his eyes blazing with rage.

"Do you know who I am son? Don't you dare treat me like this. Now get Harjes and Herold, now," he almost screamed.

From a side office another clerk that John recognized came running over waving his hand at the first teller and shaking his head no.

From the lobby a news reporter ran up.

"Morgan, don't you think that since you are being blamed for a panic that has ruined thousands of people and disturbed a whole nation, some statement is due to the public?"

John waved his cane in the air.

"I owe the public nothing," he roared and then turned to walk up the hallway.

John sat back in his chair in his hotel room. He rubbed his eyes. He looked around his hotel room: the chairs, sofa, and the pictures on the wall. He did not want to go to bed. He was having trouble sleeping lately. He hated to lay in bed trying to sleep and nothing happening. But he was growing tired. He had to get some sleep for the committee meeting tomorrow.

His game was almost complete. He turned over the next card: King of Spades.

Finally peace reigned.

John held on to the majority of the stock.

The emergency loans kept the brokers from bankruptcy. The parties agreed that short sellers could buy their shares at an agreed price of $150 per share. John could assign five new board members: he placed Harriman on the board and on the executive committee.

John was concerned that the panic had gotten so out of hand. He put rival concerns on the board of directors, he said, "Simply to show everybody concerned that J. P. Morgan & Company were acting under what was known as the community of interest plan and that we were not going to have a battle in Wall Street."

So that this sort of run should never happen again it was agreed by all parties that they would incorporate a holding company where all the assets of both the Great Northern and the Northern Pacific were placed: Northern Securities.

But there was another run from a different front. Before anyone noticed John W. Gates, Bet-a-Million Gates, fresh from being ostracized from U. S. Steel, bought up shares in the Louisville and Nashville Railroad, right in the heart of the Morgan controlled network of Southern lines.

Gates bought up the stock, which raised the price, so others sold for the profit, which allowed Gates to keep buying, the rise in price again attracted the short sellers and they bought in thinking the price surely would break soon and go down. But Gates bought to hold and the short sellers were now in a squeeze and in trouble. It was the whole situation of Northern Pacific all over again.

When he found out John was, again, furious. Why does this keep happening? Gates could do a lot of damage to the whole southern network of trust and community of interest that John was carefully building up.

He told George Perkins to go to Gates and buy it back. Get the best deal that you can but do not leave until you broker a deal. End this. I am sick of this.

It was after midnight when Perkins arrived at the Waldorf-Astoria. He went up to Gates room and began banging on the door. He banged and banged on the door. Several other guests popped their heads out to see what was going on but Perkins said 'nothing, go back to sleep.'

Finally Gates opened the door. His hair was messed; he wore a bright red robe over his flowered pajamas. The room smelled heavy of booze and cigar smoke. Opened and empty bottles littered the room.

"Mr. Gates, there is a threat of panic in the market and Mr. Morgan wants to avoid that. Mr. Morgan wants an option on your shares."

"How will that do anything?"

Mr. Morgan will own your shares, he will settle with the short sellers, and the speculation will be done."

"I'm buying the line, it's a good property and Old Pierpont knows it."

Perkins waited.

"What is your price Mr. Gates?"

"All right, since you want that stock so badly, to keep your friends in control and protect the Southern, I will let you have it. But you must pay me ten millions more than it cost me."

Perkins swallowed hard.

Three hours of negotiation later the deal was the same. Gates was having his revenge and Perkins knew it.

The deal was made, hands shook. When Perkins told John he sat silently for a moment. It would be around $43 million. Finally John just raised his eyebrows.

"We have to build security, like a moat around a castle, so that we can be immune from the ravishes of marauders. The cost of stability, even at that price, is much cheaper than the cost of chaos."

John stood up. He pushed his chair back and stood in his hotel room in naked feet. He took a long and deep breath. Out through the window he could see the sparkle of the night. Edison's dreamland made real. John went to the balcony, opened the door, and stepped out onto the balcony. The cold chill of the night rushed over his body. The balcony was ice cold to his bare feet. He stepped out to the rail. He looked out over the city, the sparkling city of lights.

Yes, Edward Harriman was a force. There was no doubt about that. There were few men like him. Perhaps even none. When the San Francisco earthquake hit in April of 1906 Harriman jumped right into the thick of it. No one asked him to, and he did not need to, but he did because he was who he was.

I have to hand him that.

John tried to imagine what it was like. He, like everyone, read the newspaper reports and saw the pictures. But how can half a city turn into a roaring flame?

John looked out and imagined the flames licking the night sky. Half the city, like all of that over there, nothing but a roaring inferno and all the smoke, massive plumes of smoke replacing the clouds and staining the whole sky with black burning embers.

And somewhere in the center of it all stood the little man Harriman with his eyes swollen behind his eyeglasses and his yellow straw hat pulled down on his forehead.

John smiled at the image.

There he stands.

Harriman stood with the others, Brigadier General Frederick Funston and his staff officers, Mayor Eugene Schmitz and members of the Committee of Fifty; they stood in the street littered with brick and chunks of concrete. On signal they held their hands to their ears. The Captain shouted.

On his command the cannon roared and kicked back from the recoil. They watched as the cannon ball blasted into the side wall of one of the mansions along Van Ness Avenue. Bricks flew in all directions.

Harriman looked up at the midnight sky; he could barely breathe from all the smoke. Black and Grey smoke curled up into the night sky. He pulled out a handkerchief and held it against his mouth. His nose and lungs were burning. The eerie reddish glow of the fires roaring across the city advanced toward them. You could hear it coming. This was where they were making a stand. Van Ness Avenue was a wide street and if they could destroy all the buildings along one side of the street it might give them the fire break they needed to stop the fires. It was a rich part of town, mansions lined the street. But they must all be destroyed to save the city.

From further down the street a loud boom echoed back and forth, and then it was followed by another one. They were dynamiting the buildings. There was no time to lose.

Next to them the captain again called out. The second cannon roared and the shell whizzed past blasting into the same side of the house. Bricks flew in all directions and the rear of the house collapsed. Dirt and splintered wood roared up from the blast mixing with the smoke. Harriman took off his glasses and rapidly rubbed them with his handkerchief trying to clear the dirty smudged glass. He smeared the dirt around more than cleaned it. When he put them back on the dust from the blast had cleared enough for him to see into the house. There had been no time to clear out the furniture. They had cleared out the people and that was all. Four soldiers had to carry a man out while he was kicking and screaming. Everything he owned was still in the house. There was no time. No sooner had they dragged him out that they fired the first shot into the house.

One of the officers, an older man with grey hair standing next to Harriman looked over at him. His face was stained with black soot. The

206

expression on the man's face was serious and hard.

"This reminds me of the war," the man said. "I was there when Sherman shelled Atlanta."

Harriman nodded to the man just as the first cannon fired again.

Harriman was in New York at home when he first heard the news of the earthquake. Telegraph messages flooded into his office from all along the Union Pacific and the Southern Pacific lines. Most of the lines in and around the city were down. He immediately telegraphed his department heads to drop all business and focus on earthquake relief. Rushing out by special train, at every stop he picked up messages and flooded the stations telegraph office with wires directing his whole network of companies to coordinate their efforts to help the city.

"I care not the cost," he wired.

He directed his general manager for the Southern Pacific, E. E. Calvin, to buy out of company resources as much food stuffs as he could acquire in Los Angeles and Sacramento and immediately ship them to the city.

From station to station his train made its way, at each station his secretary V. W. Hill rushed out as soon as the train came to a stop and ran into the telegraph office with a stack of telegrams Harriman had written since the last stop. Send these as quick as you can he barked at the teller. He only had as long as it took to take on water and wood and then they would leave. They made record time.

At one station as soon as they stopped he called for the engineer and fireman, 'I want to see them right away,' he snapped. The two men, summoned, made their way through the train to his special car. Their clothes and face were covered in coal dust. The fireman's hands were stained with oil. They mumbled to each other as they made their way to his car: what now, what's he going to yell at us for now, for god's sake we're doing to best we can. They knocked on the door. 'Yes,' was shouted from within. Once they opened the door and walked in a smiling Harriman stood up and came over to them. He shook their hands, coal dust and all, and told then how pleased he was with their progress.

"We just passed through some rugged canyons back there and we went so smooth it didn't even wake me."

Harriman shook both of their hands again and told them that when this was over he wanted both of them to take a whole week off with full pay.

"Damn fine work, gentlemen."

When he arrived in San Francisco he and Calvin toured the city. Calvin filled him in on the situation. They brought in their own dynamite and gasoline and made it all available to the fire department. Food was regularly being railed in; all the passenger cars on line were transporting hundreds of refugees out of the city.

Harriman stopped him.

"People, Mr. Calvin."

"What's that sir?"

"They are not refugees, they are people.

Calvin nodded. "Yes, sir."

On the deck of a steamship as they were coming into the bay a man approached the two of them as they stood on the deck watching the city. He told them that he and his wife had just arrived in the city a month ago to start a new life. And now his wife was dead and all their possessions were gone. He knew no one here. He had no money. All he wanted to do now was leave the city with the remains of his wife and return home to bury her. The man pointed to a policeman, he said that you can help me.

Harriman noticed that the man's woolen jack was dirty and torn at the seam. Calvin pulled out his pen and pad and wrote a note and signed it.

"Here," he said. "My name is Calvin and I am the Vice President of the Southern Pacific Railroad. Give this note to the Rail Station manager. It will provide you and your wife with free passage to wherever you wish to go."

The man stood for a moment with the handwritten note in his hand. His unkempt hair was tossed by the wind.

There were tears in his eyes when he quietly said thank you and walked away holding the small slip of paper as if it were gold.

Harriman looked at Calvin.

"How do you know the man's story was true?" he asked.

Calvin shrugged his shoulders. "I don't know," he said.

He looked straight into Harriman's eyes.

"But I think that it is better to assume it was true than to not help one in need."

Calvin spoke with the force of a conviction.

Harriman smiled. "It is well that you reached that conclusion because if you had not done so I would have taken the case out of your hands and given him the money myself."

The blast of the steamship's horn silenced them both.

There was a deeper boom down the street from more dynamite

blasts, it sounded like rolling thunder. Harriman watched as a robed man came out of the St. Mary Cathedral and walked toward them. He was a priest.

One of the Committee members leaned toward Harriman.

"Father Charles Ramm, Mr. Harriman."

Harriman watched as the Priest approached sidestepping the shattered bricks and debris that littered the street. The dust and smoke swirled all around the approaching figure.

The cannon blasted again and the ball smashed into the next house blowing a wide ragged hole into the side of the house. There was no time to waste. They had to stop the fire here because there was no where else to stop it. There was a house on fire on the east side of the street. Two steamer pumps were there and the firemen held the hoses and two streams of water were dousing the fires trying to bring it under control.

The cathedral was filled with people. What if the fire jumped the street and lit up the Cathedral?

Father Ramm was tired beyond belief. He spent the early part of the day at the Mechanics Pavilion where a make shift hospital was set up. Hundreds were there in crude liters lined in rows on the floor. The hospital across the street was destroyed and most of the medical staff killed. The injured were brought in, more and more as the day progressed. There was scarcely any water, little anesthetics. He went from liter to liter, kneeling down, giving hope and, when needed, absolution. Some clung to him with desperation, looking for answers.

He did the same everywhere he went hour after hour day and night. He made his way down Van Ness Avenue and climbed the steps of the Gothic Cathedral. He was amazed to see all the pews filled, people were sitting on the floor, on the steps to the high alter. But it was silent inside. The roar and distant rumbling of the flames were hushed. But for the mumble of prayer and the clacking of rosary beads everyone was silent, praying, waiting.

He could not rest. He knew that it had to be stopped here. Father Ramm left the Cathedral and made his way toward the cannon and the firemen. He could see a lot of men standing in the street by the cannon. Mayor Eugene Schmitz stood silent stroking his beard again and again as he watched it all unfold. Everyone was watching and waiting, quiet. Father Ramm watched as the firemen poured water onto the burning house, the flames silhouetting the men standing in the street.

Harriman watched as Ramm approached. But Ramm stopped when there was a loud anguished scream from behind him in the direction of the Cathedral.

"It's across! It's across!"

Father Ramm stood still. He did not turn around to look behind him. He did not need too. He knew what it meant.

The fire.

Father Ramm watched as the firemen fighting the burning house stopped pumping water through their hoses. They had all turned and stared toward the Cathedral. They instantly began turning their pumps around and pushing them toward Father Ramm, toward the Cathedral. As they rushed past him he could see the fear in their eyes.

"Have faith," he shouted to them as they ran passed him. How hollow those words seemed now. "There's still a chance," he only muttered.

Only the two men nearest him heard him say the last.

"We need more than a chance now, father," the tall thin one replied. "We need the damn luck of the Devil."

Harriman and Ramm: through the swirling eye piercing smoke they both stood and stared at each other. Behind Ramm people began frantically running out of the Cathedral and down the stairs into the shattered street.

Harriman watched.

He did not know what to do.

John, still standing in the cold on the balcony above the glimmering light lit city, reached into his pocket. One last one for the night, he mumbled to himself. John struck a match to light his cigar. Puffs of smoke filled the air around him. There is always a spark that starts a fire. All the underlying conditions are there but it waits until the match is struck. In the case of 1907 that match was the attempted corner on the stock of the company United Copper.

What a time that one was.

1907

New York

It began with Frederick Augustus Heinze, nicknamed "Fritz." He was one of the young crowd; fresh, passionate, successful, driven, and arrogant. Like wild stallions who have never felt any controlling reins, arrogantly thinking that they, in their youth and passion, know the secret to success, and will blaze forward with open hostility to everything in their path. But by smashing and trampling over everything for their short sided and selfish wants they will leave only rubble behind when their risky adventures collapse.

Born in 1869, Heinze stood five feet ten inches tall and weighed some two hundred pounds. It was said that he had the torso of a Yale halfback with muscles made of steel but with a face of ivory whiteness and a pair of large blue eyes. It was said he was a fine musician, linguist, and boxer. Born in Brooklyn of Irish and Jewish German ancestry, he graduated from Brooklyn Polytechnic Institute and attended the Columbia School of Mines in New York City. At twenty years old, with a job with the Boston and Montana Consolidated Copper and Silver Mining Company, Heinze left for the west to seek his fame and fortune. He landed in Butte, Montana where he lived in a small log cabin and worked for two years as a mining engineer. By 1891 he created a custom smelting operation for small independent mining concerns, raised $300,000 in capital from New York investors, and in 1893, with his two brothers Otto and Arthur, established the Montana Ore Purchasing Company.

But it was then that he turned to the courts and bribed judges to make his fame and fortune. According to state law if a vein or ore surfaced, or apexed, on your land then you can mine the vein wherever it ran, even if it was under the property of someone else. So Heinze bought small pieces of land next to producing mines, drilled down until he hit a vein, and then mined the vein under his neighbor's property. When the owners of the adjust property complained Heinze sued them and claimed the vein had apexed on his land so he had all the rights to excavate it. If declared the "owner" of the mine he would bring an injunction on his neighbor to stop them from mining and bring a law suit against them if they did not comply.

That is where the bribed judges came in handy. They, not surprisingly, ruled in his favor. He had as many as 37 lawyers working for him and at one point as many as 133 suits against various mining neighbors. By 1902 he consolidated most of his copper holdings into the United Copper Company.

One of his main opponents became the Amalgamated Copper Mining Company, when, formed in 1899 by a group of men from Standard Oil, William Rockefeller, Henry Huttleston Rogers, and stocker plunger Thomas William Lamont, they bought out the copper interest of Marcus Daly, one of The Copper Kings of Butte, Montana. They acquired other properties, including ones Heinze had under suit. Not only did Heinze refuse to sell to the growing conglomerate but he continued his legal attacks. Amalgamated counter sued and the legal battles flared and raged.

Henry Rogers himself vowed to destroy Heinze: "The flag has never been lowered at 26 Broadway (Standard Oil), and I'll drive Heinze out of Montana if it takes ten million to do it."

But it took even more than that.

Finally, in February 1906, to end it all, Amalgamated bought most of Heinze active copper interests for $12.5 million.

So, with a pocket full of money, only 36 years old, with his cultivated eloquence, swashbuckler glamour and, in the eyes of the women, good looks, with his dark curly hair parted down the middle, his loose fitting black suits with flowing tie and his hands thrust deep down into his old fashioned waistband or trouser pockets, Heinze returned to New York, sharp, shrewd and reckless, searching for his next great adventure.

Richmond

It was the Triennial Convention of the Episcopalian Church being held in Richmond, Virginia, from October 1 to October 19, 1907. John, as always, attended the convention as a lay delegate from the Diocese of New York. He and his group came down by train: Bishop William

Lawrence of Massachusetts with his wife, also Bishop William Croswell Doane and his wife Sara of Albany, Bishop David Hummell Greer and his wife, Mrs. John B. Markoe of Philadelphia, Miss Amy Townsend of New York, and his daughter Louisa. They stayed at the Rutherford family residence and John hired the caterer Louis Sherry, of Sherry's Restaurant in New York, to see to their every whim.

The program was convention meetings by day followed by luncheon and dinners at the house. In the later evening John liked to play dominoes with either Mrs. Markoe or Amy Townsend. Louisa sat working her needlepoint while others would either read or chat or retire to their rooms.

The Rutherford residence, where the group of them spent the week, was set back from the street. A three story house built several generations before, it had an old wide veranda like porch across the whole front of the house and around the left side all the way to the back. It was decked out with chairs, several sofas and deep cushioned chairs, and a two seated wooden swing attached to the roof of the veranda. Whenever anyone walked you could hear the creak of the old wooden floor, and when going inside the house the sound of the stretched springs followed by the creak and bang of the screen door.

The Rutherford family themselves were Episcopalian but were not part of the convention. When the Bishop Robert Gibson asked for rooms to rent Mr. and Mrs. Rutherford offered their entire house while they visited her aunt in Petersburg.

Two large cypress trees decorated and shaded the front lawn but people walking on the street side walk could still look over and see who was sitting on the veranda. And walk and watch the people did. The local neighbors knew that the house was rented out to the congregation attending the convention, and they knew that the famous banker J.P. Morgan was among the guests who were there. People walked by, staring, at times walking back and forth as though they had passed the first time on their way to somewhere but then remembered that they forgot something and had to walk back by to go back and retrieve what ever it was they pretended to have forgotten. Many wanted to catch but a glimpse of the famous banker.

John liked to sit on the porch in a wicker chair toward evening, wearing his white suit and shoes; his white Panama Fedora with the black band; his leg crossed over the other; perhaps a glass of sherry by his side; puffing away on his cigar. He loved the early evening when the day dissolved into twilight. He listened to the sounds of the carriages in the street, the people walking past discussing this and that, the birds in their final chatter before scattering for bed. Convention classes done members of the congregation would one by one file in or join him on the veranda, discussing what the day had brought and what the evening or the next day might bring.

John was sitting in his wicker chair when he heard from the street Bishop William Lawrence call out to him as he came up the walk.

"Morgan," he called out.

John turned to see William approach with his stiff white Bishop collar and his tall black hat. He swung a cane as he walked. The small white gate of the fence slapped closed behind him.

"Sitting there, Morgan, you remind me of pictures I've seen of the writer Mark Twain sitting on his porch in his white suit and hat chomping his cigar, as if sitting on the veranda of a paddle wheel steamship bound down the Mississippi River toward New Orleans."

John laughed.

"Then William my man you'd best jump aboard before we pull away from the wharf."

William quickly climbed the stairs and, once on the porch, tipped his tall black hat toward the sitting Morgan.

"Heave ho, my man: heave ho."

One day toward twilight John and Mrs. Markoe were sitting on the porch when he heard the white picket gate by the street open and shut. A woman walked up the path wearing a white flowered dress and a green sweater that had seen much better days. Her brown but graying hair was in a little disarray. She looked to be approaching sixty-five years old and walked with more of a shuffle than a step. Her shoes were more a soft slipper than a shoe. She climbed the stairs and headed toward the front door. She was staring at John as she walked across the porch toward the door. There were muffled voices from within the house.

"Whom do you want, madam?" John asked.

The woman stopped and turned toward him and in a forceful and direct way replied: "I want to see Mr. Morgan."

John waited a moment before he replied.

"Mr. Morgan is not at home at this time."

The woman stared at him and then walked right up to him, bent her face down toward him and stared at him directly for a second or two.

"Well," she said. "You look remarkably like his picture."

Their eyes were locked together until finally she stood up and turned and with a slight smile walked directly off, down the stairs, and down the path to the front gate. John watched her leave until she had opened and closed the gate behind her. At the gate she quickly glanced back, that same small smile on her lips.

John turned to Mrs. Markoe just as she began laughing, holding her hand up to her face. John broke into a smile, and then finally a loud laugh. They both giggled uncontrollably for several minutes until tears came to his eyes and he had to pull out his handkerchief from his coat pocket.

One day while sitting on the porch a messenger came up and asked for Mr. Morgan. When John nodded the messenger had him sign for a message. It was from the office in New York. John tore it open and read it at once. As he read the message the envelope slipped from his lap onto the wooden floor. John did not notice. Things were beginning to happen.

New York

It was in New York that Fritz Augustus Heinze met up with one Charles Wyman Morse, "The Ice King." Charles Morse was a barrel shaped man of fifty one, small, compact, portly. Born in Bath, Maine he started his career working with his father who cut, harvested, and then sold blocks of ice from the frozen Kennebec River. It was said that in his father's company his father paid him a salary but then Charles employed another man at a smaller salary to do the work, and Charles pocketed the money.

Charles came to New York with an idea. He wanted to expand the ice business and, if possible, create a monopoly. He formed the American Ice Company and, with the help of bribes and pay off's, became the only company who could land ice on New York docks, giving him a massive advantage over all other ice companies. As they began to fail he took them over.

When in 1900 he felt he had a monopoly and had the local government officials in his pocket Charles tried to double the price of ice to New York residents from thirty cents to sixty cents per hundred pounds. During the public outcry and the investigative reporting it was found that the New York Mayor Robert Anderson Van Wyck had helped Charles all along in acquiring his monopoly and that Van Wyck, on an annual salary of $15,000, owned stock in American Ice Company in the amount of $680,000. If American Ice made money then Mayor

Van Wyck made money. The scandal brought the defeat of the mayor in 1901, but not before Charles had pocketed millions.

On June 18, 1901 Charles took time out of his expanding business interest to wed Clemence Dodge, a recent divorcee from Atlanta. But their marriage was annulled in 1904 when it was found that her divorce from her husband Charles F. Dodge was not legal. She was still married. Charles, not deterred, hired the corporate lawyer Samuel Untermyer to handle the situation. The prim and proper orchard growing Samuel Untermyer handled the situation.

Next Charles tried to acquire a monopoly on shipping companies in New York. With his new found money he began buying shipping companies and acquiring banks, creating what came to be called "chain banking." By acquiring a bank with his own money he then used the assets of that bank as collateral to purchase another bank, and then used the assets of that bank to acquire a third bank, and so on and so on creating a chain of ownerships, each dependent upon the collateral of the previous.

Charles once said: Banks mean Credit, and Credit means Power.

This is where the young Fritz Heinze comes in.

Charles owned the National Bank of North America, the New Amsterdam National Bank, and was a large shareholder in Mercantile National Bank.

Fritz Heinze, with his money, bought a controlling interest in Mercantile National Bank and in February 1907 became the president. Heinze and Morse went on to either acquire or join the board of directors of up to 6 national banks, 10 state banks, five trust banks and four insurance companies.

The general feeling in America toward banks was one of distrust. Ever since Andrew Jackson dissolved the charter for the Bank of the United States in 1837 banking became mostly a small and local affair. By 1907 there were basically three types of banks functioning in the United States. First there were national banks which were larger banks authorized to receive federal deposits and issue government currency. Then there were state banks, chartered by each individual state. And finally there were private banks, some of which were international in size and scope like the Rothschild's, Kuhn, Loeb, or J. P. Morgan and Company, and some of them were small such as immigrant banks run out of a back room in a grocery store or saloon.

Regulations required small rural banks to hold 15 percent of their deposits as a reserve, and 40 percent of that reserve had to be in cash. The rest of their deposits they could place in larger city banks where they could collect interest. These city banks in turn were required to keep in reserve 25 percent of their deposits, with 50 percent of it being cash. This reserve was usually sufficient to satisfy the day to day operations of the bank. The remaining deposits they then could deposit with still larger money center banks that paid a higher interest. These larger money center banks were underwriters of securities and bonds.

As a measure of security, then, larger financial institutions pooled their resources and formed associations called Clearing Houses. If an individual bank found itself short of cash and could not honor, or 'clear,' a presented check then the bank could get a 'clearing house certificate' from the Clearing House in exchange for the check. This certificate, within the members of the association, was as good as cash and could be exchanged for cash from whichever member bank had cash to lend.

A form of state bank that was established was the Trust Company. Originally formed to perform fiduciary duties for trusts and estates, they acquired more and more the function of regular commercial banks in being able to take deposits, make loans, underwriting securities and bonds. Not as regulated as regular state banks, Trust Companies could own stock, real estate, and were only required to hold a fifteen percent reserve of which only a third had to be in cash. Thus they could invest a greater portion of their money than a regular commercial bank could invest, and thus make a higher return. They could then pay a higher interest rate on deposits and attract a greater number of depositors than a regular bank. In the ten years before 1907 assets of Trust Companies in New York had grown by 244 percent.

The Clearing House system was dominated by large, established and more conservative banks and did not like the less regulated and more risky activity of the Trust Companies. So Trust Companies were not members of the Clearing House system. Individual banks, however, sometimes acted like a clearing house for individual Trust Companies.

Fritz Heinze and his brothers Otto and Arthur purchased a seat on the New York Stock Exchange and created the brokerage firm of Otto C. Heinze & Company.

In 1902 Heinze consolidated what copper interests he had left after selling most of them to the Amalgamated Copper Mining Company, and formed the United Copper Company. He, his brother Otto, and his brother Arthur were each major shareholders in the company. Then, using their newly form brokerage house, Charles Morse purchased 30,000 shares using as collateral for the loan shares in his own company Knickerbocker Ice Company. Fritz and Otto and Arthur and Charles formed a pool and used their shares in United Copper Company as collateral for loans to buy their chain of banks.

But during the summer and fall of 1907 the stock market drifted downward and United Copper drifted downward as well. Since the shares of United were used as collateral for a whole host of loans the higher price had to be maintained. So to help support the price they started buying large quantities of the stock on margin with about twenty different brokerage houses. They had the brokerage houses 'park' the stocks, hold them without delivery, because they would have to pay cash for the certificates if delivered. The pool had outstanding loans to the brokerage houses approaching two million dollars.

Things were just not right with the market at large.

Richmond

The British embassy secretary and his wife, Charles and Claire Young, arrived at the Episcopalian Convention with a gift. It was beautiful Bible from none other than King Edward of England.

The gift was to celebrate the long and continuous heritage of the Anglican and Episcopalian church in both England and America. Mutual celebrations were already under way in Jamestown, Virginia, marking the 300 year anniversary of its founding.

But now, in addition to that, was the grand opening of the newly restored Bruton Church in Williamsburg, Virginia. Originally built in 1715, for the then British colonists, the church had became an altered and changed shadow of itself by the time the Reverend Dr. William A.R. Goodwin took over the parish in 1903. He began work on restoring the church to its original condition. Now it was done. It was the mission of the British Embassy Secretary Charles Young to present the Bible to the restored Bruton Church.

John organized a train trip to Williamsburg. He and his daughter Louisa, and Charles and Claire Young, with the Bible in hand, traveled together in the same cabin.

When they arrived at the station John started to rise. But Louisa and Claire were in conversation and did not show any sign of getting up. John sat back down and waited.

He watched out the window as people got off of the train and walked down the station platform toward the waiting cabs.

"Excuse me for interrupting but I think we should be getting off."

Louisa brushed him off.

"Not just yet, let us sit for awhile. I hate getting up with everyone else, it is so crowded. Just wait for the crowd to disperse a bit."

She turned back to their guests and continued talking.

Since both Charles and Claire did not budge, and both seemed fascinated with Louisa, John sat back in his seat. But he was nervous. He tapped his leg with his finger.

Most everyone had gotten off the train but it was not until the porter came and slid the cabin door open and said 'Williamsburg' that they realized it was time to depart.

John again was the first one up. He picked up the wooden box that contained the Bible and offered to carry it.

They all followed him out onto the platform. John walked them over to the cab station.

The dispatcher said all of the cabs were gone. They had all been dispatched. You can wait for another if you wish.

How long will that be?

Hard to say: not too long: you can wait in the station: I will call you.

On the corner, parked under a large shade tree, was an old horse drawn wagon with installed seats. It was attached to an old skinny ancient brown horse. Sitting on the front seat sat a young Negro boy, not more than fifteen, holding in his hands the reins, nothing but a frayed rope.

What about him?

The dispatcher shook his head. He's independent; not under my watch.

John turned to his guests. They were smiling, seemingly happy about traveling in America no matter what was happening.

"How would you like a true American antebellum experience like nothing you would have in England?

They both agreed.

John approached the cab. The boy nodded to him.

Charles and Claire climbed up into the wagon. The space was cramped so John set the box down on the seat next to the boy.

"What's your name son," John asked.

"Moses."

Surprised, John said: "Moses?"

"Yes sir, that's my name."

"Well, son, that is a pretty important name. Your mother named you Moses after the real Moses in the Bible?"

"Yes sir; that she did."

"Your mother must be a real God fearing woman."

"Yes sir; that she is."

The old horse turned its head around as if trying to better hear what was being said.

"Now son," John began, placing his fingers into his waist coat pockets and acting as serious as he could. "Are you worthy of such a grand name as Moses?"

The boy stared at John for a moment. He looked at John's nose but then back up to John's eyes. Then a wide smile crossed his lips. His eyes sparkled.

"My mother tells me that she found me in a basket in the woods where somebody left me behind. Never did find out who left me behind in that basket, my mother says it was like they had a Sunday picnic and when they collected up their things they left the best basket behind, but my mother says 'found you in a basket, boy, just like Moses, so that means you are bound for glory.'"

John smiled and glanced back at Mr. and Mrs. Young sitting in the back of the cab. Louisa stood next to the cab. She was covering her mouth with her gloved hand.

"Well your mother sounds to me to be a very smart woman."

"Yes sir; that she is."

"So your mother, she owns a Bible?"

"Yes sir; that she does."

"And that Bible I suppose is very important to her?"

"She reads from her Bible almost every night, she does."

"Well, in this wooden box," John said, placing his hand on the box. The boy looked down at the box sitting next to him. He continued to stare at the box as John continued to talk.

"In this wooden box is a big Bible that comes all the way from England. It is a very important Bible and these folks here themselves came all the way from England to bring us this Bible. It belongs to the Bruton Parish Church. Do you know where that is?"

The boy nodded and spoke while still staring at the wooden box.

"Yes sir; that I do."

"So can you make sure for me that these folks and their Bible both get to the Bruton Parish Church safe and sound?"

The boy looked up at John. "That's what I do," the boy said.

"What is that?"

"Getting people to where they are going. That is what I do."

"And I am sure that anyone with the honor of being named Moses does a good job of it too," John said as he pulled out a bill from his waistcoat pocket and, with the boy closely watching his every move, slid the bill into the woolen coat pocket of the boy.

"Can you do that for me?"

"Yes sir; that I can."

"Good."

There was a moment of silence as the boy stared at his woolen coat pocket. He seemed perplexed.

John watched him for a moment.

"Is there anything wrong?"

The boy looked up at John.

"That was a ten dollar bill you just put into my pocket."

"Was it?"

"Yes sir; that it is."

"That is to pay for the fare."

"My fare is not that much. I do not have change for no ten dollars."

"Well then, it is payment for the fare and for your extra protection in watching out for the safe delivery of this Bible."

The boy looked back down at the box sitting on the seat next to him.

"It must be a mighty important Bible."

"Yes Moses; that it is."

Moses looked back up at John and smiled a wide smile.

"Well then, you can trust in me."

John had to laugh.

"I knew that I could."

The boy glanced back at the two customers, asked if they were prepared, and when they nodded yes the boy turned back and slapped the old horse with the rope reins. The horse, reluctantly, started to slowly walk forward.

John and Louisa stood next to each other and watched as the party sauntered down the street.

When they were out of hearing range Louisa quietly asked: "When were they supposed to be there?"

John chuckled.

"I suppose when they get there."

New York

Otto Heinze noticed an anomaly.

In closely watching the trades being made on United Copper stock he realized that 450,000 shares were being traded, but that was actually 25,000 more shares than were outstanding.

How can this be?

How could more shares than existed be trading hands?

Otto came to one conclusion. He and Fritz and Morse as a pool had been buying stock to keep the price more elevated than stock in other Copper companies. But they did not buy the stock outright. They bought the stock on margin, meaning they borrowed the money from different brokerage houses to buy the stock. The brokerage house then held the stock certificates as collateral for the loans. But if the price of the stock declined then the value of the collateral declined and Otto had to put cash in to cover the difference. But if the price of the stock rose then the value of the collateral would be greater than the loans and they could then use the difference to buy more stock.

But speculators thought the stock price was too elevated and would soon decline in unison with all of the other copper companies. So speculators started 'short selling' the stock. This meant that they could 'borrow' a stock certificate from someone who owned the stock and 'sell' it with an obligation to 'buy' the stock later. By 'selling' the stock they hoped it would force the price of the stock to decline so that when they 'bought' the stock later it would be at a lower price and the difference would be their profit. If the stock price rose, however, then they would be forced to 'buy' the stock at a higher price than they 'sold' the stock and the difference would be a loss.

The problem, of course, was that if the person who actually owned the stock sold it while the short seller was 'borrowing' the stock then the short seller would have to immediately close his position by buying the stock.

But from whom were the short sellers borrowing stock? Otto thought he knew the answer. They were borrowing their shares from him.

Otto reasoned that he and his pool owned most of the outstanding shares of United Copper stock. Since the shares they had bought had not been delivered but were 'parked' at the different brokerage houses, he reasoned that the brokerage houses, using his shares, were lending them out to the short sellers.

Otto went to his brother Fritz.

We can corner the market on Union Copper stock.

We can make millions.

But we need some money.

Fritz arranged for a meeting with himself, Otto, Charles Morse, and

Charles Tracy Barney, president of The Knickerbocker Trust Company.

The Knickerbocker Trust Company was chartered in 1884 by Frederick G. Eldridge, a childhood friend and classmate of J. P. Morgan. Charles Tracy Barney became president in 1897. Under his leadership, through his connections of being on the board of directors of a host of companies and banks, and being the son–in–law of the financier William C. Whitney, the Knickerbocker grew tremendously. It opened several branch offices, in Harlem and the Bronx, which was a very new innovation at the time. By 1907 it had well over $65 millions in deposits from over 18,000 depositors making it the third largest Trust Company in New York City.

To help outwardly reflect their growing status the firm hired architect Stanford White of the prestigious firm of McKim, Mead & White to build their main location on the northwest corner of 34th Street and Fifth Avenue, directly across the street of the Waldorf-Astoria Hotel. It was a four story marble building fronted by four 17 ton Corinthian columns that upon completion in 1906 spoke of deep elegance and stability.

So if Otto and Fritz Heinze and Charles Morse needed to borrow money Charles Barney was a logical choice. Barney had even helped arrange the sale of his father-in-law's steamship company Metropolitan Steamship Company to Charles Morse in 1906 and sat on it's board, as well as being on the board of several of Morse's ice companies.

The earliest that Barney could meet with them was that evening at his home on 101 East 38th Street on the corner of Park Avenue. When Otto and Fritz and Morse arrived Lily Barney was in the front parlor with several lady friends. Lily, sitting across the parlor, waved at Charles Morse when she saw him. She was friends with his wife Clemence; they were on many different committees together for various causes. A servant showed the men upstairs into Barney's bedroom. When they entered he was standing at the window looking down into the street while taking off his coat. He turned when they entered.

Barney stood facing them as he hung his coat on a wooden stand. He stood with his chest out, proud. He had a short close cropped graying beard, but it overshadowed by his large twin pointed handlebar moustache. His hair was close cut and greatly thinning on the top of his head. He was well liked by many.

"Sorry for meeting you here but I am in a bit of a rush and my wife, well. . .some society meeting of some sort," he said as he brushed the air with his hands.

"We will try and not take up too much of your time."

"I must dress for the evening: an opera."

"Which one might that be," Fritz asked, trying to ease the conversation. He was a man about town, operas, shows, bars, female companions. At times his liaisons went late into the night.

"Oh I do not know. It is one of my wife's affairs. I believe it is a Gilbert and Sullivan thing."

Barney started to undo his tie.

"Please, have a seat," he said as he pointed toward his large canopied bed.

It was Charles Morse who spoke up. "Perhaps we should get right to the point. Otto?"

Otto explained the situation: their stock holdings in United Copper; the brokerage firms holding their stock; the shorts; the margin; the squeeze; the potential millions.

They, the ones in this room, owned most of the shares of United Copper. Buy now buying heavily they will drive up the price and thus dry up the shares outstanding. It will attract more short sellers thinking the stock is about to break down, causing the brokers to lend out more of his stock.

But then, by simultaneously calling for delivery of all the shares the brokerage firms held, they could corner the market and force the price to skyrocket. The brokers lent out their shares to the short sellers. If Otto called for his shares the brokers would have to get back the shares they lent out. The short sellers who held the shares would be forced to buy in a rising market and thus lose money. If the brokers can not get back the shares they need to deliver to Otto then they too would be forced to buy replacement shares, buying them in a rising market. The brokers would be forced to buy shares at a higher price and deliver them to Otto at the lower original price. That too would force the price up. And if they could not find shares to buy even at inflated prices then they would default on the call and have to pay Otto in cash what shares they owed at wherever the going price stood.

Then, at the appropriate time, Otto starts selling his shares at a higher price than he has to pay for them forcing the brokers and the short sellers to buy the same shares that Otto is selling at the inflated price. They will get killed and Otto and the pool will make millions.

Barney had been carefully listening as he undressed and redressed.

"But?" he asked.

Otto, standing, smiled as he glanced back and forth at Fritz and Morse, both sitting on the canopied bed.

"But we are a bit short of funds at the moment."

"How short?"

Otto explained that they were collectively on margin about $2 million dollars. They would have to buy what shares were still outstanding, and then start paying the margin when the brokers start delivery of their shares. But he felt all they needed was about $1.5 million to do the trick. The rest he would extract from the market as his purchasing and the buying of the shorts and the brokers drove up the price. Or, better yet, the brokers who had to default on delivery would have to pay Otto in cash.

When he finished talking there was silence in the room.

Barney, standing before his dresser and looking into the mirror, finished tying his tie.

A younger man appeared in the hallway at the door. He too was dressed for the evening. Barney could see him in the mirror.

"Yes Ashbel?"

"Sorry, father, but mother was wondering."

"Gentlemen: my son Ashbel. Tell her I am on my way down."

Barney turned and reached for his coat hanging from the wooden coat stand. He stopped before he put it on.

"I think you are wrong about the corner. You may not own as much of the stock as you think. And if it is to work you will need not only the two that you are margined, but perhaps another million at least to buy any new stock."

Barney finished putting on his coat.

"We can discuss it further at a latter date but for now I have to say that it is far too risky and I will have to decline. Now, gentlemen, as you have heard I must be off."

Richmond

One morning at breakfast John leaned in toward Bishop Lawrence.

"I do not like Bishop Doane's look. I am afraid that his heart is bothering him."

Lawrence looked over at Doane as he poked his fork at the potatoes on his plate.

"He does look a bit out of sorts."

"He is getting up there; he is seventy five years old I believe. He is a bit overweight as well."

Lawrence turned to face John and laughed.

"Morgan, my good fellow, we are all getting a bit old and a bit heavy in the waistline are we not?"

John smiled: "Speak for thyself brother."

John liked Bishop Doane even though they did not see eye to eye on things. Doane thought that a Bishops seat should not be a small parish church but should rather be a Cathedral. So, laying the corner stone on June 3, 1884, and overseeing the construction until completion in 1888, The Cathedral of All Saints in Albany New York was his crowning achievement.

Toward the end, when there were outstanding bills of $40,000 left, John, on his own, offered to front one third of the funds if he could raise the remainder from the Diocese. The funds were raised, John paid his share, and the building was completed. Doane, in jest, cut a bright new penny and sent John the two thirds piece as a charm for his watch guard and embedded the one third piece in the arch of the Benefactors' Door in the North Transept.

John, fingering the small token that he still kept on his watch chain, excused himself from the table.

At breakfast the next morning a Dr. Baldwin appeared at the door of the Rutherford house and John had him examine Bishop Doane. Outside Doane's room Louisa stopped John.

"Did you do this?"

John put his finger to his lips.

"I telegraphed him in New York and had him come down. Bishop Doane looked sickly to me."

"But why not just get a local doctor?"

"I do not know any one local. Besides, I know Baldwin and he is a good doctor."

One day Mrs. Lawrence received a telegram from Boston that a relative had died. Although she was not that close she nevertheless felt the need go. The Bishop would stay here and she could go on alone.

"Yes, indeed," John said, patting her on the shoulder. He stopped Bishop Lawrence in the hallway and insisted that he help. As she packed her bags John contacted Louis Sherry to arrange things.

Soon he tapped on her door. When she opened it John smiled and handed her an envelope.

"Here are your railroad and drawing room tickets from Richmond to Boston."

She was surprised. "Mr. Morgan, you are so kind. But William was attending to this."

226

"Yes, indeed. Now, when you arrive on the New York side of the ferry from Jersey City look for a cabman who will be standing up on his box with a white handkerchief tied to his left arm. That will be the man engaged to take you up to the Grand Central Station."

She smiled a deep and warm smile.

"Mr. Morgan, you are too kind for words."

It was the next day when a group of them went on an automobile ride to see some of the sights of the city. John never liked to sit in the front seat with the chauffeur because it was difficult to turn around and be a part of any discussion. But whenever they went as a group with two or more he insisted that he sit in front.

But as they approached the car Lawrence whispered to the others to 'keep him talking.' He then began running up ahead in order to get into the front seat himself.

John noticed what was happening.

"What are you doing?" he called after Lawrence.

"I shall be in the front today."

"Oh no, you will not," John shouted as he ran full speed to the car. John ran around the back of the car to the passenger side of the car. The spare tire was attached to the car door. John, without hesitation, climbed up and over the spare tire and into the window of the car. But then his bulk got stuck. The chauffeur in the car watched him with shocked surprise. John struggled to get over the tire and into the window.

Shouts of 'be careful' and 'are you all right' and 'what on earth' rang out.

John, laughing, tried to twist around in the seat. The chauffeur helped as much as he could, and Lawrence standing outside of the car, laughing too hard to be of much use, tried pushing him from behind.

It took a few moments of struggle but he was able to twist around and slid into the seat. His hair was in complete disarray.

"Well, then," John tried to say as nonchalantly as he could muster. "That matter is settled then." He was breathing heavily.

Lawrence piped up: "Morgan, this is not the type of activity I would suggest for a seventy year old man."

The two ladies got into the rear of the car. Lawrence, with the rear door open, stood outside looking in.

"You are a good man Mr. Morgan," one of the ladies said. "You are so kind and generous."

227

Otto decided to do it alone.

The reward was too great to let it pass him by. If they were not willing to go ahead then he would. Surely if he was in the middle of the thing his brother could find the money. He owned a bank.

On Saturday, October 12, United Copper opened in the morning at 45 1/2 and sold down by the end of the short trading day to 37 3/4. Surely that must be the action of short sellers driving the price down. Otto laughed to himself. Not for long, he thought; not for long.

He called his friend Philip Kleeberg, a broker with the firm Gross & Kleeberg, and told him to execute two separate orders on Monday. First he wanted to buy 5000 shares of United at ascending prices. That would force some short sellers to cover. Then, secondly, he wanted to issue a call to half of the brokers for all of the shares that he and Fritz and Morse owned. That would force some of those brokers to cover. The next day, after the price had shot up, he would call in all the rest of the shares at all of the other brokers. Most would not be able to cover and would have to default, they would have to pay cash for the then going price.

On Monday morning October 14 United Copper opened at 39 7/8 and drifted down to 39. Otto watched as his order hit the street.

Within 15 minutes there were 100 shares bought at 40.

Minutes later 100 shares bought at 41.

Then suddenly 100 shares bought at 49 7/8. What a jump.

This was followed by 1000 shares bought at 51.

Otto watched the ticker tape and watched the hands of the clock next to his desk.

There followed 100 shares bought at 52.

Otto clenched his fist. He was right. He was right. The outstanding shares being traded were so thin his single order for only 5000 shares was driving the price up before his very eyes.

Then there was a buy of 100 at 53.

At his office a courier came in with a bag. It was 100 stock certificates from one of his brokers. The courier needed payment for delivery. Otto issued him a check, drawn on their account at Mercantile National Bank, and took the bag. That was expected. He knew that some of the stock certificates would be delivered and he would have to pay for them. It was just a matter of how many. Not all of the brokers could deliver.

Then there was a buy of 700 at 57. That was quite a jump. The shares outstanding were dwindling, becoming scarce. That was the plan. It was working.

Another courier, more bags filled with certificates; another check. It was a big one this time. It was drawn on their account at Mercantile National Bank. Soon the couriers would be arriving at the bank to exchange the checks for cash.

He called his brother Fritz. He explained what was going on. At first Fritz screamed at him for going ahead but then Otto quoted him the pattern, the sky rocking price, and Fritz calmed down. So it was working, it was really working.

Yes.

Another courier, more certificates. I need money Fritz, I need money. Holding the phone to his ear he waved the man over, looked at the bill (startled a little by how much it was) and started writing out a check. This would be the last of what he had available.

He heard his brother on the line gasp. The ticker tape recorded a buy of 1000 shares at 59.

Fritz, he said. Did you see that?

Yes.

Another courier arrived just as the last was leaving. Otto waved him over.

He heard his brother on the line. Otto, his brother said as if not really believing what he was saying, a courier has come with one of your checks asking to cash it.

Yes, Fritz. More will be coming. I have tapped out the account and we will have to cover the buys. But Fritz, it is working. We've cornered them.

Fritz hesitated but then said that he would secure a loan, on his authority as President, through Mercantile National Bank to cover any and all checks drawn on Otto Heinze & Company.

You better be right, Otto.

I am.

When he put the phone back down into the receiver Otto slammed his fists down on his desk with ecstatic joy.

The ticker tape clicked a buy of 1000 shares at 60.

Just wait until tomorrow. Tomorrow is the kill.

Richmond

Telegrams continued to arrive for John. Whenever they arrived while he was with a group he took it, stepped aside, and then immediately tore it open and read with fixed eye and focused attention. Everyone merely brushed it aside and went on with their business. It was just the busy banker J. P. Morgan doing his business. But Bishop William Lawrence watched him. He knew John well enough to know when something was amiss. But William never interfered.

Once at dinner a message came. John tore it open and read it right there at the table. He heavily put the palms of his hands flat onto the table and fixed his steady stare at the wall opposite. Others all around him were talking and laughing but John was deep in thought.

Then someone spoke to him as if in a jolly joke.

"Mr. Morgan, you seem to have some bad news."

John shot his stare toward the man and did not say a word. After a moment the smile on the man's face dissolved and he turned to his partner to start a conversation.

John said nothing.

Two men came one day and he took them into a side room away from the others and closed the door. Louisa knew them from his office. They were in there for some time before they all came out, very solemn and quiet. The two men immediately left. Louisa stopped her father in the hallway. There were guests at either end of the hall talking. Louisa leaned toward him and whispered.

"Is everything all right?"

John tried to smile but shook his head.

"I do not know."

"Is there something wrong?"

"There are some things going on which may turn out bad."

"Do you need to go back to New York?"

John glanced down the hall as if someone could hear.

"They want me to come back to New York but if I left now it might ensure a panic knowing that I rushed back. If word got out that I was called away early then everyone will automatically think the situation is grave."

"And is the situation grave?"

John looked at her but did not reply.

"Should you rush back?"

John thought for a moment and then shrugged his shoulders.

He whispered very low, for someone was walking down the hallway toward them: "Soon, but not now."

At the convention meeting held in the State Capital John introduced a resolution to the Committee to reduce the number of lay and clerical delegates to the conventions. It sparked a sharp disagreement between those who favored and those who opposed the resolution. John was amazed at the intensity of the feelings back and forth. If he had known before the discord it caused he never would have introduced the idea to a full vote.

But a vote was taken and while the votes were being counted the debate continued with some heated exchanges.

John could not take it.

Shaking his head he stood up and from his seat on the floor he closed his eyes and began to sing.

His deep singing voice seeped into the overall dim of the arguing clamor. He sang the hymn 'O Zion, Haste.'

O Zion, haste, thy mission high fulfilling,
To tell to all the world that God is light,
That He who made all nations is not willing
One soul should perish, lost in shades of night.

One by one everyone turned to see John standing alone, singing with his deep voice, and gradually gaining volume. They began to grow quiet, listening. Some even turned toward him and began to sing the well known hymn with him. They sang the refrain: Publish glad tidings, tidings of peace; Tidings of Jesus, redemption and release.

John opened his eyes to sing the second part.

Behold how many thousands still are lying
Bound in the darksome prison house of sin,
With none to tell them of the Savior's dying,
Or of the life He died for them to win.

The debating on the floor grew more quiet. More and more people began to sing along with him.

Proclaim to every people, tongue, and nation
That God, in Whom they live and move, is love;
Tell how He stooped to save His lost creation,
And died on earth that we might live above.

They all knew the hymn. It was written by Mary Thomson one dark night in 1868 while she sat up comforting one of her children ill with typhoid fever. Death knocked on the door; she did not what to let it in.

'Tis thine to save from peril of perdition
The souls for whom the Lord His life laid down;
Beware lest, slothful to fulfill thy mission,
Thou lose one jewel that should deck His crown.

By then everyone on the floor, as well as in the balconies, had stopped talking and had begun to sing.

Give of thy sons to bear the message glorious;
Give of thy wealth to speed them on their way;
Pour out thy soul for them in prayer victorious;
O Zion, haste to bring the brighter day.

As powerful a man he was, anyone who knew him well knew how shy he was before crowds. For him to stand up alone and sing, and then to lead the congregation in song, was a remarkable event. It was one of those moments that his friends would talk about for a long time.

He comes again! O Zion, ere thou meet Him,
Make known to every heart His saving grace;
Let none whom he Hath ransomed fail to greet Him,
Through thy neglect, unfit to see His face.

After the refrain John held up his arms to conduct the long low: amen.

It was quiet. Everyone sat down. The committee chairman announced the vote. It had not passed. But no one protested. John had brought order.

All was peace.

New York

On Tuesday October 15 Otto was ready. He sat at his desk at Otto Heinze and Company. He put out a call to the entire twenty brokerage houses that held his stock to please present the certificates that day. By

232

Stock Exchange rules that meant they all had to physically deliver the stock certificates by 2:00 p.m. or else they would be in default.

But with each certificate presented Otto had to pay in cash the price he had bought the stock in order to cover his margin purchase of that stock.

That morning the stock of United Copper opened at 50 per share. It was down from the prior day but it was still up almost 11 points from the opening of the previous day. That was a 28 percent increase in price in one day.

As everyone tried to cover their short position Otto expected the price to shoot for the moon. By this time tomorrow he could be one of the wealthiest men in New York City.

But the story of the stock's price the previous day was reported in newspapers all across the country. It had soared from 39 to 60 in just one day. From everywhere people who owned stock, from New York to Butte, Montana, saw that and thought that now was a good time to sell and cash in on the high price before it came down, as it would inevitably do. Sell orders flooded in from everywhere.

The price held steady.

At Otto Heinze & Company couriers were arriving bringing bags filled with stock certificates. Otto at first wrote checks, drawn on the Mercantile National Bank account, and watched the ticker tape. More couriers, more bags full of certificates, more checks.

The price began to fall.

Otto got a frantic call from his brother. You are excessively overdrawn; I cannot cover the account indefinitely. This is a drain on the whole banks cash. You must do something.

Otto did not understand. Why did the market price not go up? There are no shares out there. I own them all.

But still the sell orders flooded in.

The price continued to drop.

The certificates continued to be delivered.

Otto closed his eyes and began to tremble.

He was wrong.

There were more shares out there than he knew. And he had created the situation where they were now coming out of nowhere and were killing him.

How could he be so wrong?

In desperation Otto began selling, selling. He had to raise cash, quickly, in order to pay for all of the certificates he had called in.

The price of the stock had briefly rose to 59 but then, as if falling off a cliff, gaining momentum as it fell, the price hit 50, and then 45, and then 36 as sell orders came in from everywhere. And Otto himself frantically sold shares to raise cash.

But he gave out.

Fritz called. He could not cover the losses anymore. It was going to bring down his whole bank. Do something.

Otto ran over and closed the door. He locked the door. He locked out the outside world and retreated back to his desk. Couriers one by one came and knocked on the door. They banged on the windows. Some shouted. Some held up certificates to the window. They kicked at the door. But Otto did not move. He sat in his chair behind his desk and shook his head at the men outside banging and kicking at the door.

Go away. I have to refuse delivery. Go away.

The phone was ringing and ringing. He did not answer.

One by one they went away. But each broker when he heard Otto refused delivery was stuck with the stock. They sold it at whatever price they could to minimize their loss. Philip Kleeberg of Gross & Kleeberg, the brokers who bought all the shares the day before, called Otto but no one answered. Kleeberg had to turn around and sell all of the shares he had bought for Otto.

The price dropped like a stone.

At the close the last sale was at 25. It had soared from 39 to 60 in one day, and then fell from 60 to 25 in one day.

Everyone knew the next day would be deadly.

Wednesday, October 16.

United Copper opened at 30. In three minutes it dropped to 20. There was a bit of calm but then it fell to 18. In the screaming and the shouting on the curb the stock dropped to 10 by the end of the day.

Otto assured the brokers and the Stock Exchange officials that he would cover all of his debts, including Kleeberg. Fritz offered $100,000, a third of the outstanding debt. He offered other debtors a 10 percent cash settlement with the remainder in three, six, and nine month notes.

Gross & Kleeberg sold the remaining shares of United Copper that they held for Otto. He had refused acceptance of 3202 shares. They then suspended all trading and closed and locked their doors. Established in December, 1904, the firm was now done.

They filed a law suit against Otto Heinze & Company for damages.

That meant that all bets were off.

Newspapers questioned Fritz Heinze, as Otto's brother. Fritz claimed that he had nothing to do with the attempted corner but then it was discovered that he had personally secured a loan for Otto through his bank where he was president, director, and majority stock holder.

Bank depositors feared that the bank itself was involved and was now in trouble. They began to withdraw their funds.

A run on the bank began.

It was reported that Fritz Heinze was seen in heated exchange with Charles Morse. Morse controlled the National Bank of North America as well as the New Amsterdam National. He was a director and vice president of Mercantile with Heinze. How involved was he, and how involved were his banks?

A run on both the banks began.

Even a rumor started to spread that even Barney at Knickerbocker Trust was somehow involved.

A run on that bank began as well.

Thursday, October 17.

At 1:00 pm The Stock Exchange suspended Otto Heinze & Company for failure to meet their legal obligations.

Also on Thursday the State Savings Bank of Butte, Montana, announced that it was insolvent. It seems that State Savings Bank of Butte, Montana was actually owned by Fritz Heinze, purchased in 1905, and it served as a correspondent bank for the Mercantile National of New York. The bank, with 6,000 individual depositors, had funds invested in Mercantile National, had loans outstanding to different Heinze interests of nearly $1 million, and had as collateral for those loans the now collapsed stock certificates in United Copper Company. Fearful that there would be a run on the bank given all the news from New York the bank decided to close instead. The president of the bank put it bluntly: The bank is insolvent.

The run on Mercantile National continued, draining its cash. On the day before Fritz Heinze appealed to the New York Clearing House (NYCH), of whom his bank was a member, for help. The Clearing House said they would stand by the bank as long as they found that the books were in good order. The bank remained open as the auditors poured over the books until late into the night. By midnight the announcement was made that they were satisfied the bank was sound and they would advance the necessary cash funds to secure the bank.

This was officially announced at an 11:00 am news conference. But there was a catch. A group of nine member banks, each putting up $200,000 to help Mercantile National, demanded the resignation of Mercantile National's board of directors, and the resignation of Fritz Augustus Heinze as President.

By now the news of the deep involvement of Charles Morse in the attempted corner was common knowledge. How involved were his banks? The New York Clearing House began investigating his banks as well for solvency. By Sunday the NYCH took drastic action. They suspended both Fritz Augustus Heinze and Charles Wyman Morse from all banking interests in New York City.

They were out.

The NYCH assured the public that everything was fine. They would take care of everything. There was nothing to worry about.

But if everything is fine then why are you firing all the top men of half the banks and pouring money in to boost the effected banks.

The runs continued.

Richmond

The last day of the convention was on Saturday. Everyone had scheduled to attend the last meetings and then leave on Sunday.

As Bishop Lawrence was walking down the hallway toward the front door John called him from his room. William stepped back and looked in.

"Yes, Morgan."

John waved him into the room.

"Bishop, I am going back to New York on the noon train."

"But why do that?"

"They are in trouble in New York: they do not know what to do, and I do not know what to do, but I am going back."

"Yes, that is fine. But why leave on the noon train? You will arrive in New York in the middle of the night. Why not get Mr. Sherry to have your two cars hitched onto the early evening train tonight? We will all pack up and go with you."

John thought for a moment. In his rush to get there he did not think it clear. He would arrive in the middle of the night and what good would that do? But if instead he left that evening he could sleep on the train and arrive home fresh and ready.

John smiled and reached out and grabbed William's shoulder.

"I had not thought of that: I do not believe it can be done, but I will try."

"My good man," William said. "You forget who you are. If you want it then it can be done."

The train pulled into Washington at around eleven o'clock. It was laid over for about an hour. Each of the group came out onto the station platform to wish farewell to Mrs. Greer, wife of Bishop David Hummell Greer. She was off to visit a friend for a few days. It was a cold night so they all said their farewells as fast as they could and then retreated back into the warm Pullman car. John waited on the platform and watched as the Bishop walked his wife to the awaiting cab. When David returned John waved him toward the door.

"Now for a good night's sleep."

"For me I think I will have one last smoke out on the rear platform," John said. "Care to join me?"

David pulled his jacket closed.

"No, it is a bit too chilly for me. I believe I shall retire."

"Well then, have a nice sound sleep."

John, alone, walked the car and exited the rear door onto the small platform. There was a small chair tucked tightly against the railing. He sat down. A small breeze rustled through the trees off to the side of the rails. Waiting for a moment, wondering, he took a deep breath. He was tired. Perhaps he should go directly to bed. But instead he pulled out a cigar from his waistcoat pocket. He lit it with a match, waved the match in the air until the fire was out, and then flicked it out onto the tracks.

He watched the trees sway, lost in thought, dozing a bit, John did not know how much time had past when he was startled by foot steps on the gravel by the rails. He turned to see a man and a woman approaching the rear of the train from across the tracks. He watched as they approached and then finally called out to them.

"May I help you?"

"Yes, please," the woman spoke. "We are looking for the Morgan train, in from Richmond."

"This is it. How many I help you?"

They came up to the steps.

"We are looking for the Bishop David Greer. Is he aboard?"

"Yes he is. He is in his cabin asleep. May I be of assistance?"

237

"It is actually his wife we are looking for. Is she aboard as well?"

"No, madam. She left a bit ago to visit a friend."

The woman looked over at the man, concerned.

"How long ago did she leave?"

"I would think perhaps an hour. Why do you ask?"

"You see sir that is the problem. We are the friends she was coming to visit and she has not yet arrived."

"I see," John mumbled.

"We live but a ten minute ride from here and thought she should surely have arrived at our house by now."

"Indeed. Come, please come aboard. I'll wake up Bishop Greer."

As John banged on Bishop Greer's door calling out his name the woman walked up the platform to the station in search of a porter. The man stayed behind with John. Finally David opened his door. He was dressed in his nightshirt. His hair was uncombed and his moustache was in disarray. He instantly saw the man standing behind John.

"Peter?"

In a second of silence he knew something dreadful was wrong.

"Let me get dressed."

David was determined to get off the train and look for her. He wanted to call a cab.

"I'll retrace the route to your house."

"We've done that."

As they were talking the engine blew a short sharp whistle. It was preparing to leave. A porter walked the platform to make sure everyone was aboard.

"I have to find her, Morgan."

But as he tried to quickly pack his bags the woman finally returned from the station house. She walked up to David. He stopped and stared at her in fear. She smiled, and then slightly laughed.

"What?" David asked.

"She is safe," she said. David closed his eyes and sat down on his bunk. He took a deep breath.

"I called several near by hotels, just in case. I finally found her at the Shoreham Hotel. She said she must have had the wrong address because she could not find our house. She said she was too tired to deal with it so she went to the hotel and would figure it all out in the morning."

One by one as the four of them looked at each other they started to laugh.

"So she is safe?"

"Yes, she was sleeping like a baby."

When the porter from the platform called out "all aboard" the man and woman rushed off the train.

"Don't worry," she called out to David. "We will gather her up in the morning."

Early the next morning as the train was pulling into Jersey City Bishop Lawrence and Bishop Doane came back to the car for some bread and coffee. They found John sitting there. He was rocking back and forth in his seat loudly singing some song holding the table tumblers in his hands. He laughed when they entered.

"What on earth is going on here?" Lawrence asked him.

"Good cheer."

"I can see that. Have you even been to bed?"

"Oh, my good man, while you were soundly sleeping we have had great adventures. But no, I am afraid I have not had much sleep."

John told them the story of the missing Mrs. Greer.

New York

When the train pulled in at the ferry house in New York it was a scene of organized confusion as everyone in the party disembarked from the train, piling their luggage on the platform, organizing lifts and porters, some going by another train somewhere else, others going by ferry, while others needed cabs to take them somewhere in New York. John was in the center of it all, organizing, explaining, helping, and calling cabs.

He had his own brougham with his own man waiting for him and Louisa. His man was securing their luggage to the back of the brougham.

As the crowd dispersed and everyone said their farewells someone in a cab called out to John as they were pulling away.

"Morgan, will we see you at service today at St. George?"

John waved to them. "Perhaps so," he said.

When he had seen to everyone else John finally got into his brougham. Louisa was already sitting inside. They looked at each other and sighed.

"Well, that is over."

John laughed. He called out to the coachman to the West Shore Ferry House. Once the cab was moving John sat back and lit a cigar. He pulled out a handkerchief and wiped his nose.

"Cold coming on?" Louisa asked.

John nodded.

"I do not suppose you would want to come up with me to Highland Falls and visit the kids?"

"No, no. As much as I would like to I need to stay here. The situation seems to have taken a turn for the worse. I fear for tomorrow and what it may bring."

"So it is bad then?"

"I have arranged for George Perkins and Charles Steele to meet me at the Library today in order to fill me in on the details."

"You will stay at the house? But Mother is in Europe. I thought it was shut down?"

"It is. I will have to stay at a hotel for now."

"Do not be silly. Our house is open. Annie will let you in. Once I get to Highland Falls I will send Herbert down. He should be there by dusk. Our house is yours."

"You do not need to go to all that trouble."

Louisa stared at him: "Father, you do as I say."

He put up his hands: "All right, all right."

At the ferry he dropped her off and said goodbye. Getting back into the brougham he told his valet to drive to the Library. As they pulled up to the curb he noticed that across the street reporters had already started lining up. They must have gotten word that he was coming back today. He told his valet to take the luggage into the Satterlee house just next door and then he mounted the steps to his Library.

John was seventy years, six months, and three days old when he mounted the steps, cigar in hand. Standing at the opened door was Bella da Costa Greene.

"Well, well: a nice welcome back to the Master."

John grunted as he passed by her into the rotunda.

"They are here, waiting in your office."

John, without a missed step walked into his office. He was at work now and there was a lot to do.

When he entered both Charles Steele and George Perkins stood and greeted him.

"Gentlemen, fill me in," John said. "I have a cold and I did not get much sleep last night so make it brief but make it thorough."

At lunchtime both Steele and Perkins left. The valet came in to tell

John that his luggage was next door at the home of Mr. Satterlee. John asked if he could bring in his table. The valet disappeared and then came back with a folding table that he opened up in the middle of the room. He placed a little silver box in the center of the table. John nodded to him and pulled up a chair to the table. Once sitting he pulled out a handkerchief and blew his nose. His cold was getting worse. John placed the handkerchief on the table next to him, then lit a cigar, and then opened the box. There were two decks of cards. He took out one of them, shuffled the cards, and then laid out a game of solitaire.

It was time to think.

Hours passed.

Toward dusk Herbert Satterlee came into the room. John looked up and smiled.

"Did you really come all the way down from Highland Park?"

"Yes I did. Louisa insisted. She said you were sick, your house was shut down, and you were facing trouble tomorrow at work."

"Well, I will have to admit that she was accurate on all counts."

"Besides," Herbert said. "I came on my own free will. Let me help you however I can. The market situation seems to be getting worse."

John nodded. "That too is true," he said.

"Come to the house. We can have dinner."

John looked back down at the table. His cards were all over the table, his game incomplete.

"No, not just yet. In a moment."

Herbert watched him. He was distant. He had seen John this way before. It was best to let his mind return on its own time.

"Whenever you wish."

But by then John was playing his cards.

Thinking.

Herbert, standing by the door, watching John and John not even realizing that Herbert was still there, thought to himself: To understand his method of attacking such a problem one has got to realize his passion for order. Undoubtedly he inherited some of this; but the story of his boyhood and youth shows that it was also cultivated. He lived in an orderly home when he was not in a school or college, and his parents and grandparents did things in an orderly way. Even as a boy he was fond of checkers and chess. When he played cards with others it was Whist, not Poker: that was his favorite game. Left to himself, whenever he had the opportunity, it was natural that he should try to create order among the cards which had been mixed up by shuffling and to build them up in the orderly sequence of suits. He wanted to substitute a pattern for disorder. That was undoubtedly why he loved all games of solitaire.

Herbert smiled. John was a million miles away. Herbert turned and left, trying not to make a sound.

Monday, October 21.

Next morning John came down for breakfast at eight o'clock. George Perkins was there waiting. There was coffee and toast, buns and cereal.

John, as soon as he sat down, began.

"George. I need a few good men, experienced men, good numbers men, who can go over the books and tell me if they are sound or not. I was thinking of Thomas Joyce, he is one of our own, and Henry Davison, vice president of First National Bank. George Baker thinks highly of him and that is good enough for me."

"You want to bring in others then?"

"Of course, this is too big. We will not get anywhere without coordination."

"Richard Trimble of U. S. Steel, I have worked with him. He is a good numbers man."

"Good. Herbert, call Davison and tell him what I want. And I want to see him in my office later. George, go downtown and talk to Joyce and call Trimble. Have all of them meet me at my office as soon as possible."

Herbert went to the phone in the next room.

"This has to be a combination. I want an inner circle of people I know and trust so we can fix this up. That means you, and that means George Baker of First National Bank, and that means James Stillman of National City Bank. I want to see all of you in my office later, set up a time convenient for everyone. Make it one o'clock."

"I can understand Baker, but Stillman? You don't really see eye to eye on a lot of things. Didn't he call you 'a back number' or something?"

"It does not matter. First National is a large bank and Baker and I get along very well, a handshake and it is done. National City Bank is one of the largest so we will need them too, and Stillman I respect, I trust his judgment even if I sometimes disagree. This situation is too large to be petty. And beside, Stillman is Rockefeller's banker. We may need to have him on board as well."

George laughed. "Good luck with that."

John just grunted.

Herbert came back into the kitchen.

"I talked with Davison and he is on board. He suggests a good detail man is a Benjamin Strong, secretary at Bankers Trust."

John looked at George searching.

"I've heard of him but don't really know him," George replied as he shrugged his shoulders.

"Well, call him. If Davidson says he is good then he is good. I need the whole lot of them."

John took a napkin and laid it on his lap.

"Now, Herbert. I need some butter for this toast. George, I will see you downtown."

But before either of them did either of their tasks John suddenly grabbed a napkin and sneezed. He looked at the two of them and shook his head. This was not the time for this.

When he arrived at The Corner and walked up into the Drexel Building at 23 Wall Street and toward his office there were three men sitting in the lobby waiting for him. He walked the hall briskly as employees nodded as he passed. In his office he took off his coat and hung it on the wooden coat stand. The top half of the wooden partitions that made up the walls of his office were made of glass. From the central location of his office he could stand and look all around the floor. But the wooden portion of the partitions was high enough that when he sat down only the persons in the very next offices could look in and see him. From his sweeping view of the whole floor before he sat down everything was buzzing busy like a hive on an active day.

His secretary waited until John sat before he approached the desk. George Perkins walked into the room.

"Yes James."

"Sir, there is a call from the National Bank of Commerce requesting an immediate call back as soon as you get in. And there are three gentlemen here to see you. They are a committee from the board of directors of the Knickerbocker Trust Company. They say it is urgent for them to see you."

"Yes, well is not everything urgent? Since they are here then show them in."

As James left the room John turned to George with a questioning look.

"The Knickerbocker Trust? What do you suppose that is all about?"

"I don't know. It seems like everyone is getting hit. They are pretty big; I hope they're not in trouble."

"The National Bank of Commerce is the clearing house for Knickerbocker. I was a vice president there until a few years ago, still on the board in fact."

"With them calling and these guys here at the same time; suppose there's a connection?"

John raised one eyebrow. "Pieces to a puzzle," he said.

"Anyway Thomas Joyce is here, Davison should be here any minute and he said that his man Strong is coming over as well. Baker and Stillman are on for one o'clock. Trimble will be about half an hour."

John grunted and nodded.

When the three men from Knickerbocker appeared at the door John stood up and waved them in.

"Gentlemen please, have a seat, have a seat. This is George Perkins."

Everyone nodded and shook hands.

"Now. What brings you to me?"

The balding man with the thin moustache spoke first.

"We represent the board of directors of The Knickerbockers Trust Company. I can only say that this is a very difficult and trying situation for us. We come to you both because of your position but also for your long standing friendly association with our bank, in particular with our founder Fred Eldridge."

John smiled.

"Indeed, Fred and I were old school mates at Cheshire back in, what; it must be 1851 or so. He was a good friend for a lot of years. A fine fellow. His son is one of your vice presidents."

The three men seemed to nod in unison. Then the younger man with the thick black moustache spoke next.

"It is in lieu of the developing situation out on the street with the announced resignations of Heinze and Morse and now the runs on their banks, as well as our own, that we had to consider their connections with our own President Charles Barney."

"Barney?" John snapped.

There was silence in the room.

"What is that about Charles Barney? I consider him too as a friend. What are you talking about? The man does not have a crooked bone in his body."

It was the oldest man of the three who had the courage to speak. He spoke in a soft monotone and used his hands a lot to accentuate his point.

"It seems that when the New York Clearing House was questioning

244

Charles Morse he mentioned that they should look around in places other than him if they were serious in getting to the bottom of this. I believe that we all can agree that Charles Morse is regarded as a dangerous and unsavory man in banking circles but unfortunately Mr. Barney chose to associate with the man both professionally and personally. Barney is director of several Morse companies including the National Bank of North America as well as the New Amsterdam National Bank. In addition Barney is on the board of the American Ice Company, is a major shareholder in the Consolidated Steamship Lines, all major Morse concerns. Furthermore the Knickerbocker Trust itself, under the stewardship of Barney, has major holdings in the Bank of North America, the American Ice Company, the American Ice Securities Company, the Butterick Company, and the Clyde Steamship Company, again, all major Morse concerns. You can begin, perhaps, to see our concern. And then there is the matter of the seat. After Morse acquired a large block of stock in our bank about three weeks ago he demanded to have a seat on the board. Not only did the board vote against the idea but several members actually threatened to resign if the matter went through. It was not only a major rebuff to Morse but to Barney as well. And now Morse is mentioning us to the New York Clearing House as a possible place to investigate further. We do not know how fully Barney is connected nor do we wish to find out."

The man stopped talking in order to let everything sink in. Then the balding man with the thin moustache spoke next.

"Rumors are flying about and we are suffering a great deal of pressure from withdraws. We have some sixty million on deposit but only ten million in cash. And that is rapidly being withdrawn. We applied for a loan with the Bank of Commerce."

The man paused. John waited.

"And?" John finally demanded.

The man glanced at the others.

"We applied for a loan but were informed that it was denied. In addition, the Bank of Commerce informed us that they would no longer serve as our Clearing House. A formal statement to the press is being prepared."

John could barely believe what he was hearing but outwardly showed nothing.

The man with the large black mustache continued.

"Therefore we have asked, and have received, the resignation of Charles Barney as president of the bank. By doing so we hope it will deflect the adverse consequences of his personal associations away from us. We cannot sustain for long a run on our bank like the one we are experiencing."

John sat still staring at the men for a moment in silence.

"Is the resignation public knowledge?"

"Not at present but it will within an hour or so. Another board member, A. Foster Higgins, will take his place."

"You may be able to ride out the Barney storm, but not the action of the Bank of Commerce. If anything will take you down that will."

"That is precisely why we are here."

"Sir." It was George, standing in the corner. When John looked over George nodded his head toward the front.

"Davison and Strong are here."

"Good."

John banged his hand down on a small bell on his desk. As he was talking his secretary James came to the door.

"Gentlemen, I would advise a meeting of the full board as soon as possible, if not this afternoon then tonight. You must figure out what your next course of action will be but by all means I would open in the morning. Do not show outwardly any panic. But meanwhile I must have complete and unhindered access to your books. I have several men here now that will get started immediately. I must know what your true position is. Now, James: show these gentlemen to the conference room."

As the three men filed out into the hallway James came over to John and leaned forward and whispered to him.

"Sir, Henry Davison and Benjamin Strong are here to see you. . ."

"Yes, yes I know," John cut him short.

"And a Charles Barney as well," James continued.

John sank back into his chair.

James left with the men. John, very slowing, rose from his chair. He turned to look out over the wooden partition and only slowly raised his head above the wood to see through the glass. Toward the front waiting room he saw Barney sitting alone in a wooden chair looking about. The chairs on either side of him were empty. He was smartly dressed, as he always did, his high white collar and black Ascot tie. His handlebar moustache was twirled into two perfect points. His hands were crossed over each other patiently sitting in his lap.

"Oh, Charley, Charley," John whispered, "what have you done?"

John sat back down in his chair.

"You can't meet with him," George said.

"I know," John replied. "I know. If I am to be seen as independent from this whole mess I can not meet with him. You know I personally own some stock in the Knickerbockers, and the company here has monies deposited there. If they go down we will lose as well. But I can not touch that if I am to be believed as an independent broker."

With his elbow on his desk John rested his forehead in the palm of his hand for a moment. He tried to take a deep breath but quickly pulled out his handkerchief and blew his nose.

"You don't look very good."

"And I feel even worse."

"What about Barney?"

James happened to walk past the door and John waved him in.

"Tell Mr. Barney that I apologize but it is impossible for me to see him at the moment. I will be tied up most the day."

"Yes sir; there is news that just came over the wires from New York Clearing House that several bank presidents have given their resignations: Orlando F. Thomas, president of Consolidated National, Edward R. Thomas of Hamilton Bank, and Charles Barney of Knickerbockers Trust. Is he the same, sir?"

"Yes, James. He is the same."

"Then that explains his comment."

"What was that?"

"Well, sir, he asked to see you and then mumbled, almost to himself, as he sat down, that these are 'troublous' times. It seemed a bit odd of a comment at the time."

John turned to George.

"A bit of house cleaning is going on. Now, fill in Davidson and Strong and get them over to the Knickerbocker and get started. Are they solvent? That is the question: are they solvent?"

John spent the entire day meeting with other bankers. He met with George Baker and James Stillman and both said they were on board with whatever he proposed. Good, John said. Good. We have a forest fire to fight and now we need to find out where to begin.

That evening he went to dinner with his partners George Perkins and Charles Steele. He wanted to dine at Sherry's Restaurant at Fifth Avenue and 44th Street. John wanted to thank Louis Sherry for his superb job in catering his whole Triennial Convention of the Episcopalian Church in Richmond. Son of a St. Albans, Vermont carpenter, when Sherry was let go from his job as a waiter in the Hotel Brunswick patrons liked him and his service so well that they helped him start his own restaurant, Sherry's Restaurant.

"He is a man who knows his wines, that is for sure."

It was said that by observing a customers bearing he could predict what course the customer would like.

When they were done with dinner they started to leave but noticed the commotion in one of the large dining rooms. John and Perkins stood to the side and watched. It was the meeting of the Board of Directors of the Knickerbocker Trust.

John could not believe his eyes. They were having their meeting, discussing the desperate emergency and the dangers that the Trust was facing, and whether the bank had enough resources to survive. But the windows and the doors were wide open and the talking and the shouting could be heard in the hallway outside the room and perhaps even in the street below. Waiters ran in and out, hearing everything. They whispered to guests. In the open dining room below groups of dinners, usually laughing and talking among themselves, now hearing of what was going on in the private rooms upstairs, wandered up and stood about in the hallway listening in on the discussion. Some even went inside the room and stood about watching and hearing.

John turned to George and shook his head.

"Why here? It is like an open town hall meeting where everyone can attend."

"Look," George pointed out. "Isn't that Brightman from the New York Times? News reporters are freely passing in and out of the room."

A couple passed by and the woman leaned into her husband. Don't we have some of our money in the Knickerbocker? Yes, we do. I think I'll take care of that first thing in the morning.

John watched as the couple walked down the hall.

Standing in a corner down the hall was a man who seemed to be one of the directors. John could just overhear him saying that if we get help overnight we shall reopen in the morning. If we don't, we won't. That's all there is to it at present. We can't tell now whether we are going to get help or not.

John closed his eyes and turned away.

"What madness," he mumbled.

"Rumors are going to fly all over town that the bank is in trouble."

"I can not watch this any more."

"I'll stay and bring you any news. You'll be at the Library?"

John grunted as he walked away, his walking cane tapping the carpeted hallway faster than he walked.

Tuesday, October 22.

By morning there was already a line formed outside the large bronze doors of Knickerbocker Trust Company. News of the board meeting at Sherry's Restaurant had spread throughout the city all night. Many went to the Night and Day Bank. It was an experiment in banking funded by Edward Henry Harriman. The concept was to stay open all night so that all the restaurants, clubs, theaters, and hotels could deposit their funds or acquire needed funds instead of waiting until the regular banks opened the next morning.

People deposited checks drawn on Knickerbocker for cash. The Night and Day Bank gathered up these checks and then sent messengers with the checks to sit outside the Knickerbocker all night until they opened. Others paid boys to wait. Boxes were brought so that those in line could sit down. Blankets were brought to protect from the windy autumn night. By an hour before they opened over one hundred people were standing in line.

Inside the bank the tellers were getting ready. They knew it would be a tough day. They piled stacks of cash in thousand dollar lots on the counter beside each teller. The bank hoped that when customers saw so many piles of cash it would settle their fears.

In the basement sat Benjamin Strong. He had been there the entire night and spread out on the table in front of him was all the books, the securities, and the statements.

Are they solvent?

That was why John sent him there. It was his job to find out.

The bank opened the doors. The customers filed in. It cleared the street. But then more and more people started showing up. They circled the lines inside the bank lobby around and around so that it would not spill out into the street. The piles of cash began disappearing. By the time the tellers could compute the interest on the accounts and stamp the voucher and count out the money more and more people arrived in line. The line spilled out of the bank, down the front steps, and down the sidewalk. Automobiles and broughams lined the street as people got out in order to get in line.

Local police began appearing and took up positions.

Across the street at the Waldorf-Astoria on the second and third and fourth floors guests looked out and watched the street below. Talk began. What is that? Do you see, what is going on? Telephone calls were made: you should see what is happening here.

News spread.

In addition to the individual depositors messengers from other banks arrived with bags and satchels full of checks drawn on Knickerbocker cashed at other banks.

Vice President William Trumbull came out from behind the cage and started to speak to the crowd. There were shouts for him to speak up. Those in the back cannot hear. He cupped his hands around his mouth. The bank is solvent, he said. We will keep the bank open until the normal three o'clock closing time. You do not need to worry.

No one left the line.

Some more loudly complained at the slowness of the tellers.

A telephone call came in for Benjamin Strong. It was from Henry Davison. John watched from across his desk as Davison talked to Strong, writing notes down onto a pad of paper. Davison was a much younger man, only about forty, clean shaven, one of the new men. Benjamin Strong too was much younger, only about thirty five. Clean shaven as well.

John held his cigar in his hand, twirling it back and forth between two fingers. He ran the fingers of his other hand through his side whiskers. He glanced at George Baker sitting silently. He was one of the old breed like himself. Huge burnsides style whiskers, colored since they were turning grey; George was in his mid sixties. And sitting next to Baker was George Perkins. He was younger, about forty five, but courted a solid moustache. George Perkins sat in a chair opposite watching every move of everyone.

Money was becoming tight as banks held onto cash. There was now a run on Trust Company of America. The brokerage firm Marcus & Mayer failed. It was announced that Luther W. Knott resigned as Superintendent of Banks of the State of New York

Henry put the telephone down into the cradle. He tapped the end of his pencil onto the pad of paper. He looked across at John.

"He said that he is not finished but from what he has seen they are short in liquid assets. In total they may have enough but most of the assets are longer term and would take considerable time to liquidate."

"And time is one thing we do not have," Baker piped in.

"No," Davison replied. "That we do not have."

Everyone seemed to stare at John, waiting.

John took a puff on his cigar and then curled the ashes off into the ash tray. He put the cigar into the tray and placed both of his hands on the desk palms down and leaned a little forward.

"Then it is done," he firmly said.

At the bank the lines were down the street. Another man, a vice president, Joseph Brown, came out from behind the cage and into the middle of the crowds in the lobby. He dragged a chair out with him and then stood up on the chair so most could see and hear him. He read something from the state superintendent of banks from September 17 saying they were solvent, quoting large numbers of assets and lesser liabilities but few understood what he was talking about. A few in the crowd cheered and clapped. That meant that they would get their money. When he was done he pulled the chair back behind the cage.

No one left the line.

Benjamin Strong walked up from the dungeons of the vault where he had spent the entire night calculating. The sunlight streaming in the window was a bit bright for his eyes. He watched the crowd. He stared into their eyes. They do not know what I know, he thought. This is the endgame. Who would be the last one? And after that: what do you do when you lose everything?

The tellers counted out the money; one small deposit at a time.

But then several messengers from different banks reached the tellers. The first was from Hanover National Bank. He had drafts for $1.5 million. Tellers brought up cash from the vault and stacked the bills as the teller slowly counted out the money.

A second messenger from a different bank stepped up to the next teller. He had a draft for $1 million. Tellers brought up what was left in the vault and stacked the cash as the second teller started counting out the bills.

Then the third walked up to the last teller. His name was John Quinn. He was the attorney for the Bank of Commerce. He presented a draft for $2 million. The nervous teller turned to William Trumbull. He looked at the draft. He knew. He shook his head no to the teller. The vault was empty. The teller mumbled something to John Quinn and then slid his teller screen down.

John Quinn then wrote out a notice of suspension and demanded to speak with William Trumbull. The notice must be immediately posted in the window. The other tellers closed their windows.

Joseph Brown dragged his chair out into the crowded lobby again and stood up on the rickety wooden chair.

"There will be no more payments today."

He stepped down from his chair.

People looked around at each other: what; what did he say; I do not understand; what does that mean? It isn't closing time. Are you going to open again tomorrow?

He pulled his chair back behind the teller's cage and closed the door behind him.

He then had to go outside and find several policemen to come and clear out the lobby. When the police cleared the people out some began shouting, with anger.

He locked the door.

People outside stood around, no one wanted to leave. They read the sign posted in the window. They tried to bang on the window but the employees pulled down the shades. Blocking out the sun with shades the interior of the bank darkened.

It was done. Eight million dollars cash disappeared in but four hours. The second largest Trust Bank in New York City was suddenly no more.

Back at The Corner John stood at the window watching the crowds outside his window. Large crowds were walking back and forth. They filled the street. Automobiles could not get through the throng of people. He stood with a cigar in one hand and a handkerchief in the other. His cold was diabolical. He wanted to just close his eyes and go to sleep. Hundreds of people were standing about in the street wondering what was going on, how this can be happening. John stood at the window with George Perkins.

James came up to them.

"Sir," he carefully said.

"Yes James."

"The Knickerbocker Trust has closed their doors."

John nodded.

"Thank you, James."

John was silent for a long time, staring out the window, holding his cigar in his hand. Spent ash fell to the floor unnoticed.

Earlier that day Oakleigh Thorne, president of the Trust Company of America came to see John. He was desperately anxious about the heavy withdrawals from his bank. He had $50 million in deposits, $100 million in assets but he was worried about the heavy withdrawals. He did not understand. Why his bank? What did he do wrong?

But Charles Barney was on the board of directors for Trust. And Barney had borrowed $175,000 from Trust with stock in Knickerbocker as collateral. That was now useless. Panic: it was spreading like an infectious disease. Was this the financial black plague?

John looked down at the chair where Charles Barney had sat earlier that day.

"I can not go on being everybody's goat," John said whether anyone was listening or not. "I have got to stop somewhere."

John put in a call to the Secretary of Treasury George B. Cortelyou. Banks from around the country were pulling their funds out of New York banks putting yet a further strain on the system. We need to coordinate what we as bankers can do and what he as the government can do. I'm on my way, he said over the phone. Cortelyou boarded a train that afternoon.

John put out a call to the National Banks, Baker and Stillman and others. He wanted to see their books. He had his men looking into the banks in trouble to see which ones they could help. But he needed to see what help was available. He was asking for unprecedented access to his competitor's books so that he could then allocate how much each could put up without injuring themselves. He was asking for a power beyond anything ever given to anyone.

But each agreed. This had to be stopped and they all knew that if there was anyone who could do that it was John.

John left his office at 6:00 P.M. He was scheduled to meet with Cortelyou at 9:00. Standing at the top of the stairs adjusting his coat and ready to walk down to his waiting brougham a reporter came up to him. Can you give us a word on the situation, sir? Usually John walked passed reporters without even recognizing that they were there. He detested them. John even bashed one over the shoulder with his cane when the man dared to snap a picture. But this time John looked at the man. There was something about him. The reporter was young, maybe only twenty, neat and clean shaven, standing there straddling the steps with his pad of paper and his pencil, with his straw hat and black band cocked back on his head, his eager face waiting for a reply from J. P. Morgan.

"We are doing everything we can as fast as we can, but nothing has yet crystallized."

"What then are you working toward?"

John waved the man off and descended the stairs.

By nine o'clock John and George Perkins arrived at the Manhattan Hotel to meet with George Cortelyou. George Baker and James Stillman were already there. They met in Cortelyou's hotel room. There would be no public forum like Sherry's Restaurant for them.

Cortelyou, with his prominent eye brows, bushy black moustache, pince-nez, and with his hair slicked back, told them that he had deposited $6 millions in government bonds at the sub treasury that the

253

national banks could draw upon when needed. The treasury was available to help in any way that it could.

Money was getting very tight. On the stock exchange call money started the day at 10 percent, by noon it had advanced to 60 percent, but then dropped to 40 but by closing stood at 70.

The talks went on for hours. They discussed in detail what could be done for the expected run on the Trust Company tomorrow. John asked Cortelyou point blank what was going to be the role of President Roosevelt. None of the bankers totally trusted his intensions. Cortelyou assured them that 'honestly' he is behind your efforts and will not interfere in any way.

John and Stillman puffed on their cigars as they listened.

The meeting ended thinking that without a doubt there would be runs in the morning.

It was two in the morning when they adjourned the meeting. As John and Perkins came out of the room and into the hotel hallway there was a swarm of reporters. How did they find this out? The reporters, standing by the elevators, once they saw John, rapidly approached shouting in the hallway for a word. John quickly grabbed Perkins arm.

"Handle them," he almost barked and then quickly turned away and started racing down the hall in the opposite direction, his cane flying as if swatting at any reporter who may be after him. They blocked the way to the elevators. John had to search down halls to find the stairs and then climbed down as fast as he could manage. He came out a back door at the hotel and had to walk around out onto the street and find Williams with the brougham waiting for him near the front door. By the time he got in he almost collapsed in the seat; he was breathing heavily, whizzing and coughing. His cold was taking over. And running down stairs and out in the autumn night did not help. He was a seventy year old man. John had a very hard time breathing as Williams raced off.

Meanwhile, upstairs in the hallway, Perkins did as best he could. Reporters were shooting questions at him from all directions. Why where the big three bankers of New York meeting in secret in a hotel room in the middle of the night with the Secretary of Treasury? What does this mean? Are we in serious trouble?

Perkins tried to alleviate their fears. It is not purposely in the middle of the night, it just happened to be the time Cortelyou arrived from Washington. Due to the lateness of the hour offices were closed, it just seemed natural that they meet in his hotel room. Yes, there is a coordinated effort by the Treasury and the bankers to alleviate the situation and rest assured that we are working very diligently toward that solution.

But then, trying to be helpful and honest, he instead dropped a match into the dry brush.

The reporter from the New York Times asked: what are some of the main issues you discussed?

Perkins replied: "The chief sore point is the Trust Company of America. The conferees feel that the situation there is such that the company is sound. Provision has been made to supply all the cash needed this morning. The conferees feel sure the company will be able to pull through. The company has twelve million dollars cash and as much more as needed has been pledged for the purpose. It is safe to assume that J. P. Morgan & Company will be leaders in this movement to furnish funds."

He had named a name: Trust Company of America. It was a 'chief sore spot.' The fact he said after that it was sound and the necessary funds would be furnished did not matter.

He named a name. It was doomed.

Once John got back to the Satterlee house he put in a telephone call to Benjamin Strong at his home in Greenwich, Connecticut. The phone rang a long time before the, until then, sound asleep Benjamin answered it. John told him to immediately get together a team of men and go over the books of Trust Company of America and give him a full report no later than noon of that day. Benjamin said he would leave immediately.

John then called Oakleigh Thorne, the president of Trust, and after also waking him up instructed him to get to the bank immediately with a key and let Strong in and provide him with whatever he asked for, for however long he asked for it.

There was a hesitation and then Thorne said: "But sir, it is almost two thirty in the morning."

"Does that suppose to mean something?" John barked.

There was a pause.

Then Thorne replied: "No, I suppose it does not."

"Fine," John snapped before he put the telephone back into the cradle.

Wednesday, October 23.

255

Herbert tapped on the door to John's room and called out his name. There was no reply. It was time for John to be up. Breakfast was waiting downstairs. The servant said that John would not answer the door.

"Pierpont, are you awake," Herbert shouted out. There was no reply. He glanced at the servant. Herbert banged on the door with his fist.

"Pierpont," he shouted out again.

When there was no reply this time Herbert tried the door. It opened.

"Pierpont are you up?" Herbert opened the door and entered the room.

John lay on the bed. His head was back and his mouth was wide open. He was not moving.

Herbert went to the bed and shook him, calling out his name. There was no response. Fear shot through Herbert. He grabbed John's hand and felt for his pulse. He did not feel any. He reached up and put his hands on John's neck under the back of the jaw. There he felt a pulse. It seemed to him weak.

"Quickly, telephone Doctor Markoe. Tell him to come right away."

Herbert kept shaking John. He put his face down close to his. He shouted out his name.

Finally John moved, he inhaled and choked and started coughing. Herbert kept trying to wake him up.

By the time the Doctor arrived Herbert at least got John awake. He was still very sleepy and seemed in a drugged state. His eyes were open but were very weak and watery. He could barely see. His voice was hoarse and he could speak barely above a whisper.

Doctor Markoe sat him up and sprayed something down his throat. He had him drink from a glass of something foaming, gargle, and then spit it out into a pan. Then drink it again, gargle, and spit it out.

It was nearly an hour before John could get up out of bed and slowly get dressed. Downstairs coffee seemed to revive him even more. Markoe said it was his bad cold, and his fatigue, and was he eating right?

"No," Herbert said.

John frowned at him.

"He's only eating cigars not food. It's one after another. I would say he consumes a good twenty cigars a day."

Markoe turned to John who sat staring up like a boy who had been naughty.

"You are not good to anyone dead."

John waved him off, saying "Yes, yes" in his hoarse voice.

Once at his office he tried to work. There was news that Governor Hughes appointed Clark Williams, a trained bank official and vice president of the Columbia Trust Company as Superintendent of Banks. Everyone regarded it as a good appointment.

John's voice was very hoarse and his eyes were so weak and watery that he could just barely read the papers in front of him. He kept wiping his eyes with one handkerchief and then rubbing his running nose with another. He occasionally had to stop and just sit with his eyes closed as if a small minute or so nap was needed for his energy to keep going. One by one he conferred with Henry Clay Frick of U.S. Steel, Thomas F. Ryan, and then Edward Henry Harriman of the Union Pacific Railroad about the developing situation.

"The Knickerbocker has gone over the dam and now the Trust Company of America is nearing the brink," he explained to Harriman.

"Is there anything I can do?"

It was James Stillman who spoke first.

"Edward, I think that you have done quite enough in public service lately."

"I agree," said George Baker.

It was John who spoke up next.

"What you did during the earthquake in San Francisco last year was remarkable Mr. Harriman; you opened up everything you had to help them. I commend your service."

Both Stillman and Baker agreed.

"And then to help repair the broken levees on the Colorado, the entire Imperial Valley in California would be under water if you had not acted. Have you received any compensation from the state; or even from the federal government for that matter? That flooding would have had major national consequences."

From the look on his face as he sat silently they knew that he had not.

"Shameful," Baker grunted.

"Mr. Harriman," John said in a way that silenced the others, "I have to say this, and I say it in front of my friends," waving his open hand toward James Stillman and George Baker, "that after all is said and done, and I know we have not seen eye to eye and have been great adversaries in the past, but beyond all of that I think you are one of the good ones. You have proven yourself to be one of the good ones."

Harriman, sitting, his hat in his hand, nodded.

"Think about the possibilities, gentlemen," Stillman said, warming to the occasion. "If you two only worked together: Harriman, with a transcontinental railroad and making inroads in Japan and China and organizing a trans-pacific shipping empire, and you, Mr. Morgan, in control of another transcontinental railroad, inroads into different industries, and your building of a International Marine shipping empire in the Atlantic to Europe. Think of the possibilities, gentlemen, if you only could work together."

Both John and Harriman sat listening, John with his cigar and Harriman staring off into space.

"What would we have then?" John asked. Indeed, he thought to himself, what would we have then? And then a sudden chill came over him. Harriman did not look well.

"Life is too short to be angry," Stillman said.

"You need to enjoy life more," John told Harriman.

Harriman glanced at John, smiled, and nodded.

Harriman stood.

"Well gentlemen," he said standing, hat in hand, "if you need anything please give me a call."

They all agreed.

John shook his hand.

"We will meet again, I am sure of it."

Harriman quietly walked off.

After Harriman left Baker spoke: "After you consider everything he is a good man. Story goes that when he and Fish took over the Illinois Central one of them had to move from New York to Chicago to run the thing but neither one wanted to move to Chicago. It was Harriman who had to move. But no sooner than he moved that his four year old son got diphtheria and died. He swore then and there that to justify the death of his son he was going to create the best railroad there ever was. Only then would the death of his son have any meaning."

John thought about it and then replied.

"The death of someone you love can be quite a motivating force. You never know what drives somebody to do what they do."

John noticed that Stillman sat smiling.

"James, you are smiling. That certainly is a rare occurrence, what are you thinking?"

"I was just remembering one evening with Harriman. It just happened by chance that we both attended an opera. After it began Harriman came to my box and whispered to me 'Stillman, I want to see you a minute.' When I came out into the hallway he waved his finger 'Come this way.' We went to the coat room, got our coats, and then outside to a brougham waiting at the curb. We drove to his house in East

258

Fifty Fifth Street. On the way I asked him, 'Well, Harriman, what do you want of me?' He replied for me to wait, we will be at his house in a moment. So we got there and he took my coat and led me upstairs to his library. Again I asked, 'Harriman, what is it?' He took out a box of cigars, handed me one, and then stood at the fireplace poking at the fire. I was growing impatient. 'Well, Harriman, I am still waiting; what is it you want?'"

Stillman, still smiling, sat silent for a moment.

"Well man, go on," Baker said.

"Harriman replied 'Oh, you must have been tired of that opera. I know I was, and I thought we might pass the time better at home.'"

"And that was it?" John asked.

"Yes."

Both John and Baker chuckled.

"But there was one important thing I learned about him that night."

John shook his head. It was frustrating at times to get anything out of Stillman. "And that was. . ."

"We chatted about all sorts of things and I asked him 'What is it that interests you most in life and gives you most pleasure?' Do you know what he said?"

John and Baker looked at each other. "No, James, we do not know."

"Well Harriman thought about it and then said 'Well, I think it is to plan some big piece of helpful work that everybody says can't possibly be done, and then jump in with both feet and do it.' That to me is the quintessential Harriman."

The runs on the banks continued, more severe. But the hardest hit was the Trust Company. Oakleigh Thorne, already inside the bank with Benjamin Strong, watched as the lines began to form outside the bank even before sunrise. When he opened he opened up seven tellers in order to get the line down. He did not want a line out the door as advertisement that something was wrong. But it did not help. Soon the line was out the door, all the way down the block and around the corner at Williams Street.

At The Corner John gathered many different Trust Company presidents and put them in the conference room. They each had to pass by the long lines outside of Trust Company just down the street in order to get to The Corner. Many were openly scared and nervous. To John's surprise many did not know each other. He had to introduce them to each other. He knew more of them than they knew themselves. If you do not know and trust each other how can you gain an acceptable agreement? How can you not know who your competitor is?

They organized a central committee with Edward King of Union Trust as chairman and Edwin S Marston (Farmers), J. N. Wallace (Central), J. W. Castles (Guaranty), John I. Waterbury (Manhattan), and John A. Stewart (United States) as committee members. John and Perkins served as advisory. John sat them down and told them to come up with a plan among themselves on how they could pool their assets in order for everyone to help everyone.

Then he went into his wood and glass walled office where James Stillman, George Baker, George Perkins and Henry Davison were waiting.

Stillman began the discussion with the news that his client, John Davison Rockefeller, has committed ten million in funds of his own money to help stop the panic.

Frederick Gates, his financial advisor, telephoned Rockefeller early that morning at the estate at Pocantico. Rockefeller stood in his bathrobe on his balcony looking out as the rising sun crawled across the moist grass. Gates thought a public statement by Rockefeller might reinforce confidence. Perhaps even an infusion of cash. Rockefeller hung up the telephone and pondered the idea, watching the rising sun fill the day with light.

Rockefeller then telephoned Melville E. Stone, general manager of the Associated Press. He told Stone that the credit of the country was sound and he was perfectly willing to give up half of all he possessed to prove the point. When he was done with Stone he called Stillman and told him to earmark ten million to help in the crisis. When he hung up the phone Rockefeller tightened his bathrobe. He was a bit chilly. Watching the birds dashing about looking for breakfast he smiled. 'They always come to Uncle John when there is trouble.'

Back at The Corner talk continued. John smoked his cigar.

James, his secretary, came in with a message that Thorne at Trust was pleading for money. He was down to $1.2 million in cash and could not hold out all day until closing at 3 o'clock.

Later James came in with the news that Westinghouse Electric & Manufacturing Company went into receivership.

Later James came in with the news that the Pittsburgh Stock Exchange suspended trading for the day.

Later James came in with the news that the New York Trust Bank might have to close the next day due to lack of cash.

Later James came in with the news that there was a heavy run on the Lincoln Trust Company.

Then James came in and said that Thorne had called again and that he was down to $800,000 in cash.

John went into the conference room.

"Well gentlemen," he called out in his sore and hoarse voice. "What do you have for me?"

No one spoke up.

He turned to Edward King, committee chairman: "Mr. King, what have we come up with?"

"I am afraid nothing of substance as of yet. There is great concern of each weakening our own cash position."

One of the bankers spoke up.

"Mr. Morgan, my reserve is down to 20 percent and I don't know what to do."

John, in disbelief, snapped at the man.

"You ought to be ashamed of yourself. Your reserve ought to be down to 20 percent or 18 percent; perhaps even lower. What is a reserve for if not to be used in times like these?"

"But we have to preserve our own positions."

"So what, we should let everyone drop one by one like flies? No, that is unacceptable. Let me make a proposal. We will need perhaps $3 million to save Trust Company today. And today means now. There are ten of you here so each of you posts $300,000. What do you say?"

Edward Marston of Farmers raised his hand: "Agreed."

No one else said a word. John, standing, his hands on his hips, looked all around the room as he sucked on his cigar rapidly puffing smoke rings into the air.

Finally he almost shouted out to them. "Talk about it and get back to me gentlemen, time is running out."

John stormed back into his office.

"Those knuckleheads in there are useless. Get Strong over here. Finished or not I want him here."

When Benjamin Strong and his helper Willard King of Columbia Trust Company arrived at John's office they were carrying stacks of portfolios and papers. There was a bit of tense look on each man's face.

"Good, you are here at last. Strong, have you anyone with you who can make a report to the gentlemen in the next room? They are the presidents of the trust companies, and when they came into the office they had to be introduced to each other, and I do not think much can be expected of them."

Strong nodded to Willard King who then walked over to the other room.

"Now, sit down with Mr. Baker, Mr. Stillman and me, and tell us about it"

Strong entered John's office and put his pile of portfolios down on the desk.

"At last count they were down to their last $500,000 in cash."

John closed his eyes and shook his head.

"What have you found? Is Trust Company solvent?"

Strong cleared his throat. "Well sir, that somewhat depends on the status of several large securities holdings they have which I feel Mr. Stillman and Mr. Baker are more familiar with."

"Get on with it," John said while lighting another cigar.

For the next forty minutes Strong went over each portfolio that he had brought with him asking the opinion of each of the bankers there as to whether they were sound investments or not. Finally, when he was done with the last one, John cleared his throat.

"Well then? Are they solvent?"

Strong looked around the room and carefully chose his words.

"I am satisfied that the company is solvent; I think their surplus has been pretty much wiped out; but the capital is not greatly impaired, if at all, although were the company to be liquidated there are many assets that will take some years to convert into cash."

In the silence everyone was thinking. John rolled his cigar around in his mouth.

"So you feel it wise for us to infuse cash to save it, cash that we will get back?"

"Yes," he said.

But then after a moment Strong continued: "If you save it now then you will get it back."

John put his cigar down into the tray and tapped his desk with his finger.

"This is the place to stop the trouble, then."

It was just a few moments later that James brought Oakleigh Thorne himself down the hallway and into John's office.

The men sitting about the office all stared at him as he entered. The fact that he himself was there could not be good news.

Thorne took off his black top hat and held it in his hands by the rim. He slowly rotated it as he talked.

"I regret to inform you Mr. Morgan, Mr. Stillman, Mr. Baker," he nodded to each as he spoke. "But I will have to cease operations within the next few minutes."

"Why?" John barked, rolling his cigar in his fingers.

"Why? Why, you ask? Because sir I have run out of cash."

"How much do you have left?"

"We are down to only $180,000 cash and have almost an hour before we close."

John stood up and turned to the others.

"Well gentlemen, I do not see anything else to do. It is up to us three."

John stared straight at Stillman who, as was his usual behavior, sat silently.

"Trust Company of America is where we must make our stand against this thing."

Stillman, silent, nodded. Baker also nodded in agreement.

John quickly turned to Perkins.

"Perkins, dismiss those clowns in there and send them on their way. I want them all to meet again tonight. Make them decide. Pick a time. I want them to meet in order to solve tomorrow. We will solve today. Tell them they must solve tomorrow."

John turned to Thorne and stood very close to him, facing him.

"You do not close. Close down to only two tellers. Tell them to count very slowly, and make mistakes in counting so that they have to start again. Delay. And you; bring over all your securities and bonds and loans, bring them here. We will determine their collateral value for an infusion of cash."

"Bring them here?"

"Here. Now. We have no time to lose."

Thorne started to run down the hall, but then turned around and as he ran backwards he called back to John.

"So there is hope?"

John, standing in the hall, put out his hands.

"Yes," he shouted.

As Perkins cleared out the conference room the bank presidents all one by one filed down the hall toward the front door. At the same time, coming in from the front door, walking up the opposite side of the same hallway, lead by Thorne, was a long line of men carrying satchels and bags and boxes. Perkins directed them into the conference room.

Willard King stood in the corner of the room. John and Stillman and Strong all came into the room.

"All right gentlemen, onto the table. All of it onto the table."

One by one each man carrying a bag or satchel, or a box filled with loan documents, stock certificates, bonds, all started to unload what they were carrying onto the large table. In no particular order they just dumped what they carried onto the table.

John motioned Strong and Willard and Perkins to all sit down. He sat Stillman down at a desk with a telephone.

"This is the plan, gentlemen. We need to raise some three million in cash and these are the collateral for us to do that. Start picking and choosing. We need it done in the next fifteen to twenty minutes."

John, with cigar in hand, sat at the head of the table.

"Someone get Thomas Joyce in here right away."

John pulled out a pad of paper and a short stubbed pencil.

"Okay; Strong, read out to me what you have one at a time. What is it and what is it worth. Thorne, get back to your bank. Messengers will be arriving with cash very shortly."

As Strong randomly picked up papers now strewn around the table he called out what it was as well as its value. John jotted it down on his piece of paper. After a moment or two John called out to stop and looked up at Joyce who was standing at the door by then.

"Get a man over to Trust with one hundred thousand, now. Strong, put that pile aside with this on top."

Strong moved the pile he had called out onto the floor and put the small piece of paper John handed him on the top of the pile.

"That is ours. Now, have you got your man on the phone?"

Stillman said yes.

"This one is yours."

John turned to Willard: "What do you have?"

Willard again called out the values of what he was gathering from the pile as John jotted them down. Then after a moment John called out to stop. He told Stillman one hundred five thousand and Stillman repeated it into the telephone receiver; Willard put that pile onto the floor and put John's small piece of paper on top.

"Perkins, this one is for Baker."

Downstairs in the vault Joyce had several tellers pulling out cash and writing down the amounts and denominations. A man stood wearing a long coat with his arms outstretched. Tellers were stuffing the counted packets of cash into his pockets and into the pockets of the coat and into a cloth bag he wore around his neck. When they were done, when they had counted out one hundred thousand dollars cash and stuffed it all into his pockets, Joyce slapped the man on the shoulder.

"Go."

They man wrapped the jacket closed and went up the stairs. Walking fast he went down the hall, out the front door, down the steps, turned and started walking briskly up the street toward Trust Company of America just up the street and firmly held his coat closed as he weaved in and out of the heavy foot traffic on the sidewalk and then out into the street between people and horses and automobiles and carriages and walked as fast as he could up to the Trust Company of America where long lines of men stood waiting to get inside to withdraw their money and then he walked up the steps and through the door where near the door stood a teller who waved him in when he told the teller that he was from Morgan and walked with him to the cage and opened it so he could walk in and then another teller waved him into the back and down the stairs and into the safe that stood wide open where Thorne and a team of tellers stood by and when he opened up his coat and opened out his arms wide they started taking out the packets of cash from all his pockets and his coat pockets and his cloth bag and they all quickly counted the packets and called out the totals to another man standing by an adding machine writing down all of the amounts as they called them out while other tellers grabbed the packets of cash as soon as they were counted and carried them upstairs to the waiting two tellers who were very slowly as slowly as they could counting out the bills one by one and carefully placing each bill down and adjusting them so that they were nice and neat and tidy and then carefully and very slowly counted out another bill and meanwhile another messenger arrived with a bulky coat who told the teller by the door that he was from National City Bank and the teller at the door took him too to the cage and unlocked it while another teller took him down the stairs into the open safe where the whole process was repeated while another messenger was brought down who said he was from First National Bank and the process went on and on and on with the same messengers going back and forth coming one after another from the three banks Morgan and National City and First National.

And at three o'clock, the normal closing time, Thorne closed the door as normal as he did everyday at three o'clock. Sorry, but it is closing time. Please come back tomorrow. Thank you.

When the last customer left and Thorne shut and locked the door with his key he closed his eyes and put his forehead against the door.

They made it.

The Trust bankers decided to meet that evening at the Union Trust Company because they had large rooms on the second floor that would accommodate them all. When John arrived that evening he saw Perkins and Davison and Strong waiting for him. They all went into a private room and closed the door. Strong gave his report from looking again at the Trust assets. He stood by his prior statement. The Trust was in the long run sound. If they get through this temporary run then it will survive and be able to pay back the borrowed funds by liquidating their longer term assets.

The four of them climbed up the marble steps to the meeting rooms on the second floor. Inside the various trust presidents had already gathered. John told them that this was a Trust Company panic, a Trust Company problem and should be handled by the trusts. They must pool their resources and defend each other.

He explained that today he and the other National Banks had 'stood the breach' but that can not continue. They, the trusts represented here, must raise the necessary funds to see through the rest of this crisis.

He had Strong give his report.

He explained that Cortelyou placed federal monies into the national banks that all the trusts could borrow from if they pass it through to the troubled trust companies.

John opened the floor to discussion. They again demurred. Talk was inconclusive. Some wanted to protect themselves and not weaken their own cash positions; others felt that if a trust failed then that simply meant more business for themselves.

John sat in a chair to the side smoking his cigar. He was very tired and it was very late.

Finally E. C. Converse, president of the Bankers Trust Company, pledged an advance of $500,000 into a fund exclusively for the panic.

John closed his eyes and his head tilted forward, his chin on his chest.

Discussion continued; all negative to the idea.

When they heard a few snores one reached over and carefully took John's cigar from his hand and placed it into a tray.

Discussion went on around and around while John slept. No one wanted to be the one to wake him.

Finally after about thirty minutes John snorted himself awake. He put his cigar hand to his mouth but then looked in confusion at his empty hand. He reached into his pocket and pulled out and lit another one.

Then he picked up a pad of paper and wrote something down. Then he looked up.

"Okay, fine. Bankers Trust is down for five hundred." He spoke as though the last thirty minutes of endless discussion did not happen. He turned his full body and staring gaze at Edwin Marston of the Farmers' Loan and Trust Company.

"And now what about you, Mr. Marston; what can I put down for you?"

After a brief hesitation he committed the same amount. As John noted it down on his piece of paper he uttered: Good.

John stared at each president one by one, calling out their name, and many committed various amounts. By the end he had raised $8,250,000.

It was midnight before John and his small group left the Union Trust building. Thorne was waiting downstairs. John told him that he had his money for tomorrow but he and Strong had to go to the bank and put together the collateral so Strong could present documentation to Edward King first thing in the morning who, as head of the committee, would release the money. Perkins will go and see Cortelyou and prepare a joint statement for release tomorrow before the bank and Exchanges open.

"We just may get through this, gentlemen."

"I certainly do hope so."

Thursday, October 24.

Strong and Thorne worked through the night and gathered together the necessary securities for the loans the trusts had committed too. Strong took a cab down to Union Trust and was there by eight o'clock in order to show King what made up the collateral. But King wanted further proof.

"Proof? Proof of what?"

"That these are sound securities."

"But you all agreed last night to commit the funds?"

"That was simply a discussion. I need full documentation that show the credit worthiness of all these before I will realize any money."

Strong stood for a moment in shock.

"You will not release the funds that were agreed to?"

King simply shook his head no.

The banks would open their doors shortly. The cash Trust had on hand would dry up rapidly. Without this money the Trust would go under. Everything they had done would be wasted.

Strong glared at the little man. It was useless.

Strong raced out of the bank and into his waiting cab.

"219 Madison, and drive as fast as you can."

When they arrived Strong ran up to the door and franticly rang the bell again and again. John was at breakfast with Perkins. When Strong burst out what had happened John banged both his fists on the table. Plates and coffee cups rattled.

"That weasel. What shallow minded men."

He had to take several deep breaths to calm himself down. He then faced Strong.

"Go to my office, gather enough of the securities we looked at yesterday, and then take them to Stillman at National City Bank and use them for a temporary loan until we get this sorted out. Perkins, call Stillman and tell him what is happening. Go."

Strong raced to The Corner, got the securities and then with a satchel filled with millions of dollars worth of securities, ran down Wall Street to the National City Bank, weaving in and out of traffic and throngs of people beginning to form outside Trust Company. With cash stuffed into his pockets Strong raced out the door and down the street to Trust. Thorne was upstairs pacing back and forth in front of the window looking down into the bank lobby. When he saw Strong enter he raced down the stairs.

"They failed me, didn't they? They have let me hang. I won't, I'm going to close at ten."

But then Strong pulled out a packet of bills and handed them to Thorne. The man's face lit up and beamed with joy.

"More will be coming."

At ten o'clock John went downtown with Herbert in a Union Club brougham. It was driven by his faithful servant William and led by a beautiful white horse. John admired and patted the flanks of the horse before they left. As they drove downtown Herbert saw that people who got a glimpse of John in the cab looked again and pointed it out to their companions. People knew John by his pictures and by all the stories in the newspapers. Policemen and cabbies who knew him called out. One called out 'There goes the Old Man!' Another called out that 'There goes the Big Chief!' People even ran along side the cab in order to peek in. John sat stone faced, settled back in his seat, with his eyes forward. Herbert thought, as he watched the spectacle, that John might have been a general at the head of a column going to the relief of a beleaguered city such was the enthusiasm he created. Although he did not acknowledge it, Herbert knew that all of it secretly pleased him.

When he arrived at The Corner crowds of people watched as he walked up the steps to enter the building.

"Save us," someone called out from the crowd.

Inside he stood at the reception area and glanced back at the large windows. People on the street were walking past all looking in and talking to each other, pointing into the building.

To James he said: "Good gracious, I am not a fish in a fish bowl."

"I think that they love you sir."

John looked at him and grunted. Then he began walking on down the hall toward his office. But James called after him. John turned.

"Edward King of Union Trust is waiting to see you. Room B."

John stood for a moment without saying a word; thinking. He took out a cigar and lit it while still standing in the hall. He still wore his black top hat and overcoat. He walked over to the room and entered. Edward King sat at a table. John walked straight up to him and placed his hands on the table palms down. He leaned in with his face very close to Edward's face. His cigar was at the side of his mouth. He watched as Edward looked at John's nose, and then, as if caught off guard, quickly looked up into John's eyes. John squinted, his eyes like knives. Very slowly and carefully John spoke.

"I am not at all pleased with what happened this morning. Everything we have been trying to do was put into jeopardy. All I have to say to you at this time is that during this crisis I am paying attention to those who are going out of their way to help in this fight, and those who are hindering it."

John stood up straight. Without taking his eyes off of Edward, without even blinking, John slowly took a puff on his cigar and held it in his hand, rolling it a bit between his fingers.

"And I will remember," he added.

"But Mr. Morgan, let me. . ."

John cut him short with a wave of his hand.

"I am done with you now. You may go."

With that John abruptly turned and walked out of the room dismissing Edward as though he did not even exist.

John went into his office. Stillman, Baker, and Perkins were already sitting together talking. John took off his overcoat and top hat and hung them on his wooden coat rack.

Stillman opened the discussion with the news that Rockefeller had transferred ten million to the Union Trust with Edward King to be used in saving the trusts that are in trouble. He wanted to convey to Morgan that up to another forty millions could be used if needed.

John raised his eyebrows and smiled.

Perkins chuckled. "Given what happened this morning let's hope King uses it for that."

"He better," said Stillman.

John flicked his cigar ash into the tray.

"He will," John finally said.

Perkins held up a morning newspaper.

"I conferred with Cortelyou last night and he has committed up to another twenty five millions in liquidity. As we speak automobiles are lined up outside the Sub Treasury building loading up boxes of gold and bags of cash all to be distributed to various National Banks that we both approved of last night.

"Good; good," Morgan said. "I saw them when I came in." John tapped his desk with his finger and a small smile crossed his face. With Rockefeller on board and with Cortelyou and the Treasury on board then there was a very good chance they were going to beat this thing. Between the government and Rockefeller John did not know which had the most money to lend.

Perkins pointed to the newspaper in his hand.

"Let me read to you what Cortelyou said: 'If everyone could reflect on the real strength of our banking institutions then confidence would return. Not only has the stability of the business institutions impressed me deeply but also the highest courage and the splendid devotion to the public interest of many men prominent in the business life of this city.'"

But the runs continued unabated. The run on Lincoln Trust accelerated. And the run on the Trust Company of America seemed just as heavy as the day before. The ten million fund from the night before simply evaporated. It was like a small pond of water in the middle of the Sahara Desert. Everyone was turning everything into cash. The stock market climaxed as new money dried up. Stocks on the New York Stock Exchange fell. Union Pacific dropped from 108 to 100; Northern Pacific from 110 to 100 Reading from 78 to 70. The volume of short selling increased. The interest rate on call money by ten o'clock was around six percent, fairly normal, but by eleven it had climbed to 60 percent.

Ransom H. Thomas, president of the New York Stock Exchange, came across the street to The Corner. Inside were a great many men milling about excited, agitated. All wanted answers, solutions, and help.

Ransom wrote his name in the appointment book and told James that he urgently must see Mr. Morgan. He quietly sat in a chair with all the angry men standing around loudly talking.

When James finally waved him in and took him back John stood at the door to his office and greeted him. Stillman and Baker and Perkins were all still there.

"What can I do for you?" John asked as he sat down in his chair.

"Mr. Morgan we will have to close the stock exchange."

"What?" John asked, taken back.

"We will have to close the stock exchange."

John glanced at the clock on his desk.

"At what time do you usually close?"

"Why, the normal time is at three o'clock."

John stood and pointed his finger at Ransom.

"Then you must not close one minute before that hour today," emphasizing each word by keeping time with his pointing right hand.

Ransom told him about the short selling, about the dropping prices, about the sky rocketing interest on call money, about the large numbers of brokerage houses that were extended beyond their means to cover. By 2:20 that day when they had to settle their accounts many houses would fail and have to shut their doors.

"Yes," John said, "but for the New York Stock Exchange to shut down is absolutely unacceptable. That would utterly destroy public confidence and completely undermine everything we have been doing. No, sir, this can not happen."

He loudly rapped his desk with his knuckles as he repeated "This can not happen."

Stillman spoke up. "Call the commercial bankers here, now. We can use the federal money being distributed. Perkins has the list of who is receiving what."

"But that is the security for the runs on the Trusts."

Stillman shrugged his shoulders as if to say yes, but right now which is the most important.

John thought for a moment and then turned toward Ransom.

"Make a public announcement. If someone is found promoting this panic and by short selling is profiting off of this then I personally will properly attend to them once this is over. I am rapidly losing patience."

When Ransom glanced at Perkins he simply raised his eyebrow. Everyone in the room knew that John could be savage when he was out of patience, and, when he was crossed, unrelenting.

"Now, put a call out to everyone on that list. I want to see them here, now."

The telephone calls were made and everywhere across New York bank presidents, when they hung up the receiver, dropped what they were doing, grabbed their coat, and made a direct line to the Corner. When J. P. Morgan called you to come you went. Especially now.

Once gathered in the conference room John explained the situation. Up to fifty brokerage houses would fail that very afternoon and the stock exchange would shut down unless they acted to prevent it. He estimated that twenty five million would for now be enough. Stillman pledged five million. As other bankers pledged different amounts John told Perkins to write it all down on a piece of paper. He said that he would supply the cash directly to the exchange since they were just across the street and the other banks would send their portions directly to him. By the end of the half hour meeting he had raised $23.6 million from 14 different banks. The money was to be loaned to the Exchange at ten percent.

Word somehow got out.

As the bankers began to leave brokers standing in the street, desperate for news, raced back into the exchange shouting and cheering. One threw his hat up into the air.

"We're saved," he shouted, "we're saved."

John, sitting at his desk reading reports, heard the shouting out in the street. He tried to see over the wooden partition.

"What the devil is that?" he asked.

James, standing in his doorway, replied.

"They are cheering, sir."

"For what?"

"For you, sir."

John just grunted and returned to his reading.

After it was reported that Rockefeller would give up half of what he possessed in order to stop the panic reporters showed up at his golf course on the estate at Pocantico. It was very early in the morning, a bit chilly, and Rockefeller and some friends were preparing for a day of golf. Tall and thin, the aging man stood on the first green, club in hand, in his grey tweed suit and kneecap high argyle socks.

"Is it true that you are willing to give half of what you own to stem the panic," a young reporter asked as a group of them stood around with pad and pencils at the ready.

Rockefeller laughed.

"Yes, my boy, and I have cords of them, gentlemen, cords of them."

Everyone laughed and Rockefeller proceeded with his game.

But it had not been a totally successful day. The Trust Company survived another day. The Stock Exchange survived another day. But the Twelfth Ward Bank and the Empire City Savings Bank suspended operations in the afternoon. The Hamilton Bank of New York ceased operations as well as First National Bank of Brooklyn, International Trust Company of New York, Williamsburg Trust Company of Brooklyn, Borough Bank of Brooklyn, and the Jenkins Trust Company of Brooklyn.

It was toward seven o'clock that evening before John and Perkins left the office. Standing on the steps again, buttoning his overcoat, a reporter approached. Perkins began to wave the man off but John stopped him. It was the same young reporter from before, neat and clean shaven, standing there straddling the steps with his pad of paper and his pencil, with his straw hat and black band cocked back on his head, his eager face once again waiting for a reply from J. P. Morgan.

"There are those who say that this crisis demonstrates the inner instability and inequality of our capitalist system. Is this the end of America, sir?"

John smiled and shook his head an emphatic no.

"No, son, it is not. It is simply a panic. If people will keep their money in the banks then everything will be alright. The man who bets short on America is a fool."

John began walking down the steps toward his waiting cab. Perkins followed him.

"But what is being done to end this crisis, sir?"

"We are believing in America," John said as he climbed into the back of the cab.

That evening there was a meeting at The Library. Multiple bank presidents came. They wanted to come up with some sort of plan to bring liquidity to the markets and the trusts and the banks without constantly needing to put together each day another loan package. They all met in the East room of the Library. John sat in on the discussion for awhile but grew weary. It was getting late. He had not slept much all week, seldom getting to bed until two or three in the morning only to be up by seven or eight the next morning. And his cold, although improved, still drained his energy away. His eyes grew heavy as one president after another rambled on and on.

Stephen Baker, president of the Bank of Manhattan suggested issuing

Clearing House Certificates as money. During previous financial crises if a bank was short of cash the Clearing House issued temporary emergency loans to member banks called Certificates. All banks within the world of a particular clearing house recognized these certificates as cash when clearing accounts with each bank each day. Since members used the certificates as cash it therefore freed up the actual cash to be used elsewhere. It in essence expanded the money supply.

John at one point stood up. It brought a temporary quiet to the room. He explained that he was tired and was going to rest in the West Room but please feel free to keep him abreast of the discussion. Please notify his secretary Belle da Costa Greene, in her office across the hall, when they wished to see him. She will show them in.

He walked across the empty rotunda, his footsteps echoing along the marble. He entered his room, his footfalls silenced by the thick rugs. It was quiet and still. Warmed by the fire in the fireplace it was cozy and peaceful. He sat down at his desk, facing the fireplace.

The walls of the room were covered in red silk damask with the repeating pattern of the coat of arms of the Chigi family of Rome. It was appropriate for John's walls. Agostino Andrea Chigi was banker to Pope Alexander VI and Julius II; he was one of the richest men of Renaissance Rome; he was patron to the arts and literature commissioning Raphael and protecting the writer Pietro Aretino.

Hanging on the walls were paintings from Florentine masters of the fifteenth and sixteenth centuries. On the bookshelves to his left was a marble bust by Michelangelo and a rock crystal bowl fashioned for Queen Christina of Sweden, patron of the philosopher Rene Descartes.

John, sitting in his red Renaissance armchair, lit a cigar and then dealt out a game of solitaire on his desk. From one wall a Madonna and Child by Bernardino Pinturicchio, a painter of the Vatican Library, gracefully watched John play while from an opposite wall Saint Lawrence and the twin saints Cosmas and Damian in an altarpiece by Fra Filippo Lippi patiently wait.

John liked to sit in the quiet of his art. Seek that which is eternal. He could hear from across the hall like distant thunder the low rumble of voices.

He played his cards and smoked his cigar.

Seek that which is eternal

Several times Belle came in with a banker. John looked up from his game: Yes? The man explained something, some solution that he had thought of, but then John, after hearing the man out and after a moment or two of thought then simply said: no, that will not work. Some then left and some asked why. John explained why he did not think the plan would work and then the man, without rebuttal, also left. Each time Belle stood by the door until the conversation was completed and then walked the man back across the hall to the East Reading Room. Once Belle returned by herself.

"Why don't you tell them what to do, Mr. Morgan?"

"Because, you see, I do not know what to do myself, but some time, someone will come in with a plan that I know will work; and then I will tell them what to do."

John loved sitting here in the room, surrounded by the Renaissance beauty of his collection; on cold winter nights with a fire roaring and crackling in the fireplace, the smooth warm of the blaze permeated the room and brushed across his skin. But it was a joy that he often shared alone. It was strange how he had to compartmentalize his friends. Some of his friends loved art, but even then some enjoyed the paintings while others enjoyed the books while others better appreciated the bric-a-brac and ceramics.

Other friends were just all business and did not really care for the art. Others loved the yacht racing, others just the sheer joy of boating, sailing along the waves. And then others enjoyed the collies and the dog shows, but not the prize cows.

And then there were all of his friends in the church, the bishops and their wives. There were his friends who delighted in the hymn singing, but not attending the opera, and the different friends who enjoyed the opera did not care for the hymn singing.

Others enjoyed a fine cigar as much as he did, and others fine wine or fine food, but not necessarily the same. Everyone liked to eat but not everyone appreciated the subtleties of fine food. This he had to reserve for discussions with Louis Sherry of the restaurant. There was his love of friends and good cheer; playing with the children on Christmas; Thanksgiving dinners with family.

And then there was his almost sacred love of Egypt. Friends, yes, liked to travel and if he went to Egypt then that was fine with them for it was the traveling they enjoyed, not necessarily the destination.

So it was odd to him that he had to compartmentalize his friends. Everyone liked something, but no one like it all. No one, that is, except him. And although that meant that he shared a lot of things with different people he always had to change his friends, like articles of clothing, in order for him to enjoy everything he loved. There was no one to share all of it with. There were people who only found pleasure in one or two things. Rockefeller, it was reported, loved his money, rode a bicycle and played golf. What kind of life it that? Golf, golf; nothing but golf.

John saw himself as blessed in that he loved so many things. There were so many paths into the heart: love of things; love of ideas; love of people; and love of places. He truly was blessed to have found within himself the love of so much. For it is love that makes you feel most alive. Beauty is everywhere, and in all things, if but you have the eyes to see it. And if you have the compassion to love it.

John sat back in his chair and looked around his room. Surrounded by beauty, luxury, Renaissance excellence, he was like a modern day Medici sitting in his villa. Colleagues called him Jupiter, noble and powerful like a Roman god and, although he knew it to be empty vanity to even think of such things, he had to admit to himself that in a deliciously evil way he did at times fantasy the thought.

But his thoughts were interrupted.

Belle called his name from the doorway. She stood at the door with James Stillman

"James," John called out as he stood up.

Stillman walked over to him.

"Here, have a seat. Please."

After Stillman sat John again sat down.

"So how is it going in there?"

Stillman, rather than answer, instead reached into his coat pocket and pulled out a cigar and placed it on the desk in front of John. John's eyes sparkled with delight.

"Where did you get these?" he asked as he picked up the cigar as if it were a precious sacred object.

"I just got these the other day. They are shipped direct from Cuba."

"Well, I am glad that something is still working right around here."

Stillman pulled another from his pocket. They both lit their cigars together.

As he was lighting his cigar John said: "Always resist everything, Stillman, except temptation."

The two of them smoked in silence for awhile. It was nice not to speak when mutually enjoying something of beauty. Words trivialize things. There are times when the experience is greater than mere words can describe. Silence can be the greatest expression of truth.

Finally, after a long while, Stillman spoke.

"I think you are wrong. The Clearing House Certificates are the solution. It is a problem of liquidity. We have too great a demand after too few dollars."

"So then just create money out of thin air. If you expand the supply of money with non money then you shrink the value of your currency into nothing."

"But as in the past it will only be temporary, it increases the supply within the clearing house environment and releases cash to be put out into the market. And if the public sees that all the demands are being met then the panic will cease."

"Being met with fake money?"

"Perception, rather than truth, counts for a great deal."

"And then what?"

"We eventually shrink back and the certificates will be retired. We then return to where we were before all of this happened."

"But we are setting a bad precedent. And if we do not retire all of them then you have polluted the money supply with baseless paper."

"It was done, temporarily in the Civil War, and then again in various panics in the past. In 1873 William Richardson bought certificates to stimulate the economy."

John grew silent.

"Let us worry about retiring them later. Right now we have a series liquidity problem and I think this will solve the problem that we now face."

John grunted. "The cure may be worse than the illness."

Stillman simply shrugged.

John took a long drag on his cigar and watched as he blew the smoke up into the air.

"If it does not work," he said, "I have half a notion to set the trusts adrift and be done with them."

Stillman nodded.

"I feel exactly the same way."

Stillman puffed his cigar several times and then popped several rings of smoke into the air.

"But you and I know very well that we will not."

"You know," John said, watching Stillman, "that is something that I never have been able to master: the rings."

Stillman smiled. It was rare for him to smile, but he smiled.

John waved his hand around the room.

"I have been sitting here, in the peace and quiet of this room with the rumble of all the voices in the other room but a distant sound."

Then he held up his cigar, admiring it. "In the midst of all this tension and complexity shines through a simple joy. I long at times for it to be

277

that simple; where the joy of a single thing outweighed everything else, such as the collapse of the whole financial system. If it were that then I could sit with Henry David Thoreau and watch as the ducks fly out over the lake in the twilight and see in it something of the greatest significance that life has to offer. Would it not be grand if it were but that simple?"

Stillman stared at John until John brought his eyes to stare at Stillman. They locked in silence for a second.

"You realize that we have worked very well together," John said. "Working together rather than against each other seems to work out just fine. Between you, me, and George Baker we could own this town."

"No, not own: run. There is a great difference."

John laughed and took a deep breath. He stood up, carefully placing his chair back. "Now, here is how we can do this thing. Let us go into the next room and get to work."

Friday, October 25,

When John arrived at his office Perkins was already there waiting for him. He met with Cortelyou at the hotel for breakfast at six o'clock that morning. In all honesty, he told John, they did not find a ray of hope in the situation. The banks were throwing millions of dollars at the situation, Rockefeller was throwing millions of dollars at the situation, the treasury was throwing millions of dollars at the situation, but it just did not seem to be getting any better. All the measures they had done all seemed to be but a delay of the inevitable.

The runs on the banks continued because of fear; he heard a report that across New York City there was no bank safe deposit boxes left. People were hoarding cash and stuffing it into strong boxes. Again, it was because of fear. Banks all over the country were pulling their cash out of the New York Banks: again, fear.

The only thing that will break this panic is to break the fear that drives it.

Perkins explained to Cortelyou that they must continue to support The Trust Company and the Lincoln Trust because that is where they drew the line. He told John that he explained to Cortelyou that:

"It was not because we were particularly in love with these two trust companies that we wanted to keep them open. Indeed, we had not any use for their management and knew that they ought to be closed, but we fought to keep them open in order not to have runs on other concerns and have another outburst of panic and alarm."

The Stock Exchange again needed money. Panic selling continued; by noon the interest rate on margin loans was 150 percent.

John shook his head.

"Are they madmen over there?"

Calls were made to King and the Trust committee to continue supplying funds for troubled trusts, especially Trust and Lincoln. Calls were made to the national banks to continue supplying funds for the stock exchange. If we can hold the situation here until this subsides then all of these emergency loans will be paid back. But if we do not hold it here, and give up, then everything we have done so far will be lost.

He called Ransom Thomas at the Exchange and told him to place a temporary order suspending all margin buying or selling.

"This is the second day of heavy selling in a row," Thomas pleaded. "How many more of these can we face?"

"As many as are needed," John sharply replied.

Perkins called Trust and Lincoln and told them to have a minimum number of tellers open; count out the cash very slowly; intentionally make accidental mistakes in counting so they have to count it out all over again.

Delay as much as you can.

Since they were just up the street John decided to personally go to the New York Clearing House offices to help solicit the funds needed for the Exchange. Herbert went with him. They had already voted to grant the issue of clearing house certificates. He told them that another fifteen million would be needed to keep the Exchange from closing. He was only able to arrange for 9.7 million, but even that was contingent that all transactions on the Exchange had to be straight cash. None of the monies could be used for margin buying or selling.

John raced back to The Corner. Herbert, walking behind him, tried as best he could to keep pace. He watched as John walked his racing walk and Herbert could only laugh. John, with his coat unbuttoned and flying open, a piece of white paper clutched tightly in his right hand, he walked fast down Nassau Street. His flat-topped black derby hat was set firmly down on his head. Between his teeth he held a paper cigar holder in which was one of his long cigars, half smoked. His eyes were fixed straight ahead. He swung his arms as he walked and took no notice of anyone. He did not seem to see the throngs in the street, so intent was his mind on the thing that he was doing. Everyone knew him, and people made way for him, except some who were equally intent on their own affairs; and these he brushed aside. The thing that made his progress different from that of all the other people on the street was that he did not dodge, or walk in and out, or halt or slacken his pace. He simply barged along, as if he had been the only man going down the Nassau Street hill past the Subtreasury. He was the embodiment of power and purpose. Not more than two minutes after he disappeared into his office, the cheering on the floor of the Stock Exchange could be heard out in Broad Street.

The Old Man had again saved the Exchange. This time the loan went out at between twenty five and fifty percent, and it proved to be enough. The market stayed open until their usual closing time of three o'clock. Six of the nine million borrowed was used. When accounts were settled Ransom Thomas called John and told him that volume the day before was one million shares, but today it was down to 637,000 shares.

"We seemed to have turned a corner," Ransom said.

John grunted and hung up the telephone.

At the Library that evening the main topic of discussion was not financial but rather psychological. The Union Trust Company of Providence, Rhode Island failed that day, and the runs continued on the Trust and Lincoln Trusts, although greatly diminished.

Many banks invoked rulings that depositors had to post a sixty day notice for any withdrawals above a certain amount.

It was agreed that they could not continue creating pools of loans to bail out the Exchange, the trusts, and now some banks.

It was also agreed that the Clearing House Certificates would greatly help, they authorized the 53 member banks to collectively issue 100 million in certificates; in Chicago, Pittsburgh and Philadelphia they were also issuing certificates, all to take effect on Monday.

And finally they all agreed to continue to save the Trust and Lincoln but they had to stop bailing out many of the smaller banks.

The next major thing that needed to be done was to restore confidence.

A committee was set up to give out assurances to the press; all information for release to the press would go through them.

A committee was set up to notify priests, preachers and rabbis to use their Saturday and Sunday sermons toward restoring hope and confidence.

It was agreed that Treasury Secretary Cortelyou would return to Washington, showing the public that the crisis was now over, let us return to business as usual. John also would leave New York and spend the weekend at his house at Cragston in Highland Falls.

"Let us turn the corner on this, gentlemen," John said as the meeting broke up near two o'clock in the morning. "There is a light at the end of this tunnel."

Once alone John returned to his office and with one last cigar, played a last game of solitaire.

Saturday, October 26.

News spread. A lot of papers carried John's message: if people will keep their money in the banks everything will be all right.

The New York Times quoted Jacob H Schiff, head of banking firm Kuhn, Loeb & Company: "We are doing everything we can to support the heroic efforts of Mr. J.P. Morgan to strengthen the banking situation generally. The prompt, decisive, and effective course of the Secretary of the Treasury deserves unstinted praise, and all must seek in every way to aid in allaying needless alarm which has sprung up and which, I believe, is already subsiding."

Andrew Carnegie was quoted: "Above all, let no man or woman selfishly lock their hoardings in private security but let them bring forth their surplus and add it to the public exchequer, so as to relieve the present famine in the money market."

It was reported that three million in gold was in route from London.

The Chase National Bank announced that two million in gold was in route from Europe.

Herbert Satterlee called the reports a "symposium of cheerfulness."

John and Herbert took the afternoon train to their homes in Highland Falls. Both exhausted, they slept the entire trip. Louisa waited on the wet platform in the rain for them to depart from the train. The crowd from the train came and passed and still she stood under her umbrella looking for them. Finally she boarded the train and walked the cars until she found their cabin. When she slid open the cabin door she saw John slumped down on one chair and Herbert sitting back with his mouth opened wide. Both were sound asleep. Snores filled the room.

"My goodness," she quietly said to herself.

Sunday, October 27.

It rained all Sunday. John slept most of the day.

Monday, October 28.

Things seemed to calm, but beneath the surface two other crises were building. As Perkins described it: "Outwardly, in the newspapers and as far as the public knew, everything was serene but four or five of us were possessed of information that made us fear that all the work we had done in the preceding week might come to naught at any moment."

First, the City of New York itself was bankrupt.

It was around four o'clock in the afternoon that Perkins came into John's office at the Library with the Mayor of New York City, George B. McClellan Jr., Herman A. Metz, the city controller, and the City Chamberlain. James Stillman with his lawyer and George Baker were already there with John.

Getting straight to the point Perkins said that he had been approached by the city the previous evening to set up a meeting. The municipal government of New York needed to raise about thirty million dollars by November 1 to meet its payroll and pay its contractors or else it would be declared insolvent. During last summer the city had tried to float bonds but only could sell forty million in short term loans, underwritten by J. P. Morgan & Company. They felt that they could pay these loans back but then with the coming of the financial crises that hope faded.

They tried to raise bonds over the last week but were hindered by the fact that they could only pay six percent bonds, whereas loans now in the crises were paying ten and in some cases as high as fifty percent. No one would buy their six percent bonds. Perkins explained: "To raise even one million dollars seemed about as possible at that moment as to move a mountain."

But to have the Trust Companies fail, and then the banks fail, and then the Stock Exchange fail, to now have the City itself fail certainly would be too much for the public to take.

"How much fuel would be added to the flame if the credit of the City of New York should be questioned at such a moment?" asked Perkins.

John sat with his cigar and listened.

He agreed they could not raise a bond issue in Europe; they were panicked by the panic so no one would buy. And they could not raise a bond issue here because in this environment the going rates were too high, so, again, no one would buy.

John thought as everyone discussed. He looked at Stillman and Baker and then turned in his chair to face his desk. He took out a piece of Library stationary and began writing. Everyone became quiet as John wrote. He silently continued writing without stopping, a continuous flow of words, he did not even stop as he slid the sheet of paper to the side and pulled out a second sheet where he kept writing without a break and then did the same when he pulled that sheet of paper aside and continued writing on a third sheet of paper. Finally he stopped, picked up the three pages and sat back in his chair and began reading them to himself.

No one spoke during the entire time.

Finally John held out the papers to Perkins.

"See what Baker and Stillman think of that."

As each of them read the plan was laid out in perfect detail. J.P. Morgan & Company would take thirty million of city bonds with optional terms of one, two, or three years, with six percent interest.

"But you will take a tremendous loss if the situation does not improve."

John planned to turn the bonds over to the First National and National City Bank in exchange for Clearing House Certificates. That would release thirty million dollars of cash to the city, to pay out to employees and contractors who would then put that cash back into the banking system. Doing what he was doing would itself help the situation to improve. It was a dramatic vote of confidence.

John smiled. "It is bullish to bet on America."

After all had read and discussed the handwritten document they all agreed. Stillman's lawyer nodded.

"It was practically perfect both from the standpoint of an offer and the concise manner in which it had been put."

They adjourned the meeting; the city would get their money the next day.

With the stroke of a pen John created thirty million dollars.

He finished the evening with a cigar, a brandy, and a game of solitaire.

Thursday, October 31.

Foreign exchange of Gold changed from net import to net export. There was a great need to get cotton and grains to tidewater wharves for England and Europe greatly needed cotton and grain. If they could get to the ships then foreign bills of lading could be issued and the gold payments for such shipments could again begin to flow.

But the rail shipments of these were stopped. The progressive and anti-money interest Roosevelt administration had passed laws which strictly forbid railroads to discriminate in their shipments of product.

The government knew better than the market place what products should be shipped. According to the government everything shall be shipped equally, to ship only products that are needed is to discriminate against the products that are not needed.

So England and Europe were calling for grain and cotton but the railroads could not ship enough of it to port. That would be discrimination.

"This is absurd," John said, talking on the telephone to Robert Bacon, now Assistant Secretary of State. "Does the government want the markets to work or not? Apparently the government bureaucrats think they know better what is needed than those who need what they need."

Bacon tried to answer but John cut him off.

"We need cash, we need gold reserves. We are in a crisis of liquidity, we need cash. But by restricting the railroads from shipping the products that Europe will pay us for in gold we are simply aggravating the crises. How stupid can we be, and for what, what end?"

"We must look into the situation. . ."

"Look into it, what do you mean? Get the government out of the way so the market place can get on with its job. Let the railroads ship what the market place wants us to ship so we can get paid. We are bleeding cash in a cash crisis because the government won't let us do our job. You honestly think a committee of bureaucrats in Washington knows better what is needed than the markets that need what it needs?"

In the end Robert Bacon talked with Secretary of Treasury Cortelyou who talked with President Roosevelt who said that he would order an exception and that the railroads could, for now at least, ship products that the market was buying, and therefore discriminate against the products that the market was not buying.

"Think about it," John raged at his forever faithful George Perkins. "The government sets up all these silly rules to make it look like they are punishing us for something, but then when it does not work and it comes back to haunt them they then have to make exceptions so that it will work the way it is suppose to work without letting anyone know that they were wrong to block it in the first place."

"Government control of business seems to be the direction that we are headed."

"Why does government hate business? Business is what America is."

"I think it is power. Perhaps they just want to own that power themselves."

"Then woe to us. We are doomed if this is the direction future presidents are going to take."

Saturday, November 2.

Early in the morning Grant Schley, co-owner of Moore & Schley, one of the largest brokerage firms on Wall Street, and Lewis Cass Ledyard, of the law firm Carter, Ledyard & Milburn, came to the Library to see John. John knew both of them. Moore & Schley was a leading underwriter of corporate mergers, perhaps second only to J.P. Morgan & Company itself, and Grant Schley was married to the sister of George Baker. He had worked at the First National Bank from 1874 to 1880 and was a large stockholder in the bank. Lewis Cass Ledyard was an avid yacht race participant. John met him at many of the races and knew him well.

"You know my associate George Perkins; Perkins, this is Grant Schley and Lewis Ledyard."

Each shook hands and then they sat themselves in a small circle around John's desk.

"How can I help you gentlemen?"

The two glanced at each other and then Ledyard laid out the situation. The firm of Moore & Schley was in trouble and on the verge of collapse. They owe about $35 million to various banks, including your own, and it had used as collateral the stock of the Tennessee Coal, Iron & Railroad Company, a steel producer based in Birmingham, Alabama. However the firm itself does not own the stock directly. A thinly traded stock, Schley had organized a syndicate of buyers in 1905 to purchase a controlling interest in the company. The firm lent monies to these investors, taking the stock as collateral, for them to purchase the stock. It then used this stock as collateral for the loans they incurred from various banks.

Schley and a member of the syndicate, one George Kessler, a wine merchant, used the stock to secure loans for themselves. Mr. Kessler became over extended and the banks called his loans. He could not pay. Now, in his opinion, because the dealings of Mr. Schley is tied to Mr. Kessler, and because due to the recent trouble the value of the stock has dropped well below the assumed value, these banks are calling his loans and will not accept as collateral any more shares of the stock.

"What is the value of the shares?"

"They were purchased at $130 per share, and since it is so thinly traded the true value is unknown but steel industry experts put the value at around $60."

Ledyard continued that Mr. Schley himself, due to recent reversals, is overextended and owes money to other firms, friends, and banks. His obligation to First National Bank was two million, and to J.P. Morgan about one million. We have word that on Monday several banks to which both he and his firm owes money are, due to the current situation where they are desperate for cash, calling in many loans. This includes Mr. Schley and his firm. He cannot meet the call and will have to close.

John, listening to Ledyard, was tapping his finger on the desk. Finally he stopped. He cleared his throat.

"It is very serious," John said. "If Moore and Schley go, there is no telling what the effect on Wall Street will be and on financial institutions of New York, and how many other houses will drop with it, and how many banks might be included in the consequences."

"Yes," Ledyard agreed. We could be at the beginning of an entirely new round of panic."

"What are your requirements?"

"We estimate twenty five million."

"A loan of that much is out of the question, given how overextended he and the firm are already."

"That was my thought as well. I actually represent not Mr. Schley but another syndicate member, Oliver Hazard Payne."

John raised his eyebrow at the mention of the name.

"You, I understand, worked closely with Mr. Payne during the consolidation of United States Steel."

"Yes, of course."

"Well, it is his suggestion that the syndicate should not secure a loan but rather, in his words, 'sell the Tennessee Coal & Iron and be done with it.' He greatly feels that there is only one potential buyer and that is U.S. Steel. It is in that capacity that I am here: to open negotiations."

John sat frozen for a very long time without saying a word. His cigar sat in the ashtray burning down untouched.

Thinking.

It was Schley who next spoke.

"The majority shareholders agree they would be willing to sell at par value, one hundred per share."

It was quite awhile before John spoke. He turned toward Perkins.

"Call Trimble at U.S. Steel and Tommy Joyce, I want to see them right away. Call Elbert Gary and Henry Clay Frick and have them meet me here immediately. Tell them also to organize a full Finance Committee meeting here by no later than two thirty this afternoon."

Perkins picked up the telephone. John then turned toward Schley.

"I want you to go with Mr. Trimble and Mr. Joyce and give them complete access to your books. Spare nothing. I want them to tell me exactly where you are.

By three o'clock the Finance Committee meeting was under way. The situation was explained to the members in detail.

Debate began.

Tennessee Coal, Iron & Railroad Company was an independently owned steel producer in Birmingham, Alabama. It possessed coal and steel properties throughout Alabama, Tennessee, and Georgia and owned an estimated 800 million tons of iron ore and two billion tons of coal as well as various reserves of limestone, dolomite and other minerals. It owned 17 blast furnaces, including 4 of the largest 200 ton furnaces in the town of Ensley, 3256 beehive coke ovens, 120 Solvay coke ovens, 15 red ore mines, as well as a large network of railroads.

And all of the company ore mines were within 25 miles of their furnaces so transportation costs were significantly below that of other competitors. It was a leading southern steel manufacturer and gave anyone a great opening into that market. It was a great competitor to U.S. Steel, and had recently received an order for 150,000 tons of steel from E. H. Harriman for his railroads, an order not given to U.S. Steel.

And, as a show of confidence, the company was one of the first twelve companies listed in the industrial average that Charles Dow and Edward D. Jones put together in May of 1896.

But there were problems.

There were repeated stories in the newspapers of mismanagement. The new owners, the Moore & Schley syndicate, had spent heavily to modernize the plants but it forced the company into heavy debt.

Henry Frick was adamantly opposed to the acquisition. He felt that it was inefficient and had too high a cost of production. Because of high phosphorus content in the ore the resulting steel was of low quality. The Harriman order of steel was produced at a loss of $4 a ton and much of it had to be returned as defective.

But, John pointed out several times, just the coal and ore mines alone were worth the price. And it allowed U.S. Steel into the southern markets.

"Think in the long term, gentlemen; always think in the long term."

As the discussion continued Trust Company and Bank presidents began to gather. There was to be meetings all evening. John moved the Finance committee into Bella Greene's office toward the back of the Library while putting the Trust bankers in his office in the West Room and the Bank presidents in the East Room. Each group had different important things to discuss and cover while John played the maestro of the financial symphony as he moved from room to room.

East Room.

The runs had continued on Trust and Lincoln. The pace had slackened but the banks had to still set up pools of loans to keep them afloat. It had to come to an end. The trust companies had to set up a mechanism to support themselves without the national bankers continuing bailing them out. Everyone in the room was in agreement on that.

"I will not provide the solution," John insisted.

John looked around the room: they were all bankers like he was; old, established, consistent, careful and conservative bankers. He personally knew them and could do business with them all for they all followed the same rules.

"These trusts are not banks and therefore are not regulated as banks are. Their wild and immature actions will be the death of us all unless they are organized and operate in an orderly manner. To use public funds for wild speculations like trying to corner the market on some stock is reprehensible."

They all nodded in agreement.

Perkins added that he had been trying to get a complete statement from the trust companies on their financial condition but, he said, "I had obtained nothing that was satisfactory." Tomorrow was Sunday so the banks are closed, and Tuesday was an election day so they would be closed again. He felt that the trust problem should be solved by then or else, as he phrased it, "there was no use in making any further fight for them and that they would have to close."

288

Perkins had assigned Strong to study the accounts of Trust Company again to see if it is still viable. He was scheduled to give his report later tonight.

"So why save them?" one asked. "Let them face the consequence of their actions. If you open a business and run it poorly then you fail; it is as simple as that."

Stillman shook his head no.

"I believe," he began, "that the greatest possible service to mankind, rich or poor, was the establishing of sound financial institutions as the foundations of business. We are the stewards of that stability. It is the National Banks who have the major accounts. The majority of the depositors in the trusts are common working men. They can ill afford to lose all of what little they have."

"But is it up to us to protect them?"

There was a moment of silence before Stillman again spoke.

"Who else?"

John, who had been silently twirling his cigar, finally spoke.

"I agree. But I am enabling the trust presidents to not do anything because I keep solving their problems for them. Now is the time; tonight no one leaves until it is solved by them, not me."

Belle Greene Office.

It was reported that U. S. Steel had had cash reserves of $76 million and had reported quarterly earnings surpassing $43.8 million: it was the second most profitable quarter in its history. Elbert Gary, nicknamed 'Judge,' as chief executive had just last Tuesday, October 29, said while talking to the board of directors: "There has existed during the last week a delirium of excitement. The feeling in a large measure has been without cause, and there is already a change for the better. If all of us do everything in our power to maintain a high standard for the conduct of affairs in our charge we can be of great benefit in restoring the confidence necessary to success."

What better way than to keep a major brokerage firm from failing, and acquiring useful assets for U.S. Steel in the mean time?

Just yesterday, Friday November 1, the company announced plans to pay their payroll 20 percent in cash from their own cash fund and the rest in checks drawn on different banks. With a payroll of $3 million a week that certainly helps relieve the cash strain on banks.

Why not use some of that cash for the purchase, there by putting more cash out into the strained system?

But is the scheme not mostly a way to protect the syndicate? It gives relief to a group of wealthy who do not need it and gives U. S. Steel a chance to gobble up a competitor? The public will see it just as that, not as any kind of public service.

"No one wins, gentlemen, unless everyone wins," John finally piped up as he sat mostly silent listening to the discussion smoking his cigar.

Several still grumbled.

"This is our chance. There may be some other way of saving Moore & Schley, but this one will work. Do not see what is but instead what can and will be."

The Committee decided on two actions: either loan Moore $5 million on the equities presented, or else buy controlling interest in Tennessee Coal, Iron & Railroad for $90 per share in cash.

John looked around the room at everyone and when no one objected he slapped his hands down on the desk

"Then make the offer to him."

West Room.

John told Edward King of the Union Trust Company that they must take action now, provide $25 million to support the Trust Company and Lincoln or else "the walls of their own edifices might come crumbling about their ears."

"It is time that you look after your own," John forcefully said standing over the sitting King while dangling his cigar over King's lap and letting the ash purposely fall.

But the trust company presidents were still reluctant, they wanted to talk it all over with their board of directors because without them they did not have authority to commit the banks to such heavy commitments, and they needed cash themselves.

"Have you gentlemen not already done so, it has been a week, are you not observing the ground falling away at your own feet?"

John paced the room back and forth as he talked, waving his cigar for emphasis.

They were convinced that it was their fiscal responsibility to their depositors to conserve their own assets for the good of their own bank in order to weather the storm.

"You do not see the larger picture here. We save ourselves collectively or we go down individually."

Standing in front of the fireplace John waited for a moment as he looked around at everyone.

"It was Benjamin Franklin during the Revolution who said it best. We must hang together or we will surely all hang separately."

John waited again.

"That is the situation that you are in today."

Belle Greene Office.

Perkins brought in word that Schley made his reply. Neither of the offers presented would solve the immediate problem for Moore & Schley. They would still have to close their doors. Therefore, with all due respect, he must reject both of their offers and seek solution elsewhere.

Where else is elsewhere?

East Room.

Many had said about John that his refusal to admit defeat was his greatest strength. But he could not continue to help people who did not help themselves. That is not admitting defeat, that was recognizing an impossible situation and coming to grips with it.

John paced the floor puffing on his cigar, bent forward slightly, staring at the floor as he paced.

James Stillman tried to steady him.

John felt like letting the trusts fail because they would not help themselves. John: "They must deal with it as they see fit. I have gone with it as far as I can."

James nodded with John as he joined the pacing, placing his hands behind his back.

"Perhaps," Stillman began softly, clearing his throat before he continued. "Perhaps we should see this matter in a bit of a longer perspective. Where will it end if we do not end it where we have already been ending it?"

Benjamin Strong arrived at the Library with a handful of folders.

While word went to John that he was there Strong sat in a lounge along the wall. He was exhausted. He had been going over and over the books and the collateral securities of both the Trust Company and Lincoln Trust for days as each day the situation changed. He watched as about forty or fifty men walked about the large room arguing and talking. He recognized some of the bank presidents and presidents of the Clearing House, but did not recognize many of them. Was the thing growing and effecting everybody everywhere?

Henry Davison came over and sat next to him. Early in the day Davison had told Strong of the Tennessee Coal & Iron situation. By the look of the room and the agitation it seemed that something was wrong.

"What is going on? Is the Tennessee deal done?"

Davison put his finger to his lips as he carefully looked around. He leaned in and whispered.

"Many do not know about the deal, so shhh."

Strong nodded.

Davison went on: "Morgan is in the back with Judge Gary, Frick and Ledyard. Schley turned down the first offer."

"That's what I thought."

"They are working on a second offer. And Morgan has the Trust presidents in the West Room working on a bailout for themselves. Morgan thinks they need about twenty five million. They need to solve it themselves so he can get on with the Tennessee deal. Wait here until he calls you in."

Davison got up and left.

Strong sat silent looking in disbelief at the hustle and bustle of the men dashing all around. Completely surrounding them on the walls and on the shelves stacked to the ceiling was the art work and the books; the thousands of precious books. The whole scene seemed so incredibly incongruous. On the floor anxious bankers rushed about in panic about their withering earthly goods while above them, silent, lofty and magnificent tapestries hung from the walls, while rare Bibles, books of ancient and eternal wisdom, and illuminated manuscripts of the Medieval and Renaissance world of knowledge sat serenely in elegant glass cases; in another room other panicked bankers shouting and yelling beneath walls where hung collections of early Renaissance masters like Andrea del Castagno or Michelangelo's teacher Domenico Ghirlandaio or the leading painter of the Umbrian school Pietro Perugino: an Adoration of the Magi, a Madonna and Child, a portrait of the lovely Giovanna Tornabuoni; if the paintings could speak of what they have seen.

Like the School of Athens by Raphael, men were milling about each lost in thoughts of themselves. It was in the Renaissance Florence of the Medici Bank that modern capitalism as we understand it began, so it seemed appropriate that Morgan the Modern Medici of New York, patron of the Renaissance arts, was here trying to save it from collapse.

West Room.

It was around midnight when Edwin S. Marston, president of Farmers Loan and Trust Company, was summoned to the back office where John waited.

When he returned to the West Room he looked very grave.

"What is the matter?"

"Morgan has informed me of another serious matter that has come up. He can not at this point tell me what it concerns but he says that it is very serious."

The others banks grew silent. They watched Marston for clues. What can it be, they all thought?

"He said that he had to handle the matter himself. But doing so will tax his time and his financial ability to do anything else."

"What do you mean?" someone asked.

"He said that for him to insure the success of his problem required our own resolution of our situation. If we fail and collapse then the whole matter that he is facing will collapse as well."

"But what is it?"

"He could not say for fear it would jeopardize the whole situation. But he did inform me that its failure could be catastrophic. That is the word he used: catastrophic."

"It means that we are truly on our own to solve this issue?"

Marston nodded.

"He said it was imperative we solve this for now we are not just a danger to ourselves but to a situation much greater and dire in its consequences."

"What are we to do now?

East Room.

Benjamin Strong, still sitting on the lounge, could not help himself.

Without realizing it he dozed off. He did not know how long he slept but he woke up with a start. Looking to his left James Stillman sat next to him. Stillman was smiling as he stared at Strong.

"How long have you been sitting there?"

"A few minutes."

"Sorry," Strong said as he shook his head trying to get fully awake.

"When was the last time you have been to bed?"

Strong thought about it.

"Thursday morning. All Thursday and Friday I was at both the Trust Company of America and Lincoln."

"And today?"

"At Trust again."

"Well, I don't think that the country is going to smash if you go home to bed."

"After I give Morgan my report on Trust I will."

"I'll see if I can hurry it along."

"Thank you."

It was near three o'clock in the morning before Strong was summoned into Belle Greene's office to give his report. The Trust Company is still solvent enough at this time but not if the situation lasted too much longer. It had equity of about two million and could still exchange that for the necessary cash to pay off its depositors in time but the Lincoln Trust was short of at least one million and needed loans to stay solvent.

John dismissed him. Strong walked out and headed for the front door. When he tried to open the front door he could not. He tried several times. Davison came up behind him.

"It's locked. Morgan orders. And Morgan has the key in his pocket. No one leaves until he says so."

Davison shrugged his shoulders and laughed.

"Settle in for the night, it is going to be a long one."

Strong was exhausted. He sat back down in the lounge.

West Room.

John, followed by Stillman and Baker and Perkins, walked into the crimson colored room in single file. The trust presidents all turned to watch as they all entered. The conversation came to a halt.

294

John stood in the center of the room. All that could be heard was the crackling of the fire.

"Well gentlemen. You have been briefed of what Benjamin Strong has reported. You have had all night to discuss it."

John turned his gaze at Edward King.

"What do we have?"

King said nothing. He tried not to look directly at John.

John pointed to a piece of paper that Perkins held in his hand.

"This is an agreement that states that each of you will offer your weighted share of twenty five million that will be placed in a fund for use in helping struggling trusts during this crises. I am sure that your various boards of directors will approve of such measures and if they do not then I will convince them that they will."

John nodded to Perkins who then proceeded to read the document. When Perkins was done he handed it to John. John walked over and put the paper down on the desk. He waved his hand toward the paper as he stepped back and looked around the room.

"There you are gentlemen: signatures."

It was a statement, not a question. No one moved. No one spoke. John waited.

Finally John put his hand on the shoulder of Edward King and slightly pushed him forward.

John pointed to the paper.

"There's the place, King."

John pulled out a gold pen from his waistcoat.

"And here's the pen."

King stared down at the pen in his hand. He looked up at John. John raised one eyebrow.

Slowly King walked up to the desk and signed the document. One by one each of the trust presidents signed. John nodded with a smile to each one as they approached.

The timepiece on the desk chimed: it was 4:45 am.

John finally walked over and unlocked the large bronze doors. Everyone could finally go home. John stood in the foyer as they all started to leave, putting on their heavy coats and walking out into the cold November morning. Baker and Ledyard took John aside.

"And what are we to do about our matter?" Ledyard asked.

John smiled and patted Ledyard on the shoulder.

"You look tired. Go home and get a good nights rest, but be back here at nine o'clock sharp!"

"Tired is too timid a word for how I feel."

"Tomorrow will be a better day."

Sunday, November 3.

The meeting began in the West Room at four thirty that afternoon. Since the previous day Thomas Joyce, of the Morgan firm, and Richard Trimble, of U.S. Steel, was reviewing in detail the books of Moore & Schley. Perkins, with Grant Schley and John Topping, president of Tennessee Coal, Iron & Railroad, spent the day reviewing their books. All were on orders to present their findings later that night.

John sat at his desk facing the warmth of the blazing wood fire. The fire had crackled and popped with flame since Friday without stop. A table was set up next to the desk where sat Stillman and Baker and Steele. As time passed Perkins joined them, as well as later Grant Schley, Elbert Gary, Henry Clay Frick and Lewis Ledyard. Others were contacted by telephone.

What to do with Moore & Schley?

John told them: "I have done what I can. I have never been more concerned over a situation than I am over this. I think this is the most serious thing we have had to meet in this panic yet."

He thought U.S. Steel should buy Tennessee but he could not force them, it was their decision to make.

Gary and Frick were against.

Debate continued. The new point of objection was the United States Attorney General and the Bureau of Corporations. After this purchase U.S. Steel would own up to sixty percent of the countries Steel manufacturing capacity. Would it violate the Sherman Anti-trust law of 1890? The administration was very aggressive in curtailing such concentrations.

They broke for dinner.

John, with Baker and Stillman, met privately with Thomas Joyce and Richard Trimble. They gave their report. John sat silent while listening to what they presented. It was a bit bleak. There were no good securities left in the company, all that they had were used to borrow money during the panic.

"So, in your estimate, how much is needed for Moore & Schley to remain open?"

Joyce answered: "About seventeen or possibly eighteen millions, sir."

Trimble nodded in agreement.

John looked at Baker and Stillman.

"We must raise the money at once. I will take a third interest in the subscription, the complete subscription not to exceed eighteen million; perhaps you two could each carry the same, until U.S. Steel arranges to take it over."

Baker thought for a second and then said that he would take a third.

But Stillman hesitated.

"I don't know about this. I am not pleased."

"What?"

"Why, you haven't had time to study those figures."

John glanced down at the papers presented by Joyce. He then looked back up.

"Well, I know my man," John replied.

After dinner everyone returned. Perkins and John Topping presented the fact that the company was actually stronger than the committee thought. A new rail producing mill was near completion which estimates said would bring down production costs.

Debate continued.

Finally the U.S. Steel finance committee agreed to a new proposal to purchase Tennessee Coal, Iron & Railroad. They would buy a majority of the company but not with cash, as had been discussed. U.S. Steel would exchange their own 60 year, 5 percent sinking fund gold bonds for 100 shares of Tennessee. Everyone wins. There would not be a cash strain on the already cash strapped markets, Moore & Schley could pay their obligations off with U.S. Steel bonds, payable in actual gold, and U.S. Steel got a controlling interest in their major competitor.

But Gray and Frick demanded three conditions.

First: the Roosevelt administrations must not object to the acquisition, by prior approval.

Second: this transactions must 'unquestionably save Moore & Schley' from failure.

Third: the problem with the trust companies must be solved.

John assured the committee that the third condition was already in place by the agreement drawn up and signed last night, or, actually, this morning. And he personally would ensure the second condition. So the only thing remaining was the first.

Grant Schley, on behalf of Moore & Schley, accepted the deal.

John Topping, on behalf of Tennessee, accepted the deal.

That left the government.

"Before we go ahead with this," Gary said, "we must consult President Roosevelt."

John was confused: the Attorney General, yes; the Bureau of Corporations, yes; but Roosevelt?

"But what has the president to do with it?" John asked.

"If we do this without consulting the administration a bill in equity might stop the sale, and in that case more harm than good would be done. He cannot say that we may or may not purchase, but we ought to know his attitude since he has a general direction of the law department of the United States."

Frick: "What he leads they will follow."

Gary: "I consider Roosevelt a friend of mine. I feel it best to speak directly with him."

John tapped his lips with the tip of his cigar several times without putting the cigar in his mouth.

"Can you go at once?" he finally asked.

It was already ten o'clock at night. Gary called William Loeb, Roosevelt's private secretary and requested a meeting first thing tomorrow, Monday. Perkins called the dispatcher for the Pennsylvania Railroad in Newark New Jersey for a special train with a locomotive and one Pullman sleeper car for immediate dispatch for Washington D.C.

It will leave at midnight.

As Gary and Frick were leaving John gave them one last warning.

"It is imperative that this is resolved before the markets open tomorrow because without word the loans might be called and Moore & Schley will collapse.

Monday, November 4.

John, after going to bed after two in the morning was up at eight. He sent Perkins to his office to await a call from Gary and Frick as to their meeting. Cables from London said that the market was falling and so the American markets would most likely fall as well. That would put a strain on the whole situation. The stock value of Tennessee would drop and increase the demand for reimbursement from Moore & Schley.

Gary and Frick arrived at the White House at eight o'clock.

But William Loeb refused to let them in. Roosevelt was at breakfast and would see them at ten o'clock.

"But that will be too late," Gary insisted.

"I am sorry but I cannot schedule you before ten."

"But this is s serious matter and I think that if you will tell him just what Mr. Frick and I are here for, he will see us."

"No, I am sorry but the President says ten and that means ten. Now please excuse me."

Loeb walked away.

Gary and Frick stood in the hall.

They were in shock.

What could they do now?

From the doorway there was a call.

"Judge Gary, what brings you here?"

Gary turned. It was James Garfield, the Secretary of the Interior, just arriving.

"James!" Gary screamed out to him.

Gary, in the hallway, in a rushed flood of words, told Garfield the situation.

"Can you please help, it's very important."

Garfield nodded. "I'll see what I can do. Wait here."

After about ten or fifteen minutes Garfield appeared. He took Gary and Frick upstairs to Roosevelt.

Roosevelt was eating breakfast. He was still in his robe. There were papers strewn about the table with photographs of him hunting. He explained that he had just gotten back from a hunting trip in Louisiana and was writing an article about it for the magazine 'Outdoor Pastimes.'

Oh, how nice Mr. President.

"So, what can I do for you?"

It was 8:45.

Perkins waited by the phone at The Corner.

He waited.

The market opened at 10:00.

It opened down.

At 10:15 the phone rang.

It was Gary.

"The President is still considering the situation but seemed favorable. I just wanted to get word to you. I have to go back in."

Perkins called the Exchange.

He told them there was a plan in place to save Moore & Schley. Details would follow.

Perkins called John.

Perkins again waited.

The phone rang at 11:00.

It was Gary. He read to Perkins Roosevelt's written reply: 'I answered that while of course I could not advise them to take the action proposed, I felt it no public duty of mine to interpose any objection.'

Perkins called the Exchange. The government is letting the deal go through. Moore & Schley is saved. The trust companies are backed by an agreement from all the trust companies that each will save each other.

Perkins called John.

He heard John laugh over the phone. He laughed.

It turned out to be the best day on the stock exchange for over a month.

The center had held.

Thursday, November 14.

It was about ten in the morning, a cold crisp November morning. Lily Barney sat in the upstairs front bedroom with her friend Susan Abbott Mead chatting. Susan had just returned from a trip through Europe two weeks ago and was telling Lily all about what a wonderful time she had in Europe. Susan stood by the window looking out onto Park Avenue as she talked. The winter trees were stark, stripped of their leaves.

"Aren't the trees in winter so sad looking, stripped so bare," she said.

"Yes, indeed. They are certainly not like in the spring."

Suddenly there was a loud bang.

They both jumped in fright from the noise.

They looked at each other in shock.

"What on earth was that?" Susan asked.

It was so loud, and it sounded like it was in the next room. Susan immediately went out and crossed the hall to the other bedroom at the rear of the house. Lily followed. In the bedroom was a large brass bed with posts and a canopy.

Susan walked into the room but then froze.

Lily came in after her. Charles Barney, her husband, stood by the chest of drawers in his pajamas. They could see themselves in the mirror behind him. There was an incredible pained and shocked look on his face. He looked toward his wife. His breathing was heavy and labored. She rushed toward him. As she approached he fell forward into her arms. She helped him ease down onto the floor.

"What is it? What's the matter?"

Charles, lying on the floor, heavily moaned.

Their son Ashbel was downstairs when he heard the loud noise. He immediately ran upstairs and saw both his mother and Susan kneeling down over his father.

His mother turned to him.

"Call Doctor Dixon, quickly, something is wrong."

Ashbel ran to the hall telephone and dialed up Doctor George Dixon, he then returned to the room.

With the help of Lily and Susan they got Charles up onto the bed.

It was then that Susan saw the revolver on the floor, and the blood.

When Doctor Dixon arrived and looked at Charles he instantly called for Dr. Louis Stimson and Dr. Joseph Blake. With the three of them there Dr. Dixon gave Charles ether and they began exploring the gunshot wound. The shot entered the upper left quadrant of the abdomen. The bullet traveled upward through the intestine and traversed the entire left lung coming to rest in the left shoulder near the collar bone.

They tried to stop the bleeding that was soaking the bed sheets crimson.

Charles lasted until two thirty.

Dr. Dixon then called the coroner.

Newspapers put out afternoon extras.

John was in his office reading reports. James walked in with a newspaper in his hand. John kept reading.

"Sir," James quietly said.

John looked up at him.

"Yes, James."

James placed the newspaper on the desk. John picked it up and began to read. He read it: Charles Tracy Barney. . .Knickerbocker. . .dead from gunshot wounds. . .his wife Lily found him. . .financial problems. . .apparent suicide.

But John stopped when he reached the quote from, of all people, Charles Morse: "Mr. Barney's heart was broken by the cruel treatment of his associates; that is the cause of his death."

John put the paper aside. He put both elbows on the desk and buried his face in his hands.

Oh Charley, oh Charley; what have you done?

James stood quietly watching.

It is hard to hold on.

"Are you all right, sir?"

John took a deep breath. He sat back in his chair and placed the palms of both hands on the desk. Sitting back he closed his eyes and then opened them again.

"Yes, James," he answered staring straight ahead, "I will be all right."

The Trial

The two lawyers arrived. It was early. There was a small knock on the door. Jack answered the door.

"We should go now," the one with the handlebar moustache said.

"Yes, I agree," Jack said. "We want to get this over with as soon as possible."

John sat at the table engrossed in his game of solitaire. The cups and plates from breakfast room service sat beside him. Louisa came over and touched his sleeve.

"Father," she said.

John looked up at her.

"Yes. What?"

"It is time to go."

John glanced over at Jack and the two lawyers standing by the door. The three of them were staring at him.

John grunted and then looked down at the cards. He was not done.

"They are waiting," she said.

"Yes, yes," John snapped.

He stood as Louisa held out his coat. He let her help put his coat on, while still staring at the cards.

"Well, then," Jack said as John walked over to the door. "Shall we?"

The two lawyers filed out into the hallway followed by Jack then John then Louisa. Once John was in the hall Jack leaned in toward him.

"Lamont and Davison are already in the lobby."

John walked on without acknowledging what Jack said. They all filed down the hallway single file. John passed the door where the boy was the night before. John glanced over. The boy was gone.

They all squeezed into the elevator. They were all silent on the trip down. Finally, when the elevator came to a stop, one of the lawyers spoke, the young one with the black hair.

"I think you will do just fine, Mr. Morgan."

John said nothing. He stared at the elevator door. No one spoke as the porter slid the door open.

Once they came out of the elevator into the lobby Jack directed everyone toward a group sitting on a set of couches. As they approached everyone rose.

As he passed by John glanced up at the photograph on the wall. Curtis: the Indian. He watched it grow smaller and more distant as he walked away from it. The Indians; they were all gone now.

"We will need several cars, I thought Father and Louisa and I would go in one and then the rest of you in other cars as you see fit."

Everyone nodded in agreement as they gathered their things: coats, leather briefcases, thick portfolios filled with papers. John watched it all with a certain feeling of detachment. All that I am, or what they think I am, neatly summarized into a portfolio of papers.

He did not feel that well. His cold was still there. He knew what he had to do but he just did not want to be here.

People standing and sitting around in the lobby of the hotel all watched and pointed and whispered wondering what was going on as the whole group of John's party all walked one by one toward the main entrance:

John Pierpont Morgan Jr., Jack, partner at J.P. Morgan & Company;

Thomas W. Lamont, another partner at J.P. Morgan & Company, with his wife;

Henry P. Davison, another partner at J.P. Morgan & Company, with his wife;

Joseph H. Choate, former U.S. Ambassador to Britain's Court of St. James and former President of the Bar Association for the City of New York, considered one of the leading corporate attorneys in the country;

John C. Spooner, former Senator, Wisconsin's railroad attorney;

Richard V. Lindabury, attorney for U.S. Steel Corporation;

De Lancey Nicoll, former district attorney general for the City of New York;

William F. Sheehan, former lieutenant governor of New York;

George B. Case of the New York law firm of White & Case;

Frances L. Stetson of the law firm Jennings & Russell;

Louisa Satterlee, daughter;

John Pierpont Morgan Sr., partner, chief officer of J.P. Morgan & Company.

They moved like an army on their way to battle. John, tapping his mahogany cane on the tiled floor as he walked, pulled out a handkerchief from his coat pocket. He blew his nose as he walked.

Eternal sickness, he thought. It never seems to go away.

At the entrance to the hotel, as Davison held the door open for everyone to pass through, John turned his head and looked back. From across the lobby, toward the bar, he tried to hear the piano from last night, distant, wandering out across the muffled sounds of voices and the hustle and bustle of the hotel lobby. But there was no piano. It sat silent, unplayed.

John came out of the hotel and stood on the top of the steps. A long row of taxis were lined up along the curb; the drivers held open the doors as different members of his party got into different cars. Crowds of people were passing by on the sidewalk. John watched it all with distain. His cold was sapping what energy he had. He did not want to deal with crowds of people right now. He just wanted to get to the committee hearing and get it all over with. Jack stood by one of the taxis and waved him over. Louisa began to descend the stairs ahead of him. A group of reporters, standing around and watching as everyone filed out of the hotel, recognized John. They all, as if on a common cue, rushed over to him. They all began firing questions at him at once.

"Could we have a word?"

"What is up, are you testifying on the existence of your money trust?"

"Are you, as suggested, the leader of a large money trust?"

"How much of the banking system do you control Mr. Morgan, are they going to bust up your trusts?"

"What will the Pujo Committee find as they dig into your finances?"

"Will the committee find a conspiracy among New York bankers to control the money supply?"

John waved them off with sweep of his hand and began down the steps to the sidewalk.

There was the flash of a camera and John raised his walking cane into the air as if to hit the cameraman. Jack appeared at his side and took him by the arm guiding him toward the waiting car.

Jack shouted out to the reporters flocking around his father: "We have no comment to the press at this time, please let us pass."

He led John to the opened back seat door. Louisa had already gotten in and slid over to the other side.

"Please let us pass," Jack repeated as John stepped into the car. As soon as he could Jack shut the door and got into the front seat.

"What do you have to say for yourself, Mr. Morgan?"

Jack turned to the driver: "Leave now."

The driver turned the wheel and pulled away from the curb and into traffic.

"Where are you headed?" the driver asked.

Jack, looking back at the crowds on the sidewalk, said: "Go up to the Hill."

"Where sir?"

"The Hill, the Hill; to the Capital Building."

John sat silent. He watched Jack's frustration. Louisa placed her hand on his and when he glanced over at her she smiled.

The car arrived at the steps to the House of Representatives. The steps to the Capital and the area around it were strangely empty. John watched from the back seat. Jack looked around.

"There is only one other car. We should wait for the others."

"Is there strength in numbers?" Louisa asked, smiling.

"Exactly," Jack replied. "I don't want a repeat of outside the hotel."

John looked out the window. There were only a few people standing around, wrapped in heavy overcoats, and they all seemed focused on other things. It was cold outside.

It was, after all, December. It was the time to tally all the things up, time to close the books and tally up all the transactions for the year, see where we stand, what we have done, and then see what there might be for the next year.

"Looks a bit deserted to me," John said.

Wrapping her coat tighter around her chest Louisa said: "Maybe it's the cold. People would rather stay home and be warm."

She leaned toward her father, smiling. "Maybe you are not as important as everyone fears."

John looked at her. "If only that were true."

The driver turned off the engine.

There was a deadening silence. Everyone could hear themselves breathing.

"Well," Jack began, "still the same I can not get over the disrespect those reporters showed. Once there was a time when gentlemen were respected, men of position revered, and they were treated as such. Now they seem to treat you almost like a common criminal."

"Let's not go that far, Jack," Louisa spoke up.

"I just find it appalling, that's all."

"Well, tensions are a little high right now over this committee hearing."

"And their behavior simply helps to enflame the situation."

"Yes, but when did newspapers ever not enflame any situation that may sell more papers?"

Another car pulled up behind them.

"It just seems that we are under attack from every angle these days," Jack said.

Others began getting out of their cars as a third car arrived. John could hear from outside and behind him car doors slamming, voices floating in the cold air.

Jack, watching out the window, spoke in a tone of deep reflection. "What is to become of all the good we have done? Is that to be ignored and brushed aside?"

John, looking out his window watched as people began to assemble. Jack kept talking.

"What about in 1895, the country was out of gold and was about to default on their obligations. But who saved the whole country from defaulting: you. Is this how you are to be repaid?"

John and his son's eyes met. They stared at each other for a long time. Finally, Jack looked away.

"Well, we best go in," Jack said.

John, sitting in the car, had been watching as others gathered outside his window.

John opened the car door. It swung open. The cold air rushed it.

Outside on the curb John put on his black top hat, buttoned the top button of his overcoat leaving the rest open, and then touched the ground with his walking cane. Louisa held her fur in her hands in front of her. Jack came around the side of the car with his black derby and walking cane. The three of them walked toward the entrance.

In sharp contrast with the outside, inside the hallways leading to the committee room were filled with people. They all stood to the side and watched as John and his group made their way down the hall.

It was extremely crowded in the committee room. John made his way with the rest of his entourage to the side of the room where there were a few seats. John stood as his group struggled with getting enough chairs for everyone. He looked at each of the sub committee members one by one as he stood waiting. Some glanced his way; others did not know he was there yet.

Standing at his table stood Samuel Untermyer gathering together sheets of paper. John knew of Samuel Untermyer. Sharply dress, impeccable, with his tiny trimmed moustache and his plucked orchid in his lapel. He raised orchids as a hobby and could be seen almost everywhere with a fresh orchid flower in the lapel of his suit. He raised orchids and he raised show collies. That was how John knew of him. One year Untermyer's collies won best for show over all others, including John.

John did not like to lose.

At the end of the show John watched as Untermyer strutted out of the show area with his orchid in his lapel and a smiling smirking look of superiority on his face.

John did not like to lose.

At another show John won; Untermyer lost. Untermyer left the show angry and foul.

Samuel Untermyer did not like to lose.

They finally got John a chair and he sat down.

John studied the men sitting in judgment, a committee of professional politicians who will determine the right or the wrong of business decisions. How is that right? How many of them actually have any business experience, but yet they are to pass judgment?

A court of law can pass judgment on a case, do these facts fit a particular law, because the judges are trained in the rule of law. A doctor can pass judgment on an illness because he is trained to study illness. But what laws are there in business; who is right when it comes to saying what is right and what is wrong? Would not a business man know better what is right and what is wrong? First, what works is right. But then what works with the least harm to all parties involved is more right.

That is exactly what John had tried to do all of his professional life. But now a career politician who caters only to getting re-elected is to pass judgment on him. What makes the man think that he knows? What next? Will bureaucrats pass judgment on how a doctor treats a patient?

John sat silent waiting to be called. He was not used to waiting. People waited for him, not the other way around. But that was the way with the government. You waited. It was like when he waited watching President Cleveland wondering how to solve the gold crises with the least political damage while John sat there with the solution but could not speak. Cleveland was more concerned in placating a hostile congress than solving the crises with the correct solution.

John had testified at a lot of governmental hearings. It seemed of late that no matter what anyone did there was a congressional investigation into it.

But the blow fell on February 19, 1902. President Roosevelt and his Attorney General Philander Knox announced that they were bringing a lawsuit under the Sherman Act against the Northern Securities for illegal restraint of trade.

After the Northern Pacific raid and battle between Harriman and John they had formed the Northern Securities pooling the assets of the

Great Northern Railroad, the Northern Pacific, and the Union Pacific Railroad together in order to bring harmony in the Northwest railroad industry and block from happening exactly what had just happened. Now the government was going to break it all up again and return to the chaos of before.

John was stunned. He was taken totally by surprise.

Upon the announcement the stock market fell and, over the next several weeks, grew weak.

John, with Senators Mark Hanna and Chauncey Depew, went to the White House to see President Roosevelt and Attorney General Knox.

He asked why there was no prior announcement. They worked in private exactly so there would not be any leaks to Wall Street.

"But why was I not informed?" John asked, as head of Northern Securities.

Roosevelt answered that warning Wall Street was "just what we did not want to do."

"If we have done anything wrong, send your man to my man and they can fix it up," John replied.

Roosevelt quickly shook his head no. "That can't be done."

"But why not?"

At this point Knox spoke up.

"We don't want to fix it up, we want to stop it."

John sat silent.

This was dangerous. They meant it. And with the full force of the United States Government behind them they could not be ignored.

"Are you going to attack my other interests, the Steel Trust and the others?" John finally asked, realizing the direction that they were going.

"Certainly not," Roosevelt replied, "unless we find out that in any case they have done something that we regard as wrong."

After John left the room Roosevelt turned to his Attorney General.

"That is a most illuminating illustration of the Wall Street point of view. Mr. Morgan could not help regarding me as a big rival operator, who either intended to ruin all his interests or could be induced to come to an agreement to ruin none."

"He is old and set in his ways. He does not understand where the world is heading."

On March 14, 1904 the Supreme Court voted five to four in favor of the government suit. The Northern Securities would have to be broken up and put back the way it was before the merger.

John, in his office, laughed when he heard the news.

"Well," he said. "Have fun unscrambling that omelet and putting the eggs back into their original shells and then putting the eggs back into the hens."

James Hill shook his head.

"It really seems hard that we should be compelled to fight for our lives against the political adventurers who have never done anything but pose and draw a salary."

"Well, Jim, the time is coming when all business will have to be done with glass pockets."

Then, on October 27, 1911, John was at home sick with another of his eternal colds. He and his brother in law, Herbert Satterlee, were sitting by the fire. He heard that men had come to his office that day and then to his library with papers for him. Now, that evening, they rang at his home. John himself answered the door and then after a moment returned to the parlor. He sat back in his chair before the fire. He had several papers open in his hand.

"What was it?" Herbert asked.

John did not speak for a moment but then turned toward him.

The government had brought a lawsuit under the Sherman Act against U. S. Steel. Now they want to break that apart.

For a full ten minutes John sat and stared at the fire, glancing now and again at the papers he held in his hand.

The cigar he held in his other hand burned out unpuffed.

Finally, with a weariness and defeat in his voice he turned to Satterlee.

"Well," he said. "It has come to this."

The government brought a suit against Standard Oil and had it broken up.

The government brought a suit against U. S. Steel and wanted to break it up.

The government brought a suit against Harriman and the Union Pacific and wanted to break it up.

The government under the Interstate Commerce Commission brought several suits against several of Harriman's railroads and wanted them broken up.

Since the Civil War businessmen had made America rich, but now the benefactors of that wealth thought those same businessmen were evil.

And now John was here. The Pujo Committee. They were trying to show that the major bankers, with Morgan as the central lynchpin, were a vast interlocking money trust that controlled the entire finances of the

United States.

And then proving that point, they wanted to bring suit against all of the major banks and break them up.

"The Committee calls J. P. Morgan."

John stood and walked over to the table. He felt the eyes of everyone in the room.

John sat in the wooden chair. He tried to sit back as best he could, spread out his legs. It was not a comfortable chair. He watched as Untermyer bent over talking with one of his assistance. Then, with a small nod, Untermyer turned and approached John. The room grew quiet. Untermyer smiled to John. John nodded in return.

"Where do you reside, Mr. Morgan?"

John cleared his throat.

"New York City."

"Are you senior member of the partnership or firm J. P. Morgan & Co., bankers, of New York City?"

John held up his head. Proud.

"I am, sir."

John could see various people in the room looking back and forth. The great battle had begun.

Untermyer questioned him on the basic structure of his firm, the different branches.

"Does your New York house do a general banking business?"

"We try to, sir."

"Do you take deposits?"

"We do."

"You do the business that is done by a bank?"

"Exactly; so far as we can."

Untermyer paced in front of the table in front of John.

"And you receive as bankers, in that way, deposits of interstate corporations, do you not?"

"We receive the deposits of any corporation."

"You mean you have, among others, large deposits of interstate corporations——that is, corporations engaged in interstate commerce?"

"Yes; I suppose we do. I do not remember any distinction between them."

"The distinction between them is that certain corporations engage in commerce between the States and others engage in commerce only within the States. For instance, the Interborough Co. engages in business only within the State of New York."

"Yes."

"Whilst the Southern Railroad engages in business between the States."

"That is it."

"You receive deposits from both classes of corporations?"

"We receive deposits from any corporation that we think good."

John glanced over at Joseph Choate, sitting taking notes. Interstate Commerce is where he will attack, Joseph said last night. While John was playing cards and everyone in the room were discussing what to expect, Joseph said Interstate Commerce. If you are a private business or only transact business in one state then the federal government does not have control over you. But if you do business across State lines then they can regulate you, they can control you. The Interstate Commerce clause in the Constitution is the front door through which they will come and they will try to widen that door as much as they can until they can classify everything everywhere as interstate commerce.

John watched Untermyer close. Does he think I do not know the difference? It is only an issue with you, sir, not with me running a business.

Untermyer turned.

"Mr. Morgan, do you think these great corporations engaged in interstate commerce, that have their securities scattered broadcast, ought to be permitted to make their deposits with private bankers?"

"I do, sir."

"As a rule?"

"Not as a rule. I do not know that every private banker. . ."

But Untermyer barked in before John could finish.

"Do you not realize that there is no supervision over a private banker by any State authority? There is not, is there?"

"No," John replied. But why should there be any government supervision over a private entity?

Untermyer kept pacing back and forth, more actively now. Maybe he thought he was closing in onto something.

"On the whole," he carefully began, "taking the question as one of policy, and considering the broad question rather than a question personal to any particular banking house, do you not think——"

Pacing back and forth, John followed him with his eyes.

"As a matter of policy——"

"It is a mere matter of judgment, I should say."

"As a matter of policy——" Untermyer began again, emphasizing every word.

"As a matter of judgment, I should say. . ."

Shaken, Untermyer almost shouted out: "I do not think you have heard my question."

John sat silent. He felt the grain of the wood on the table with the fingers of his left hand.

Untermyer began again.

"As a matter of public policy, concerned with the regulation of interstate corporations that are owned by the public and whose shares are widely scattered, you are of the opinion that they should be permitted, without restriction, to make their deposits with private bankers just as readily as with banks that are chartered?"

John waited for a few seconds to make sure that Untermyer was done with his question. Then he answered.

"If their directors so decide."

There was a slight look of disgust in Untermyer's face.

"Do you not think that anybody other than the board of directors has an interest in that subject?"

"If it is a company it can be examined at any time."

"But the private banker who holds their funds can not be examined, can he? The private banker can not be examined either publicly or privately?"

"Yes; if the public claim the right to do it, they can be examined."

"You do not mean to say that an interstate corporation depositing with a private banker would have any right to find out the means of that private banker?"

John shrugged his shoulders.

"Then they need not deposit with them."

Untermyer shook his head.

"But the question is whether they ought to have the right to do such a thing?"

"I should think that was left to the board of directors."

Untermyer stood still for a moment staring at John. John was expressionless. He moved his left hand back and forth across the wooden table.

"That is all you care to say about that, is it not?"

"Yes."

Untermyer turned and walked back to his table. His aide handed him some papers.

John glanced over at Joseph Choate. Joseph winked.

Untermyer turned back toward John.

He asked a whole line of questions about J. P. Morgan & Co. acting as agent and selling their securities, is that not a conflict of interest?

He asked a line of questions concerning the independence of the board of directors if they were appointed by the fiscal agents.

He asked a line of questions concerning competition for securities and was J. P. Morgan & Co. not curtailing that competition by being both agent and seller of securities.

But then he turned on U. S. Steel.

"Who decided that J. P. Morgan & Co. should be the depositary of the United States Steel Corporation?"

"That was rather ex officio, I think, sir."

"You mean you decided it both ways?"

"When the company was formed, J. P. Morgan & Co. had the whole company at that time, and I think that is the way it came."

"You thought it was a good business, and so you thought you would take it?"

John shook his head no.

"No; I did not know whether it was going to be good business or not at that time."

Untermyer smiled and raised an eyebrow.

"It proved pretty good?"

John nodded in reply. "It did; very good indeed, sir."

"You did not think you were taking many chances on its being good business when you took it up, then?"

"No; but I began to have doubts when the stock went to $8 a share afterwards."

"Your doubt did not interfere with your buying heavily?"

"No; I bought all I could."

"You did not have any doubt, did you?"

John sat up in his chair and held his head up.

"Never; not for one moment," he replied.

"You were getting the advantage of other people's doubts at that time?"

John leaned forward in his chair. John's eyes narrowed and focused direct at Untermyer. He held him in his stare for a moment. Then, carefully choosing each word, John responded.

"Nobody ever sold it at my suggestion," John replied and then ended it with a sharp "sir."

Untermyer raised his hands up and waved them in defense.

"No; I did not mean to assume that."

Still leaning forward and still staring intensely at Untermyer John simply said: "I know."

314

"My question does not imply that."

Again, John answered: "I know."

"It only implies your confidence in the company at that time?"

"I always had it," John replied and then, after a second delay, once again ended with "sir."

Untermyer then asked about the buying and selling of U. S. Steel securities. When you put together a syndicate of banks and investors do you have a list of such members, a list to which you return again and again for different issues?

He asked questions about his friendship with George Baker, president of First National Bank.

He asked a long line of questions on voting trusts.

He kept asking questions about control of credit; concentration of power and credit.

At several times John had to stop and blow his nose. It was running now. He had to keep sniffing and wiping his nose.

Untermeyer kept up the questions, power and control, power and control.

The afternoon dragged on and on.

John did not feel well; he grew tired.

Then, in the late afternoon, Untermyer tried to close in. He boldly walked up to John.

"Commercial credits are based upon the possession of money or property?"

John, thinking of something else, returned.

"What?" he said.

Untermyer, with a touch of irritation in his voice, asked again.

"Commercial credits?"

"Money or property or character."

Untermyer was a bit puzzled.

"Is not commercial credit based primarily upon money or property?"

John shook his head and spoke with boldness.

"No, sir; the first thing is character."

The words seemed to echo across a quiet chamber.

"Before money or property?"

"Before money or anything else. Money can not buy it."

Several committee members glanced back and forth at each other.

Untermyer paced to one side moving his hands as he talked.

"So that a man with character, without anything at all behind it, can get all the credit he wants, and a man with the property can not get it?"

Untermyer turned his head to look back at John.

John nodded. "That is very often the case."

Untermyer paced back to stand directly in front of John. "But that is the rule of business?"

"That is the rule of business, sir."

"If that is the rule of business, Mr. Morgan, why do the banks demand, the first thing they ask, a statement of what the man has got, before they extend him credit?"

"That is what they go into; but the first thing they say is, 'We want to see your record.'"

Untermyer, carefully, asked "Yes: and if his record is a blank, the next thing is how much has he got?"

John shook his head no. "People do not care, then."

"For instance, if he has got Government bonds or railroad bonds, and goes into get credit, he gets it, and on the security of those bonds, does he not?"

"Yes."

"He does not get it on his face or his character, does he?"

John held his head high, forceful.

"Yes; he gets it on his character," John replied, nodding his head to reinforce the point.

Untermyer paused for a moment.

"I see," he began to speak with a superior tone of voice, "then he might as well take the bonds home, had he not?"

John glanced over at several of the committee members who were smiling as if suppressing a laugh. Even Untermyer had a certain gleam in his eye.

John, very carefully, very deliberately, sat forward in his chair and with a penetrating stare glared directly at Untermyer. The gleam in Untermyer's eyes seemed to melt away. And then, with a slowly exacting tone, John spoke.

"Because a man I do not trust could not get money from me on all the bonds in Christendom."

Untermyer did not immediately respond.

He turned away.

Ships Sail

Corsair.

That evening they were all on board waiting for him when John arrived. On the upper deck under the canopy they sat around in a circle, some on the cushioned seats along the railing, and some on wicker chairs pulled up from below. Evening was coming on. They were all going up on his yacht the Corsair for a dinner at his home at Cragston. Even his favorite cushioned chair sat empty waiting for John to arrive.

When John finally walked on all of the guests cheered him. He laughed and circulated around each of the twelve guests to individually say hello.

When John completed shaking everyone's hand and saying hello then Bishop William Lawrence waved his arms in the air, taking charge.

"Well everyone, please take your seats so that we can get this tin can under way. It is on to Avalon I say."

"Cragston," Jack corrected him.

"Indeed," William replied.

As everyone sat down William turned toward J. Bevor Webb.

"So, Mr. Webb, what is it like working on the Corsair for the old man?"

"Working on the Corsair is rather strange. You all know that there have been three versions of the Corsair. Each boat is larger and improved over the previous one, but yet almost exactly the same. It is so much so that when we built this one, the third, he wanted exactly the same rugs downstairs as he had on Corsair II. The problem is that they were no longer made so we had to have them especially weaved just for this. His philosophy I think is do not get rid of the old and loved simply for the new but make the old and the loved into the new."

"Sounds like Morgan," William said.

"It is like working on the same boat, and a different one, at the same time. It is always the Corsair even when it is new."

"All things change but remain the same. Do you mind if I use that story in a sermon?"

"But I must say that when the Spanish War started and the Navy Department impounded the Corsair II for service Mr. Morgan was heart broken. He offered to build them another ship but they insisted on taking his. So the Navy took it, all of the polished mahogany was ripped out, she was commissioned as the U.S.S. Gloucester, and she sailed off to war."

"Knowing how he loved it I'm sure it was almost like losing a child," Julia said.

"But it saw good service. On July 3, 1898 through rapid gunfire it sank the Spanish ships Pluton and Furor. The Seawanhaka Corinthian Yacht Club held a celebration for the victory and Commodore Morgan was persuaded to go only if he did not have to speak because, as we all know, he is intensely so shy in public."

"Oh, are you so charming," Julia Lawrence said.

John, sitting on his cushioned chair with his cigar in his hand, held up his hand in acknowledgment.

"Two sailors who were on the ship that day gave a speech describing the event. They concluded by saying, 'And our ship was absolutely unhurt.' After the applause Commodore Morgan, much moved as we could all see, stood up. He addressed Ensign Edson. 'Of course, you don't mean the Corsair was not hit. I have at home a piece of her mast showing where a Spanish shell hit it. The Navy Department gave it to me.' He went on in a very emotional speech for some ten minutes about his boat and what it meant to him. But then, suddenly, as if he only then realized that he was speaking in public, he stopped and sat down."

"Sounds like Morgan," William repeated.

Two stewards dressed in white pants with black jackets approached John. They each held in their hands bottles of wine. They presented them for his inspection. He looked at each and then nodded.

"Quite by accident we will actually be sampling two Spanish wines this evening, I suppose in honor of Corsair's service."

"Sounds quite lovely," Herbert said, glancing at his wife Louisa.

It was Jack who spoke next.

"The last story reminds me of a story. My father, as you may all know from knowing him as you do, is actually a very quiet and solitary person. Even in our family circle he can fall into long periods of silence, as we can see even now."

Everyone looked over at John and laughed. He nodded and smiled in return.

"Well it was when I was at Harvard, I invited a classmate up to spend the week end with us at Cragston. 'My father is coming up in the evening on the Corsair. Just hop aboard, tell my father who you are, and come along with him,' I said. My friend found my father in an armchair on the forward deck reading a newspaper and introduced himself. My friend then took out a newspaper from his satchel and sat down and himself began reading. They sat silently reading the entire trip. I was at the dock waiting for them and when my father got off, out of ear shot of my friend said 'Son, I am glad you asked that young fellow up. He is one of the nicest chaps I have ever met.'"

"Sounds like Morgan," William repeated again.

The stewards meanwhile had popped open the bottles of wine and began circulating with trays of glasses and bottles of wine. Each guest eyed the selections and then picked one.

There was a sudden shaking of the boat as they untied the ropes and the boat, free, pulled away from the dock.

"I assume everyone is on board," William said.

"It will be too late if they are not now," his wife Julia answered.

There was a loud horn blast.

"Goodness."

"Talk about how my father is silent, you do realize that he can talk up a storm under the right conditions," Louisa commented.

Attention turned to her.

"There was one time when an old class mate of his at Cheshire School named Joe Wheeler showed up at our house. Now this Joe Wheeler was a Major General and had served as an artillery officer during the Civil War and again in the Spanish war so one can imagine the horrible things he may have seen or experienced. But there they both were like little school boys again talking and laughing on and on through out the evening about do you remember this, or do you remember that. I have never seen Father so talkative."

"And did they reveal any dark childhood secrets?" William asked.

"Well," Louisa began.

"Yes, go on, don't mind him," William said waving his hand toward John.

"Well they talked about the school bell high up a tower where it was an act of the utmost bravery to carve your initials. As they were talking about it I imagined them carefully climbing up the wall of the school, or maybe by a tree near by, in the dead of night or maybe by the light of a full moon, and speaking in but whispers filled with fear of being caught, and then holding on for dear life so not to fall and reaching out ever so far and with his jackknife that he got from his Grandpa Pierpont he carefully carves out his initials JPM on the wooden beam supporting the bell."

William turned toward John, sitting in his chair with his glass of wine and his cigar.

"And Commodore, tell me, if we went to do that ever so treacherous climb today would we be rewarded with the wonderful sight of your everlasting initials?"

John shrugged his shoulders.

"Bishop, some things are best left unsaid."

"True, true indeed."

The boat swayed sharply to the starboard as bells rang out. Florence Lamont, standing, almost lost her balance.

"Steady there," Jack said.

"I am afraid I do not have sea legs," she said.

"Are you sure," William piped up, "that it doesn't have to do with the half empty wine glass you are holding?"

Everyone, including Florence, laughed.

When the laughing died down Herbert Satterlee then took his turn.

"Since we are talking about it I too have a Corsair story. I have a story about the great sailor. It was just after he built Corsair number three. Fanny had spent the summer in England with Jack and Jessie and the children and she and I came back home on the maiden voyage of the Oceanic, which is a wonderful ship by the way. When we sailed into New York Harbor the Corsair was there waiting for us. Morgan and all of the family, Louisa and Anne and Juliet were on board waving and waving at us as we sailed in. It was a wonderful sight. I waved back shouting. So we docked at Quarantine and waited for the Health Officers to give us clearance. As soon as the doctor went over the side and started down the rope ladder with the small wooden rungs I saw a launch leave the Corsair and come over. There was a group of us watching as the doctor went down the rope and drop into his waiting tug. No sooner had it pulled away than the launch came up to the ladder and there stood Morgan. Now the water was swirling rather badly at just that moment and when Morgan reached up to grab the ladder the launch pulled away."

"Oh no," Julia Lawrence gasped as she put her gloved hand to her mouth.

"It is alright dear," William Lawrence piped in. "He is still here with us."

"I know, but. . ."

"So when the launch pulled away he was left hanging onto the rope ladder. It swung and he banged against the side of the boat. Looking down over the railing from above I watched in horror. If he let go of the rope he would have fallen into the churning water and who knows what would have happened. He pulls himself up onto the ladder and places his feet on the bottom rungs. Now picture the scene. He was then around sixty two years old, two hundred plus pounds, clinging to the end of the robe with a large cigar in his mouth and a straw hat on his head."

Herbert had to stop for a moment as he laughed at the memory.

"What did he do?"

"So he looks up, probably grunted, secures his straw hat more firmly on his head, clenches the cigar firmly in his mouth, and starts climbing the ladder. Now mind you this is a climb of over sixty feet straight up the side of the ship."

"I could not watch," Louisa laughed. "I had to turn away."

"So he climbs, slowly but steady never looking up or down or sideways, rung after rung. There were those on board watching who took bets on whether he was going to make it or not. When he reaches the top he pulls himself over the rail, waving off anyone who tried to help him. Standing there on deck, the sweat dripping off of his face, without taking the cigar out of his mouth, he barks at the steward 'Where is Mrs. Morgan.'"

"Mr. Morgan, what were you thinking?"

John pulled his cigar out of his mouth and held it in his hand.

"I was thinking that I was a better climber than a swimmer."

"My goodness."

Louisa piped in: "We made him swear that he would never do it again."

A steward came over to John and opened a humidor. John selected a cigar and waved the man to offer them to everyone else. John took out his lighter from his coat pocket. Looking at the unlit cigar John smiled.

"Speaking of cigars I myself have a story," John said. "Now everyone knows how I love my fine Cuban cigars. I was coming aboard the Corsair one day and I had forgotten my lighter. I went up to one of the workers on the pier and asked for a match. He kindly gave me one of his so in return I offered him one of my cigars. He was delighted. 'Thanks to you,' the man said, 'I was just out of tobacco.' Then he proceeds to pull out his pipe and he crushes the cigar into bits and stuffs the tobacco into his pipe."

"That was the best smoke he ever had," William said.

"I was taken aback but then, I thought, everyone has their way."

As the steward walked around with the humidor some took cigars. There was a pause as cigars were lit.

"Of course there is another family story on his athletic exploits that we in the family have all heard," Jack said, holding up his cigar.

Everyone's attention turned toward Jack.

"Story goes that he was going on a train trip with his grandmother. She was in her cabin and he was outside on the platform saying goodbye to friends when suddenly the train started moving. Grandmother screamed out at him but it took a minute before he realized what was going on. So he runs alongside of the train and instead of climbing up the stairs at the end of the car he instead runs to her open window and just as the platform was giving out he leaps up head first and flies through the window. He pulls himself in head first and with his head on the floor of the cabin and his feet dangling outside the window he looks up at his frightened grandmother and says: 'Hello.'"

"Oh Morgan, you are impossible," Florence Lamont laughed, picturing the scene in her mind.

Standing by a small cabinet Florence pointed at some miniature portraits on display in the cabinet.

"These are very nice, Mr. Morgan, and assume they are valuable, but shouldn't they be in a safer location like the Library?"

"Yes, you are quite right, of course, but I like to indulge myself now and again by having things with me."

"It is a touch of beauty for your soul in the everyday world?"

"Something like that. But I have to tell you the story of how I got those particular ones. I usually deal with the art dealer Henry Duveen. But one day his nephew Joseph Duveen, now of course a leading art dealer in his own right, thought his uncle was not taking full advantage of me. Knowing my propensity to buy objects in bulk he put thirty miniatures on a velvet tray. Six were valuable, those six you see, and the rest were mediocre. I looked them over and then asked the price for the whole lot. He glanced at his uncle with a sly smile on his face. The price was for much more than he would get if he just sold me the six. I looked them over again and then carefully picked out the six valuable ones and slid them into my pocket. I then told him to take the price he offered for all thirty, divide by thirty to get the price for one and then multiply by six for the six I took. 'Send me a bill for that,' I said and then walked out. It was for much less than I would have paid if he had just offered me the six. I heard later that as I turned and left Henry turned to his nephew and said 'Joe, you're only a boy. It takes a man to deal with Morgan.'"

"How delightfully funny," Florence said.

"In addition to their beauty that is what I think of when I see them."

"And this carpet is so stunning," she said, pointing down to the rug that covered the sitting area. "This is Persian is it not?"

"Yes it is," John said, proud that she asked but also intrigued that she asked.

"I bought this particular carpet in Egypt from this old Coptic Christian. They are still there, the Christians. He was an old man and was lamenting the fact that he had three daughters and could not give them away in marriage. He asked me if I wanted one but I declined; 'thank you but no. Not today.' That I found out was a mistake for he then looked at me with this hopeful look in his old face and he says to me, 'Well then, maybe tomorrow?'"

"Well, it is so wonderful to be surrounded by such beauty."

"Indeed," John said slightly nodding. "It is."

Julia Lawrence spoke up.

"We spoke a moment ago about his shyness but there is one area that he is not afraid to show himself: singing church hymns."

It was John who spoke up in protest.

"At this I must file a protest. Everyone has their gifts but I'm afraid that when the Good Lord came around to me he was fresh out of singing voices."

People laughed.

"We already know this Father," Jack chimed in.

"The Good Lord just patted me on the shoulder and said sorry son, move along."

"But you try and that certainly means a lot," Julia said.

"Oh yes," John replied. "Perseverance is not a virtue I lack. I feel that all men are equal in their desire to sing; it is just that not all men are equal in their ability."

"I remember when St. George's hired that Harry Burleigh in the choir, just a heaven of a voice. But there were those who were appalled just because he was a Colored Man. Morgan stood up to them and said: I care not for the color of a man's skin when he carries within him the voice such as his. God has gifted this man with the voice of an angel so who are we to complain about the color of the container."

"I remember that," Julia said.

"Rector Doctor Karl Reiland tells me that he has come into the chapel and found you all alone sitting in quiet prayer or singing by yourself filling the empty chapel with your voice," William said directly to John.

"Yes, I find that an echo of my voice sounds much better than the original."

"You have a deep soul, my friend," William said.

Others nodded in agreement in the quiet that followed.

"You have said it very well," Louisa said. "My Father does indeed have a strong sense of the sacred. There is a letter that he wrote to my mother when he visited Jerusalem. He writes that when he entered the Church of the Holy Sepulchre there was a slab of marble said to be where the Saviour was anointed for burial after the crucifixion. There was a deep stillness he writes, and I remember his words vividly, 'awestruck and impressed you stand almost breathless upon what must always be the most sacred spot on earth. I cannot attempt to describe my feelings, words fail me entirely.'"

Louisa smiled toward her father.

"He wrote that 'impelled by an impulse impossible to resist you fall on your knees before that shrine.' I think that is why we are leaving next month for Egypt, as we have many times. He must return to those places that are sacred. I must tell you that at Karnack by moonlight my father wept. He has a soul few are witness to."

"And there is a depth of compassion as well," Doctor Markoe added.

"I do not know if you have all heard the story of the Lying-In-Hospital. I and Doctor Lambert and Doctor Davis all helped organize the Midwifery Dispensary. The birthing conditions for immigrants at the time were quite appalling and most had no access to medical care at all. The dispensary was in one of the tenement houses but we still had to work in the homes of the patients. One evening in 1893 I arrived late at a dinner party where Mr. Morgan was attending. He listened while I explained that I had to perform a Caesarean operation on a Hungarian woman who lived in a tenement room about ten feet square and was destitute. It was the first caesarean we had performed. I was worried about her for she needed extra care that the dispensary could not provide. Before the evening was done Mr. Morgan took me aside and gave me $500 dollars and said to help the woman with whatever she needed and he would fray the cost."

"How awfully kind," Florence Lamont said, quite taken.

"And from this he set up a fund which helped to build in 1902 an entirely new, state of the art, Lying-In-Hospital. It is open to everyone regardless of their ability to pay and I am proud to say we service thousands of women every year. And that, to me, is the depth of his compassion."

Several of the members held up their glass as if to propose a toast.

Stewards circulated with bottle of wine filling everyone's glass.

The boat cruised along the river.

"Look out at the city everyone," Louisa said. "I love this view at night whenever we come this way."

The skylight of the city glowed with pulsating lights. The lights stretched across the river waves in a delicate glistening dance.

"It is simply beautiful and serene," Herbert said.

"Father had a lot to do with creating this. Think of how dark all of this used to be before Mr. Edison."

"True, true indeed," Herbert agreed.

"And on such a clear cloudless night with all of the stars," Julia said.

"The stars are trying to outshine the city lights," Herbert said.

"Herbert," John spoke up, "the sky is the Lord's doing and I think the stars have no competition from us."

"Still, it is such a beautiful combination."

There was a long moment of silence as each stared out into the night. A breeze, seemingly out of no where, came across the deck.

"If I may enter here," Thomas Lamont spoke up, "I am new to the Morgan circle of friends but I was taken aback by a similar story when I first began working for him. On January 2, 1911, my very first day of work, I arrived to find two gentlemen in my office, Paul Cravath and Bradley Martin. They represented the Nineteenth and Twelfth Ward Banks. The banks were in danger of closing due to some mismanagement of funds of a company they were heavily involved with. They knew that Morgan had no connection with either bank but they were approaching him for help due to the nature of the depositors. With the collapse of the company involved there would be runs on the bank and they lacked the funds to cover their depositors. After a careful analysis of the assets William Porter and I concluded that there was not sufficient capital to warrant a loan. We were sorry but we could not help. Do you remember this sir?"

"Yes I do remember," John replied.

"When we briefly explained the situation to Mr. Morgan he asked: 'Wait a moment, Porter. How many depositors have these two banks?' 'About thirty thousand.' 'And what is the character of them?' 'Mostly Eastsiders, working people, small tradesmen, dressmakers.' 'Well,' said Mr. Morgan, 'some way must be found to help these poor people. We mustn't let them lose all they have in the world. Suppose that, at worst, we were to guarantee the payment of these deposits in full. You say the total is only six million. That means that the firm can't lose more than six million, doesn't it?' 'Yes.' 'Work something out.' So we worked with

325

Henry Davison and several days later I and Davison went to Morgan's home with the details for his approval. When Davison started to explain it Mr. Morgan just brushed him aside. 'Davison, I don't care to see the paper. Whatever you think is right I will approve, but, whatever happens, don't let those poor people lose their money.' So the banks posted a sign in their windows which read: 'To our Depositors. We have received the financial support of J. Pierpont Morgan and can assure you that your money is now safe in this bank. F. B. French, President.'"

Thomas Lamont stopped for a moment.

"The mere mention of his name was enough to save the banks."

"But then the newspapers twist the whole story around," Florence Lamont added to her husbands story. "What was that headline that upset you so much?"

"Yes, it read 'Morgan Grabs Two More Banks.' Nothing could be further from the truth. There was never any equity share in the banks whatsoever."

Doctor Markoe shook his head.

"Those newspapers are relentless with falsehoods. Even with the Hospital they cannot say a kind word. They write that he built the Lying-In-Hospital for the purpose of sending his used mistresses whenever they get into trouble."

"That is so horrid," Florence said.

"You are absolutely correct, Doctor Markoe," William said. "I dare say that most of the time the critics are simply wrong but why should that ever stop them? They do not have their facts correct nor do they understanding the situation, but nevertheless spout off as if they do. I know of one case in particular."

William turned toward John.

"John may not want me to tell this story but I think that it is important for everyone to understand. I am speaking of your friendship with the Rector of St. George's Church: Reverend William Rainsford."

William Lawrence cleared his throat and then told the story of William Rainsford:

John sat in his parlor with the vestry members of St. George's Church: David Dows, John Wood, Charles Tracy, J. Noble Stearns and Harvey Spencer. The church was in trouble. Attendance was down, the Parish was shrinking, the missions set up had failed, there were less and less paying pew holders, and there was a $35,000 floating debt.

They needed a new Rector.

Several of the members had seen William Rainsford in tent revival meetings and were impressed. "He is a bit radical in his social beliefs but he is a just man who whole hardily believes in the Brotherhood of Man." So he was summoned and came to the meeting to meet the gentlemen. They told him of their situation.

William Rainsford explained the situation as he saw it. The problem was much greater than their one parish. Times were changing but the church was not changing with them.

"The Evangelical revival had saved religious life in England in the Eighteenth Century," he explained in his strong Irish accent, but now in the later Nineteenth Century it had lost its way.

"But the Church of Jesus, who came to the poor, understood the poor, and talked to the poor, had let the poor go——had lost touch with them. And when the Church's voice did reach them, in the din of the factory or the unhealthful crowding of the slums, it did nothing but call on them to seek a future salvation from a distant catastrophe, and had no word of understanding sympathy, nor hands of ready help, to save them or rather help them to save themselves, from the cruel despotism of an unjust economic condition and an environment that made a mockery of all hoped of home."

Rainsford continued as they all sat silently listening to his explanation.

"I would make my church a great free church, open to all, not in name only, not by profession only, but in actual operation. I would make it a church of the people, a truly democratic church."

He stopped for a moment to look around at all of the wealthy gentlemen gathered in Mr. Morgan's lush parlor.

"But I fear, in any church, what probability was there that the vestry had either the will or the power to act with me; nay, more than that, act under my direction in a course so novel and so revolutionary in its change? I fear not a chance in a hundred."

Rainsford prepared to leave. The meeting was over and done as far as he could see. These gentlemen would not in the least be interested in what he offered.

"Gentlemen, that is the only sort of church I would care to be rector of, but frankly I think your church has gone too far to be pulled up. In any case, I do not think I am a big enough man to pull it up."

Rainsford looked about at the different faces.

John, silent until now, also looked around at the various faces in the room. He then turned directly to Rainsford.

"Mr. Rainsford, will you be our rector? If you consent I will do what I can to help you carry out this plan."

John turned to the others, "Gentlemen, do you agree with me?"

327

No one replied but John turned to Rainsford again.

"Will you accept our unanimous call?"

Rainsford was surprised but replied all most immediately.

"I will on three conditions."

"Name them," John said.

"First, you must make the church absolutely free. Buy out those who will not donate their pews. Second, abolish all committees in the church except the vestry, and only reappoint such as I shall name. Third, I must have an annual fund of $10,000 for three years, independent of my salary, to spend as I see fit on church work. My salary I leave to you."

The room was dead silent.

Rainsford waited as John again glanced around the room. Then, to Rainsford, John said: "Done."

They became the best of friends and co workers for the faith. The pews became free and working class people began to attend. Rainsford set up outreach programs for the poor and invited them into the church. Pierpont became senior warden after the death of his father in law; Pierpont passed the plate every Sunday that he was in New York; when Rainsford was not available Pierpont arrived at the church a half hour early in order to greet everyone at the door, both the known and the unknown alike; there was Sunday service followed by hymn singing Sunday evening at either the church or at John's home; every Monday morning Reverend Rainsford came to breakfast.

"And don't forget about the trust fund," Julia Lawrence broke in.

"What was that dear," William asked, surprised at the interruption. He had been telling his story to the group as if it were his Sunday Service sermon.

Julia poked her husband, as if trying not to look in John's direction. "The trust fund," she whispered.

"Yes, well that as well."

Julia broke in: "It was after Reverend Rainsford had his collapse. He was trying to get back into things but was desperate for money. So one day Mr. Morgan drew him aside and slipped him a piece of paper. 'Don't work too hard; you ought not to have to worry about money. Don't thank me and don't speak of it to anyone but your wife.' It was a small trust fund that Mr. Morgan set up for him."

Then, toward John, she said: "I know that you don't like to talk about things like that Pierpont but people should know that about you, especially your friends."

"Well, with that, my dear," William went on, may I continue with the story?"

But she kept on instead.

"And at the Triennial Convention in 1895 in Minneapolis there was discussion of sending Bishop Peter Rowe to Alaska, and everyone agreed, but there were no funds for his yearly salary. But then William announces that 'a layman' had put up the money so off Bishop Rowe goes. And who might that 'layman' be?" she asked as she motioned with her head toward John.

"Yes, and now dear, might I proceed?"

Julia waved him on.

Rainsford, to better realize his plans to expand the Church and the scope of its congregation, wanted to increase the size of the rectory in order to better represent the mixed working class make up of the congregation. But one evening at a vestry meeting John stood up and announced: "I have a motion to make, Mr. Chairman, and I think that the vestry will agree with me it had better be passed without debate." The motion was to reduce the size of the vestry from eight members to six.

Rainsford was stunned. He had no advanced warning that the motion would be made nor of its makeup. He demanded an explanation.

John, unwillingly, stood.

"Rector, we are all more than satisfied with what you have accomplished. You have done your part well. Yours is a spiritual responsibility. Your part is to teach the Christian religion, and all that implies, to the congregation. The vestry part is fiduciary. Our obligations are financial. This vestry should be composed, in my judgment, of men whom I can invite to my study, and who can help me to carry the heavy financial burden of the church. The rector wants to democratize the church, and we agree with him and will help him as far as we can. But I do not want the vestry democratized. I want it to remain a body of gentlemen whom I can ask to meet me in my study."

To Rainsford it was clear: would the vestry be representative of the congregation or not? Long hours of debate followed until finally the vestry sided with Rainsford and voted John down, voting to increase the number to eleven.

John stood and said: "Rector, I will never sit in this rectory again."

He walked out.

The next day John gave Rainsford his resignation and asked it be submitted to the vestry without delay.

The following week Rainsford went to the Monday morning breakfast as usual. There was nothing mentioned.

The following week Rainsford went to the Monday morning breakfast as usual. Nothing was mentioned.

Finally on the third week when Rainsford arrived for the Monday morning breakfast John asked.

"Have you submitted my resignation?"

"I have not, and I will not."

"Why not?"

"Because I will not now or ever put you in the position of going back on your pledge to the rector and the vestry of St. George's Church."

"What do you mean?"

"You know what I mean. When I first came to you I came because you gave me your hand and your promise to stand by me in the hard work that lay ahead. I told you I was a radical. I told you I would do all I could to democratize the church. I am only keeping my word. I certainly shall not now, nor at any time, do anything to help you break yours."

There was stone cold silence. Rainsford lit his cigar and walked away.

It was several weeks later that John left for one of his European vacations. Rainsford went to the ship to see him off. When he went up the gangplank he saw John in a group of friends. John saw him. John excused himself from the group and waved Rainsford to follow him. Silently the two of them walked down the hallway to his cabin. He followed Rainsford inside and then closed and bolted the door.

William sat back in his chair. Everyone's eyes were on him but William sat silently.

"Well," Doctor Markoe asked, "what happened then?"

"Yes," others said. "What happened?"

William, smiling, watching John who sat in his chair silently, replied.

"We do not know. When I asked Rainsford later he simply said: 'We never had another falling out.'"

"But," William continued, raising his finger in the air, "to return to the important point that Doctor Markoe raised about critics. It was said at the time that this behavior showed that Morgan was a snob, an elite, he only wanted to mix with members of his own class and could not care about the wage earners of the world. But you see they do not understand. But we all know the real reason. The vestry members at times have to put out monies for the church and he wanted only those who could be counted on with out embarrassing them. He actually, in his way, was protecting the less well off from obligations they could ill afford."

Several of the ladies complained that it was growing chilly.

"Perhaps we should all retire down below out of the wind," Louisa said. Florence nodded in agreement.

The lights along the embankment were thinning out. The boat proceeded up and away from the city. Bells chimed out, directed at a passing boat on its way down stream. They watched it steam by. William waved.

John was tired. His eyes grew heavy. He turned and glanced a bit behind him. Belle, sitting back in her cushioned chair, noticed his glance. They smiled. She raised one eyebrow. That was enough.

John turned back. He was contented, content in just knowing she was there. He settled back and took a deep breath.

"There is one thing that we all know about Mr. Morgan," Julia finally said. "And that is that he always gets what he wants, don't you."

John shook his head. "If only that were true my dear Lady."

"Well, I was told a story about you from Bishop Potter. It seems that Bishop Potter was spending a Sunday afternoon up at Cragston. Now the Highland Falls station, where Cragston is located, is a side station so the fast trains do not stop there. The Bishop had to return to New York for an evening service so he was going to leave by some local lines, which left just before supper. But Mr. Morgan said no. 'But that is the only train,' Potter said. 'Oh no, there's a train after that one. Of course you'll stay for supper.' Potter, looking at his train schedule, said 'I don't see any train and I really must get to town in time to conduct an evening service.' 'There's an express,' Morgan says. 'I'll have it stopped for you.' Potter, looking amazed, asked 'You can do that?' And then Morgan brushed him off. Then, several hours later after a nice supper and after it had grown dark, Morgan took Potter down to the station in his carriage. But at the station it was all dark and there was no one around. The Coachman got out and tried rattling the door. It was locked. The Coachman came back to say it was locked and that the agent went home for the night. Then they all heard the train whistle far off but approaching. Frantic, Morgan jumped out of the carriage and with a frightened Potter behind Morgan ran to the station. 'Quick,' he said to his Coachman, 'break in the door. Take that large stone and smash it in.' Potter and Morgan watched as the Coachman smashed the door several times with a large boulder until he broke through the wood. Morgan reached in and fumbled with the lock until the door sprung open. 'Quick,' he shouted again as he entered. Potter waited outside, listening to the train coming closer. Morgan finally came out with a lantern and a box of matches. He lit the lantern. 'Alright Bishop, come with me.' Morgan stood in the middle of the track and waved the lantern frantically back and forth signaling to the train. Potter heard an awful squealing roar as the train came screeching to a halt just before Morgan. He heard Morgan shout out: 'It's the wrong train.' It was a freight train and not the express. Soon the Engineer came out of engine and the Conductor came running up from the darkness. They were both shouting and furious. 'What do you mean by stopping this train,' the Conductor. Morgan, still standing in the center of the tracks with the lantern told him who he was. 'What should that matter to me? I don't care a damn who you are, you've got no business. . .' but then he stopped short. 'Why there's an express following us, they could very well crash into us,' he shouted. Morgan, meanwhile, waved Potter to follow him and as the Conductor followed them shouting Morgan brought Potter to the Caboose. 'Now, Bishop, hop on board and ride the caboose all the way into New York.' When the Bishop climbed on board Morgan turned to the fuming Conductor. 'Be off man, there's an express coming on your tail.'"

By the time she had finished talking everyone was laughing.

"And I say it again," William said again: "It sounds like Morgan."

Conversation drifted as the group broke up. Several different conversations started up independent of the others.

John, sitting back in his chair, content, his wine by his side, his cigar in his fingers, surrounded by his art, by his friends, by his family, and by the glistening lights across the water, and by the canopy of stars, John closed his eyes.

Before long different people noticed his drooping head and nudged others smilingly pointing to the sleeping John. Everyone began to speak softer, in hushed whispers.

Louisa was the first to stand.

"I don't know about the rest of you," she said, "but I think the night chill is going to drive me downstairs."

One by one each of them stood, agreeing and chatting. They filed downstairs one by one, glancing at the sleeping John as they passed by.

Soon the deck cleared. There was only John asleep in his chair and one remaining steward standing off to one side. John's limp hand still held his lit cigar. Ash dropped off onto the carpet. The steward walked over with a small broom and tray. He swept the ashes away. He carefully took the cigar from John's fingers. Kneeling the man looked up at John's face. The man had a permanent scar across his cheek, a saber slash at Chancellorsville when he was barely eighteen.

The man took the tray of ash and cigar over to the trash can.

The boat slipped on with muffled voices from the deck below, the darkness of the embankment now almost complete.

John slept.

Egypt.

John sat under the canopy on the top of the boat.

They made their way up the Nile.

It was a bright day, as it was here on the Nile, and the shade from the canopy was nice.

Louisa came up behind him and placed her hands onto his shoulders. He looked up at her as she bent over and kissed his forehead.

"How are you doing?" she asked.

"Fine," he said, smiling up at her.

"Are you happy?"

"That is very strange," he replied, looking back at the horizon of desert.

"In what way?"

"You are not the first to ask me that recently."

"And what did you reply when asked before?"

Louisa by now had walked over to the edge and leaned onto the railing. She stood half in the sun and half in the shade of the canopy.

"I do not really remember," he replied.

Louisa looked out across the water of the river, and out across the desert. John was happy that she was here with him. They traveled well together.

But he first asked Belle to come with him. He was happy, supremely so: the Pujo hearing was done; he was back at home; and it was Christmas morning, 1912. John loved Christmas. John walked into the Library singing at the top of his lungs, with the full accompaniment with his waving arms, the Christmas Choral 'O Come all ye Faithful.' His booming voice echoed across the Library.

When he entered Belle's office she watched him as he finished his song and tossed his hat and cane into a nearby porphyry sarcophagus. He threw his arms around her in a large bear hug and kissed her on both cheeks. Laughing, she broke away. 'You look happy and about seventy years younger,' she said. 'I am,' he replied. He asked her if she would come to Egypt with him. They were to leave on January 7. She said no. Both of us should not be away from the library at the same time. John, disappointed, but nodding in agreement, said that he would then ask Louisa.

But when it was time to leave his mood had changed.

It had completely changed.

On the day before leaving John went to see George F. Baker at his office. Once before when he was leaving on a trip abroad, just after the Panic of 1907, John visited Baker. It seemed to be a pattern: exhausted, worn out, depressed, waves of mortality washed over him before each of his rejuvenating trips. The last time he went to tell Baker how he felt about him.

"If anything happens to me, I want you to know that my association with you has been one of the most satisfactory parts of my life—especially during the last six months. I have had many pleasant things in my life, but none more pleasant than this—I want you to remember it always."

This time he went into Baker's office, just the two of them. When John left Baker came out to his secretary Frank Rysavy.

"Take a memo: conversation between J. Pierpont Morgan and myself. 'I am going abroad, and as my health has not been all I would like, I must consider the possibility that I might not return. I have settled everything at the office, I believe, except one thing, and that is why I come to see you. My partners have often found themselves with different conclusions as to a course of action the firm should take. When they could not agree, they have always laid the matter before me and let me make the final decision. We have all been wondering what to do if I should not be here. I have told them, and they agree, that in such event they should come to you and let you make the final decision for them. Will you do it?'"

When Rysavy finished writing he looked up at Baker.

"And your reply, sir?"

"My reply was yes."

Belle sat with John in East Wing of the Library the night before his trip. They talked. They talked about what was up and coming, what there was to do while he was away. There would be fresh purchases; there were fresh purchases whenever he went on one of his trips. Hordes of dealers flocked around him like locust.

He looked weary: tired.

He stared down at a letter for far longer than required for him to read it. She noticed that his hand was shaking a little bit. But then he looked

334

up at her. His eyes were soft, usually so fierce and penetrating, but now soft and gentle. He reached out across the desk with both his hands and held her hand in his.

"Belle," there was a hint of desperation in his voice. "If only it had been."

She smiled. They had talked about this before, many times before. She knew how he felt.

Belle brought his hand up to her lips and lightly kissed it.

"We still have what we have."

"Yes, I suppose so."

"Well," Belle sharply said, breaking the mood.

"I have to go," she said, "and you have to retire so you will be fresh tomorrow when you leave for your trip."

Belle stood up and gathered the few papers she had before her and then looked across the desk at him sitting there.

"Will you be all right?"

"Yes, yes," he waved her off. "Go, go."

She turned and walked to the door. As she passed through she closed the door behind her. As she closed the door she looked back and could see him through the crack of the half closed door. He sat and stared off into space. It did not look as if he were looking at anything in particular, he simply stared. Blank. She always knew him to be so full of energy and drive, he was always doing something. She once wrote Bernard that John was so exhausting. 'He is the most exhausting man I have ever known,' she wrote. 'Just being in the same room with him and feeding off of his energy tires me out.'

So it was so strange and foreign to see him so listless, so sunken. He was like a proud and noble and fully rigged clipper ship at full sail in a hard full wind plowing the seas ever forward, but now the winds have died down, the sails collapse and droop and the ship glides forward until it finally comes to a complete stop in the middle of the sea.

She noticed, not for the first time but perhaps for the first time fully realizing the meaning of it, she noticed his face and his hair. His hair was white, thin, balding and a bit unkept. His side whiskers were grey and need of trim. His face was deeply wrinkled, his nose a distorted mangled red. He was portly, his clothes tight around his bulk, and he sat with his shoulders slumped.

It suddenly struck her how old he was.

It pained her to see him like this.

Belle walked back into the room and walked over to him. He did not notice her until she stood next to her. She leaned over and looked into his eyes.

"Are you alright?"

He smiled. A sparkle returned to his eyes. He nodded his head yes.

"Are you sure?" she asked.

"Yes, everything is fine."

She could see in the old mans face his old self flickering beneath the surface. It was like a small fish at the bottom of a clear lake darting to and fro. It was like a small open flame in a breeze woven room.

She put her hand onto his shoulder.

"Are you happy?"

John thought for a moment as if confused by the question, confused by the meaning of the question.

Then he simply nodded.

She raised one eyebrow as if to ask the question again, a deeper question.

"Yes," he replied. "Really, I am happy, I am happy."

Then, in a slower tone, "I am just apprehensive of the inevitable."

"What is the inevitable?"

John did not answer.

"Oh, go on," she said, slapping his shoulder a little. "You are so cantankerous you will live to be a hundred."

They laughed.

She had brought it back.

"I think not but it is wonderful to think so."

"And what is it you hope to find in Egypt this time?"

John replied after a moment.

"Eternity." He held out his open hand and then closed it into a fist. "I want to hold it in my hand."

"Are you sure you do not need anything, any help with anything for your trip?"

"No, nothing."

"Then I will be off," she said and then leaning in closer to him and with a stern hand and her pointing finger, "and I will see you when you return. We still have an art collection to finish and it is far from complete. The world is still full of treasures."

"I fear there is more beauty in the world than time to enjoy it."

She softly kissed his forehead.

"Good bye Mr. John Pierpont Morgan."

"Good bye, Belle."

With that she turned and left the room, without looking back, leaving him behind, alone.

John looked down the length of the boat. Others in his party were near the rear talking and laughing. The women where fanning themselves. John sat near the bow, his arms crossed on his chest, and his white fedora hat pulled forward on his head. Louisa raised her hand up to shield her eyes from the glare of the sun as she tried to stare off as far as she could see.

The day was winding down, the sun descending.

He could hear the sound of a saw from the shore. Several men were building a small cabin.

He could remember: 1909, Arden. It was the last time he saw Harriman.

The car arrived at the front entrance. It was Arden, the home of E.H. Harriman. Coming down the beautiful tree lined drive John looked out of the window of the car into a thick fairyland like forest. Birds were active dashing about and through the trees John saw a dear standing watching him.

He and Harriman were different in that way. Harriman loved nature, walking, taking expeditions to Alaska, Japan and China. And here, at his home, he had bought a large tract of land to save it from the loggers. Adding onto it over the years it was now a retreat, and animal preserve, a virtual Eden.

John, on the other hand, liked buildings, cities, architecture, and vacationed in Europe, museums. His only touch with the natural world was in Egypt and even that was filtered through the ruins of Ancient Egypt.

As they came into the courtyard at the house John could see the scaffolding. The house was under construction, never ending. Is paradise ever completed?

John stepped out of the car onto the gravel. He was glad he wore boots, Harriman said to wear boots. John adjusted his coat and his white fedora hat and walked toward the front door. As he approached a Porter came out of the house and stood on the top of the cement stairs.

"Are you Mr. Morgan," the elderly Porter asked.

"Yes."

The man waved his hand to the side of the house.

"This way, Mr. Harriman is expecting you. He is on the patio."

John followed as the man walked around the side of the house, through a gate, and then further back toward a raised patio. John was apprehensive. He did not know exactly what to expect. Harriman was dying, that was for sure. It was near the end. He battled the cancer for years and traveled throughout Europe for cures. But in the end it was to no avail. Harriman had called and asked to see John, 'perhaps for the last time' was the way he phrased it. To John it felt like a stab wound.

As they walked they came underneath some scaffolding. John could hear some workers above him, toward the roof. He could hear the sound of a saw cutting through wood. Ahead of him, as they came up the steps to the patio, he saw Harriman. He was lying down on a small cushioned sofa. He wore a straw hat and was covered with a blanket. He was shriveled and worn down, his face drawn.

Above them, up near the roof a workman looked down.

He said to his fellow worker, pointing to Harriman: "I feel sorry for the old man, being so sick an all."

"Why, he's richer than everybody ever will be."

"But he's dying, have some respect."

"Yeah," the second man said, stopping for a moment to look down. "All that millions an' it don't help him much now, does it."

The first man then sees John walking in toward Harriman. His coat tail flapped to the side as he walked, walking briskly and sure.

"Heh, that there is that Morgan fella. Yeah, I'm sure of it, that there is J. P. Morgan."

"Why are you surprised, all them rich fellas stick together."

"Yeah but I know him cause I worked on building his library."

"You, a library? I didn't know you can read."

The first man shook his head as the second man laughed.

"Come on," the second man said. "We gotta get up on the roof."

The first man watched as John came up to Harriman. Harriman turned his head. Without getting up they shook hands. John pulled over a chair.

"Come on I tell ya," the second man called out to him.

It was the better part of an hour when the two workmen came back to the scaffolding. The first man looked back down to where Harriman and John were. John was standing. The two of them, again, were shaking hands. Then John leaned down and they embraced. They held the embrace for a long time until John stood up again. The workman watched as John walked away. Harriman turned his gaze toward the garden. Shade and shadow from the sun through the trees danced about the ground. John stopped and looked back. He stood for a long time watching Harriman lying on the sofa. John then turned and walked away and out of sight. Shade and shadow from the sun through the trees danced about the ground.

It is done.

Dappled in sun and shade the day drifted away.

"I am so glad that you could come," John called over to Louisa standing by the railing of the boat.

"Well, so am I. It was so different when I got married and you started using Anne as your companion."

"Yes, I know," John abruptly said.

Louisa turned to look at him.

"She does not like to tolerate your companions?"

John grunted.

"But I do not approve of them either, Father."

"Yes, but you let it pass. You do not shower me with disapproving looks every time I see you. It ruins the trip."

"Still, it was nice to see her when we left port."

John nodded.

Louisa was careful in what she said next.

"I am glad to see that you two have seemed to patch things over."

John, staring off at the far distant mountains, grunted in reply.

Anne. She had been a precocious child, unpredictable, and, as Louisa once said 'irresistibly funny in spite of her naughtiness.' One evening at a formal dinner party at the house the maid brought the very young Anne down to share in the dessert. She sat next to her mother and as Fanny stroked her hair and she ate her piece of pie and other dinner guests smiled and chatted with her she suddenly announced to the party that she was never going to get married.

Conversation halted. Guests glanced back and forth at each other, some giggled surprise, as John, sitting back in his chair at the head of the table, stared down at little Anne. He was not amused.

"Well then," he asked in his blunt and direct manner, "what do you intend to be when you grow up?"

Anne, unshaken, stared back at him.

"Something better than a rich fool anyway."

John watched as the boat passed a small landing extending out from the shore. Several children, playing and fishing from the pier, waved as he passed. He waved back.

"We must do something for them," Anne said once.

She was standing in the dining room, one hand on the table. Sunlight streamed through the window. He could hear the small clock on the side cupboard tick away. It was just he and she standing in the dining room. It was just before she began to cry.

That echoed in his memory of her.

She had her causes; she wanted to save the world from suffering.

On a previous trip, as the 'Khargeh' was tied to a dock loading supplies, John stood on the second deck near the top of the stairs and threw coins out into the shallow water by the embankment. Young boys dove into the water and retrieved the coins, when they surfaced they proudly held them up so all their friends could see. He shouted out to them, and they to him. One of the guests from a different boat stood by watching. John did not know him that well and did not really like him. He was trying to impress John too much.

"Throwing crumbs to the birds?" the man asked, smiling a slightly superior smile.

John turned to face the man. 'We must do something for them' echoed in his mind.

"Yes," John said. "But they are only crumbs to me; to them it is gold."

John returned his attention to the laughing and splashing children.

Anne and several of her friends (Helen Hastings, wife of architect Hastings, Helen Barney, daughter of banker Charles Barney, and Daisy Harriman, first cousin by marriage to E. H. Harriman) determined to open a club exclusively for women, fashioned after the Metropolitan and the Union Clubs for men, as a place to meet friends, have dinner out, complete with athletic facilities, lecture halls, and swimming pools and squash courts.

Anne roped John into both financial support and membership in the men's advisory committee. She helped sign up 550 members, bought a large lot on the corner of Madison and 30th Street, and hired as the architect Stanford White of the firm McKim, Mead and White. They hired Elsie de Wolfe as the interior decorator.

It was called the Colony Club. John was present, with Charles Barney, on opening night March 9, 1907. He helped greet members at the front door when they arrived. One woman, shaking his hand, was overjoyed.

"I've waited for this evening all my life. I've just telephoned the boys. 'Don't wait dinner. I'm dining at my club,'" she giggled. "Oh, isn't it all so exquisite?"

As the early evening wore on John whispered to Charles that he would be right back: he had to visit the washroom.

"Good luck," Charles laughed.

John went into the Colony Club but came back out after a few minutes.

"They would not let me in," John told Charles in surprise.

"Well, Morgan, it is an exclusive woman's club."

"I do not know if I like this. I helped build it."

"But you are not a woman my good man," Charles said as he patted John on the back.

As the evening wore on and the arriving guests thinned out Charles and John took the time to talk. It did not take long before the topic of Sanford White came up. It was Charles who first brought it up.

"It is such a shame that Stanny did not live to be here celebrating his creation."

"Yes," John answered sharply.

John stood with Stanford White on opening night of the Metropolitan Club, February 27, 1894, greeting the arriving guests. John had been a member of the exclusive Union Club and one day brought in John King, president of the Erie Railroad, for membership. But the club blackballed King. He was too coarse; he had at one time been a common day laborer. William Vanderbilt brought in his brother-in-law Dr. W. Seward Webb for membership but he too was blackballed.

John was furious. He helped organize a protest with over one hundred other members. They met and decided to form their own club. They picked Stanford White as the architect. "Build a club fit for gentlemen," John demanded, "and damn the expense."

And it was built. On opening night the two of them greeted the guests into the club. White was radiant but he said he was 'nearly driven to death to finish it.' John knew White but they were not close friends. John preferred his other partner Charles McKim, and would use him to design and build his Library. There was always talk of White's endless affairs with young women. But John told White he had to slow down. He was working too hard.

"You need to rest," he said.

"Haven't the time."

Charles nodded to two young ladies as he held open the door for them to enter The Colony Club.

"He was in his fifties and she was just sixteen. My God, man, how can older men let their passions get away from them like that?"

John did not answer. He did not want to think about it. How could it have happened?

She had long black hair, full lips, and dark eyes. Evelyn Nesbit was her name, and she was sixteen at the time. White met her, dined her, rented a room for her and her mother, and brought her up to one of his secret apartments where it is said there hung from the ceiling a red velvet swing beneath Japanese fans.

The affair was short lived. She met and married soon to be rich Harry Thaw. But Harry was not quite right. He was obsessed with the fact that White had 'taken' Evelyn before she married him.

June 25, 1906. It was a hot day. That evening there was a performance of the musical 'Mamzelle Champagne' on the roof of the Madison Square Gardens, the same Madison Square Gardens that Sanford White had designed and J. P. Morgan had financed. Hundreds sat at tables enjoying dinner and watching the stage. In the audience sat Evelyn Nesbit and her husband Harry Thaw. Toward the end of the production, as Harry Short was on stage, surrounded with chorus girls, singing the song 'I Could Love a Thousand Girls,' the elevator opened and Stanford White stepped onto the roof. With the song in the air White walked down the aisles toward his reserved table near the stage. A large and tall man, with flaming red hair and a huge moustache, many in the audience recognized him. Stopping to talk to some, waving to others, White reached his table and sat down. Immediately Harry Stevens, the Garden's caterer came over and they chatted, White at one point threw his head back in laughter. When Stevens left White turned his attention toward the stage.

Some thought it strange that another man making his way toward the same table was on such a hot night wearing a black overcoat. When Harry Thaw got to just three feet from the table he stopped and pulled out a revolver from his coat. He held it at arms length aimed at White. White turned to look up at the man standing next to his table. Thaw aimed for the eyes and fired three shots.

White tried to stand but then fell across the table to the floor taking the tablecloth with him. Silverware and wine glasses and plates spun and shattered on the ground next to him.

The music stopped, the chorus girls froze in place.

There was complete silence.

Then someone screamed. Others screamed. People stood, some ran for the exits.

Harry Thaw, standing over the body, calmly held the revolver up in the air and emptied the chambers. One by one the unspent bullets dropped and bounced on the ground next to the body.

Standing at the door of The Colony Club, traffic rushing back and forth, John tried to understand. What was happening to the world? The shooting death of Jim Fisk so many years ago he understood. Low men of that type like him lived in that filth. But Stanford White, a partner in the most prestigious architecture firm there was; Stanford White was one of us. He was a man that John would have a brandy with at the club.

It was all breaking down. The higher elements of society were being corrupted down into the base rather than the base being uplifted into the higher. Was all of life being torn down into the lowest common denominator?

It was through the Colony Club that Anne Morgan met Elsie de Wolfe, the interior designer, a pixie woman with unbounded energy and joy, and her companion the literary agent Elisabeth Marbury, a larger, more sedentary figure. Whenever Anne was in France she stayed with her two new friends. They had a home in Versailles called the 'Villa Trianon.' On one trip when John was in Paris Anne asked him if he could stay at the Villa Trianon one night before heading off for Aix les Baines.

He agrees.

Early morning. John hears their voices downstairs in the patio. He looks down, with his face close to the glass, and can see into the patio and garden. They are preparing for breakfast. John would soon be down. He watches them. Elsie and Elisabeth and the Vanderbilt girl are sitting having tea. Anne in a white dress stands in the grass bending over a bed of roses. She holds one up and smells. She turns and smiles back at the group. John watches as Elizabeth stands up and walks over to Anne. They smell the rose together. But then Elizabeth curls her arm around Anne's waist. Anne turns into her. They kiss. It is a long and passionate kiss.

It suddenly hits him.

He understands.

"Maurice," he calls out. John stares at himself in the mirror.

"Maurice," he calls out louder than before. John takes a towel and wipes away the shaving cream still on his face.

Maurice, his driver, enters.

"Get the car around."

"Now, sir?"

"Yes."

"Sudden change of plans, sir?"

"Yes, get the car around," he snaps.

John sits on the side of the unmade bed as Maurice leaves. He can hear laughter from below in the garden. He does not care to look. Finally John quickly gathers his things and stuffs them into his bag. When Maurice comes back John motions to the bag.

"Put it into the car, we will leave at once."

"Yes, sir," Maurice says as he picks up the bag.

John leaves the room, walks down the short hallway and then down the stairs. As he walks through the parlor toward the front door Anne comes in from the patio and sees him.

"Father?"

John stops in the door way. She comes over to him. He notices that she is barefoot.

"Father, are you leaving?"

"Yes, something has come up."

"But breakfast. What has come up; is it that important?"

John turns his head and looks at her. Thoughts raced through his head. Louisa was always the favorite, he knew that, and Fanny had said more than once that he should be careful. What effect do you think that will have on the others? What effect indeed; what does she feel knowing that she was not the favorite of his affections?

"I saw," he says. He almost could not bring himself to say it.

"You saw what?"

"I saw you, just now in the garden. Is it true?"

"True, is what true, Father?"

"I thought, you are a single woman, it was only natural that you would be with other women. I would disapprove if you were with other males. There would be talk. But it is safe with other women. I had no idea it was, it was, much the opposite."

"Opposite of what, Father? Opposite of what? Opposite of a normal relationship? What do you think is normal? To fall in love and marry an appropriate man someday. Is marriage so normal? Normal, like your marriage perhaps, you think we don't know of your indiscretions against mother?"

344

John rages. He steps toward her but she does not flinch. He sees the fear in her eyes but he also sees the determination.

"You want me to fall in love," she begins with as steady of a voice that she can, "you want me to fall in love if the reason to fall in love is to be married, or to be happy in my life and fulfilled?"

Her voice cracks a little toward the end.

"Have you ever really been in love?"

John stands silent.

"Love knows no such distinctions," she continues. "Are you afraid of talk or of scandal?"

"Yes," he says but then immediately bites his words.

"No, no," he quickly says.

They stand facing each other for a moment.

"At first that crossed my mind," John begins, "but really, no, that is not what I feel."

"Shame then?"

John is silent for a moment. He stares into her. What have I done to you, he thinks.

Finally, quietly, he speaks.

"I feel that your heart will suffer the pain of it."

A question crosses her face. Anne did not immediately respond. It was not the answer that she was expecting.

"Society will not let you be complete."

"Someday perhaps."

John turns away.

"Must you go?" she asks, the tone of her voice pleading.

"Yes, I cannot face them now, knowing."

"Knowing that I have finally gained happiness?"

"Have you, with them? Knowing that I have been fooled, have you realized that yourself?"

"You are wrong. I think you knew. I was never like the others."

"Anne, I have sat across the table from the hardest men alive, I had to face down the most back stabbing and conniving men there are. How can I be defeated by my own daughter?"

John went out the door. The car was waiting in the driveway. They drove off and he did not look back. She watched from the doorway, watching him go.

"You know, Father, I've been thinking about you," Louisa said.

John, sitting in his chair on the deck under the veranda, looked over at her. He pushed his white fedora hat up on head a little bit so to see her better. She stood leaning against the railing. Behind her he could see the whole sweep of the blue sky. Little puffs of white clouds seemed so small and so alone in such a sea of blue.

"Yes," he said.

"You are such a divided man. Much of what you are is so conservative and traditional, and you are stuck in your ways, you are a strong church member, you love singing hymns, your marriage, the great respect you showed for your father and others, you are a man of this time."

"Is that a bad thing?" John asked.

"No, it is not at all bad. But then again so much of you is not of this time. You are made up of a future time perhaps: your innovations with electricity, building a different structure to business, even in your own companies by issuing financial statements so nothing is hidden, letting workers buy stock for their own enrichment. But it goes deeper than that, it means your open heart, hiring such a woman as your librarian, and now accepting your daughter and her different ways of seeing things."

"Perhaps," John said.

"Today is different. The world is opening up, social norms are changing. Our society is quickly changing and you have in yourself both elements of that change, the old as well as the new. You are helping to create a better world, a better future, by enriching the new with the best of the past."

"Well, this new government does not see that in me."

Louisa shrugged it off.

"What do they know? They only see half of the story."

The boat drifted on.

They grew silent as Louisa once again stared out at distance. The sun was behind the distant mountains. The day was dying away.

John listened to the churning of the engine, the slap of the paddle against the water.

Evening was coming on.

From the shore, from the reefs, John watched as birds flew up and ascended into the sky. A long white egret flapped its wings as it took flight. It flew parallel with the boat, flapping its long white wings, as it rose higher and higher into the growing night sky.

Louisa walked over to him and stood behind him. She leaned over, placed her hands gently on his shoulders and kissed his cheek.

His hand was shaking.

"Where do they go?" he asked her. He held out his shaking hand, pointing.

"I do not know," she whispered.

They watched as the long white bird flew off higher and higher into the sky.

"She told me about it," John finally said.

"Told you what?"

"The fire."

"Anne?"

John nodded. "She was quite shaken."

"I know. Father, night is coming on," Louisa said. "Do you want to come inside?"

"Leave me."

Louisa stood up straight. It was the tone in his voice.

"Leave me," he said again.

Louisa stared down at him for a moment and then turned and walked into the interior of the boat.

"I saw them Father. I saw the bodies."

John and Anne stood in the dining room.

Over the last several years Anne became politically involved with the shirtwaist workers, she became involved with the garment district strikes in the summer of 1909, and supported the Triangle shirtwaist workers strike in November. In December she and Elizabeth Marbury arranged for some of the strike leaders and some of the workers to give talks at the Colony Club about their plight.

"We can't live our lives without doing something to help them."

But then it struck. March 25, 1911. The Triangle Shirtwaist Factory.

Anne was trembling standing in the dining room, her hand holding steady on the table. The sun streamed in.

"I talked with Frances Perkins just after it," she told John as he stood in the doorway to the hall. She looked ahead, not at him, talking as if to herself alone.

"She was near and heard the fire wagons. She ran to the site. She said the whole top three floors, the eighth ninth and tenth was all ablaze. And all of the screams. She watched some of them jump, jump ten stories to the pavement. She said you could hear them crack when they hit. They were burning to death. Burn to death or die by jumping ten stories to the cement below. They only had seconds to decide."

Anne stopped for a moment. She had to swallow hard and then wait.

The small clock on the sideboard chimed a small chime.

"They say the doors were locked so that no one would try to get off work early. There is something like a hundred and forty of them."

She had to catch her breath.

John cleared his throat.

"The horror of it is beyond comprehension," he said.

Anne looked at him, searching with her eyes.

"I saw them father. I saw the bodies. They picked up the crushed ones off the street and took the burned ones out of the smoldering building. They took them all to the wharf and lined then up in boxes in a warehouse. I went there that night. The wooden wharf; the smell of the harbor, I watched as loved ones came to try and find their missing children. People were silent as they walked down the rows, feet shuffling, police held up lanterns in the dark warehouse so you could see them, one after another. Some of the bodies were crushed from jumping for their lives, others were burnt. They were black, their skin was burned black like an over done steak."

John saw the horror in her eyes.

Anne was shaking as she talked.

"We must do something for them. They need something more, father. It needs to be different. This is not right."

She began to cry, standing alone crying for the dead.

John walked up to her and held his hands up, hesitating. Then he held her; then he pulled her into him and held her.

Louisa came back. She was with Robert Giles. It was very nearly dark. You could barely see the embankment of the river. There were no lights in the desert, only deep blackness. John sat with his eyes closed. Louisa leaned over with her face near his. She touched his forehead; it was warm to the touch. He opened his eyes.

"She is right," he mumbled. "It is not a game. It is deadly serious."

Louisa was confused.

"What is that?" she asked

"That is where he is wrong. The one who wins is not the one who dies with the greatest wealth. It is the one who leaves the greatest goodness and compassion behind."

Louisa glanced at Robert with a confused look on her face.

"Father, I think that it is time to come in."

John looked up at her.

"I must keep moving," he said with a growing desperation in his voice. "Never sit still, always moving, changing, otherwise it will catch me."

"What will catch you?"

"The sickness."

"The what?"

"Grandpa Pierpont struggled with it, my mother, dear soul, succumbed. But I must fight it and be ever a step ahead, ever a step ahead, otherwise it will take over."

Louisa looked over at Robert who leaned forward trying to make out what John was saying.

"Come on, Father," Louisa said as she pulled on him to stand.

John, reluctantly, stood up. Louisa noticed his shaking hand.

"Come on, you are tired. You need to rest."

John walked toward the cabin door. The lights were already lit inside. He stopped for a moment and stared out at the distant horizon. The darkness was now complete. He looked up at the bloom of the stars.

"It has come down to this," he whispered.

"Go on Father. You do not want to be here."

John slowly went inside the cabin. Louisa stared at him as he entered. She and Robert exchanged glances. Their looks seemed to speak. He seems so much worse. She was afraid. Maybe we should turn back. Was there never any real rest?

As they all entered the cabin the boat steamed up the dark river and was slowly swallowed by the desert darkness.

The swirling darkness enveloped all.

In the whiteness of the bed sheets Louisa leaned forward to hear his words. John opened his eyes and stared up toward the ceiling. He tried to point. His face and forehead glistened with sweat. His hand shook. His breathing was labored. She listened closely and made out his words.

"I've got to go up the hill."

The night closed in. The small boat with the tiny lights sailed further up the darkened river as the deep blackness of night soaked through the whole fabric of the dying day. In the eternal vastness of the desert night the tiny light of the boat grew dim, dim, and then disappeared.

Louisa cabled her brother using the code name for their father.

Charcoal died today twelve five.

NOTE TO READER

Many sources were consulted for this work of fiction. The major books used are as follows:

ALLEN, FREDERICK LEWIS, THE *GREAT PIERPONT MORGAN.* New York Harper & Brothers, 1949.

ARDIZZONE, HEIDI, *AN ILLUMINATED LIFE.* New York: W.W. Norton & Company, 2007.

BRUNER, ROBERT F. & CARR, SEAN D., *THE PANIC OF 1907.* New Jersey: John Wiley & Sons, Inc., 2007.

HOVEY, CARL, THE *LIFE STORY OF J. PIERPONT MORGAN.* New York: Sturgis & Walton Co., 1912.

KLEIN, MAURY, *THE LIFE & LEGEND OF E. H. HARRIMAN.* Chapel Hill: The University of North Carolina Press, 2000.

ROTTENBERG, DAN, *THE MAN WHO MADE WALL STREET.* Philadelphia: University of Pennsylvania Press, 2001.

SATTERLEE, HERBERT L., *J. PIERPONT MORGAN, AN INTIMATE PORTRAIT.* New York: The Macmillan Company, 1939.

SINCLAIR, ANDREW, *CORSAIR, THE LIFE OF J. PIERPONT MORGAN.* Boston: Little, Brown and Company, 1981.

STROUSE, JEAN, *MORGAN, AMERICAN FINANCIER.* New York: Random House, 1999.

TARBELL, IDA M., *THE LIFE OF ELBERT H. GARY.* New York: D. Appleton and Company. 1925.

WENDT, LLOYD & KOGAN, HERMAN, *BET A MILLION! THE STORY OF JOHN W. GATES.* New York: The Bobbs-Merrill Company, 1948.

WHEELER, GEORGE, *PIERPONT MORGAN AND FRIENDS.* New Jersey: Prentice-Hall, Inc., 1973.

WINKLER, JOHN K*., MORGAN THE MAGNIFICENT.* New York: The Vanguard Press, 1930

ABOUT THE AUTHOR

With a Masters Degree in Philosophy, John is a writer, owns an accounting firm, is married to an accomplished photographer and performing musician, has a best friend who is the daughter of a famous abstract painter, and also has an artistic photographer as a friend.

He lives in and experiences multiple worlds. This gives him a unique blend of practical and artistic insight that carries over into his novels and stories.

John is a highly eclectic writer. His short story collection *Pillar of Stores* ranges from the literary to horror to travel to comedy. His historical novels, like *J.P.*, his novel of the banker J. P. Morgan, are fast paced and plot driven narratives. However his more literary novels, such as his four volume *Fire in Winter*, are very character driven, slower paced, and richly dense symbolic works.

In his output there is something for everyone.

www.ingramcontent.com/pod-product-compliance
Lightning Source LLC
Chambersburg PA
CBHW051228260626
47162CB00002B/327